THE
MEMORY
WALL

Also by Lev AC Rosen

Woundabout (with Ellis Rosen)

For Adults

Depth
All Men of Genius

THE MEMORY WALL

Lev AC Rosen

Alfred A. Knopf
New York

THIS IS A BORZOI BOOK PUBLISHED BY ALFRED A. KNOPF

Visit us on the Web! randomhousekids.com

Educators and librarians, for a variety of teaching tools, visit us at RHTeachersLibrarians.com

Library of Congress Cataloging-in-Publication Data is available upon request.
ISBN 978-1-101-93323-7 (trade)
ISBN 978-1-101-93324-4 (lib. bdg.)
ISBN 978-1-101-93325-1 (ebook)

The text of this book is set in 13-point Adobe Jenson and 9.5-point Caecilia.

Printed in the United States of America
September 2016
10 9 8 7 6 5 4 3 2 1

First Edition

For my brother.

ONE

THE GAME *comes out the day we're taking Mom to the home.*

Nick had laughed when he realized that a few weeks ago, when they'd picked a "check-in date" for the home, like it was some sort of hotel. He didn't know why he laughed—he was just sitting at the table, reading one of his game magazines, and he'd noticed the release date in an ad, and that was the first time he'd realized it, and he'd laughed. Mom and Dad had looked at him, confused, but hadn't asked anything. Mom had even smiled. She didn't know it wasn't a happy laugh.

Nick thinks now he probably shouldn't have ordered the game with release-day shipping, but they hadn't known then—or at least *he* hadn't known—that Mom would be going to a home. And he hadn't known it would be today. He sees the yellow padded envelope on top of the pile of mail in the hall and he knows he should walk by it, that today is Serious and Dad is going to get upset, but then he thinks, *Screw it.* He kneels down and grabs the envelope and tears it open on the floor. He hates everything about today. He doesn't want today to happen. He doesn't think it needs to happen. He may as well do something to try to make himself happy.

He takes the game out. It's wrapped in that insect-wing-thin plastic, and he immediately starts trying to pick it off, but then he stops and looks at the front of the box. He already knew what the cover looked like—he'd seen it on all the spoiler-free websites, in the spoiler-free reviews—but to be holding it is something else. Knowing he could be playing it in a matter of hours—once the mistake of today is done—makes him feel a lot better about everything. It frees him, for just a moment, from the sad, angry, weak, too-heavy-to-move way he's been feeling for months. All of it lifts, then crashes back down again like a tidal wave.

The cover shows the mountain city of Wellhall, capital of Erenia, homeland of the gray elves. This game is the fifth in the series. Each installment happens in a different homeland, hundreds of years apart, so each new game is familiar but still fresh. This one has all sorts of new tech, too: next-gen graphics, AIs so real you can't tell them from people, and online capabilities—he doesn't know yet if that last feature is a good thing. But it's the gray elf homeland, and that's exciting, because he always plays as a gray elf—a treasure hunter/explorer named Severkin (his own name, Nick Reeves, spelled backward but with some letters taken out, because when he first made him four years ago he thought that was cool; he still thinks it's sort of cool). The mountain city on the cover looks like a spiral into the clouds. Carved staircases wind up the city, and stained-glass windows shine like embedded jewels. Above it is the title of the game in carved letters:

"What are you doing?" Dad sticks his head into the hall from the kitchen. They live in one of those suburban houses where the ground floor has archways, not actual doors, so Dad can do that without Nick's noticing. Dad's 'fro bobs like a sea creature: his head is tilted a little, and it's the only part of him showing, like he's playing a spy on a kids' show. Nick would laugh, but seeing Dad makes him remember how angry he is at him for letting this happen.

"Just getting the mail," Nick says, and picks up all the letters and brings them into the kitchen. Mom is sitting at the table, looking out the window. Mom is white—like, *really* white. She's from Germany, and she's so blond that you don't notice where she's going gray unless you look really closely. In the light, her face is like the carved ivory cameo she used to wear when Nick was little. She has a bowl of soggy cereal in front of her, half eaten. Not a great last meal.

"You should eat, Mom," Nick says. She turns to him and smiles, then winks, which is a thing she does, and then takes a spoonful. Once, the winks were supposed to be reassuring, like a shared secret, but now Nick doesn't know what they mean. He looks down at his hands and realizes he's still holding the game, and for a moment he forgets what's happening and he wants to sit across from Mom and open it and look at the in-struction booklet with her. Mom plays the game, too—well, she played the last one. She won't be playing this one with him.

"You should eat, too," Dad says. He's drinking coffee by the stove.

"I'm not really hungry," Nick says, and he wants the words to sound cold and mean, but Dad just nods, unaffected, as usual.

"I get that," Dad says. "Me neither." He pauses and takes off his glasses to polish them and then looks at Mom. Nick looks at Mom, too. Mom looks out the window. The light on her face makes her phantom-pale.

"You want to get going, Sophie?"

In the game, there's this poison—ragebrew. You prick someone with it and they get crazy angry, start attacking everyone in sight. Severkin uses it to cause distractions when he needs to get into well-guarded ruins or private collections, like when he'd liberated the Shield of Chalaak from the hidden crypt in the Royal Jungles of Aneer. One dose and the guards patrolling the jungle—open only to the royal family— were distracted by one of their colleagues as Severkin leapt from tree to tree, following the directions on an ancient map.

When Dad asks that question, it's like Nick has been pricked with the poison. He can feel anger as a bright white liquid pouring into his blood and making it fizz. He can't explain it, but he hates the way Dad asks it like a question. Like there's a chance of backing out now.

"We're going to Sunrise House today," Dad says after Mom doesn't look at him right away.

"I know," Mom says. She's still got this faint German accent that makes her words sound like heartbeats. "*Gehen wir. Bevor ich komplett zerfalle.*"

Nick realizes he's holding his breath and clutching the game so tightly it's sticking to his skin. For a split second he had thought maybe she'd say, "No we're not, I've changed my mind." But that's not happening.

So Nick says it: "You don't have to."

He knows the moment it leaves his mouth that it's a mistake. It's the same old argument they've been having for months, since his parents said Mom would be going to the home. For two years, really, since they sat him down and said, "Mom has early-onset Alzheimer's."

"*Nick*," Dad says, his drawing out of the i like a warning bell.

Nick's not blind. He knows Mom has been a little off for the past few years, and she's had some bad days. But they told him Alzheimer's meant forgetting things, and he said okay and went upstairs and googled it. Forgetting things apparently meant forgetting everything—also, changes in personality, weird fits, needing to be bathed, cleaned. Mom wasn't like that. She still isn't.

"Nicky," Mom says before Dad can start telling him he's being immature and needs to accept things. "I love you. I will see you. And I'm doing this for you. I promise, one day, when you're ready, you'll understand why. But right now you just need to trust us. You're still young. I want you to enjoy your youth, not worry." The same clichés she's been spouting for months. Hearing them again should make him angrier, but instead of a fire inside, he feels hollowed out and wet.

"I'm going to worry anyway," Nick says. Mom stares him in the face, her eyes bright blue and a little sad.

After he'd googled "Alzheimer's," he googled "Alzheimer's misdiagnoses," and after Google had corrected his spelling, he found a lot more. He found articles by doctors saying that half of all Alzheimer's cases are misdiagnosed. Or at least one in five, which is a lot. And that usually whatever the problem really is is curable. The big one, a condition called normal pressure hydrocephalus, is curable. It's just some pressure on the brain because something isn't draining right, so someone sticks a big needle in and drains it. Well, not anyone—a doctor. And that's just the most common possibility—there are so many others: Wilson's disease (symptoms go away with regular treatment), uremia (curable with dialysis), hypothyroidism (symptoms fade with regular treatment), and more.

There are even people called "the worried well"—people who think they're sick because a relative has been, but who are fine, it turns out, and are just getting older. Nick had brought all this back to his parents, but they'd shaken their heads. Mom definitely had Alzheimer's. They knew because her dad had had it.

As if these other conditions—and he'd brought them dozens—couldn't be what had actually been wrong with her dad. As if doctors couldn't have misdiagnosed Alzheimer's thirty years ago in Germany. As if it weren't more likely a misdiagnosis than a correct one. They hadn't had the best doctors or tests back then. Nick argued with them for months. Mom was a little weird sometimes, but she was fine otherwise. She didn't have any of the ten key symptoms of Alzheimer's. His parents said he was in denial, and had to accept his mom's condition. They offered to send him to a shrink. He told them no.

Nick found those ten symptoms on the Alzheimer's Association website. He included the "normal behavior" (not Alzheimer's) descriptions, then made the symptoms into an interactive desktop for his computer—a little program with check boxes. Every time Mom showed a symptom, he checked it. If she didn't show it again the next day, he unchecked it.

❶

☐ **Memory loss that disrupts daily life.**

☐ Normal: Sometimes forgetting names or appointments, but remembering them later.

❷

☐ **Challenges in planning or solving problems.**

☐ Normal: Making occasional errors when balancing a checkbook.

❸

☐ **Difficulty completing familiar tasks at home, at work or at leisure.**

☐ Normal: Occasionally needing help to use the settings on a microwave or to record a TV show.

❹

☐ **Confusion with time or place.**

☐ Normal: Getting confused about the day of the week but figuring it out later.

❺

☐ **Trouble understanding visual images and spatial relationships.**

☐ Normal: Vision changes related to cataracts.

❻

☐ **New problems with words in speaking or writing.**

☐ Normal: Sometimes having trouble finding the right word.

❼

☐ **Misplacing things and losing the ability to retrace steps.**

☐ Normal: Misplacing things from time to time and retracing steps to find them.

❽

☐ **Decreased or poor judgment.**

☐ Normal: Making a bad decision once in a while.

❾

☐ **Withdrawal from work or social activities.**

☐ Normal: Sometimes feeling weary of work, family and social obligations.

❿

☐ **Changes in mood or personality.**

☐ Normal: Developing very specific ways of doing things and becoming irritable when a routine is disrupted.

Nick had told himself that if she showed all the symptoms in one day, or even just one symptom for three days in a row, he would accept it. But she never did. And two years later, she was going to the home. He even keeps track of how often the boxes are checked. In the past year, she's had box 1 checked twice, when she forgot to pick him up from school, and that one really bad day in the spring; box 2 checked once; box 3 checked a lot—sometimes two days in a row; box 4 checked ten times, but never in a row; box 7 checked about a dozen times; box 8 checked once, for that bad day again; box 9 was never checked, though he's not sure if that's fair, with her quitting her job (anthropology professor at the local college, where Dad teaches African American studies) just after he made the checklist. Boxes 5, 6, and 10 have never been checked.

But this isn't enough for them. Nick showed them the checklist a few months ago, when they started talking about the home. They said he wasn't seeing everything. As if he could stop—as if every move Mom made didn't make him go through all the symptoms in his head.

"Let's get going, then," Dad says. Mom sighs, and stands, and Nick follows them because he doesn't know what else to do.

Outside it's bright, in a cheerless sort of way, like bad video game graphics. Two Rivers is a suburb of Manhattan, wealthy and mostly white, with what Dad calls "an artsy, intellectual community," which Nick thinks means it's rich but liberal, and people are willing to pay too much for stuff. Free-trade coffeehouses in every little shopping center, good schools, the smell of cut grass and suntan lotion sweeping in every summer and hovering there in a haze of self-satisfaction.

They get in the car, Dad driving because Mom gave up her driver's license at the end of last spring. When Nick goes to fasten his seat belt, he realizes he's still holding the game, and starts picking at the plastic again.

"What is that?" Dad asks, turning his head around.

"It's the new game." Nick finally manages to tear away a corner of the plastic. He puts his finger beneath the rip and pulls up, trying to rip more of it.

"Why did you bring it? Go put it back."

"Let him keep it," Mom says. "He's been looking forward to this game for almost a year."

"So have you," Nick says, finally pulling a crack in the plastic and tearing the whole thing off. He looks up at her, but her eyes are staring ahead of her. He reaches out and puts his hand on her shoulder and she turns slightly, her face in profile.

"I'll be sorry to miss it," Mom says as Dad starts the car. "But you can tell me all about it when you come see me."

"Yeah." It won't be the same.

At this point, Mom is better at the game than he is. She used to just watch him play when she was getting dinner ready, and she'd point out how this quest or character was based on a Greek myth or that this traditional ceremony of the trolls was clearly inspired by the Japanese tea ceremony. She gave the story a lot of layers. And then one day he asked her if she wanted to play, too, and she said yes. And she was really, really good. She'd even played when he was at school, set up these little quests in the game and given him clues in the form of little notes hidden in his room. She did things like that before the game, too, clues to lead him to candy and birthday presents, but it was even cooler when she did it for treasure in the game.

Nick knows it's dorky or lame or whatever, and it's not something he'd ever tell his friends (if he still had any), but he likes playing the game with Mom. He likes having her nearby commenting on the quests he does. And he likes that she gets so into the story, like he does.

"It's such a beautiful day," Mom says from the passenger seat. "Just like the day we brought you home from the hospital, Nicky."

Dad drives the car through the funnels of Two Rivers: Easter-egg houses with picket fences and then a large park, a mall, a hospital. They drive by Lincoln Middle School, where Nick graduated in the spring, and Reagan Junior High and High School, where he starts seventh grade in just over a week. No one talks. Mom just keeps looking out the window, her hands in her lap, and Dad stares forward, driving. They both must know how much happier Mom would be at home—they'd watch her favorite movies and eat popcorn on the couch and listen to her jazz records.

Nick doesn't know what his grandpa did that she's so scared that she wants to lock herself up. He asked once, but she just shook her head, and Dad told him not to talk about it.

"It's such a beautiful day," Mom says as they pull into the parking lot of the home. "Like the one when we brought you home from the hospital, Nicky."

"Yeah, Mom." Nick pops open the case the game is in, but then snaps it shut again. Repeating sentences isn't on the checklist. But it could be a symptom of Lyme disease (curable with antibiotics).

Sunrise House is an old-fashioned white mansion, the kind that looks like the plantations in the photos Dad is always showing Nick while telling him "Our ancestors were slaves there." It's been painted bleach white, and the grass around it is trimmed carpet thin. A tall white gate rises up like a prison's between the grass and the parking lot. Dad parks the car in a lot of finger-size pieces of bone-white stone. They crunch under the tires. The fence and gravel are the same shade, like the fence rose out of the stone, a skeletal hand.

"This is wrong," Nick says. He knows he's repeating himself, but he has to keep trying.

Mom turns around in her seat to look at him. She's wearing leather gloves even though it's warm out. "Remember last spring?" she asks.

Nick nods. "That was just a bad day, though. You said so."

"There are too many bad days," she says. "And they are getting worse than bad. I don't want you around for them anymore. I don't want you to come home one day and find I've forgotten you."

"You won't forget me, Mom," Nick says, crossing his arms. "And what other bad days? What are you talking about?"

No one says anything; no one ever says anything except Nick. Or maybe they say it, but not when he's around. Dad keeps his hands on the wheel, staring in front of him, and for a moment Nick really hopes he's going to back out of the parking lot and say "Screw this, you're staying at home," but he opens the door instead, and starts getting out.

"It's a nice place," Mom says, finally. "Let's go in. You'll see."

"I've seen it already," Nick says. They've visited—"as a family"—twice over the past month. Mom doesn't say anything, just opens the door and gets out. Nick's the last one still in the car, and so he finally gets out, too.

Nick grabs the game, getting out. He can read the instruction booklet while they're checking her in. It will be better than participating in his mom's imprisonment. It'll be like a form of peaceful protest.

There are stone paths weaving through the grass, and a big porch with lots of chairs on it. A handful of people sit out on the chairs, staring at Nick and his parents as they walk in. Nick doesn't know if it's because they're new or if it's just the usual stares they get as a mixed-race family. All the people are old, so it could be either. Inside smells like lemon cleaning supplies. The floor has a rose-colored carpet, and the walls are white, with photos all over them. There's a bulletin board and a high wooden counter that a few people in scrubs sit behind. They look up when Nick's family comes in, and one of them picks up the phone and says a few low words before hanging up and standing. She smiles broadly and extends her hand. She isn't much younger than Mom, and wears teal scrubs with a thick brown cardigan over them.

"You're the Reeves family, right?"

Dad shakes the woman's hand. "Yes, I'm Lamont, and this is my wife, Sophia, and our son, Nick." He turns to look at Nick, and his eyes furrow into the expected glare when he sees the game. "Nick, why did you bring that game?"

"Peaceful protest," Nick says. His dad taught him that term, but he just looks confused when Nick says it now, and then more annoyed. Nick tries not to smirk. He likes that Dad can finally be angry today, that Nick isn't the only one.

"What are you talking about?" Dad's voice rises. "Don't you get what we're doing here? Can't you take it seriously?"

Mom puts her hand on Dad's shoulder. "Relax. It's okay. You can keep your game, Nicky."

The woman in scrubs has been smiling pleasantly through this in a plastic sort of way but uses the moment of silence to speak up again. "I'm Maria Lopez, one of the nurses here. I oversee the daily care of patients, and I supervise the early-onset patients, especially. So I'll be a person you see every day, Sophia."

"Sophie is fine," Mom says.

"Why don't we all go and sit down in the lounge and we can talk about what you like to do, Sophie, so I can make sure you're in all the right activity groups and we give you the best possible schedule."

She walks them to the back of the lobby, to the only other door, where she swipes a card over a panel. There's a buzz like an insect and she heaves the door open.

"You'll have to get an aide to swipe you in when you visit, but someone is always here for that." She smiles again and leads them through the door into a wide room that branches into a few hallways and a large staircase. She starts down one of the halls, and Nick's parents follow her like happy sheep to slaughter. Nick goes after them. It's a narrow hall, and on one side of it is an old woman in a wheelchair, her head bobbing wildly up and down, a smile on her face. Her mouth is wet, like she's about to start drooling, and her eyes follow Nick as he gets close.

"Jimmy?" she asks. Nick shakes his head, keeps his eyes down, tries to keep walking. "Yes, Jimmy," she says louder. "I know it's you. You get so dark in the summers. I told your father not to marry an Italian, but he wouldn't listen and that's why you get so dark."

"I'm not Jimmy," Nick says, and he feels bad because it came out nasty-sounding and this woman is clearly sick. "Sorry," he adds quickly. She looks confused and then starts more frantically bobbing her head, like a basketball being dribbled, clutching the arms of her wheelchair. Nick takes a step backward without meaning to. His legs feel shaky and throbbing, like his heart is sucking up the blood from them.

"Yes! You are! I know!" she shouts at him. Her voice is loud and screeching, an angry seagull.

Maria turns around at the shouting and hurries back down the hall to the old woman, then kneels down so she's at eye level. His parents wait down the hall.

"This isn't Jimmy, Mrs. Wach. Jimmy is thirty now and married, remember? You have a great-granddaughter, Rosemary, named after you?"

The woman's bobbing slows down a little and she focuses on Maria.

"I remember," she says. But she looks so confused, Nick doesn't believe her.

"Good. Why don't you just wait here until Steve is done getting Mrs. Goldman out of bed, and then he can take you both outside. Does that sound like something you want to do?"

"Yes," the woman says after a moment.

"Good. Steve will be right here."

The woman nods again, her head bobbing only a little. Maria stands and walks to a nearby open door. Nick watches her, sticks his head into the room. It looks like a hospital room, with a curtain down the center. Mechanical, cold, not a home, not even a hotel.

"Steve," Maria calls, "Mrs. Wach is getting impatient."

"Okay, thanks," comes a voice from behind the curtain.

Maria turns to Nick, an uneasy smile wavering on her face. "Sorry about that," she says. "Mrs. Wach tends to see her grandson everywhere if he hasn't visited in a while."

"That's okay," Nick says, because what else can he say? And Maria seems cool. He thinks maybe she'll get it. "My mom's not like that, you know. She doesn't get people confused."

"That's great," Maria says. Her smile is blank, like she understands what he's saying but doesn't feel any particular way about it. It doesn't change her mind the way it should.

"She shouldn't be here." Nick straightens his neck and shoulders out, like a wall, waiting for Maria to disagree, to tell him that she knows Mom better than he does.

"Maybe she shouldn't," Maria says. "But she wants to be." She's making the PityFace, that face some teachers and parents were giving him toward the end of last year, after the thing that happened in the spring.

Nick rolls his eyes. "She's afraid of something. With her dad. She won't tell me what. And my dad is letting her shut herself away. It's messed up."

Maria just shrugs. "I don't know how your parents operate, or how they decided this, but I know your mom was part of the decision, or she wouldn't be here. Your dad loves her, and he's trying to do right." More clichés. It's like since Mom's (incorrect) diagnosis, everyone talks in greeting cards, the ones marked "Sympathy" in the store. *As long as she's in your heart, she's with you. Love transcends goodbyes. Sorry for your loss.*

When they pass by those cards in the drugstore, Nick fantasizes about tearing them all up, about slicing the display down the center with Severkin's daggers.

"Come on," Maria says, "let's get back to them. I need your help, anyway. You need to tell me the sort of things your mom likes to do."

They head down the hall to where his parents are waiting in front of a closed door. Maria leads them inside, to what looks like a lounge, or maybe a conference room. Round tables, chairs. Maria sits down, and his parents sit down next to her. Nick takes a seat farther away.

"So," Maria says, looking at them like they're contestants on a game show, "let's talk about your day-to-day activities, how you like to spend your time. What did you do for a living?"

"I taught," Mom says. "College—"

"Anthropology," Dad interrupts. He's been doing that a lot lately. When Nick interrupts, he has to apologize. Not Dad, not when he interrupts Mom.

Nick looks down at the game he's still holding and opens the box. Inside is the disc and the instruction booklet. He takes out the instructions and closes the box with an audible click. No one says anything, and he smiles. He starts flipping through the instruction booklet. He's happy there even is one, and that it's thick. Most games have only digital instructions these days.

"And your accent," Maria continues. "You're from Germany?" Nick looks up and sees Mom nodding. "We have foreign-movie showings sometimes in the afternoon. I'll be sure to let you know if we show anything German. Your family might even be able to come watch with you."

"That sounds fun," Dad says. Nick looks back down at the game instructions and keeps flipping through them as they talk about stuff Mom likes: reading, painting, nature documentaries, according to Dad, though Nick has never seen her watch any. Listening to all this is making him angry.

"She likes watching me play my game," he says. So much for peaceful protest and non-participation.

"We have some game consoles here, actually," Maria says, which is cool, but he wonders what for. He imagines the old wet-lipped woman in the hallway with the bobbing head trying to play a video game, yelling at it when it doesn't do what she wants. "So you can come play together, if you want."

"That'd be cool," Nick says. The room is warm. They should open a window.

"What about keeping her academically challenged?" Dad asks, like Mom isn't in the room. "Anthropology—can you provide her with the latest papers and books? And read them to her, if . . ."

"Yes," Maria interrupts as Dad trails off. "If you give me a list of publications, we can make sure she sees the ones we subscribe to. And you can direct her subscriptions here, of course."

Nick shakes his head. For a moment he has a vision of Mom in a wheelchair, her head bobbing. He doesn't voluntarily think of it, it just appears in his head, and suddenly he can't breathe and his eyes sting. He feels the instruction booklet in his hands, the stickiness of the pages, and looks down at it. He takes a deep breath and blinks the image from his mind and focuses on the words in front of him. The online play is optional, the booklet says, but makes the experience more fun. He doesn't get how. He likes getting lost in the game's world. It's open, and filled with adventures, and the other open-world games he's played with people online—the

MMORPGs—are filled with people talking in slang and joking out of character, which immediately takes him out of the world and the story. It's like everyone is just pretending, instead of experiencing the story.

Nick doesn't want to miss out on anything, though. The booklet says the game has online servers dedicated to people who have their characters speak only in character, in appropriate language, and where anyone who violates those rules will be tossed off. Maybe he could do that. He'll try it, but the moment he sees "OOC" or "LOL," he's shutting it down and going back to single-player, off-line play.

The other big change to the game is that you can play as a dwarf. Nick isn't sure how he feels about this, either. The dwarves had been bad guys in all the others (in fact, the main bad guys in the first one), but now there's an uneasy truce, so everyone can take on the newly awoken giants together. But Nick was used to fighting the dwarves. They had these huge underground cities that Severkin had to sneak through, sniping in the dark, fighting off their machines.

"How about you, Nick?" Maria asks.

Nick looks up from his booklet. "What?" he asks.

"Can you pay attention?" Dad asks.

"I was just saying that you should visit before sundown," Maria says. "And that if you plan to visit after, you should let me know. Is that okay?"

"Sure." Nick shrugs. "I have to come with Dad, anyway. I can't drive yet."

"Maybe a friend could drive you," Dad says. Nick almost laughs. Like he'd ever bring a friend here. "Well, we'll come every weekend. Right, Nick? At least. Every day if we can." Dad reaches out and takes Mom's hand.

"Yes," she says. "We can come as often as you'd like."

Nick looks up at Mom. Dad is staring at her, too. There is a long moment, and she smiles, and Dad smiles back at her, but Nick can tell it isn't a real smile. Nick knows this is a checkbox moment, but he isn't sure which. He decides on number 4, "Confusion with time or place." Currently, it's empty. One check doesn't mean anything.

"Except for the first week," Maria says. "No visiting then. It's best if we get her used to the routine without interruptions."

"Oh," Dad says. "Will that be okay, Sophie?" Mom nods, and he pats her hand. "Then we'll be back in a week."

Nick flips through the booklet to see if there are any major control-play changes, but there don't seem to be any besides a few more moves. They all seem like natural controls, though, no button switching. Severkin uses a bow and a pair of daggers. The bow is great for sniping while hidden, so he can take out enemies in ruins without disrupting the actual ruins. The daggers—long and curved—are for when he can't snipe. He uses disguises, too, to get past guards into off-limits areas, where he shouldn't explore. He's badass. He was a street urchin, a pickpocket as a child. An orphan. Swift hands were important for treasure hunters. Old locks that needed picking, traps that needed removing, and sometimes artifacts, owned by people who didn't appreciate them, that needed to be "liberated." Severkin isn't above theft. He's even a member of the Thieves Guild, although he never takes from the poor. Nick has worked hard on Severkin. He turns back to the front of the booklet to make sure he can carry his old character over to the new game. He can. Good.

Nick goes back through the booklet to see if he's missed

anything, and then he notices a new subrace: underelf. A gray elf raised among the dwarves. Nick didn't know such a thing even existed. But that's not Severkin. Severkin was raised by a human in the overworld.

"That all sound about right to you?" Maria asks. Nick looks back up. They seem to be finishing. His parents are nodding.

"So let's take you to your room," Maria says, getting up. Nick puts the game and booklet away as everyone rises to follow, then grabs his mom's hand, holding her back a little, so they're walking behind, out of earshot. It feels silly, holding mom's hand, but it feels sort of good, too, like a cure for the rage poison, or a healing spell. She looks down at him, as if also confused by the handholding.

He opens his mouth to say something, but suddenly he feels like his throat has a film over it. Mom stares at him, waiting.

"Please don't do this," he says, after his breath comes back, but it's taken so long it feels stilted, silly. "Please, please, please," he says. "Don't lock yourself up. Tell the doctor to test for other things. It's something else." He squeezes his mother's hand so tightly, her fingers start to turn pink. "I've researched it, I have a checklist, I know it's something else."

"I love you, Nicky. Don't you forget that," his mother says quietly, and squeezes his hand back. Nick doesn't respond. He's going to rescue her. Bring her home. She walks back into the hall, not letting go, pulling Nick with her, and though he could resist, he lets himself be dragged along. Out in the hall, where the nurses and other patients are, Nick lets go of her hand.

Dad looks back at them, and Mom hurries to catch up with him. Nick follows, a little behind, watching his parents hold hands. They walk up the wooden staircase they'd seen when they first came in, then down a hall. Up here, the carpets are blue. They take her to a room at the very end of the hall. It's like an old-fashioned hotel. There's a bed with white sheets, some drawers, a closet, a bathroom, and a big window—the kind with a seat built in—that looks out on the lawn in front. Nick goes and sits in it, looking out. A nurse is walking down a path in the lawn, a man with a walker hobbling next to her. He turns back to his family. His parents are quiet, looking at the room. Maria stands in the doorway, watching them.

"This is very nice," Mom says, sitting on the bed. Dad sits down next to her and lays his head on her shoulder, something Nick doesn't think he's seen Dad do before. He has a sudden flash of memory—he was very little, maybe six, and Dad laid his head on Mom's shoulder after a long phone call. Later that week was his grandmother's funeral. Nick looks back out the window. The man with the walker hasn't gone very far.

"Do you have bags or anything?" Maria asks. "I can get them for you."

"Yes. In the trunk. Nick, go help her." Nick nods and gets up from the bench at the window and walks out of the room. The nurse follows him out to the parking lot, where he opens the trunk. There are three suitcases. Mom's whole life.

"This isn't easy for your dad, either, you know," Maria says.

Nick clenches his jaw, feels a prick of the rage poison. "He acts like it is," he says, grabbing one of the suitcases with more force than he means to. It leaps out of his hand and falls onto the white gravel. He bends over and picks it up again. "He's given up. Some doctors start saying Alzheimer's and Mom can't remember where her keys are and suddenly she has to move out!" He's shouting. He doesn't mean to, but he also doesn't care. He sits down in the parking lot without knowing why. The stones are sharp on his ass. He probably looks like an idiot. He should apologize for yelling. This isn't Maria's fault. Maria looks down at him, and Nick stares up at her, expecting PityFace, but instead she looks unimpressed. Like she expected more from him.

"What?" he asks in a soft voice.

"You know it's more than that, right? You know what this disease does. You have access to the Internet. You must have googled it, if your parents didn't talk to you."

"I did," Nick says.

"So," Maria says, "you must realize how hard it is for your dad, too. You should tell him how you feel. He probably feels the same way."

"If he felt the same way, we wouldn't be here," Nick says, standing up. "I told them—I said there are a thousand other things it could be. They didn't even test her for normal pressure hydrocephalus."

"Hydrocephalus," Maria says, correcting his pronunciation. The *a* at the end sounds more like an *e*. "There must have been other tests," she says.

Nick shakes his head. "Not for her. She said her dad had early-onset Alzheimer's, and everyone just nodded and said you have it, too, now leave your family." Nick grabs another of the suitcases from the trunk and walks away, his game tucked under his arm. He hears Maria slam the trunk behind him, and she rushes to catch up, holding the last of the bags. He walks faster but then realizes how rude he's being—childish. She meets him on the porch.

"Sorry I yelled," he says.

"That's okay," Maria says, in a way that sounds sincere. They go inside and start walking. "I'm not going to lecture you anymore," Maria says. "But if you need to talk—and you don't want to talk to your dad—"

"Thanks," Nick says. "But I'm so tired of people asking me to talk."

Maria nods but doesn't say anything, and Nick is grateful for that. When they get up to the room, his parents are exactly as he left them, frozen like statues, Dad's head on Mom's shoulder, their hands clasped together in her lap.

"We have the stuff," Nick says, and puts the bags by his parents' feet.

"Thank you," Mom says, and then takes a breath, a pause, sounding as if she means to say more, but doesn't.

"Thanks, Nick," Dad says, standing and lifting one of the bags up onto the bed, where he unzips it and starts unpacking things.

"Oh, we can do that," Maria says. "It's good if the staff knows where everything is."

Dad takes a few framed photos out of the bag anyway and puts them on the nightstand by the bed. Nick smiles at his dad's own small peaceful protest, forgets how angry he is at him for a moment. One of the photos is of Mom and Dad before he was born. One is of Mom's parents, who'd died before Nick was born, too. One is of Nick. The last is of all three of them together.

"You see, Nicky?" Mom says. "It's just like I'm staying in a hotel."

"Yeah," Nick says drily. "Just like that."

"Don't be rude," Dad says.

"I think maybe it's time you boys leave me," Mom says. Nick stares at his mother. She's still sitting on the bed, looking down at her hands. He wants to control her like Severkin and make her stand up and walk out of this place. He knows part of her wants it, too. But she keeps looking at her hands instead. Nick feels his jaw clenching and his hands fold tightly, and for one breath, he hates her for not standing.

"Fine," he says, and walks out, his heavy footsteps muffled by the blue carpet.

Dad takes a while getting to the car, but Nick waits in the backseat, looking at the game. He runs his hand over the spine of the case, where the plastic wrap had been glued, and where leftover flakes still ripple under his touch. When Dad does get in, he says nothing, but slams the door. Then he pulls out of the parking lot and starts driving home.

"I know this is hard for you," he says as they pass the mall. There are a bunch of kids Nick's age hanging out in front, smoking. "But you should have said something to your mother. Given her a hug. She's going to miss you." Nick doesn't say anything but runs his hand over his cheek. It feels rubbery, cold. "Well, you can say something when we visit next week."

He drives a while longer in silence.

"Tomorrow we should go by Traci's and get your books for school. That sound okay?"

"Sure," Nick says. They're close to home, and he doesn't want to be talking when Dad parks.

"Good."

Dad pulls into the garage, and before he's turned the engine off, Nick is out of the car and up the stairs to his room, where he closes the door and turns on his game console. He slips the Wellhall disc into it, the hiss of the tray sliding shut somehow relaxing his shoulders. He grabs his controller and sits on his bed. There's not much else in his room—a desk in the corner with his computer, a closet, a few big posters of Chichén Itzá, where they'd all gone together two years ago, before they'd told him about Mom's misdiagnosis. He'd walked the pyramid steps as Mom told him about the Mayans. He'd touched old carvings, just like Severkin. It had been one of the best weeks of his life. And he's going to go back there with Mom and Dad, once she's out. Or maybe someplace else, like Rome. Someplace ancient, where Mom knows all the stories.

The game has to install, which could take a while, and for a few seconds, Nick watches the little percentage bar creep closer and closer to 100. Then, before he forgets, he goes to his computer and checks off box number 4 for his mother— "Confusion with time or place." It's the only check on the screen. Dad knocks and opens the door without waiting for a reply when the game's loading screen is at 76 percent.

"I'm playing my game, Dad," Nick says without looking up.

"Okay," Dad says, standing in the doorway. "But if you want to talk about anything, I'm here, okay?"

"Yeah." He looks up at Dad, who is lingering, holding on to the doorframe like it's a mast and his ship is going under.

"I'll just order us a pizza tonight."

"Good." The bar is at 98 percent.

"Want anything on it?"

"Olives," Nick says. Olives are usually Mom's favorite, but he wants them. The bar is at 99 percent.

"Okay," Dad says, and leaves without closing the door. If

Mom were home—or even if she weren't home, if she were at work, if things were normal—he'd probably invite his dad to watch. Dad never got into the game as much as Mom, never really understood it, but he would have stayed ten minutes, asked some stupid questions that Nick would have answered and laughed at, and said how cool the game looked. Something about graphics and how it's like a movie. He would have sat next to Nick on his bed and squeezed his arm as he left, and told him, "Have fun, but don't go all crazy and start trying to pickpocket people in real life," or something. Nick would have smiled. Nick wishes they could still do all that, but without Mom there it's like she's a ghost in every room, floating between them, reminding Nick that his dad has given up. And Nick feels sorry for him, feels sorry because he knows today was hard for his dad, too, but he's also so disappointed in him for not fighting harder. He can't even look at him.

The bar reaches 100, and finally Nick gets to play the game.

TWO

SEVERKIN INHALES deeply. The ship rocks beneath him, and the air tastes of salt and the deep smoky flavor of sunset.

"Are you going home, gray elf?" asks an elderly human woman beside him. He's seen her a few times since the journey began, but she's never spoken to him.

"I'm not from Erenia," Severkin says. "I was born elsewhere. This will be my first time seeing my people's homeland."

"Are you fleeing the quakes, too, then?"

"Quakes?"

"In Arrowsrest. My family farm was swallowed by a sinkhole after the last quake. They say it's the giants, waking up underground. That's why the dwarves have made peace. They know the giants are awakening."

"Giants are an old myth," Severkin says. "But I'm sorry you lost your farm."

"Everything is an old myth till it's real again," the woman says.

Severkin looks forward to seeing his people's homeland at last. He's explored so many ruins, seen so many ancestral tombs and forgotten palaces—but always those of others, never of his own people. He had begun to suspect his people didn't have a history. But he'll find one here.

When the sun is half submerged beneath the waves, Severkin feels a slight tremor under the ship. Not like the waves they coast through—something different, like a stone dropping in a pond. It unsettles him. And then it happens again.

"Something is wrong," he says to the woman. He turns away from her and runs up the deck to where the captain is steering the wheel. "Did you feel that?" he asks. "We need to stop, make landing. Something is wrong."

"Calm yourself," the captain says. "We're just a few hours from our destination, see?" He nods out at the water, and in the distance, Severkin can see what he assumes is Wellhall, a huge gray mountain rising up through the clouds. It glows from within, windows punched in the stone firing out beams of colored light into the darkening sky.

The ship shudders again, this time so strongly that the other passengers stumble. Someone shouts.

"See?" Severkin says.

But the captain isn't focused on Severkin. He is looking off at the horizon to their right, where a shadow is emerging from the water. It's dark against the navy sky, but visible: a head with long dripping hair, shoulders like rocky hills, heading for Wellhall. As it moves, it grows, walking out of the water. A chest becomes visible, and stone-tower arms, then a stomach and legs, nothing covering them but shadow. A giant man, easily taller than the huge redwoods of Arrowsrest.

"I told you," screams the woman who had been speaking to Severkin earlier. "The giants have returned!"

As if he hears her, the giant turns to the ship and regards it. The captain is spinning the wheel and barking orders, trying to turn the ship around, but Severkin knows it is already too late. The giant pounds a flat hand on the water, and a huge wave rises up and flies toward the ship. The froth on the edge of the wave flies over them, blocking out the sky and falling over the ship almost silently. The world goes sideways, suddenly filled with screaming and the snap of breaking wood. Severkin holds his breath and spins wildly about, his world blackness and water.

⊙   ⊙   ⊙

SEVERKIN OPENS his eyes. His vision explodes in circles of bright white and he closes them again. He aches everywhere, but he's experienced worse, like the time he fell from the Tower of Kariska, or when he failed to notice the rockfall trap in a tomb beneath Umai. He opens his eyes again, slowly, then stands and takes inventory of his situation. He still has his bow and knives, though they've seen better days, and his leather armor is torn but still functional.

He is standing on a red sand beach—if it's big enough to be called that. The beach itself doesn't run more than a few feet from the water before it hits a red cliff face. But there's another beach, a few feet through the water, and another and another, all around him, each beach a ring around a column-like cliff. He feels as though he has been shrunk down and is at the foot of a cluster of small red mushrooms. The mushroom-cliff tops are far above him. Down here, it's all rushing salt-water and stems—with no end in sight. He doesn't see any of his fellow passengers, either. He tries calling out, but only the sound of the waves responds.

He needs to get a better view of where he is. He tries grabbing on to one of the stalklike walls to pull himself up, but the rock crumbles under his hands. He's a good climber, but he can't do much with a surface like that. He'll have to find a more solid wall. He starts exploring, wading from stalk to stalk and testing the rock. They all crumble, until the fourth, where there's a rope ladder suspended from above. He gives it a tug and it holds firm. He climbs up it.

Up here, the tops of the stalks look much like they had from below—small, circular plateaus, with a long drop to the water in the spaces between them. Luckily, someone has laid down wooden planks between many of the mushroom tops. They aren't very safe-looking and have no rails, but using them would be better than jumping. In the distance, perhaps six planks off, Severkin can see where the plateaus end and a smooth meadow begins. There are no people around. No sign of who'd thrown down the ladder or put up the planks.

Carefully, he walks the planks to the meadow. There in the grass lies a large stone; carved into it is the word BRIDGE-FALL and an arrow. He wonders how many shipwrecks had happened here before they'd set this system up. He looks out over the horizon—he could go anywhere. But he needs to get new equipment, more arrows. He heads in the direction of Bridgefall.

The sun is high in the sky by now, nearly noon, but it has

a paleness to it that Severkin finds disturbing. It doesn't feel warm. The plains stretch out in front of him like a wasteland of green. There's no road, just patches where the grass has been worn thin and sandy. He had thought somehow that his people's homeland would be more welcoming than this—that it would feel instantly like a long-lost home, the sun a roaring hearth, the grass whipping at his ankles like embraces from family. Instead, he feels as though he's experiencing it from behind glass, as though he isn't really there. Then again, the welcoming committee had been a giant.

He's only walked a little way when he feels the ground shake. He instinctively takes a combat-ready position, his feet wide, his blades drawn. He grips the ground through his shoes, feeling his toes wrap around the dry soil. In the distance there's a cloud of sand coming toward him. It fades, then explodes out of the ground again, closer to him. And in front of the cloud of dust is a shadow, a person running toward him.

Severkin looks around for higher ground or something to hide behind, but the best he can see is a large rock, barely taller than himself. Still, it's something. He runs for the rock and leaps up on top of it. Then he crouches low and draws his bow, focusing on the shadow and the dust cloud rising behind it.

He can see that the dust cloud is a creature, chasing someone. It looks to be the size of an elephant, and it sometimes dives into the earth as though it's water, popping up again to the surface a few feet farther along, as it chases its victim. The dust obscures the monster's features, but Severkin can see that the creature has a long, sinewy tail, like a giant rat's, and huge claws in front that it uses to dig into the earth. Its victim is easier to spot: a dwarf in leather armor, with a huge sword that he sometimes swings at the beast. But the beast is too quick for him, so the dwarf runs on, trying to gain some ground, some advantage.

Severkin considers letting the beast kill the dwarf. He doesn't like dwarves. They'd been his enemies for ages, tucked away underground, only sometimes popping up to lob explosives at him or at other overworld dwellers. He's raided more underground dwarven keeps and labs than he could count, whispering through the darkness, bow drawn. But the dwarves are the overworlders' allies now. He knows he should help.

The dwarf and the beast come close to Severkin, and he can see the monster's form—part rat, part mole—with its two huge white eyes like curdling milk, and a mouth made up of tentacles, pink and dripping with saliva. It claws at the dwarf, who dodges out of the way again, and Severkin lets fly an arrow at one of the beast's milky eyes, hitting it dead center, causing it to burst like a wineskin.

The beast rears up on its hind legs and lets out a sound like a dying horse. The dwarf sees his opening and takes it, hacking at the creature's front legs. Severkin reaches back for another arrow to find his quiver empty. Damn. He must have lost most of his arrows when he washed up on shore. He hooks his bow around his back and draws his knives, leaping down from the rock.

Severkin dashes to the side, trying to flank the beast, but it turns and smacks him to the ground with its tail. He rolls to his feet, but now the creature has him, its fleshy tentacles sloughing mucus, its breath a thick fog that smells of carrion.

The dwarf dives in front of him, sword aloft and swinging

at the tentacles. The beast makes a sound that's both a shriek and a snarl, and backs up.

"Thanks for the assist there," the dwarf says.

"We're not done yet," Severkin replies evenly.

The beast charges at them again, but now Severkin is on his feet and ready. While the dwarf swings at the creature's mouth, Severkin rolls below its chin and, rising up, slashes with both knives at its belly. The skin is as soft as fine leather and cuts open easily, pouring ichor and blood down on Severkin. The monster coughs, then screams, and Severkin thrusts his hand up through the open wound, striking his knife where he thinks the heart is. He feels the creature begin to die, its muscles clutching at its last heartbeat, its last breath. The beast begins to fall on Severkin, but the dwarf pulls him back in time to watch the thing topple forward.

"That's some fighting," the dwarf says. Severkin turns around and looks him over. He wears lightweight leather with a copper badge in the shape of a mountain on his chest. He has a short black beard and a leather helmet that covers his nose but has two huge openings for his eyes.

"You too," Severkin says. "You also run pretty well."

The dwarf laughs. "I would have never taken an under-smelk on by myself. I was out patrolling—didn't expect it. They say the giants stirring is what's driving them overground, making them angry."

"I'd believe it," Severkin says. "I saw a giant last night. It rose from the ocean and made a wave so huge my ship was dashed on the rocks. It was headed for Wellhall."

The dwarf nods, his mouth a grim line. "They call that one Grimwater. He's huge, and the only one we've seen from the sea. He's been attacking Wellhall nightly for three days, but they drive him off with their cannons and ballistae. He keeps coming back, though. It's a good thing he's the only one from the sea awake so far. The land giants are smaller. Still need an army to take one down, but at least they *can* be taken down."

"So it's true? All the giants are waking?" He'd hoped the one in the ocean had somehow been an oddity, an aberration.

"Aye." The dwarf nods. "We dwarves have felt them stirring for years. It's why the peace was made. We need to fight together. But we can talk more of that in town. You look like you need some mead in you, or a shower at least." Severkin looks down at his blood-soaked clothes. "And, as a member of the National Guard, I can reward you for your valor in slaying the undersmelk. That'll help you get some new clothes."

"Thanks," Severkin says. He doesn't trust the dwarf, not really, but he needs more arrows. "I'm Severkin."

"Rel," the dwarf says, shaking his hand. "C'mon, I'll take you to Bridgefall."

THREE

NICK WAKES up to Dad knocking on the door of his room. He opens it before Nick can reply. Mom always waits until he says it's okay to come in. Waited. Will wait. He conjugates his mother's presence in his head, trying to figure out what state she's in.

"Bookstore today," Dad says quickly. "Better get ready." Then he closes the door, leaving Nick alone in the dark, rubbing his eyes. He'd only played the game a little, just through that first big fight, before he'd felt crazy tired. He'd gone to sleep, wanting to play in the morning, take it all in with fresh eyes. But now he feels guilty. He should have been looking up more symptoms, maybe searching his parents' room. He thinks maybe if he can find out what Grandpa did, he can prove that it didn't line up with Alzheimer's. He'd told himself he'd do that today. He'd forgotten about the bookstore. If they get it over with quickly, he can come home and maybe sneak into their bedroom then. But the bookstore never goes quickly with Dad. Dad will have to sign any copies of his book they have, and chat with Traci, and agree to come in and give another talk. Nick sighs, and rolls out of bed.

The boss fight had been awesome. He could practically feel the creature's breath through its tentacles and that moment where he had rolled under the thing and killed it by stabbing upward had made him feel amazing and powerful. The controls were ten steps ahead of anything else on the market—it was like they'd been able to sense what he wanted to do. The graphics were so intense he could feel the world—smell it, taste it. It was nice to be in a reality where he got to be Severkin again. And Severkin is even more of a badass now. If Severkin's mom needed rescuing, he'd break her out in less than a day. But Nick isn't Severkin.

He showers and dresses and heads downstairs to eat. Dad isn't in the kitchen, so Nick pours himself some cereal and milk and eats alone, not looking at the stove, where he can hear Mom cooking and humming, but instead staring at the seat Mom usually sits in, wondering if this was what it was going to be like for the rest of his life.

Dad comes in and looks down at him.

"Ready for the bookstore?" he asks. Cheerfully. Just his tone is like a prick of rage poison in Nick's blood. Nick feels his hand clench into a fist as he turns slowly to look up at Dad.

"Sure," he says. The school will give him his books at the beginning of the year, but Mom and Dad always wanted him to buy copies of the novels and history books he would be reading, so he could write in them, highlight them, and keep them. He has shelves of books from middle school that he doesn't think he'll ever look at again, but they make his parents happy.

"Well, let's get going, then." Dad makes a "come with me" motion, and Nick takes a deep breath and unclenches his hand. "Bowl in the sink," Dad reminds him. Nick leaves his bowl where it is and follows Dad outside.

They drive to the bookstore in silence. Nick gets to sit in the passenger seat. The seat isn't quite comfortable—usually Nick pushes it back a few inches, but he doesn't feel like it today. He just stares out the window. When Dad pulls the car into the large parking lot that's shared by the various stores and restaurants of the shopping center, he turns to Nick, his face all solemn, so Nick talks before his dad can.

"Let's get my books," Nick says, opening his door. "I want to get home and play my game."

The bookstore was called A Place for Learning when Nick was little, but six years ago it had been bought out by a chain. The same woman still runs it. Traci is working the register when they come in, and puts her arms up as though she's rejoicing in church when she sees them. She's older than Nick's parents and wears her hair in long braids that are almost entirely gray.

"Lamont!" she calls, her voice half fangirl scream, half singsong. People look over at Nick and his father, and Nick looks down at his shoes. Traci runs out from behind the counter and gives Dad a huge hug, then gives Nick one, too. "We have plenty of your new book in stock," she says, pointing at a nearby display. "If you want to sign them." The display shows the latest of Dad's books, its bright black-and-white cover with the chain of red hearts: *Across the Line: A History of Interracial Love and Marriage in America*. It's his fourth book. In his first one, *I Go Back*, he traced his own heritage all the way back to Africa and recounted what it meant to him. That one landed him on *Oprah*, where he traced her heritage, too, and became a bestseller. Then came *Before We Were Free*, on the history of pre–Civil War civil rights activists, and *Stories Across the Ocean*, where he took traditional African folktales and showed how they transformed into American Southern tall tales and fables—that one is Nick's favorite.

Sometimes, when he's just with his family, Nick's dad jokes about being a professional Black Man. Nick liked it more when he was younger, how famous Dad was, hearing the stories over and over again about where he came from, about how his great-great-great-grandfather was one of the first black men in the army, and how his ancestors before that fought back against their white masters in the South, and even before that, about where in Africa his ancestors came from. He still likes it, but it's become less impressive some-how. Dad has all the answers, but only on one subject, and Nick's questions all fall into other realms.

It's not that he doesn't appreciate it. When Nick was little—like ten or younger—and kids in his class would say something racist, like "You can't be Luke Skywalker, you're black," he would say that wasn't true and then call over a teacher to confirm it. But as he's gotten older and has had to say the same things over and over, teach the same lessons to the same people, he's gotten tired of it and has just stopped. If Dad wants to educate, let him educate. It's not Nick's job to make white people stop being racist. It's theirs. He doesn't know how Dad has kept it up for so long.

"I'd be happy to sign some books," Nick's dad says, a big smile on his face. "But we're here doing a little school shopping. I have Nick's book list. . . . Maybe you could give us a hand?" Dad takes the book list from his pocket with a flourish.

"Of course, of course," Traci says, still smiling. She looks at the list. "Junior high? Seventh grade? Are you really that big now, Nicky?" She takes a step back, as if evaluating him.

Nick sighs. "Yeah," he says.

"Oh yeah, he's a teenager," Traci says with a laugh.

Nick tries to smile. He likes Traci. She's silly, and fawns over Dad too much, but she's smart, too, and used to read him books when he was little.

"Where's Sophie?" Traci asks suddenly. Nick shivers and wanders over to the display of Dad's books, to look at the covers.

"Ah," Dad says delicately. "She's at Sunrise now."

There is a long pause, and Nick fingers the corner of one of Dad's books. It's sharp as a razorblade. He bends it back and forth, listening to the tiny rustle it makes, like a stifled sob or a sigh.

"Oh, Lamont," Traci says. She pauses, and Nick can tell she's looking over at him. He opens the front cover of Dad's book and reads the dedication: *For Sophie, the love of my life and the most amazing inspiration I have ever found.*

"I'm so sorry," Traci says finally. Nick feels his shoulders relax, and he closes the book and puts it back.

Nick wants to say she'll be coming home soon. Soon as he figures out what's really wrong with her. But he can't open his mouth.

"Thanks," Dad says, and Nick wonders why he says it. "Do you want me to sign some of these books?" Suddenly Nick feels Dad's hand on his shoulder; they've followed him over to the display. Dad rests his hand there for a moment, and then squeezes. Nick takes a deep breath and pulls his attention from the book display. Dad's hand is warm on his shoulder, comforting as sunlight. He doesn't know why it shattered him to hear Dad tell Traci about Mom, but he feels more broken than he did before, like pieces of glass being ground into sand. Dad's hand holds him together for a moment, until he can rebuild. He doesn't know how Dad knew he needed that, but he's thankful.

"Sign as many as you like. You can come sit behind the table if you want, and I'll have someone bring them over."

Dad once told Nick he tried not to sign them all, in case Traci couldn't sell them all. But Traci loves Dad. She invites him to speak every month, and he always goes. Nick and Mom go, too, and they sit in the back as Dad reads from his book and talks about black history and answers the questions from the couple dozen black people who live in the area and all get together for this. Sometimes people come and talk to Mom and ask Nick how proud he is of Dad, which is a question he can't really answer without sounding like a really little kid. But it's a lot. Or it was. He's not sure now.

Dad goes and sits at a counter, a stack of books with him, and takes out a pen from somewhere—he always has a pen prepared when they come—and starts signing. Traci brings another pile to him, then looks at the book list again.

"I'll go get these. Nicky, you want to give me a hand?" Nick nods and follows Traci around the store, picking out the books from the list.

"Junior high," she says, shaking her head and looking at the stacks of thick, glossy books. "You're making me feel old, Nicky."

"But I'm not making you look it," Nick says. Traci laughs, a heavy bell-ringing sound that Nick loves. "You are too charming, just like your father." Nick smiles, but he knows this isn't true. Traci is the only one he can charm. And only by repeating things Dad has said to her before and she's forgotten. She forgets all the little compliments within days, but no one is locking *her* up.

"Let's see," she says. "*A Streetcar Named Desire, Dr. Jekyll and Mr. Hyde* . . ." She plucks the books off the shelf and stacks them into a pile in Nick's arms. "I think I'll have another get-together soon, you know. Your dad can read again. It'll be good for him, and you, to be around the community."

"That sounds cool," Nick says—politely, he hopes. He doesn't want another one of those gatherings right now. It's not that he dislikes them—he actually thinks they're sort of interesting, and there's a good feeling to them, to being in a room filled with people who look like him. But he wouldn't know what to do without Mom to sit with in the back. He wouldn't know what to do every time Dad said "She's gone to Sunrise House" and Nick would shatter again.

"I'll make sure to invite the Clarkes, too, and tell them to bring their daughter," Traci says, half to herself. "She'll be entering Reagan this year, too."

Nick nods and swallows. Usually he's the only one under thirty at these readings. He's not sure if it's better that way.

"Here we go, that should be the last of your books," Traci says. "Let's see how many books your dad has signed." Nick carries his books back to the register. Dad has signed about a dozen books but seems to be talking to some customers. A few of them are looking over the book.

"Nicky and I agreed it's time for another little get-together, if you're up for it," Traci says to Dad. "Maybe . . ." She goes around to look at a calendar hanging on the wall behind the register. "Thursday? That good? You want to come read a little, talk to the usual folks?"

"Sure, that sounds nice," Dad says.

"We'll be allowed to see Mom by then," Nick points out. He knows other things will happen by then, too—school will start, his friends will ignore him in the halls—but he feels weird scheduling something when they should check with Mom first. When does she want them to come? Every day? Shouldn't she be the priority?

"That's okay, though, right?" Dad asks. "We're going to have to give her a break from us now and then."

Nick wants to say no, it isn't, but he thinks Dad should be able to realize that. Why would she need a break from them, after all? She hasn't needed one before. He feels the ragebrew in his veins again, a sudden desire to burn all Dad's books, watch those dedications dissolve in the smoke. But he folds his arms instead. "Sure," he says.

"It'll be nice for you, Nicky," Traci says, putting her arm around his shoulders. She smells like paper and coffee and a little bit like flowers, and Nick nods and says "Sure" again, and is surprised to feel the poison begin to drain from him.

"Good, now how about we get you rung up? I hope you learn something this year, with all these books you're buying."

• • •

At home, Nick runs upstairs before Dad can say anything. He knows he should be snooping for information about his grandfather, but all he wants is to lose himself in the game. Everything outside the game is so sad now, so gray. The absence of his mother is everywhere, reminding him she needs to be rescued. And he can't rescue her yet, isn't sure how. But Severkin can slay giants.

He turns on the console, but Dad opens the door without knocking, before Nick's last save even loads. Dad comes in with the bag of books and sits down on the bed.

"You want to talk about anything?" Dad asks.

Nick thinks Dad has asked this a thousand times since yesterday, though he knows it can't actually have been that many. "No," he says. The game is taking a long time to load. Nick hopes they fix that with a patch soon.

"It's going to be weird, without your mom, I know that. But I'm going to try, Nick, to be the best dad I can. You know that, right?"

"Yeah," Nick says. The game's loading screens are pictures from the game, first a view of Wellhall, then a farm, then a dwarven city. Under each of the pictures is a little information about the game. *You can organize your inventory by pressing O at any time in the inventory screen. Wellhall is the capital city of both the gray elves and the dwarves. Remember to recruit companions! It's easier to slay a giant with friends.*

"Okay, well." Dad stands, taps his foot a few times, crosses and uncrosses his arms. "I'll be here if you want to talk."

"Thanks, Dad," Nick says without looking up. Dad leaves, and Nick hears him go downstairs. The game is only 20 percent loaded. It's taking forever. Nick puts down the controller and stands. His parents' bedroom is just across the hall, and he can hear Dad downstairs, watching TV. Nick walks quietly across the hall and opens the door slowly, so it whispers. The room is in disarray. Closets are open and empty, the armoire's doors hanging out like the arms of a defeated knight. How much had they managed to squeeze into those suitcases? Nick pads over to the closet. Mom had kept an album here, and a shoebox. When he was little, she'd take them down and show him things—photos of his grandparents, a piece of the Berlin Wall, a lock of her hair from when she was a baby. But they're gone now. At the home? Dad couldn't have thrown them out, could he? He looks at the bottom of the closet, under the bed, but he doesn't see them anywhere obvious, and he feels the shiver-tingle of fear—he's been in here too long, Dad could come in. Nick pads back to his own room. The game is 99 percent loaded. Nick sits down to play. Where is Mom's stuff?

FOUR

BRIDGEFALL ISN'T much to look at from where Severkin is standing. They've come to it across the plains, and it's just a bridge connecting two cliffs over a huge ravine. It's a big bridge, very big, with houses on either side of it, and still wide enough down the center to march an army, but Severkin had expected more somehow.

"You gotta look at it from over there," Rel says, as if sensing Severkin's disappointment. He waves Severkin away with his hand, and Severkin walks down the side of the cliff to look at Bridgefall from the side. And then he *is* impressed.

Under the bridge, hanging like wind chimes, are platforms, dozens of them, each larger than a house, all suspended by thick ropes and connected to one another with smaller bridges and spiral staircases. There are platforms hanging from platforms, and against the sides of the cliff are more platforms, built out like shelves. And this is where the life of the city is. There are inns swaying in the breeze, smithies and taverns, and people scurrying up and down the stairways. The lowest platforms hang just over the river at the bottom of the ravine, and the people there cast nets off the side and haul up fish. The city sways in the wind, but no one seems to mind.

"Nice, innit?" Rel asks.

"Impressive," Severkin says, nodding. "No one worries about falling? Something breaking?"

"Oh, we worry about it. . . . But the water is fresh, the air is cool, and the company is good. So we check the ropes every day and we trust in the gods, if you're inclined toward them." Severkin doesn't say anything. "C'mon, I'll take you to the guardhouse and give you that reward you've earned. I may have a little job for you, too, if you're interested."

"I'm interested in any work I can get," Severkin says, following the dwarf.

"Good. It'll be a simple job. We're expecting a team with a package to show up soon—a special artifact we've recovered from one of the ruined dwarf cities—and we'll need someone to deliver it to Wellhall. And, if you can do that, I'll even send along my recommendation that you be allowed to join the National Guard."

"The National Guard?"

"We have chapters in every city; we do what our orders tell us, and get paid well for it. You wouldn't have to take a full-time position if you're the wandering type, though. We have plenty of what we call freelance members. Approved to work for us on a fee-per-job deal." They walk out onto the bridge, and Severkin follows Rel to a spiral staircase leading down toward the wind-chime platforms.

"Like a mercenary?"

"Yes, but with a fancy badge." Severkin raises an eyebrow.

Mercenary with a fancy badge. That sounded like a useful job title for getting into forbidden ruins and the like. "O'course, it won't let you break the law, if that's what you're thinking." The platforms sway, but only a little. It's like being on a boat.

"No," Severkin lies. "Just wondering about the system."

"It works for us. And with most of us being called back to Wellhall to defend against the giants, we have lots of work for freelancers these days."

"Sounds like there's no downside."

"There isn't." Rel has led him over a few platforms, and they stop now in front of a large wooden building adorned with a symbol of a mountain over the door, like the one Rel wears on his armor. "This is our chapter here in Bridgefall."

The inside is just like any other guardhouse, with practice dummies on one side of the room, a dining table on the other, and armor and weapons displayed all over the walls. Rel leads him upstairs. There are bunks up here, and a small office. Rel's office, Severkin realizes as they go inside. Rel opens a small safe and presents Severkin with a few hundred gold coins.

"Your reward. You interested in the job?" Rel asks.

"Yes," Severkin says. "And I'd like to join the guard."

"Good," Rel says with an approving nod, and sits down at the small desk in the corner. He takes out paper and ink and writes a short letter, folds it up, and hands it to Severkin. "You'll need to bring this letter to Wellhall—give it to Rorth, in the upper city. Don't give it to Elega, in the lower city. She can approve you, too, but she doesn't like elves. She doesn't really like anyone with the nerve not to be a dwarf."

"Thanks," Severkin says, taking the letter. "But . . . what is the lower city?"

Rel smiles. "Don't know the history, do you?" Severkin shakes his head. "Well, Wellhall is really two cities. Above is the capital of the overlands, where your folk, the gray elves, rule. Down below is the capital of the dwarves. It used to be one big city, all of us living together, hundreds of years ago before the wars. Then we sealed the lower part off from the upper—until two years ago, when we dwarves felt the giants stir and hammered through the seal to make peace. So it's one city again, but of course it's not, not really. Many don't like the peace. On both sides. That's why I asked to transfer out of there. I'm a dwarf, but the way I see it, there are folk who break the law and folk who don't. And monsters, of course." Rel strokes his chin for a moment and chuckles.

"That's very enlightened of you."

"Don't flatter. I can tell you're no great lover of dwarves, and that's fine, since you came to my rescue anyway." Rel waves him off with a hand. "I'm just telling you how I see it. Maybe you'll see it that way sometime, too."

"Maybe," Severkin says, thinking it might be true.

"Good. Now, as I said, I have a package for you to take to Wellhall, too, if you're willing."

"I am."

"The team isn't here yet, though. So go wash up and get some new armor with all the coin I just gave you. Stop by tomorrow or whenever you're ready and I'll tell you the details."

"Thanks," Severkin says. "I will."

Severkin leaves the guardhouse and walks to the edge of the platform, then looks over. It's a long drop. He straightens his shoulders and takes a deep breath. He has to get some arrows.

Severkin finds a weapons shop a few platforms down, and an armor shop across from that. He has enough gold to get a slightly better class of equipment, but not as much as he wants. Luckily, the blacksmith at the armory needs some hyena skins, and Severkin is happy to go out of town and hunt a few down.

It seems everyone in Bridgefall has some tasks that need to be done: the herbalist needs herbs from a particular nearby cave, a fishmonger has lost his wedding ring while fishing, a pretty young gold elf who approaches him on the street wants an escort to her husband's grave, where a herd of molevores have made their home. Severkin is happy to tackle all these jobs and more, taking the coin and rewards and using them to upgrade his weapons and armor, as well as practicing his archery and hunting.

Once he's done nearly everything that seems to need doing in Bridgefall, Severkin returns to Rel. He has new armor, new knives, and a new bow. He's carrying hundreds of arrows. He feels ready for anything. He finds Rel in the upstairs office of the guardhouse. He's talking to a woman, a gray elf. She's older than Severkin, maybe old enough to be his mother. Her hair is white and pulled back into a long braid, which makes the lines on her face seem more severe. A long spear is strapped across her back. When Severkin walks in she regards him like an appraiser.

"Severkin!" Rel says. "Ready for that job?"

"Yes," Severkin says.

"Great. This is Reunne. She'll be going with you. She has the package."

Severkin looks the woman over again. Rel had said there

was a team bringing the package—is she it? She's clearly a warrior, all muscle and worn hands, but he much prefers to work solo. "I can do this alone," he says.

But Rel shakes his head. "Sorry. An approved guardsman needs to go with the package. Reunne has to go. But she'll need your help."

"*Need* is a strong word," Reunne says. Her voice is deep and slightly accented. She folds her arms and leans to one side.

"Well, you'll *appreciate* the help, then," Rel says. "You were just saying the shortcut you know would be dangerous on your own. Now you won't be alone."

"Perhaps you and I have a different definition of *alone*," she says, raising an eyebrow. "He's so scrawny, I'm not sure he counts as a person. And I round down." Rel stares at her blankly. "Fine," Reunne says. She turns to Severkin. "We're clearly both loners, but I'll give it a shot. You willing?"

Severkin nods. "Sure."

"Good, then follow me. I know a shortcut."

FIVE

NICK SAVES, then turns the game off. It's late, and he doesn't want to get started on the next part of the quest right now. And even without his mother telling him, he knows he should sleep. The first day of school is tomorrow.

He's been living the game for almost a week now. Dad hasn't bothered him, either. They've barely spoken, just eaten together, and then Nick goes back upstairs to play. Dad hasn't left the house, except once, to go to the grocery. Nick explored some more while Dad was gone—looked in the hall closet, the downstairs cabinets—but he couldn't find anything about Mom or her dad. Any clue to prove she's got something that isn't Alzheimer's. Maybe he can search her room at the home.

He crawls into bed and sets the alarm. He focuses on the game, instead of Mom. He wonders if that new elf, Reunne, is an NPC or another player—a real person somewhere out there. She looked older, but then, some of his friends (not really friends anymore, he remembers like a punch in the face) like playing as old wizards, so maybe there are people out there who like playing as older women warriors, too. And she'd had a sense of humor—joking about how thin Severkin was. NPCs are never really funny—they don't get jokes, the way Rel didn't get Reunne's jokes. She's probably a person. He hopes that she's not mad he turned off the game, though, and that she'll wait for him to finish the quest. There are probably plenty of other quests for her to do in the meantime.

He turns out the light. He doesn't want to go to school tomorrow. He wants to keep playing. But he knows that's not an option. When he visits Mom next week, she's going to ask how the first day of school was, and he can't say he didn't go. So he closes his eyes and tries not to think about how it's going to be tomorrow. Instead, he thinks about what he's going to do in the game when he gets home.

• • •

Nick has already been inside Reagan a few times, for some sports events and field trips. But he has a locker here now, and has to remember where the classrooms are.

He sees people from Lincoln. Some are even people he used to hang out with, but mostly now they turn away from him and whisper to each other. Some of the girls give him PityFace, but when he smiles at them, they look away. After the thing last spring, he'd lost all his friends, but in a way that had made it clear to him he'd never really been close to any of them.

The first day is mostly orientation, with a big assembly, and then they're divided into groups and instructed to tell each other their names and favorite subjects and stuff. It's pretty boring. At lunch, Nick sits with some of the people from his group who hadn't gone to Lincoln, but they talk among themselves on the other side of the table while Nick stares at his lunch.

After lunch they have twenty minutes in each of their classes, so they know where their classrooms are and so the teachers can introduce themselves. The teachers seem to fit the standard roster of "enthusiastic" and "weird," none of them too scary or special, except for Ms. Knight, for world history, who is really young for a teacher, or at least looks and acts it.

And dresses it, Nick thinks, looking at her long yellow polka-dot skirt and T-shirt. She has giant eyes and long red hair and talks with her hands a lot. She's very excited.

"So, what we're going to do," she says, "is figure out where each of your families interacted with a famous moment of history! For the first quarter, you're all going to do a research project based on some historical event that your family, or ancestors, were part of. It could be slavery, or the War of the Roses, or . . . anything!" she says, making a giant circle with her hands. "So you guys should start talking to your parents, and figure out what bit of history you'd like to do." Nick sighs, and puts his head down on the desk. Dad is going to love this. "Oh, and don't forget to put your email on this sheet. I want to be able to contact you about the project." Nick puts his Severkin email down instead of his student email so he doesn't have to check more than one.

Luckily, history is the last class of the day on Wednesdays. He shrugs his backpack on and leaves the classroom, headed for the buses.

"Hey!" comes a voice from behind him, but he ignores it, assuming it's for someone else. "Hey, Severkin!" the voice says again, and Nick turns. There's a girl he doesn't know running toward him. When he turns she stops and smiles. She has eyes like huge, soft hills, and lots of freckles on her fawn-colored skin. Her black hair is piled up behind a blue headband, and then falls down her back like a horsetail. It's streaked with chlorine blue. Her eyeliner flies out from her eyes in wings and she wears a shimmery purple dress. He's staring, and a girl is talking to him, and he realizes he hasn't learned that skill yet—talking to girls.

"I'm Nat," she says, extending a hand. Her other hand clutches some books to her chest. Nick shakes her hand, swallowing. "I recognized your handle on Ms. Knight's email list. I've seen you on the message boards. For the game. I always thought it sounded fun to say—'Severkin.'" She says the name like a serpent coiled around a sword. Nick feels his body warm slightly. "I love Wellhall—have you been playing it?"

"Yeah," Nick says, smiling. "I think I've done every side quest in Bridgefall. And my real name is Nick."

"Nick, right," she says, shaking her head. "I was totally prepared to just call you Severkin for the rest of your life."

"So where are you?" Nick asks, pulling his backpack straps higher on his shoulders.

"I'm all over the place. Not too far in the main quest, though. What server do you play on?"

"The Character one," Nick says.

Nat's eyes go wide. "Hardcore," she says. "Wanna play together?"

Nick thinks about it. He's played with friends before, but

that was always just taking turns watching each other play. Same when he plays with Mom. Played with Mom. Will play.

He doesn't know how it will work with someone else. A girl with freckles and blue streaks in her hair.

"Okay," he says. "I've never . . . I mean, I don't usually play MMORPGs, so I might not be good at it."

"Well, you play on the Character server, so I just won't tell you who I am," she says, smiling.

Nick laughs. "That doesn't seem fair," he says.

"It isn't," she says, still grinning. "But it'll be fun for me."

"Okay," he says. Cold hands tickle his stomach from the inside. He doesn't know if she's being sincere or just pretending to like him.

"Oh, I gotta get outside or I'll miss my bus. I'll see you in history tomorrow?" She bites her lower lip.

"Yeah," Nick says, smiling back. She runs off, and Nick stares after her, the phantom of freckles and blue streaks left behind like fireflies.

• • •

He takes the bus home and eats potato chips in his room. Dad's semester has started, too, so Nick has the house to himself. He thinks of searching his parents' room, again, but knows it's pointless—he's given the place a once-over, as Severkin would say. He's found all the treasure. There are no secret doors or puzzle-locks here. No notes left from Mom.

He looks down at the homework he has for tomorrow. There is way too much of it for the first day of school. He puts it on his desk, then goes to turn on the game, but his finger hovers in front of the power button, and he can hear Mom saying he needs to do his homework first. If she were here, he'd complain and say he'd get to it later, but somehow her absence makes him pull back his hand.

It's mostly reading. English, math, history, bio, Spanish. It's slow going, too. He keeps looking up at the power button on his game console and thinking of Nat saying she'd find him. He finally turns it on when he's halfway through his homework, but before his game can load, he hears Dad pulling into the garage. Nick's just following Reunne out the door of the guardhouse when Dad knocks and comes in.

"First day of school!" Dad says, smiling. "That means we're going out to eat. Turn that thing off. Tradition."

Nick sighs, and turns the game off, not even bothering to save. His parents used to always take him out on the first day of school to this burger place he loved as a kid but since he grew up has found kind of sad. The jukebox and the stuff on the walls just look like junk now. And he feels bad for the waitresses, having to wear those big skirts that don't really fit between the tables. But he knows he can't get out of it. Can't complain, either, without Dad saying, "It's for you! It's about you!" So he doesn't. He just follows Dad downstairs to the car, and they drive to the burger place and get a table for two. Nick orders a burger with curly fries, and Dad orders the same, but with cheese, and they eat, staring at each other and trying not to talk about how Mom should be there.

Nick wonders if Mom was the one who kept the conversation flowing. He doesn't remember ever being this awkward and silent with Dad before.

"So, how was the first day?" Dad asks. "Classes all look good?"

"Yeah," Nick says.

"Teachers?"

"Yeah," Nick says again, and takes a bite of his curly fry. He doesn't mean to be terse, but he doesn't know what else to say. It was one day—it all seemed fine.

"What are you reading first in English?"

"*Romeo and Juliet*," Nick says. "I have to finish Act One by tomorrow."

"Junior high. They're not going to go easy on you anymore," Dad says, his head bouncing.

"Because it's been so easy for me before this," Nick says, half joking, half mean. Dad just looks sad, though, even when Nick smiles.

"I meant teachers," Dad says.

"I know," Nick says, and sips his soda.

"How about history?" Dad asks.

Nick pauses. He doesn't want to tell Dad about the assignment and get another lecture on his black roots and where he comes from. He doesn't want Dad to be excited about a project Nick isn't even excited about. He doesn't want to do this project on Dad, *for* Dad—but the only alternative is doing the project on Mom. Which, the moment Nick thinks of it, makes perfect sense. It's a brilliant plan.

"World history, teacher seems young," Nick says, then quickly, before Dad can ask more: "What part of Germany is Mom from?"

Dad leans back, looks a little surprised. Nick can use the project to question Dad, and hopefully Mom, too, about Mom's past. Figure out what happened that makes her think she has to get locked up. It's an excuse to go digging, and maybe get them to tell him the whole story. And from that, figure out how to rescue her.

"You doing recent history?" Dad asks. "Germany?"

"I think we're doing all of it," Nick says drily. "That's why it's called '*world*.'" He doesn't want to seem too eager.

"Yeah." Dad smiles. "Yeah, of course. Your mom is from Berlin." He pauses, bites into his burger while Nick eats another fry. "East Berlin," Dad says, when he's swallowed.

Nick furrows his brow. That means something, he knows. The eighties, and the big wall that was covered with graffiti and then came down, and the fall of communism, or the cold war, or something. He doesn't remember, exactly. He's not sure if it could have anything to do with Mom's being locked up, either. He'll have to google it tonight.

"Oh," he says.

"She doesn't like talking about it much. She came to America the first opportunity she could. Came to study anthropology. Met me." He grins. "I told her I was another culture she could study."

"Ew." Nick rolls his eyes.

Dad laughs. "Everything was new for her here, back then," Dad says, more solemnly. "She saw everything as wonderful, even the bad stuff, because she could learn from it. It's why I fell in love with her."

Nick looks down at his plate. "Then why did she want to go to the home?" he asks. *Damn.* He didn't mean to say that. The words were just bubbling in his mind and overflowed for a moment. His body goes numb, and he feels like he's about to get pushed over a cliff edge and is just waiting for the fall. He hopes this won't ruin his plans, won't make his dad tighten up and lock the truth further away.

Dad sighs, and looks at the empty chair where Nick's

mom should be sitting. "It's complicated, Nick. But your mom wanted it, in her lucid moments. I . . . didn't want her to go, but I know she had to."

"Lucid moments"—Nick doesn't know what that means. All Mom's moments are lucid, by checklist standards. He's been keeping track. Still, Dad doesn't seem mad. He's even opening up a little. Maybe he feels guilty. Nick peels away some of the moisture on his soda cup with his finger, trying to look bored.

"Had to?" he asks as casually as he can.

"Your mom wanted to protect you. And . . . I do, too."

Nick scowls at the table—light blue, flecked with mica—and the silver napkin holder. It's cheap, everything here is cheap. And he knows he's not getting anything else out of Dad. Once they say "protect" it all goes to nonsense and "You'll know when you're older." Why not just chant *Your fault, Your fault* over and over?

"Protect me from what?" Nick says loudly enough that the people at the next table look over for a moment. He doesn't care. "And why didn't you ever ask what I wanted?"

"Because you don't get to decide," Dad said softly. "None of us do, really."

Nick looks up, ready to yell some more, but he sees Dad's eyes are wet, like he's about to cry, and Nick feels himself blushing, and he quickly takes a drink of his soda. The bubbles beat against his throat like an onslaught of arrows. He keeps sucking through the straw, inhaling the soda because he's not sure if he can breathe otherwise, and his chest feels squeezed empty. The straw makes dry sucking sounds at the bottom of the empty cup, and Dad doesn't tell him to stop, like he normally would. He shakes the cup so that the ice clatters against itself, like plastic jewelry falling on the floor and breaking.

"Next year, let's go somewhere else," Nick says.

"Okay," Dad says.

· · ·

At home, Nick looks at the game again but then turns on his computer and googles Berlin. A city divided down the middle by a wall. It reminds him of Wellhall.

When he's read all the Wikipedia articles and some others on the Berlin Wall and East and West Berlin, he realizes it's late, and he finishes his homework and goes to bed without turning on the game. He lies in the dark, facing the game and feeling bad that he didn't meet up with Nat. But how would they do that, anyway? He wouldn't even know it was her.

SIX

THE NEXT day is real school, full-length classes, teachers asking questions, being expected to do math on the board in front of the class. Nick is tired but tries to pay attention. He mostly succeeds. He has English and gym and math and bio before lunch, and he can do all that, but when he goes into the lunchroom—five times the size of the one at Lincoln—he realizes that he has nowhere to sit. He's an embarrassing teen movie cliché come to life, and worse than that, he's still standing there, and people are starting to look at him. The entire cafeteria murmurs like a swarm of insects, all talking about him. He swallows slowly because his throat feels dry.

"Severkin!" shouts a voice. He turns. Nat is here. Eyeliner, hair in a huge beehive behind a lime headband. She waves him over, and he takes a deep breath. She's sitting with a few other kids, all talking among themselves, but she turns away from them when Nick sits down.

"You can call me Nick at school," Nick says. "Sorry I didn't turn on the game last night. I forgot my parents always take me out to eat the first day."

"That's okay," she says, peeling an orange. She seems to mean it, too, which Nick is thankful for. "Hey, guys, this is Nick," she says to the rest of the table, who nod or wave. Nat says their names, but Nick forgets them within minutes. "He plays the game," Nat says.

"Oh, thank god you found someone else to talk to about it," one of the guys says, and everyone at the table laughs, but in a friendly way, and Nat smiles, too, before sticking her tongue out at them. Then she turns back to Nick.

"Also," Nat says, popping an orange slice in her mouth, "I teased you about it before, but you really wouldn't know if it was me. So you could have just, like, walked away or ignored me. On the hardcore server, you can't talk out of character at all."

"Yeah," Nick says. "That's why I like it. I can still get lost in the world."

"Escapist." Nat nods. "Well, I picked a character to play on the hardcore server. Elkana. She's a troll sorcerer. And you're Severkin, right?"

"Yeah. Gray elf treasure hunter. A *troll* sorcerer?"

"I like to play against type," Nat says with a grin and a shrug. "So, you want to meet up in Wellhall?"

"I haven't even gotten there yet. But I'm headed there now."

"Okay, cool. There's a pub in the overcity called the Silver Roof. Let's try to spend time there between quests. We'll be sure to meet up eventually, right? Why don't you text me when you're close? Then we won't wait forever for each other."

"Okay," Nick says, nodding. She takes out her phone and Nick takes out his and they quickly exchange numbers. Nick realizes he hasn't eaten anything yet and stares at his soggy, Dad-made salami sandwich, then takes a bite. It's not as awful as he'd expected, but still pretty bad.

"It's so well thought out, the way they did it. I wish they'd given more interviews and stuff, and told us where they got their ideas. They say they're going to talk all about it for the first time at the GamesCon in the city in a few weeks." She leans in close, conspiratorial. She smells like oranges. "I got tickets. My parents are taking me."

Nick swallows, and he can feel his eyebrows rise.

"Jealous?" Nat asks, grinning widely.

Nick nods. "Will you . . . tell me about it? After?"

"Absolutely!" Nat says, acting like it was a foregone conclusion. "You'll probably be begging me to shut up about it." She twirls a small pendant she's wearing in her fingers.

"Only, no spoilers," Nick says. "I don't usually pay too much attention to the behind-the-scenes stuff—it's harder to really get lost in the game that way—but I feel like I'm going to have so many questions."

"You want to sit before the sages of the Forever Quest?" Nat asks.

"Yeah," Nick says. He imagines the sages—really Canadian tech nerds and artists—talking about inspiration and culture the way Mom talks about the mythical basis of the game when she watches him play it. That thought suddenly makes his throat dry and his cheeks hot, and he drinks some of his juice. He should be trying to bring Mom home, and here he is talking about the game, almost forgetting the trouble she's in.

"It's such a good game," Nat says. Nick nods. He tries to smile. He can't do anything for his mom here, and he doesn't want Nat to see how upset he is. He doesn't want her to know about his mom.

"The game play is amazing," he says. "I feel like I'm there."

"Yeah," Nat says, nodding. "I want to talk about the main quest and my favorite side quests, but I don't want to spoil anything, either."

"I was thinking the same thing. I don't want to ruin anything, so I don't want to ask you anything."

Nat laughs. "Okay, okay. Let's talk about something else, then. . . . Um, you know what you're doing for your history project yet?"

Nick looks down again, thinking of his mom. "Well, my dad has written all these books about the African American experience and the parts of history my ancestors were involved in," he says.

"So you have it easy. Lucky," Nat says.

"Well, I think I want to do my mom's side of the family, though," Nick says. "She was in East Berlin for the fall of the wall. I think that could be cool."

"Your mom is white?" Nat asks.

Nick nods.

"You're mixed, too!" She almost jumps out of her seat. "Another *hapa*."

"Oh, now she's never going to leave you alone," one of the other kids at the table says, and the rest of them laugh. They're all white, and Nick notices that this time Nat doesn't smile and act as though the joke is funny.

"*Hapa?*" Nick asks.

"It's the Hawaiian word for half," Nat says, shaking her hands in front of her like she's having a fit. "People who are multiracial, though, they've taken it on as a sort of community word, to express what it's like. Don't you feel like you're not really part of either side of your family?"

Nick shrugs. "I think I'm just black," he says.

"Half black," Nat corrects.

Nick takes another bite of his sandwich, his leg bouncing a little. The other kids aren't paying any attention to them now. "I don't think my dad would agree."

"Sorry," Nat says, calming down. "I don't mean to tell you what you are. You're what you are. I just got excited. I'm the only *hapa* I know, in real life. Mostly I just talk to others online. My dad is Jewish, and my mom's Chinese," she adds. "'Nat' is for Natalie Asher-Woo."

"That's cool," Nick says. "I mean, I guess you're kinda right. I do sometimes feel like I'm not totally black. Or like my dad's history has sort of eaten up my mom's. That's why I want to do this project on her side."

"Well, I can give you the *hapa* spiel, if you want," Nat says. She clearly wants to. It's practically bursting out of her. It's like he can see words pouring over the rim of her bottom lip, like an overflowing dam.

"Okay," Nick says, because he thinks if he says no, she might cry. She smiles and takes a deep breath.

"Well, I guess I told you the basics. It's half. Most people take it to mean, like, half Asian or Pacific Islander and half something else, usually white, but people of all mixed races are starting to use it, which I think is cool, 'cause we usually have more in common with each other—with other *hapas*—

than we do with people who are totally one race. 'Cause, like, my mom's parents, they all speak Mandarin when we go to visit them, and I know some Mandarin, but then they'll notice me and they'll start talking in English. And I think they talk about different stuff, too. Like, I always think they're talking about me when I leave, like I'm not really one of them. And that doesn't mean they don't love me, 'cause I know they do. I'm just . . . different. And it's the same on my dad's side. My grandmother was surprised when she got the invitation to my bat-mitzvah. I was like 'Why do you think I went to Hebrew school for five years?' and she said, 'I thought you were just trying to be more Jewish,' like I was trying to study my eyes straight or something." She takes a deep breath. "Sorry. I'm talking a lot."

"She always talks a lot," one of the other girls at the table says.

Nat rolls her eyes. "I do, though," she says in a low voice.

"That's okay," Nick says, and for some reason he feels embarrassed, like his face is tingling. "I don't mind you talking." He looks down at his food. "And, I mean, I guess I know what you're saying. I go to my dad's readings, and it's all the black people in the area, and they're really nice, but I just sit in the back with my mom. They all come up to me and talk to us, too. . . ." Nick tilts his head. "I mean, I'm black." He shrugs. "I don't think I'm really mixed the way you mean, sorry. But it's really cool that you are. And I do get what you're talking about. Maybe it's different 'cause I've never met my mom's parents. They died before I was born."

"I'm sorry," Nat says.

Nick shrugs again. "I never knew them," he says, because

what else is there to say? Also, *my mom's in a home for people with Alzheimer's and dementia, and I think she's scared more than anything, and it has something to do with my grandparents, but I'm not sure, and I know she shouldn't be there.* No. He takes another bite of his sandwich and holds it in front of him, studying the burned edges.

Suddenly a hand comes down and slaps his sandwich out of his grasp. He looks up into the laughing face of Charlie. A few other kids stand behind him. He and Charlie had been friends before last spring. Charlie is dressed differently now, with a sideways baseball hat over his blond curls, and an oversized red jacket.

"Hey, freak," Charlie says, grinning. "Your mom learn about waxing yet? Or did she learn and then forget again?"

Nick goes cold. The kids behind Charlie laugh. He doesn't even know some of them. But they know him, he guesses. They walk away, and Nick realizes he hasn't moved, hasn't responded, hasn't stood up for himself or his mother. He feels like an ice statue just starting to melt. Nat is staring at him. So is everyone else at the table.

"People are *drek*," Nat says. Nick wonders if she knows. He wonders if Charlie has told the whole school by now.

"I should go," Nick says. His sandwich is flat on the table.

"Okay," Nat says. She gives him PityFace, but only for an instant, and then she smiles. "I'll see you in history next period, anyway."

"Right," Nick says. He gets up and leaves. He feels like the whole room is looking at him. He hears a burst of laughter from behind him and it goes through him like an arrow.

Outside the lunchroom he takes a deep breath. He goes to

his locker and stares at it, trying to remember the combination. Eventually he does, and he gets his books out and goes to history. The room looks empty, the lights are out, but the windows are open and everything is gray in the light from outside.

"You're early," comes a voice from the teacher's desk. Nick turns to see Ms. Knight, eating a salad from a plastic box. She hunches her shoulders slightly, looking embarrassed, then dabs at her mouth with a napkin.

"Sorry," Nick says. "Can I just . . . sit here? Till class starts?"

"Sure," Ms. Knight says, bobbing her head in a nervous nod. "I just . . . I'm going to eat, so I don't know if I can talk. I mean, I can talk, but my mouth will be full, and that's never polite, so if I don't answer any questions, it's just 'cause I'm chewing," she says in a long rush.

"I don't want to talk."

"Okay." She looks at him like she wants to say something else but then hunches her shoulders again and picks at her salad with a fork. She takes a few more bites, and Nick looks down at his desk and wonders if he's going to go through all of junior high and high school as the freak kid with the freak mom. It was just one really bad day, at the end of spring, and he doesn't know why he needs to be punished for it. It wasn't his fault. It wasn't her fault, either.

"I really hate salads," Ms. Knight says. Nick looks up. "But I eat them, because I'm supposed to eat them, y'know?" She sighs. "I'm close with this woman—she's studying to be a physician's assistant and working as a nurse's aide—real healthy type, you know? And she *always* eats salads." She closes the plastic container and leans back over her chair and tosses it into the small trash bin behind her, glaring at it for a moment. "You're Nick, right?"

Nick nods. He wonders if she knows, too. Do teachers listen to that stuff? Is it in his file somewhere?

Ms. Knight points at him suddenly, narrowing her eyes. Nick holds his breath. "Your dad is Lamont Reeves, right? I saw that in your file."

Nick nods.

"So you're going to have an easy time with this family assignment," she says, grinning. "I mean, he pretty much wrote it for you."

"I'm thinking of doing my mom's side of the family," Nick says softly.

"Oh? What's her background?"

"She's from East Berlin." He sees Ms. Knight's eyes widen slightly. "She was there when the wall fell."

"Wow," she says after a moment. "Have you asked her about it?"

"No," Nick says, shaking his head. "I just found out, actually. She doesn't talk about it much."

Ms. Knight nods. "Well, if she doesn't want to talk too much about it, don't push. East Berlin was sort of a scary place, and it's sometimes hard for people to talk about what it was like there. But there's lots of research you can do."

"I know," Nick says. The classroom door opens and Nat comes in, holding some books to her chest.

"Hi, Ms. Knight," she says. She sits down next to Nick, and her books fall with a bang on the desk. "You okay, Nick?"

Nick looks over at her. She's drawing her eyebrows together like nuzzling sheep. He wants to smile and he wants to look away all at the same time, because she's cute, and he wants to go to the movies and try putting his arm around her. But right now, she's his only friend in the world. So he won't. He decides right then. He won't try anything that could lose him a friend. His *only* friend.

"Yeah," Nick says. "I'm okay. Sorry I ran out. I shouldn't have let him get to me."

"Don't worry about it," Nat says. Ms. Knight has stood up and is starting to write on the board, giving them some privacy, for which Nick is grateful.

"You don't . . ." Nick pauses. He doesn't know if he wants to ask. "Have you heard anything about me? From the people I went to middle school with?"

Nat shakes her head, her hair wobbling slightly. "No. Have you heard anything about me?"

"No."

"So we're strangers," Nat says, smiling. "Screw what other people say." Ms. Knight turns around at this. "Sorry, Ms. Knight. I didn't think you'd mind my saying 'screw.' You're not an old teacher." Ms. Knight shakes her head, but smiles, and goes back to writing on the board.

"So you wanna try to meet up in the game tonight?" Nat asks.

Nick nods, then remembers. "I can't," he sighs. "I have to go to this reading my dad is giving."

"That's okay," Nat says. "Tomorrow?"

"Tomorrow." Nick pauses. He's seeing mom tomorrow. "I can't tomorrow. But this weekend—absolutely on the weekend."

"Okay," Nat says. Other kids have started to come into

class. "Just text me when you know when you'll be playing. Although, that'll be so long from now, I'll probably be, like, twenty levels ahead of you, and I'll have to keep reviving you and reviving you."

"I never die," Nick says, smiling.

• • •

Nick's dad picks him up after school. Nick looks around before getting into the car, searching for Nat's blue-streaked hair so he can maybe wave goodbye to her and prove that he really does have to go to Dad's reading. But he hasn't seen her since history and doesn't spot her in the lot. He goes to get in the backseat before remembering his mom isn't there anymore, so he gets in the front seat next to Dad, his legs uncomfortably close to the dash.

"This'll be fun, right?" his dad asks.

Nick shrugs. He'd rather be playing the game.

He stares out the window as they drive to the bookstore.

"Have fun in school today?" Dad asks.

"Yeah," he says. He doesn't want to tell Dad about Charlie. "My friend Nat plays the game, too."

"Is Nat from Lincoln?"

"No." Nick is watching the other cars on the road.

"I'm glad you're making new friends," Dad says. "Maybe you can bring him over one of these days. Play the game at our place?"

"It doesn't work like that, Dad," Nick says. "You play together from separate places, with your own version of the game. If you're in the same room, you can't *both* play." Nick pauses for a moment, considering pointing out that Nat is a she, not a he, but decides not to. He's not sure why, but he wants to keep that a secret for now.

"Sorry," Dad says. "So . . . I know your mom used to play the last game with you. She said it was based on Greek mythology?"

"Yeah," Nick says, nodding, "but I wouldn't have known if she hadn't told me."

"Is this one a Greek myth, too?"

Nick shrugs. "I don't think so. I haven't played it long enough yet."

"Okay, well . . . I'm happy to watch you play, if you want." Nick looks over at Dad. It's a weird offer, and it's said in a weird voice, but it makes him smile.

"That's okay," Nick says. He knows it wouldn't be the same, and somehow that would make it worse. "I'll tell Mom about it tomorrow. She can tell me if it's from Greek myth."

"Good," Dad says. "Good idea, I mean."

"It's okay, Dad. You don't have to do everything Mom did." He hears Dad sigh a little, trying to hide it. "But you could learn to cook better."

Dad laughs. "You pick out a cookbook or two at the store today, then. We'll make something."

They get there before the official start of Dad's reading. Traci is setting up the part of the store where they have events. When Dad reads and talks, Traci drags out a podium and sets up all the chairs facing it, like in an auditorium. She makes punch and puts it in plastic pitchers on the tables in the back, next to the paper cups. She smiles at Nick and his dad when they come in.

"Come help me set up these chairs," she says—clearly to Nick, and not Dad. "Young strong man like you probably has energy to burn."

"Go help her. I'm going to go over my notes," Dad says. Dad goes to the table at the back and takes a copy of his book out of his suitcase. He has folded pages stuffed in the book, and there are Post-its sticking out between pages. Nick goes to Traci and starts putting the chairs out with her.

"What is he going to talk about tonight—do you know?" Traci asks.

Nick shakes his head.

"Oh well. School going okay?"

"Yeah," Nick says. "I have to pick out cookbooks. Do you know any good cookbooks?"

"Is your dad trying to cook now?"

"He orders pizza a lot."

Traci chuckles. The chairs are all set up. "Here, I'll take you to the cookbooks. Just pick out what looks like the food you like. I'll let you know if you pick something bad. Try to start simple, though. Stuff with words like *quick* and *easy* in the title. Not *gourmet*."

Traci walks Nick to the cookbooks, then leaves him alone to browse. He picks up a book called *German Meals*, but the recipes all look disgusting, and he puts it back. He chooses one called *Chinese Cuisine for Beginners* and one called *Classic Italian Meals*, and walks back to the front of the store to show Traci but pauses at the display of Dad's books. He looks around to make sure no one is watching, then takes one off the stand and sits down next to the display. He flips to the index at the back of the book and looks for the word *hapa*. He finds it, but there's just one page number after it, 46. He flips to page 46 and scans the text. He finds the reference:

> Sadly, though there were many relationships between Caucasians and native Hawaiians, none of them were legally recognized. This made it easy for the white partner—almost always the man—to leave the woman for a more socially approved wife. This resulted in many Asian and Pacific Islander women who had never been legally married but had given birth to half-white, half-Asian children (who became known, derogatorily, as *hapa haole*—"half-white"). In fact, many such women were imprisoned for having these children.

Nick scans some more, but that's all he sees on *hapa*. The book is mostly about marriage, after all, not as much about the kids that come from the marriage. He understands what Nat was talking about, though. Sometimes when he meets new people—kids his age new to school or even older college kids hanging in the video game store at the mall—they take him for not-black, because of his light skin and some features like Mom's. He doesn't look white, either—no one ever thinks he's white—but something else, which they try to guess, throwing out ethnicities like they're on an old game show: *Latino? Middle Eastern? Maybe one of those dark Italians? What are you?*

Nick knows that if he dressed more like what they expect of a black kid, they wouldn't be confused. It's his lack of uniform—which indicates not-uniform interests—that throws them off. But he likes his video game T-shirts with gray elves and his polo shirts with the Wellhall symbol stitched over the heart. And though he often feels bad—like he's done something wrong in being so difficult to categorize on sight, like he's made these people's lives harder—he's starting to get over that. He's starting to roll his eyes and think *racist*, in a flat, dull tone when people say, "Oh, you're black? I thought you were something else."

He stands and puts the book back and then brings the cookbooks to Traci, who looks at them both approvingly.

"He shouldn't burn the house down with these," she says. "Oh, look, there's Dina and Mike!" She waves at the couple who have just come in. People are starting to show up for the reading. Nick lets Traci greet them, then heads for the back of the speaking area, pours himself some punch, and sits down.

People arrive over the next fifteen minutes or so. There're usually between a dozen and twenty people: all black, well-to-do suburbanites, interested in their heritage and history. Dad's done genealogy charts for lots of them. Nick likes to imagine all the charts framed, hanging over fireplaces throughout the neighboring counties.

The listeners—the community—all say hello to Nick, and Nick says hi back. Some ask him how school is going, and he says fine, and they nod, and then there's an awkward silence before they go say hi to someone else. Nick doesn't know if any of them have kids. He assumes some must, but they never bring them. Nick doesn't think he'd be here, either, if it weren't Dad's reading. This is adult stuff.

But then Traci ushers in a couple with a girl he recognizes from his history class. She's pretty, and wears a light pink dress and a green headband, and her hair is so perfectly curled, Nick thinks it could be a wig. Traci practically pushes the girl toward Nick, where he stands in the back.

"Nick, this is Emma," Traci says. Emma's mouth pinches into a smile, and she nods. Nick nods back.

"I think we're in history together," he says. She nods again.

"I guess you have a lot to talk about, then," Traci says before zipping off to talk to another person who's just arrived.

"You want some punch?" Nick asks after a moment. Emma looks at the little paper cups and shakes her head. Nick nods, not sure what else to say.

"Did your parents make you dress up for this, too?" she asks after a moment.

Nick looks down at his clothes—slacks, polo shirt. "No," he says, shaking his head. He tries to remember what she wore in class today. Short denim shorts and a tank top with shiny stuff, he thinks.

"Oh," she says. She leans back on the punch table, sighing loudly.

"My dad is the one reading," he says. "He wrote the book."

"Oh," Emma says, tilting her head. "That's cool. My mom said he's been on TV?"

Nick nods. "So, what are you doing for the history project?" he asks, feeling braver now that she's said Dad is cool. Cool is genetically transferable, he tells himself.

"Oh," Emma says, and waves her hand like she doesn't want to talk about it. "Something about slavery or something. That's why my parents made me come. They said it would help with my project."

"Cool." Nick nods. He waits for her to ask him about his

history project, but she doesn't. "You like Ms. Knight?" he asks, to fill the silence.

"She's okay," she says quickly. "Do you like Ericaceae?"

Nick frantically scans his mind for teachers or students named Mr. or Ms. Ericaceae but can't think of any. "I don't think I have her," he says finally.

Emma gives him a look like she smells something bad. "She's an R&B singer. She's on the radio all the time."

"Oh," Nick says. "I don't listen to much modern music." Emma smiles, but not in a nice way—more like she's dealing with a crazy person she just wants to go away. "Do you play video games?" he asks, because at this point he knows he has nothing left to lose. Her eyebrows shoot up into unimpressed arcs and she opens her mouth, then closes it again. Luckily, Dad starts reading then, and everyone focuses on him, up front. They sit down, Nick with Emma on his right and the empty chair Mom usually sits in on the left.

Dad talks about Frederick Douglass and his second wife, Helen Pitts, who was white. He talks about how Douglass's children disapproved of the marriage and how Pitts's parents stopped talking to the couple, despite her parents' being abolitionists. When Dad's done reading, Nick wants to raise his hand, ask if they had any children, but the adults are asking their questions more loudly than Nick would have been able to, and soon they're all laughing and talking history and Nick doesn't want to say anything.

"This is not going to be helpful to my history project," Emma says softly, crossing her arms. "What do white women have to do with slavery?" She turns to Nick, her eyes reptile narrow, as if this is his fault.

"My mom is white," he says, hoping it will make her feel bad. Instead, she looks him up and down, her lips pursed.

"That explains it," she says. She turns back to the front of the room, where the parents are talking, and sighs. Nick looks at the empty chair next to him and feels very alone. He knows he shouldn't feel that way—he knows these are his parents' friends, the "community" that Traci talked about, but without Mom here, it feels incomplete. And he wishes everyone else would notice it, too. He wishes Dad would say something, anything, about how it's not the same. His dad wouldn't even have to mention Mom. Nick feels as though someone has pricked him with the rage poison again, and he tries to take deep breaths to make himself calm down.

Dad steps down from behind the podium, then takes a chair and turns it to face everyone, so they're talking more in a circle now. Some of the people get up to grab punch. Emma uses the hustle of the room as an excuse to leave.

"If my parents ask, tell them I'm in the bathroom," she says. Nick watches her walk out of the bookstore. An older man comes back to where Nick is sitting, and as the man pours himself some punch, he turns and smiles at Nick.

"I try to get my son to come to these things," he says. "I tell him he should know his history, his heritage. I didn't know any of mine growing up. You're a lucky kid, having a dad who can tell you about your whole family, going back generations, at the drop of a hat."

"It's not all of my history," Nick says, and it sounds like the growl before a battle cry. The man nods and goes back to the group.

It ends just over an hour later. People say they have to get home for dinner and start leaving, and Traci takes the empty punch pitchers to the restroom to wash them out.

"Thanks again for having us, Traci," Dad says as he puts his book and papers away.

"Anytime, Lamont. Oh, and I have those cookbooks up here."

Dad looks down at Nick. "You're really going to make me cook, aren't you?"

Nick nods. He wants to say something, yell at Dad about how Mom isn't here, but instead he looks over at the book display, with all the covers' red hearts like chains.

"Okay," Dad says.

Traci rings up the cookbooks, and gives Nick and his dad hugs before they leave. Dad chats most of the way home, commenting on something interesting someone said at the reading, and saying he should write about something else in his next book. Nick doesn't pay much attention—Dad usually talks to himself after readings—but the familiarity of the talking, the way it fills the car, even Mom's empty space, is comforting, like warm cocoa on a cold night. Nick flips through the cookbooks by the light of his cell phone and finds a recipe he likes for pasta with tomatoes and spinach. The dish seems hard to mess up.

At home, he shows Dad the recipe, and they check the kitchen for supplies, of which they have very few. As Dad leaves to go to the store, he turns and tells Nick to do his homework. Nick nods, then heads upstairs. He takes out his books, but instead of opening them, he looks over at the game console. He'd told Nat he'd meet her in Wellhall, and he still

has a mission to do before he gets there. And after that reading and Emma, he deserves this.

He shoots Nat a quick text:

> My dad's reading didn't last too long, so I'm going
> to try to sneak some game in now. I don't know if I'll
> make it to Wellhall, but just in case, keep an eye out.

Then he turns on the game.

SEVEN

SEVERKIN LEAVES the guardhouse and looks around for Reunne. He spots her already a ways off, and wonders how she walked so fast. He jogs to catch up.

"What took you so long?" she asks. "I've been waiting forever."

"Sorry," Severkin says. "I just wanted to make sure I had everything before we left. What's this shortcut of yours?"

"It's through an old dwarvish colony," Reunne says as they climb the stairs to the top of the city. "I hope your night vision is good."

"It is," Severkin says. All gray elves have night vision to varying degrees, but he has honed his. "Is the colony dangerous?" And, more important, he thinks, are there any forgotten treasures there?

"Yes," Reunne says as they leave the city. "It was abandoned decades ago. It was experimental . . . and got out of hand."

"Have you traveled through it before?"

"No," Reunne says. "I just heard about it. And I once ventured into it to see what it was like. I fought some . . . creatures there but left the way I came. If my information is correct, though, it will get us to Wellhall in a day instead of a week. We'll be well commended for bringing this quickly." She pats a small satchel strung on her belt.

"What is it, anyway?" Severkin asks.

Reunne shrugs. "An old relic. Part of a weapon, supposedly, though it seems small." Severkin's ears perk up at the word "relic."

"Can I see it?" he asks.

She pauses, then reaches into the satchel and removes a silvery orb and holds it out. Severkin takes the object—it's perhaps the size of a fortune teller's crystal ball, and covered with deep carvings of symbols he doesn't recognize. There are usually repeated themes in pictorial languages, and given enough time, he could probably figure out part of this one, but Reunne is standing there with her hand outstretched, and he hands it back to her. "Fascinating," he says. "Is that an ancient gray elf language?"

Reunne shrugs, and slips the orb back into the pouch. "All I can tell you is that it was well guarded—lost my partner getting it. That's why Rel insisted you go with me. This isn't supposed to be a solo mission. Look out—coyotes."

Severkin ducks low, sneaking through the grass toward the pack of coyotes Reunne has pointed out. He unlatches his bow and aims an arrow at the largest of them. Reunne, he is pleased to see, hangs back, waiting for him to strike first.

He shoots, hitting the coyote squarely in the flanks and sending it falling. The rest of the pack turns on them. Reunne leaps out in front, her spear at the ready, and starts to fight them off. She spins the spear, striking out at the first coyote to come into range. Despite her age, she fights with ferocity. Severkin backs away and aims his arrows at other coyotes at her sides. Reunne's reflexes are quick, and she takes out three of the beasts while Severkin gets two more with his arrows. When they've all fallen, Reunne puts her spear over her back and smiles at Severkin.

"Nice," she says. "If we keep that strategy up in the caves, we should be fine."

"Just be careful in narrow tunnels," Severkin says. "I don't want to hit you."

"That's very kind of you," she says. "Come on, the entrance isn't far now."

EIGHT

NICK HEARS Dad pull into the garage downstairs and quickly saves his game and shuts the console off. He feels guilty that he keeps putting off Reunne, that whoever it is playing her keeps waiting for him to come back so they can get on with the mission. Her dig about his being late pretty much confirmed that she's a real person. At least she's waiting for him, though. The colony she mentioned is probably too dangerous for a solo player.

"If I'm going to do this, I'm not doing it alone!" Dad calls from downstairs. "Bring your homework down here."

Nick brings his work downstairs and starts to do math problems at the table while Dad deals with cooking prep. But after a few minutes of Dad's holding up two sizes of pans and asking which to use and then taking out the spinach and looking at it as though it were an alien, Nick realizes that if he wants to eat, he's going to have to help.

They choose a pot and boil some water in it; then Nick

starts chopping the spinach, and Dad turns on some music—the old jazz he and Mom dance to (danced to; will dance to)—and he hums along, chopping tomatoes, taking the chopped spinach from Nick and putting it in a bowl, grinding pepper. He squeezes Nick's arm and Nick smiles, realizes he's humming along, too, that he hasn't thought about Mom for fifteen minutes. Then he feels guilty. They're creating a new family tradition, a new thing for them to do together, without Mom. But then Dad's knife slips and he almost chops his finger off but doesn't, and Nick laughs. Cooking together isn't wrong, he decides. This is something he and Dad can do even once Mom is home. They can cook for her while she waits on the couch.

"Did we do everything right?" Dad asks, looking at the ingredients laid out on the table in brightly colored stripes of red and green. The water is boiling like the sound of rain on the window. The smell of garlic, tomatoes, spinach, and olive oil fills the room.

"Yeah," Nick says. "We're doing good so far. But now we need to actually cook. Think you're up for it?" he asks Dad.

"I can handle it," Dad says confidently. "But you should probably read everything aloud as I do it." Nick laughs, and starts reading from the cookbook, making sure they boil the pasta for the right amount of time, and sauté the garlic a little first before adding the spinach. It doesn't take too long, and when they're done, they sit and eat—and the food isn't too bad.

"Pretty good," Dad says.

"Thanks, Dad," Nick says.

Dad gives Nick's arm another squeeze as he helps himself to seconds. "We're a good team," he says.

Nick looks at the empty chair and shivers from a sudden chill. "Yeah," he says.

. . .

In history the next day, Emma is pretending like Dad's reading never happened, like she doesn't know Nick, which he tells himself he's fine with. He has Nat to sit next to.

Ms. Knight hands out a questionnaire to the class. "By now you should have started asking your parents about their heritage and what, if any, roles in history your family has played. Don't worry if there's nothing dramatic or exciting. This questionnaire should cover almost every sort of family. It's very general, but it's a good place to start. Ask one or both of your parents all the questions. If they can't answer, don't worry about it. At the end, you can tell me, based on the answers, what moment of history you'd like to do your paper on. But if you don't know, don't worry, just leave it blank, and I'll look over the answers and email you some suggestions. This is due Monday, so you just have the weekend."

Nick flips through the questionnaire. It is six pages long. Next to him he hears Nat murmur, "Oy vey." Suddenly he has a memory of a similar homework assignment when he was little—in grade school. A list of questions about himself that he had to write the answers for: favorite color, favorite food. For the first one, he wrote "blue" in blue crayon, just to show how much he loved it, but he wasn't sure about his favorite food, so he looked up at Mom. They were in the kitchen and she was at the stove.

"Mommy, what's your favorite food?" he asked, hoping she would help him decide between mac and cheese and chicken nuggets. Mom turned away from the stove, where she was making mac and cheese. The smell of it filled the room, yellow and salty. She wiggled her eyebrows and grabbed a piece of paper from the notebook on the counter and wrote something down on it, then tore off the page and folded it up.

"Close your eyes," she said. Nick closed his eyes. This was his favorite kind of game—with little tricks and riddles, hidden messages. Sometimes there were notes under his pillow, sometimes before dessert he was given a drawing of three objects and he had to figure out where in the house was an area of equal distance from each of them. "Okay," Mom said, and he opened his eyes. "Now, where do you think I would keep my favorite food?"

Nick looked around the room, and at first headed for the refrigerator, which he could get open with a strong pull. He looked on the shelves and in the drawers at the bottom, but there was no piece of paper. Then he tried the pantry, the big closet with the cereal and potato chips, but there was no paper there, either.

Suddenly it dawned on him, and he ran up to Mom. She was wearing a hoodie with a kangaroo pocket in front, over her belly, and he reached into it and took out the folded paper. He unfolded it and sounded out the word.

"Pie-kles," he said. But that wasn't right. "Pickles!" He scrunched up his face. "Ew."

"I used to love pickles," Mom said, stirring the pot on the stove. "They were hard to get, but I loved them."

Nick went back to his questionnaire and wrote "mac and chese" in orange crayon.

"Did you decide if you're going to do your mom or dad?" Nat asks in a whisper, bringing Nick back to the present.

"My mom," Nick says.

too," Nat says. "She was born and raised in Chinatown ̶y, and her family still owns a restaurant there . . . but ̶ I know. I don't know when or why exactly they came ̶̶ything. Grandma doesn't talk about it."

"Does your mom cook?"

"Yeah. She's the head chef at Chinatown Palace, and she owns it, too. You know, it's in that little shopping center off Green Street?"

"That's where the bookstore my dad always reads at is," Nick says, too loudly, because Ms. Knight clears her throat and glares at Nick. "Sorry, Ms. Knight."

"So, you all read up on the causes of World War One last night," Ms. Knight says. "Or were supposed to. Anyone want to explain them?"

• • •

After history, Nick and Nat walk to lunch together.

"That's awesome that your dad reads there," Nat says. "Next time, you should come over for dinner after. I can tell you what's good on the menu." Nick nods but isn't sure he's ready to go to Nat's restaurant, explain why his mom isn't there. He'll do it after he gets her out of the home.

They get in line for food—Nick has another Dad-made sandwich, but he needs something to wash it down with. Something strong, probably. "If your mom's a chef," Nick says, "why don't you bring lunch from home?"

"Oh," Nat says, looking at the tater tots, "it's weird. I mean, I like the food my mom makes, but it smells funny and I eat it with chopsticks, and in middle school the kids used to make fun of me or gawk at me or kvetch about the smell, so I stopped."

"I don't know how to use chopsticks," Nick says. He takes a bottle of cranberry juice. Strong flavor.

"Come to the restaurant and I'll show you," Nat says. "I usually hang out there after school until my dad gets home from work. You should come tonight! On Fridays, dad is always home for dinner. I bet you and your parents could come, too."

"I can't tonight. I have a thing," Nick says. He thinks about saying he's going to see Mom, but he doesn't want to explain where or why or anything, so he just smiles apologetically. "Next week, maybe," he says.

"Let me know when—I'll save you the best table," Nat says, smiling. They go sit down at their own table. Nick twists open his bottle of cranberry juice, and just as he does it, he feels a light smack on the back of his head, making him spill juice on his tray in a small puddle, like blood.

"Hey, freak," says Charlie. His new friends from the other day are with him, like a band of hulking highwaymen.

"Don't call him that," Nat says. "Just go away."

If Nick were Severkin, he could handle this. But he's just Nick, and he can't even look Charlie in the eye. He feels frozen, stiff as a corpse. He can feel Charlie turning his attention on Nat, and for a moment he feels grateful—not to Nat, for standing up for him, but to Charlie, for ignoring him. And then he feels guilty and weak.

"Did someone take a dump on your face?" Charlie asks Nat. The boys behind him laugh. "Seriously, though, was it a dump? It doesn't look like dirt."

"They're freckles, you *schmuck*," Nat says. "And don't think I haven't heard all these lame jokes before. You wanna play connect the dots on me, too? 'Cause I don't think you're smart enough to remember the rules."

"You think I have trouble remembering things," Charlie laughs. "I'm fine at that. Nick's the one with memory problems. So if you were hoping he'd play connect the dots all over your body . . . well, like you said: He'd have to remember the rules."

"Piss off," Nat says. Her voice is strong, but anyone paying attention—and it feels like the whole cafeteria is—knows it's a weak response. It's not Nat's fault. She doesn't understand Charlie's weapon. She doesn't know how to counter or block it.

Charlie and his friends laugh and then move on like a herd of animals. Nick just stares at the spilled cranberry juice on his tray.

"God, what a jerk," Nat says.

"He wasn't always such a bad guy," Nick says, watching Charlie trail off with his new pack.

"I find that hard to believe," Nat says, shaking her head.

Nick shrugs. "We were friends. Then it changed." There's silence for a while. Nick doesn't want to explain why it changed, about his mother's bad day. Not yet. Maybe not ever.

"So," Nat says, her tone light, dispelling Charlie's existence, as though she's restarting from a previous save. "I couldn't find you last night. How long did you get to play?"

"Not long. I didn't want my dad to catch me playing before I'd done my homework. I think I can probably only play on weekends now, with school."

"Yeah, me too. School sucks. And we still can't talk about the game."

"Not till we meet in the game." Nick nods. "But school isn't so bad, right? I think Ms. Knight is okay."

"Oh yeah," Nat says, pushing a stray curl behind her ear. "I just mean it sucks that we have less time to play the game. Oh, and Mr. Wredge. He sucks."

Nick laughs. "I don't have him," he says.

"You're lucky. You have Briggs?"

Nick nods, and they talk about whether or not they think Briggs is going to be a good English teacher, and they compare other teachers and classes. Nat tells him about her grade school, and Nick tells her about his, and Nick forgets how weird his lunch tastes and forgets about Mom and just enjoys the talking, the way Nat's face scrunches up and her mouth moves, and then they go to their next classes, and Nick feels pretty good.

· · ·

After school, Nick finds Dad in the parking lot and gets into the car. They don't say anything, but Dad starts driving, and Nick turns the AC down because he feels chilly.

"It might be a little weird," Dad says after driving twenty minutes, "seeing Mom now. She has a new routine, you know?"

"Yeah," Nick says, though he wants to roll his eyes. She's staying at a hotel, he wants to say. She's fine.

"Just don't be upset by anything, okay?"

"Okay," Nick says.

When they show up at the home, Nick realizes he's sweating, and wishes he hadn't turned off the AC. They pull into the white gravel parking lot and walk to the porch. Mom is waiting there, sitting on the swing and sipping lemonade, talking with one of the aides. The aide sees them first and points. Nick's mom turns and smiles.

"My family," she says. She gives Nick a big hug. Nick feels a sudden relief, like he'd been holding his breath and now he can release it. But Mom smells different. She still has the smell of mint and orange, but she also smells a little medical, like a hospital. "I'm so happy to see you," she says, then lets go of Nick and kisses Dad for a long time. Nick looks away, but he thinks he hears Mom sigh a few times. He hopes they're not going to kiss like this every time now that they live apart. They never did before.

"Come upstairs," Mom says. "I can show you everything I've been doing." Maria, the nurse who checked them in, appears in the doorway, and Nick's mom smiles and hugs her. "Maria, my family is here! Wonderful, isn't it?"

"It's great," Maria says, nodding at Nick, who nods back.

"We're going upstairs," Mom tells her.

"Okay, but I think they'll probably have to go in an hour, okay Sophie?"

"Oh," Mom says, and looks down, sad. "Right. Of course. Well, let's hurry then."

They follow Mom upstairs. She's all smiles, and sometimes she cocks her head to one side in a girlish way. In her room, Mom sits on the bed and throws her arms up.

"You seem really happy," Dad says.

"They're very nice here," Mom says. "I miss you, though."

"We miss you, too."

"Look, I did some paintings in an art class I take." She goes to the large windowsill and takes a pile of papers from the sill and puts them on the bed. Nick isn't looking, though—his eyes are darting around the room, looking for the shoebox, some photo albums, clues. Something. But, like a hotel room, the place is immaculate—every drawer closed, the closet shut. He'd probably get in trouble if he just started flinging everything open in front of his parents. But how to sneak in here alone?

"Mom," Nick says, his eyes still scanning the room, "I have to do this project for history class. I have to find out how my family was involved in some sort of historical event."

"Oh, of course!" Mom says. "You started seventh grade. I'm sorry I forgot. How are classes? You're so grown up, Nicky."

"Classes are good," Nick says. "But like I said, there's the project for history class. And I thought I could interview you about the fall of the Berlin Wall. You were there, right?" Mom's smile fades. Nick takes off his backpack and takes out the questionnaire Ms. Knight gave them.

"Oh, I don't think I want to talk about that," Mom says.

"Please, Mom? I'm curious. It's for a project."

"Why don't you just interview me, Nick? Our family has been involved in lots of historical moments. You know your great-great-grandfather was one of the first black men in the army?"

"Yeah, Dad, I know," Nick sighs. "I know everything. I want to know about Mom. So, Mom," he says, looking at the questionnaire, "first question: Were there any historical events you personally lived through? Well, I know the answer to that one. . . . Let me find something more . . ." He flips through the questionnaire, past all the initial questions he already can answer, looking for something that might give him some real answers. "Here. Mom, what do you remember about your life before the fall of the wall? How did your parents make a living?"

"Oh, Nicky . . ." Dad sits down next to Mom and puts his arm around her shoulder. Mom takes a deep breath. "Well. What I remember is fear, Nicky. It was terrifying. You didn't know who you could trust. I had a friend—I don't remember his name. And he . . . Why can't I remember his name?" She pauses and shakes her head. "*Scheisse*," she says in a deep growl. "Sorry. I . . . This man, he was taken away one night. None of us—my other friends. We didn't know what he had done, or if we would be next. It was like that, all the time. But also, wanting to escape . . . I had another friend, she . . ." Mom sighs.

"Why don't we let her think about it, Nick?" Dad says. "She can write down things as she remembers them and give them to you next time you visit. Okay?"

"The questionnaire is due Monday . . . ," Nick says. He looks at Mom. Her hair has fallen into her face in smoky wisps, and her face looks like it's covered with a spiderweb of lines and white hairs. She looks so sad.

"I bet I could answer a lot of the questions for you, Nick. Tomorrow, okay?"

"Okay," Nick says. Mom is silent.

"Oh, look, Nick, Mom did a painting of you." Dad takes the top painting off the pile his mother had brought over and shows it to Nick. It's a reproduction of the photo of him she has on her nightstand. It's well done, in watercolors, so his edges seem to bleed out a little into the background. It's careful, though. Loving.

"That's really good, Mom," Nick says. Mom smiles at him.

"Oh, and this one," Dad says. "Beautiful, Sophie. And so imaginative."

Nick takes the second painting from Dad and stares at it. His body is pricked by a hundred icicles, and he thinks he should shiver, but he can't move. It's another watercolor. It shows a bridge over a ravine, bright blue water rushing under it. On the bridge are some buildings, and below it, suspended by wet lines of brown, are platforms, with other buildings on them. People, small blurs of color, walk between the platforms on bridges and spiral staircases. Some men on the bottom platform are fishing in the river.

"It's Bridgefall," Nick says finally. "From Wellhall. Have you been playing the game, Mom?"

Mom furrows her brow. "What game?" she asks. She turns to Dad. "What game?" she asks more forcefully.

"Nick's video game," Dad says, stroking her hand. "Your painting reminds him of his game—high praise indeed, since he spends all his time with it. Oh, and look, this one is beautiful. And this one."

Nick looks at the next painting, a mountain rising high into the sky, stained-glass windows cut into its sides, stairways curved along the outside: Wellhall, just like on the box the game came in.

"That's from the game, too," Nick says. "Are you playing it?" he asks again. "We could play together, if you are."

"I'm sorry, Nicky." Mom shakes her head. "I don't know what game you mean."

"*Wellhall*, Mom. The one we always play together," Nick says, feeling confused, and angry that he is confused. She's supposed to be fine. She's supposed to remember the important stuff. "This is from the game!" He shakes the painting in her face, the sound of it like thunderclaps and the feeling of its moving back and forth in his hand like gusts of wind. And then he realizes what he's doing, and he stops. His mother has drawn back from him, as if struck. Her eyes are different, confused-looking. He remembers how her eyes were a few years ago, blue and sharp as a wave smacking you in the face. But now the water is calm, rippling as though something underneath were moving, but invisibly, because the water just reflects your own face back at you. He takes a deep breath.

"Sorry," he says.

But then, for an instant, his mother meets his eye, and she winks. It might just be a flutter of eyelashes to someone not paying attention, but Nick is looking at her, and her eyes go from calm water to ocean waves again, sharp as knives, totally aware of what he's asking, and planning a secret puzzle to give him the answer. And then her eyes go calm again. Nick wonders if there's a disease that can split a person in two—take who she is and wrap her in a fuzzy-cloud layer of confusion while the real her can only struggle to get out. The real her is trapped inside, communicating only for moments, through winks and watercolor paintings of the things that will speak to her son. The real her is playing a game, just like she's always done, with hidden clues, and Nick has to figure out what the clues mean if he wants to save her. Because the real her—real Mom, trapped in the cotton-candy mass of whatever it is—can't get out until he pulls her out.

NINE

"IS SOMETHING the matter?" asks Maria, suddenly appearing in the doorway. Nick stares at his mother a moment longer, and she blinks, then her eyes change again and they're dark and sharp, and she smiles. Not scared and confused anymore, but not with the wink he had seen for just a moment. Nick isn't sure what box to check for this, but he goes over the other diseases in his mind—which one could compartment his mother off from herself? He knows some drugs can make a person look like they have Alzheimer's. Maybe the ones they've given her have made it worse, since she never had Alzheimer's to begin with. That's another Alzheimer's look-alike: drugs (curable by stopping taking the drugs).

"Sorry," Nick says again to his mother, who seems more relaxed now. Then, to Maria, he says, "Everything is fine . . . but could you tell me—you said you have game consoles here. Do you have Wellhall? Has Mom played it?" Has she hidden clues in the game, like she used to? Is she trying to tell him something?

Maria tilts her head. "I don't usually monitor the video game playing. It's during lounge time. But it's possible. I don't know about the game you mean, though. Is it new? We don't have many new games."

"She has to have played it," Nick says.

"It's possible," Maria says, nodding. She looks quickly at Nick's parents, then smiles at him. "I think maybe you should give your parents a little time alone. Want to come sit on the porch with me? We have some good lemonade. It's not the powdered stuff." Nick looks back at Dad, who nods. Mom is staring at Dad and stroking his arm.

"Okay. I'll be back in a little bit, Mom. I'm going to see if I can find the game. And then we can play it together. Okay?"

"Okay, Nicky. That sounds nice."

Nick follows Maria back downstairs and outside to the porch. He sits down on one of the benches, and Maria goes inside and comes back with two glasses of lemonade. Nick sips his. It's cold and sour.

"You okay?" Maria asks.

"I'm okay," Nick says, and nods. "But she should know the game. I've been talking about it forever. We played the last one together."

"I'm sure she remembers spending that time with you," Maria says in a voice that would match PityFace.

"Can I see where you keep the games?" Nick asks.

Maria laughs. "You can see it . . . but they're all mixed in with movies and out of order. We never really worked at keeping them in order at first, and when you have a bunch of patients with memory problems . . . things are in the wrong boxes, or not in boxes, and they're not arranged. I found a

DVD in the bathroom next to the extra toilet paper the other day. I keep telling the boss we need more of a library system, but they don't want to take away from the homey environment. So I can show you, but . . ."

"Yeah," Nick says. "I'm sure you have it. Mom probably saw someone play it or something. It's really cool looking. The graphics are great. I bet she decided to paint it and then forgot where she'd seen it. Like a dream." She's played it, he knows. She's trying to tell him something. But if he tells Maria or Dad that, they're just going to give him PityFace and tell him it's all a fantasy. He needs to get proof first. He needs to find her in the game.

"Like a dream," Maria says in agreement.

Maybe he can find her. He takes out a piece of paper from a notebook in his backpack and writes down the name of the server he uses and "Severkin," so she knows where he is. She'll understand. She's probably already guessed—he wouldn't be on any other server than the Character one.

"We can probably go back up now, if you want," Maria says when they've finished their lemonade.

"Okay," Nick says.

"It's important your parents get some alone time, you know," Maria says as they head back upstairs. "I know you love your mom, but just try to remember that, okay?"

"Yeah," Nick says.

Back upstairs, Nick sees his mom is laughing and Dad has turned on some jazz music and they're dancing. Nick remembers how they used to all dance together when he was little, though he remembers it more as bouncing around his parents while they swayed. Mom and Dad both had always hummed along, and if Nick held on to their legs, he could feel the vibrations from them. It had been like he was inside the vibrations, like they were *all* inside them.

"Nicky!" Mom shouts, smiling. "Come dance with us!" Nick rolls his eyes but is smiling. He takes the piece of paper with the server name and "Severkin" on it and puts it under the framed photo of him on her nightstand, weighting it in place, and then he goes over to Mom and they all dance together for a while. Nick feels silly, but he feels happy, too.

When they have to go, a little while later, Nick gives Mom a big hug and tells her he loves her.

"I love you, too, Nicky," she says, and Nick thinks she might be crying, but when he looks at her, her eyes are dry.

"I'll meet you downstairs at the car, Dad," Nick says. Nick's dad nods, and Nick heads downstairs and outside, waving at Maria as he passes her. In the parking lot, he heads toward the car but stops when he sees Ms. Knight, his history teacher. It gives him a weird sensation, seeing her outside the classroom. She is standing off to one side, out of sight of the porch, and is holding hands with a woman in scrubs. They're talking closely and smiling at each other. The woman rubs her hand over Ms. Knight's arm. Nick knows teachers have lives outside school, but he feels like this is something he's not supposed to see. He turns away, heading for the car, but then he hears Ms. Knight's voice call his name—"Nick!"—half question, half the noise you make when you're hit in the stomach. Nick turns and smiles at her.

"Hi, Ms. Knight," he says. He tries to sound respectful. He stares at the white stones of the parking lot.

"Hi," she says. She looks confused, and Nick thinks she

probably didn't mean to call out his name. "Um, this is Jessica. Jess, this is one of my students, Nick Reeves."

"Hi," Nick says, extending his hand. Jess shakes it. She's tall and thin, and her hair is in thousands of thin black braids pouring back from her high forehead. Her scrubs are grass green and covered in a pattern of happy bees, leaving loop-de-loop dotted lines where they've flown. She has a huge smile. Nick tries to think if he's seen her at one of Dad's readings. He thought all the black people in Two Rivers came to them, but he doesn't know her. Maybe she lives farther away, or doesn't know Traci. It's odd to think that the community Traci talks about doesn't really include everyone. It makes him feel like he's taking someone else's spot—someone who wouldn't just stand in the back with Mom.

"Nice to meet you, Nick," Jess says.

"So, why are you here?" Ms. Knight asks.

"Just . . . visiting," Nick says.

"Oh," Ms. Knight says. Everyone stands there smiling at each other for a while in silence, and Nick scratches his ankle with his foot.

"Hey, is it okay if my dad helps me answer some of the questions on the questionnaire, even if I'm doing the project on my mom?"

"Sure, sure," Ms. Knight says, nodding. Then she looks up at the big white house behind Nick. She purses her lips but doesn't say anything. She looks at Jess. "We can talk more about it on Monday, too," she says. She takes a deep breath. "So . . . who are you visiting here?" She looks away from him when she asks it.

"Who are *you* visiting?" Nick asks.

"I'm visiting Jess," Ms. Knight says.

"Are you guys girlfriends?" Nick asks. "It's cool if you are. My dad says that the fight for gay marriage is like the fight for interracial marriage was back in the day."

"Well, we're not at the marriage stage yet," Jess says with a laugh. "But nice dodging of the question."

"You don't have to tell me if you don't want to," Ms. Knight says, and Nick can tell she means it. Nick looks down at the white gravel parking lot. The small stones aren't actually all the same. Some have gray flecks, and some have points.

"I . . . she just moved in," Nick says finally. "She's way better than everyone else here. I don't think she even has Alzheimer's. She's young, and she only gets a little weird sometimes." Nick thinks of the way he'd just yelled at Mom, and kicks a few of the stones. He has to remember to check box 1 when he gets home, "Memory loss that disrupts daily life." And erase the check in box 4—no sign of confusion with time or place today.

"Is it your mom, Nick?" Ms. Knight asks in a low voice. Nick feels the words go through him like icicles.

"Don't tell anyone at school, please?" Nick says. "I won't tell anyone you're gay."

"I don't care if anyone knows I'm gay," Ms. Knight says, sounding a little angry. She sighs. "And I won't tell anyone about your mom. Of course not. But it does make me wonder why you're doing your project on her. It must be hard for her to answer your questions."

"I want to know before . . ." Nick stops and clears his throat. He looks her in the eye. She's not giving him PityFace, and for a moment he really likes her because of that. Thinks she might be his favorite teacher. "I already know everything about my dad's family. 'Cause of his books. I wanted a challenge."

"Let's see how your questionnaire goes," Ms. Knight says. "If your dad knows enough, or if you can do research, then maybe—"

"My mom isn't that bad," Nick interrupts. "She's only been here a week. She still remembers stuff."

"Okay. Then no problem," Ms. Knight says. "I just don't want this to be . . . painful for you, Nick. Or for your mom."

"No, it'll be cool," Nick says. He spots Dad coming toward them through the parking lot. "Dad!" he shouts. "This is my history teacher." Dad comes closer and smiles at Ms. Knight and Jess.

"Hi," Dad says.

"We're both big fans of your books," Jess says, shaking his hand. "I'm Jess."

"And that's Ms. Knight. She's my history teacher, but she's pretty cool so far."

Ms. Knight, Jess, and Dad all laugh at this.

"Hillary," Ms. Knight says, shaking Dad's hand. "I haven't read your most recent book yet—someone has been hogging it"—she elbows Jess as she says this—"but I'm really looking forward to it."

"Oh, don't worry about that," Dad says. He opens his briefcase and takes out a copy of his book and his pen. "Hillary, right?"

"Really?" Ms. Knight asks. "You don't have to—I'll wait till Jess is finished. Or buy another."

"Nick says you're pretty cool so far," Dad says, signing the book. "That alone should earn you a library." He hands her the book. "And I often do readings and talks at the bookstore over in the shopping center. I'll have Nick let you know next time I give one."

"Thank you," Ms. Knight says, taking the book. She hugs it. "Nick's pretty cool, too, so far." Nick rolls his eyes. "And, Nick, thank you for telling me. It means a lot to me that you'd trust me like that. I know your project on your mom will be great. I'll help you, if you need it, okay?"

"Okay," Nick says. "Thanks." He looks up at Dad, hoping it's time to leave. Ms. Knight is being really nice, and even though she might be his new favorite teacher, it's getting weird.

"All right, we're going to head home, ladies. Nick is probably dying to play that new game of his."

"Which one?" Ms. Knight asks.

"Wellhall," Nick says.

"Oh, I love it!" Ms. Knight says. "I just got to Bridgefall."

"You play, too?" Nick asks. She is absolutely his favorite teacher.

"When I have time, yeah," Ms. Knight says, smiling. "We adult types like video games, too."

"Cool," Nick says, though suddenly he wonders if he could have bumped into her in the game—she'd recognize him from his email. That would be weird.

"Anyway, go play. It's got a great background in Norse mythology, from what I've seen. Totally educational." She wiggles her eyebrows at Dad, and Nick rolls his eyes. "See you on Monday."

"Bye, Ms. Knight, bye, Jess," Nick says. Dad is chuckling, but he says goodbye to both of them as well, and gets in the car.

"They seem nice," Dad says. "And it's good that she knows about your mom. Happy coincidence."

Nick turns to look at Dad. His ears are ringing like he's been punched.

"Happy?" Nick asks.

They're pulling out of the parking lot. Dad sighs, and keeps his eyes on the road. "Bad choice of words. Sorry. I know that nothing about this is happy."

Nick looks at Dad and thinks about how well he's been handling it all week, how he seems to have adjusted so quickly. How he's not fighting, like Nick is, to prove that Mom should come home. Maybe he *is* happy. Nick doesn't know how that could be possible, but as they drive home, Dad starts to hum the jazz song they'd been dancing to, and Nick thinks maybe he's just happy for right now—happy for having seen Mom.

· · ·

At home, Nick goes upstairs to his computer and stares at the checklist. Box 4 is still checked from when they took Mom to the home. He unchecks it. She didn't show any confusion about time or place today. Then he puts a red check mark in box 1, "Memory loss that disrupts daily life." It's probably the scariest box, but that's why he knows he has to find out what's really causing her occasional memory lapses.

He goes back over some of the other Alzheimer's look-alike diseases. Depression is a big one. He knows depression is a mental problem, like one that you cure with a shrink and sometimes pills. He wonders if depression could trap a person in her head, like Mom is trapped, like those Russian dolls where inside each one there's another identical-except-smaller doll, over and over again. There are probably pills for that. She could be home in a week, once he proves it.

He wants to play the game. He wants to find his mom there. He leaves his computer, goes over to the game console, and turns it on. He smiles a little at the idea of bumping into Ms. Knight and not knowing it's her. He'll have to be careful—make sure he remembers that anyone Severkin meets could be someone Nick already knows.

TEN

REUNNE HAS vanished for the moment, and Severkin kills time by hunting a few hyenas before she reappears.

"Sorry," she says, emerging from a cluster of trees. "Nature called." Severkin shrugs. "The cave is this way," she says, and heads off toward a shallow cliff in the distance. It's a short hike, but when they arrive, the cave is barely a hole in the rock. Severkin isn't sure he would have seen it without her. They have to crouch down, practically crawl into the hole and through a long tunnel of stone and dirt. But at the end, the tunnel opens out into a cave so big that Severkin feels dizzy for a moment. *Cave* might not even be the right word, it's so huge. He's standing on a balcony made of carved stone that looks out over a glowing green lake stretching beneath them, as wide and flat as a battleground. There are houses around the lake, a death drop below where they stand, and he can see more paths and balconies winding around the walls and down through the buildings. It's as big as Bridgefall, this cave. It's a city.

Or it was. Even with his night vision, the place feels dark and gloomy. The lake glows green because it is coated with algae, and shadows seem to shimmer beneath its surface.

"What is this place?" Severkin asks in a low voice.

"It's an abandoned dwarven colony, like I said."

"I didn't think it would be so big."

"Dwarf colonies are cities. This was supposed to be a farming colony, providing food not just for everyone here but for half the dwarves in Wellhall." She starts walking carefully along the balcony. It slopes downward toward the city. Severkin follows Reunne, threading an arrow into his bow.

"What would they farm here?" Severkin asks.

"The algae in the lake. Mushrooms. That's all there was to eat down here until the peace. You surface dwellers don't know how good you have it. You've been eating mutton and bread; we've had mushrooms and mole-rat meat."

"We?" Severkin asks, but Reunne throws up a hand, silencing him and pointing ahead into the darkness. On the narrow road of the balcony, a few dozen feet ahead of them, is a strange creature. It has brass, spiderlike legs that make hissing mechanical noises Severkin can hear in the silence, and its top half is a glowing green tentacle, flapping about wildly like a tongue searching out a stray crumb.

"What is—" Severkin starts to say, but Reunne again gestures for him to stay silent. Another creature emerges from the darkness. This one also has a brass lower body, but instead of spider legs, it seems to have rusted wheels, squeaking along. And its top half is a dome, glowing green, and faceted like an insect's eye.

"Damn," Reunne says. "Can you shoot the wheeled one from here? Kill it in one shot?"

"I don't know how powerful it is," Severkin says. "I don't know what it is."

Reunne draws her spear from behind her back as silently as if she were drawing it out of water.

"Try," she says. "And if it doesn't go down in one shot, be prepared for more of them. It's some sort of telepathic brain—it can call more."

Severkin draws his arrow back and inhales the sweet sweat of the hide bowstring. He holds his breath and aims directly for the center of the strange glowing sphere and then lets the arrow fly. He hears the soft musical *twang* of the arrow leaving its string, and he and Reunne watch it sail through the air and strike its target. The sphere thing lets out a noise— part screech, part the hum of a swarm of insects. It begins to deflate, oozing black liquid, but now the other creature has turned its attention to them, its spider legs hurrying toward them, its tentacle waving in front like a whip. Reunne is up, though, prepared for this, and slashes at the thing with her spear, her braid of hair whipping behind her like a pennant in the wind. Severkin nocks another arrow and checks to make sure his first target, the sphere, is dead. It isn't moving, it has completely deflated, and its glow is fading, so he turns back to the tentacle.

It's still dueling with Reunne, weaving out of the way of her thrusts as it tries to whip her legs and grab her spear. Severkin takes aim at the tentacle thing and hits its base, right where the green membrane flows into the brass. Severkin's arrow bounces off it with a clang, but the tentacle briefly turns its attention to him, and Reunne takes the opening, sweeping the blade of her spear through the middle of the tentacle.

The top of the tentacle flies off into the air and lands like rotten fruit, but the base of it still moves, and the creature begins to flee.

"Shoot its green part!" Reunne hisses, and Severkin quickly loads another arrow and aims it at the fleeing thing, hitting it square in the stump. It clatters forward, tripping over its own legs, and finally collapses, dead.

"What *were* those things?" Severkin asks. Reunne holds up a hand, scanning the area for more enemies. When none are forthcoming, she nods and starts walking forward again, quiet and stealthy, eyes peeled.

"This colony was supposed to be a farming colony. A huge lake to grow algae in, many machines to harvest it. A mage promised the dwarven elders he could make the algae grow faster, feed more. He came here and worked his magics, but it didn't go as planned. And when the farmers sent machines to harvest the algae, the machines didn't come back."

"The algae took the machines over?" Severkin asks. "We were just fighting enchanted algae and rogue farming equipment?"

"Yes," Reunne says, her voice a steel whisper in the low light. They've reached the end of the balcony, which slopes downward like a hill. When they step off it, they are at a crossroads with a sign at the center. Two-story buildings, long abandoned, rise above them. Severkin can hear the distant clattering noises of more machines.

"How do you know all this?" Severkin asks in a whisper. "Before, you referred to the dwarves as 'we'—what did you mean?"

"I'm one of the gray elves that stayed below," Reunne says. She glances at him as if waiting for a reaction.

Severkin shakes his head.

"Don't you know your history?"

"I'm not from here," Severkin says. "I was raised far away."

"Ah," Reunne says, perhaps a little sadly. There's a sound of mechanical rattling again, this time closer. Reunne looks up at the walls, carved with dwarven symbols, then heads off down a narrow alley between two large buildings. Severkin follows. "You know the history, though, right?" Reunne asks in a whisper. The walls are close here, and claustrophobic. "That Wellhall was once a huge city both above and below, where gray elves and dwarves lived together in peace?"

"Yes," Severkin says.

"Well, when the dwarves closed themselves off from above, there were a few families of gray elves—noble families, too—whose estates were in the undercity. They knew the divide was coming but chose not to move. They stayed below."

"And you're from one of those families?" Severkin asks.

"Yes." The alley twists sharply, and Reunne peeks around the corner. She holds up one finger, then points to where she is looking. Severkin loads his bow and looks around the corner. There is another of the algae machines, another tentacle with spider legs. Severkin shoots it, and it collapses with a metal *clang*, never even knowing Severkin was there.

"So you might as well call yourself a dwarf," Severkin says. He almost spits the last word. A dwarf who looks like him.

"No," Reunne says as they move on through the alley. "I'm a gray elf from the undercity. I grew up with my family among the dwarves, but we are proud of our heritage. We have a huge wall on our family estate where the name of each new family member is carved, showing whose child it is, mapping our family all the way back to before the divide."

"But you lived with the dwarves," Severkin persists. "You

must have been part of their culture." They turn another corner and come onto a wider street, paved with broken cobbles. Stone pedestals that look as though they once burned like torches line the road.

"Well, yes," Reunne admits. "Part of their society, anyway. We kept our own culture, our own gods. But we worked alongside the dwarves, true."

"Did you work to fight the abovelanders?"

"No," Reunne says, and turns to him, looking him in the eye. "You see that, don't you? We stayed out of that conflict. The dwarves couldn't trust us to fight our own kind even if we'd been willing. I'm an elf, Severkin. Like you." She holds his eye, and Severkin believes her.

"Very well," Severkin says after a long pause. Reunne turns back around and they head farther down the street. They're more in the open now, though they are clinging to the sides of buildings. This must have been a main road at one point. Judging by the faint glow he sees coming from the lake, which is hidden behind buildings, Severkin guesses they're moving around it. He assumes they don't want to get close to the edge. It must be like these things' . . . home? Breeding pit? Severkin doesn't want to think about it.

"More," Reunne whispers, and ducks low. But this time it's too late. Four of the tentacles have emerged from an alleyway and are heading for them, and above them, diving off a rooftop, is another creature, this one a pair of green bat wings holding a rusted sawblade.

"I'll get the flyer," Severkin says, and ducks down, tracking the thing with his bow. It dives for Reunne, aiming to plunge its blade into her back, but Severkin shoots it through the wing and it spirals to the ground. Severkin looks to the front lines, where Reunne is dealing with the four tentacles herself, spinning her spear around her like a whirlwind. He crouches and takes aim, striking, but not killing, one of the tentacles. Reunne slashes it, and it falls, leaving three to defeat. Severkin notches another arrow while Reunne parries a blow from one tentacle, but then she's hit squarely on the chest by another, knocking her to the ground. Severkin lets fly his arrow, killing another of the creatures, and then draws his knives. The tentacles are quick. They make a sound like rustling leaves and rain as they move. One knocks him in the shoulder, and it stings, but he rolls and stabs it in the back. It lets out a high-pitched squeal and dissolves into water and dead plant life under his touch. Reunne is up again and quickly slashes the last creature, ending the battle.

Severkin puts his knives away and takes a deep breath.

"Thanks for that," Reunne says, leaning on her spear like it's a walking cane. "We're a good team."

"I think so," Severkin says, wiping sweat from his brow.

"But we should move. There might be more. The sooner we're away from the lake, the better."

Reunne hurries down the path and Severkin follows, both of them letting their feet fall as quietly as they can. Reunne ducks into an alley, where it feels safer to talk again.

"So what was it like?" Severkin asks.

"What?" Reunne whispers back.

"Growing up with dwarves?"

Reunne chuckles softly. "If I asked you what it was like growing up with elves, could you answer me?"

"No," Severkin says. "I was raised by a human. But I

take your point. I've just never met anyone like you, so I'm curious."

"Dwarven society is . . . dark. Paranoid. It's why they cut off ties from the overland to begin with. Everyone spies on everyone, and if you put one foot out of line, you disappear in the night, taken by the Sword and Shield. And you're lucky if you come back."

"The Sword and Shield?"

"Guards who pretend they are not guards. Spies." Reunne looks around quickly as she says this, and Severkin isn't sure whether she's scanning for monsters or spies. "Their goal is to know everything. They keep files on everyone."

"But surely not the elves?"

"Us, too. We could get away with some, but not much. We could be taken away in the night, too. Disappeared. No one could prove the Sword and Shield had taken us."

"That sounds difficult," Severkin says, but it sounds familiar.

"It made me vigilant," Reunne says. She says it in a way that ends the conversation.

ELEVEN

SINCE THE spring, Nick has been having occasional night-mares about his mother's bad day. He doesn't tell anyone about them, because he doesn't think there's anything any-one can do. He just relives the incident, twisted into some-thing worse, then wakes up and gets on with life.

In reality, it happened like this: There was an end-of-the-year dance for the sixth graders. It wasn't anything fancy, just some punch and a DJ in the gym, which had dimmed lights and balloons. Nick hadn't asked anyone to the dance, but he'd gotten to dance one song with Sadie Merrick, who he'd always thought was funny and good-looking, if not quite as cute as Jackie Dalhause. He hadn't gone for girls, though; he'd gone because everyone was going, and he thought it ended up be-ing kind of fun. Not like the masquerade balls that Severkin sometimes went to in the game, but Severkin was usually there to steal something from a museum and often got chased by guards by the end of the party, so Nick thought maybe it was okay that this party was a little boring.

As the dance ended, the kids all went outside to wait for their parents to pick them up. It was late May, and the night was warm, but there was a strong breeze that made Nick cross his arms. Charlie asked Nick to go with him around the corner, out of view of the chaperones, where Charlie was going to smoke his Second Cigarette Ever because Charlie's dad had just sent him an email saying he and the girlfriend he'd left Charlie's mom for had set up Charlie's room in their new place in California for when Charlie visited. He wanted Nick to take a drag, too, but then Nick's mom's car pulled up.

It arrived with the sort of screech that always precedes a car chase on TV, and his mom didn't park in one of the parking spaces but rather at a slight angle through two of them, right across the dividing line. The door flew open and Nick's mom stepped out.

"Oh, Nicky," she said, "I'm so sorry I'm late. I forgot all about the time." She wasn't really late—only a few people's parents had already shown up. But weirder than that, she was wearing her bathrobe, turquoise and ragged and cinched around the waist with a belt but, still, low-cut in the front. Nick felt a strange fear in his stomach, a cold nausea and dizziness. It was like when there was a glitch in a game that made you walk through a mountain and fall into a sky that wasn't supposed to be there and you died. Except it was happening in real life.

"Your mom has a nice rack," Charlie snickered.

Nick ran over to her. "It's okay, Mom, you're not late," he said. He knew he needed to get her into the car, and get away. He looked behind him, and everyone was staring. The teachers, his classmates, some of his classmates' parents. He looked back at Mom as the wind picked up and blew the bottom of her bathrobe out behind her, showing that she was naked underneath. There was laughter behind him, but it was quickly silenced. His mother looked down at him and smiled, seeming not to notice that her body was on display.

"I'm sorry," she said. "I won't be late next time."

"Get in the car, Mom," Nick said. Mom got back into the car and Nick walked around to the passenger side, his face burning, his eyes a little watery. He heard footsteps behind him.

"Um, Mrs. Reeves?" It was his English teacher, Ms. Ford. "Are you sure you're okay to drive? We can call a taxi for you."

"She's fine," Nick said, turning around. He had said it in almost a roar, and his hands were clenched into fists. Ms. Ford looked at him with an expression Nick had sometimes seen on white people's faces when his Dad walked by. That weird combination of confusion and fear, and an unspoken *What is this person doing here?* And now Ms. Ford was looking at him the same way. He turned away from her and got into the car, slamming the door.

"Let's go," he said.

In the nightmare he's been having, the incident plays out like it did in real life, except that when the wind comes along and lifts his mother's robe up, the laughing doesn't stop. His classmates and teachers laugh and point, and his mother laughs, too, and suddenly her hair is askew, and her lipstick is messy, and her eyes are heavy with mascara, and she looks like a clown or a crazy old woman from a cop show, laughing and lifting up the bottom of her bathrobe and dancing as though everything were wonderful, and Nick begs her to stop, but she doesn't.

In tonight's dream, though, when Mom goes to lift up her bathrobe, she tears it off and throws it into the wind, and along with the bathrobe, her skin and hair come off, too, and underneath is Reunne, gleaming in leather armor, her spear in one hand. She smiles at Nick, then looks behind him. Nick turns, and his classmates and teachers are mechanical spiders with glowing tentacles, and he reaches into his quiver for an arrow and takes aim.

· · ·

"Nick!" Nick wakes up to Dad calling his name and knocking on his bedroom door. "I made pancakes!" Dad sounds really excited. "And they're only a little burned!"

Nick sits up in bed, his eyes crusty from sleep. The smell of burned pancakes—like an oven on the self-cleaning setting—wafts through the door Dad left open. Nick rubs his eyes and hops out of bed. He looks over at the game console. He'd been hoping to play again this morning. He was so close to Wellhall, but he had played till 2 a.m., and he wanted to be awake when he finally saw Wellhall, so he could appreciate it. So he'd saved and shut down, hoping again that Reunne wouldn't mind. He'd had to wait for her before going into the colony, after all, so it seemed fair.

He pulls on some clothes and heads downstairs. The smell gets stronger as he walks, but the burned part fades. Instead, it's the full, sweet smell of pancakes.

"Hey," Dad says as Nick comes into the kitchen. Dad's at the stove, and Nick swears he can see a shadow in the shape of his mother just behind him. "Go get that survey from your class that you want to give your mom. Let's see what I can help you with."

"It's too early for homework," Nick says.

"It's eleven o'clock, and it's not work for you. Just asking questions. I'm the one who has to answer them. Go get it." Dad flips a pancake into the air. It lands on the counter and he quickly scoops it up and puts it back on the stove. "Five-second rule," he says to himself. Nick sighs and goes back upstairs. The questionnaire is wrinkled and in his backpack, but he digs it and a pen out and brings them downstairs. Dad has put the pancakes in a large pile on one plate in the center of the table.

"Help yourself," Dad says, handing him a plate. Nick sits and takes one of the pancakes, inspecting both sides of it for burned bits or hair. It seems clean, though, so he starts eating. It's a little tougher than it should be, but it tastes good.

"Not bad, Dad," Nick says, nodding. Dad smiles, then sits down and takes one and cuts into it before reaching over Nick's hands and grabbing the questionnaire.

"We should talk about yesterday," Dad says.

"What about it?" Nick asks.

"You . . ." Dad pauses, pours some syrup on his pancake. "The way you talked to your mother. I think you were being a little emotional."

"I just wanted to know if she was playing the game. And I thought it was weird she didn't remember. Do they have her on some new medication or something?" Nick has seen TV shows where hospitals keep their patients docile and stupid through their medication.

"Yes," Dad says, using his careful voice. "But she forgets things, Nick. That's what the disease is."

"She'd remember the game," Nick says. He knows arguing that Mom isn't sick, not the way they think, will just prolong the conversation. But the information about the meds confirms a new possible alternative to Alzheimer's. He takes another pancake. He can feel Dad's eyes on him but chooses not to look over. "So can you answer any of the questions for homework?" He eats as Dad looks it over.

"Well, something she 'remembers hating about her childhood' is the food, I know that."

"The food?"

"In East Berlin, they got only certain brands of food—really cheap stuff, and what they had at the store varied wildly from week to week. And, of course, they were only allowed to buy so much. They used ration coupons, I think. But what there was was crap. Your mom used to have to do a lot of the cooking after her dad got sick." Dad stops talking for a moment and stares at his pancake. Nick looks over at him. The room feels very hushed now, like the strange quiet of a church. Nick holds his breath, hoping Dad will say what exactly his grandfather was like, hoping there'll be some clue. "Anyway," Dad continues with a shake of his head, "she came here, and she was thrilled to be able to cook with all these different, higher-quality brands—all these new foods. That's how she became such a good cook. I was never allowed in the kitchen—she wanted to do it all."

"That's what she hated the most?" Nick asks, annoyed that nothing more has been said about his grandfather. "Not her friends vanishing in the night or being cut off from the world?"

"Well . . . that's what she talked about to me," Dad says. Nick takes another pancake and cuts into it with his fork. The bottom of this one is burned, and crackles as it breaks. Nick takes a different one. He thinks of how the dwarves and elves below Wellhall had nothing to eat but algae and mushrooms.

"Did Mom . . . protest?" he asks Dad. "I've seen some videos online, of people marching and the wall coming down. Was she there?"

"No," Dad says, and shakes his head. "She didn't want to get arrested. But she marched a few times, at the very end. She wanted to get out of there really badly, to run away, and she couldn't do that if she was arrested. Her dad was a cobbler—made shoes. And her mom was a secretary. By the time your mom was ten, though, her dad wasn't working, so her mom had to work long hours, and it was just her and her dad. And then her mom died five years later." Nick opens his mouth to ask what that was like, but his father, staring at his pancakes, just keeps talking. "Her life was hard, and really scary. Scarier than you can imagine, I think. That's why you have to be careful about asking her about that sort of thing. It reminds her of the stuff from her past. We don't want to remind her of that. Okay?"

"Okay," Nick says. But he knows that it's fear that's keeping her in the home—that's what she has to overcome. "You and Mom said that Grandpa—Mom's dad—that he had Alzheimer's, too, right?"

Dad nods.

"So is that why everyone thinks she has it?"

His father looks up at him, his eyes narrowing like he's just caught Nick saying a dirty word. "Mom does have it," Dad says, and stands up. He puts his fork on his plate and takes it to the sink.

"But is that why Mom went into the home?" Nick says, trying to get the conversation back on track. "Even though she's not that sick? Was taking care of her dad hard? Does she just not want that for me? Because I don't mind taking care of her if she forgets her car keys or something. I can start putting that stuff away, so I remember where it is. And we had fun cooking the other night, so she doesn't have to do that any-more. I mean, you probably shouldn't try pancakes without me. . . ." He trails off, staring at his father. Dad's back is to him, but Nick can see his shoulders hunch over, slowly, like stone settling after an earthquake.

"Nick," he says, without turning, "just trust that we know what's best for you." Nick can't see his dad's face, but his voice isn't angry. It cracks like the old ropes of Bridgefall, creaking in the wind, holding up a great weight. Nick's de-sire to fight back, to demand answers, fades at this. He is left silent.

"Let's see," Dad says in his normal voice, turning back around. "What else is on here?" He sits down at the table and picks up the questionnaire again, and Nick stares at him for a moment. He won't get answers this way, he knows. He'll still have to find the answers on his own.

They go over the questionnaire for about an hour, but Nick doesn't feel like he learns anything new. Maybe a little about East Berlin, but nothing about Mom. People were poor, the secret police were terrifying and controlled not just the people but also the information that got into the country. The news was twisted so that capitalism always looked like it was failing. And that all sounds awful, but Nick doesn't know what it has to do with Mom.

"That place was like a disease," Dad says. "That's what your mom used to say. She said East Berlin was like a disease."

"Okay," Nick says. He leans back in his chair. There's one pancake left, but Nick doesn't want it.

"Is that enough?" Dad asks.

"I'm supposed to talk to Mom about this," Nick sighs. "I know you're trying to help. But this is about Mom, not you. Can we go see her?"

Dad picks up Nick's plate and walks it over to the sink. "I thought we'd give her a day to rest up," he says, putting their dishes in the dishwasher.

"Rest up from what?" Nick asks.

"Well, just seeing us," Dad says, closing the dishwasher and not looking at Nick. "It can be a little exhausting, you know, hosting people you love after you've moved."

"She saw us every day until a week ago," Nick says.

"It's different now," Dad says, turning around. His voice is steelier.

"Fine," Nick says. "I'm going to go play my game." He gets up and walks away from the table. He feels the ragebrew again, the prick of the needle a clear throbbing on the back of his neck. He rubs at it as he walks up the stairs.

"And do your homework!" Dad calls after him.

Nick ignores this, walking up the stairs with heavy foot-falls, like a marching soldier. The questionnaire is squeezed into a spear in his hand. He opens the door to his room and slams the door shut, making his room cave-dark. He doesn't know why he's so angry, or even who he's angry at. He knows he should feel a hundred other things—sadness, fear—and he does, but somehow the anger always comes rising to the top, red and boiling. He feels it swell up in him like a tide, and so he takes a deep breath, sits down in front of the TV, and turns on the game.

TWELVE

THE UNDERCITY skyline seems to be made of small glowing eyes. Every building in the huge cavern—and there are easily thousands of them—is outlined in dots of light that quiver in place. But they're only little oil lamps, Severkin sees as they walk through the carved arch that marks the border between cave and city. A few dwarves with large axes and full metal-plate armor stand on either side of the gateway and eye them warily, but Reunne flashes her guard badge and this seems to appease them.

"Where do we drop off the package?" Severkin asks.

"I want to show you something first," Reunne says. "Just follow me."

Reunne leads him through the undercity of Wellhall. The buildings and the cavern towering over them are all the same brown earth color, and the oil lamps keep the city in perpetual twilight, carving shadows into every corner and street. Severkin's instinct to hide tells him this would be an easy place to do so. The shadows are thick as wool. He could already have passed a dozen invisible people, all watching him, and he wouldn't have known. They hadn't spoken much after Reunne had mentioned the Sword and Shield at the farm colony.

Something about the way she had talked of the Sword and Shield made him nervous, and unwilling to continue the conversation as they made their way to the city. He doesn't feel much safer here, but she does, apparently. He wonders what she wants to show him.

Almost everyone here is a dwarf. Severkin feels the hairs on his neck stand up. He's been in dwarven encampments before, of course, but he was always lurking, invisible. And none were ever as big as this place. He can't see the ceiling, just oil lamps growing smaller and smaller above him, like winking stars.

Reunne leads him past the blocky buildings, all confusingly alike, down street after sand-and-dirt-covered street. Windows are tinted, muffled brown glows with only fuzzy shadows behind them. Severkin can't tell if he's actually being watched or if it just feels that way.

He notices there are fewer dwarves on the streets Reunne leads him down. They're emptier. The windows in these houses aren't glowing, and it's quiet enough to hear every footfall. Severkin spots a few other gray elves, but they don't look up. They scurry around, keeping their heads down like slaves.

"This is the gray elf district," Reunne explains. "And this is my home." She pushes open a narrow gate and gestures for Severkin to go inside. They are in a small courtyard, better maintained than the rest of the neighborhood, with a bench and a low, bubbling fountain. The house at the end of the courtyard is very dwarvish-looking—square and narrow, more like a guard tower than a house.

"Nice," Severkin says.

"There's another place like this for sale just down the road," Reunne says, unlocking the front door, which seems to be made of woven roots. "It'll need some fixing up to get as nice as mine, though." She opens the door and walks in. Severkin follows. Inside is a strange melding of dwarf and gray elf: the traditional gold-and-brown stone tiles of the dwarves and walls strung with gray elf tapestries, not dwarven weapons. A fire is already burning in the hearth.

"I have a maid who keeps things tidy while I'm away," Reunne explains. "She's the only one who stayed when they opened up Bilrost Hall and we could go to the overcity. Most of the elves left."

"But not you," Severkin notes.

"I'm going to show you why," Reunne says, walking to the back of the entry room they're in. There's a stairway leading up, but Reunne walks around it to another stairway, leading down. Severkin follows her downstairs to a small room that reminds him of the gray elf shrines to the god Wodea. There are dried flowers strung from the ceiling and a ceremonial staff sticking up out of the center of the floor. The dirt smells smokier here, and floral from the incense. He knows many gray elf families have shrines like these in their homes, but usually there'd be an altar of some kind. Here there is only a huge stone wall.

"This is my family's memory wall," Reunne says, gesturing at the wall. It's a huge slab, and carved into it is a pattern of some sort. Severkin walks up to it, careful to sidestep the small incense burners on the floor. "We've kept track of where we come from, for generations, since the split." Severkin examines the carvings. They're ornate, with names carved in high gray elf script, connected by lines, and surrounded with flourishes and small symbols Severkin recognizes as representing birth or marriage.

"It's a family tree," Severkin says. The names are carved in feather-fine lettering, and they go on forever—hundreds of names. A few feet from the bottom is only one, though: REUNNE.

"We don't have trees down here," Reunne says. "Roots, but no trees. All the gray elf families who stayed have memory walls. Many left them behind when they went to the overcity. I couldn't. This is my family, my history. This is everything I am."

"I see," Severkin says. But he doesn't, really. He had no parents, no sense of family aside from his late mentor. He'd always been alone. But looking at the wall, Severkin still feels a strange tug in his chest, as though it's somehow calling to him. He stares down at Reunne's solitary name. He doesn't think it would be hard for him to leave it, but maybe he can see how it would be hard for her to. "It's powerful," he says. To know your place, to be a part of something—he has never had that.

"I just wanted you to see. I know you find me an oddity. A lot of people do now. Since the cities were connected, so many elves went back up top. But I wanted you to know I have my reasons for staying, and I wanted you to know that though we may have had different upbringings, we are kin."

"Kin?" Severkin says. The word feels strange.

"Aye," Reunne says. "I know you weren't raised here, but look—" Reunne reaches forward and touches her name. "This is me," she says as she follows the lines up, name after name, tracing them with her fingers so quickly that Severkin feels sure it is something she's been doing since she was a child. "This one, he helped create the original device that put the giants to sleep. This one is Morara, the warrior priestess who single-handedly fended off the Orcish invasion. . . ." Her hand traces up and up, her wrist gently spiraling like breath on a cold day. "And here," she says, touching a name on the top, "is the one we call the Grayfather, who founded Wellhall, over a thousand years ago. All gray elves can trace their lineage to him. So can you, even if you don't know it. We're kin."

Severkin knows the legend of the Grayfather, though he's not sure he believes it. But at that moment, watching Reunne's hands—old hands, worn like porous cliffs by the sea—and seeing her fingers tap the name of the Grayfather, he wants to believe in him. Wants to believe that he's found family after so many years alone—that he's found kin. The desire swells in him like being hit with a heavy charm spell, but like a charm spell, the connection feels unwieldy—too much too soon. And, after all, the Grayfather is just a myth.

"I just wanted you to understand," Reunne says. "We're not so different."

"I understand, Reunne," Severkin says, reassuring her. He smiles.

She reaches out and pushes some of his hair back behind his ear, then quickly pulls her hand back. "I haven't had another elf in here in years," Reunne says, shaking her head.

Severkin stares at the memory wall, his eyes falling back to Reunne's name. It's alone, no brothers or sisters, and her mother's name has a mark next to it showing she's passed on. But her father has a symbol next to it he doesn't recognize.

"Is your father living?" he asks.

Reunne stares at him a moment, then looks at the incense burners on the floor. "I'm not sure. He disappeared." She picks up one of the incense burners from the floor and looks inside it. "Empty. I'll bring it up." She heads back to the stairs, and Severkin follows. He wants to ask about her father, but she clearly doesn't want to talk about it. As they leave the place, the cloying smell of old roses fades and Severkin feels colder, a little more alone. He watches Reunne walk up the stairs and wonders if maybe they *are* kin—not in the way she means—but in their spirits. Her loneliness resonates with his, and that might mean more than lines on a wall.

Reunne places the incense burner on the upstairs mantel. "I guess we should deliver this," she says, patting the satchel on her belt. "You want to come? You can apply for the guard while we're at it."

Severkin purses his lips, remembering what Rel had told him about applying for the guard in the overcity, not under.

"Actually, you can do that alone, if you don't mind. Can you take me to the . . . staircase? The way to the overcity?"

Reunne looks disappointed but nods. "Rel warned you off Elega? Probably wise. She's not so bad once you get to know her, though. And you'll have to talk with her eventually if you want to advance in the guard."

"Still," Severkin says, tilting his head slightly, "perhaps if I can delay that meeting . . ."

"Good idea," Reunne says, one corner of her mouth turning up. "I'll walk you to Bilrost Hall."

Reunne leads him out of the house and locks up before taking him back into the labyrinthine city. This time she leads him to a new part of town, one that looks different. There are statues here, and large open squares with fountains. The buildings are wider and have domed roofs covered in gold tiles.

"That's the guardhouse, where Elega is," Reunne says, pointing at a particularly sharp-looking building with a huge carved snake coiled over the door. "And that's our palace," she says, pointing at the largest of the buildings, one with a courtyard and fountain out front. It seems softer than the other buildings, and the gold tiles cover all of it, so it looks like a huge mountain of treasure, studded with gems here and there above the windows.

"Impressive," Severkin says.

"And here we are," Reunne says, stopping at what seems to be a small wooden door placed haphazardly into a huge wall of natural stone. It's practically hidden amid the intimidating buildings that surround them.

"Seriously?" Severkin asks.

"When the lower city shut themselves off, they put up this wall. Through there were guards, traps, beasts, and another wall. Now it's all dirt." She opens the door and Severkin follows her, hunching over slightly to get through the door. There are a few guards standing just inside, but they don't say anything. In front of them is what looks like another courtyard, but as Reunne said, it's just dirt. Reunne walks across it to another wall, and Severkin follows. This is a more ornate wall, with huge metal doors, already slightly open.

"We should take down the outer wall," Reunne says with a sigh. "It would make trade between above and below easier. But some things are slow to change, even now." She slips through the opening in the metal doors, and Severkin follows. "Some things change too fast, though," she says.

Severkin looks up at Bilrost Hall. *Hall* isn't really the right term, he decides. It's a tower, completely filled by a spiral staircase wide enough to lead eight horses up, side by side. But the scale of the staircase isn't as fascinating as the material it's made of—it looks to be carved from solid white opal, and it glimmers in pearl and rainbow hues, glowing from within. Set up along the outer wall of the staircase, against the edge of the tower and ascending with the stairway as far as he can see, are stalls displaying jewelry, spices, dried roots, fruit, all calling out to Severkin to buy them. Most of the merchants here are elves, selling fruit and vegetables from the overworld, but most of the people purchasing are dwarves. Severkin remembers that dwarves ate nothing but algae and mushrooms for centuries. They must find the apples and leeks from the overworld to be exotic.

"Just think of all this, locked away from the rest of the world. The stairway is a beautiful piece of craftmanship, isn't it?" Reunne asks.

"What is it made of?" Severkin asks.

Reunne shrugs. "We think it's smelted opal—from an old, magical technique of the dwarves. Lost ages ago. The overlanders say it's a solid rainbow—old lost elf magic. We all have our stories, but no one really knows."

"And the merchants?"

"They moved in weeks after we opened it up. They heard

there were dwarves who had never seen an apple. If you want an apple, I'd recommend waiting until you get to the overcity—cheaper there."

"Thanks. You going to walk me to the top?"

"I wish I could," Reunne says with a sigh. "But Elega has eyes everywhere, so she must know I'm back by now. If I go to the overcity before delivering this"—she taps at the pouch— "I'll be in real trouble. And I don't want trouble with Elega. But I'm sure I'll see you again. I hope to, anyway."

"I hope so, too," Severkin says, grasping Reunne's hand and shaking it. "It was a pleasure to meet you. You're a great warrior. And thank you . . . for showing me the wall. I don't know much about my bloodline, but I feel perhaps we are even more closely related than your wall shows," he said, thinking of their kinship of spirit.

"I think so as well," she says, and her eyes glisten slightly. She squeezes his hand. "I'd gladly fight by your side again. I'll even request you for future missions."

"It would be an honor," Severkin says. They stand there for a moment, staring at each other. Severkin is waiting for her to go, but she seems unwilling. "Farewell," he says finally, and takes a step back.

"And you," Reunne says, smiling. The wrinkles on her face crinkle up but seem shallow in the strange light of the staircase. She turns around and slips out the metal doors, leaving Severkin on the stairs. He takes a deep breath and starts walking up.

The stairs feel cool under his feet, even through the soles of his shoes. But they're not as solid as stone. They feel like a plush carpet, stiff with frost, but still slightly yielding.

Severkin is grateful for this, because the climb is long, and his legs and feet soon begin to ache. As he goes higher, the stalls' goods change, and the merchants, too. Now they are dwarves, bellowing out their wares—gold and silver trinkets from a trip to the underworld, pendants showing hammers and shields, small glass reproductions of the palaces Severkin had seen below.

He's nearly at the top when a slim woman runs up the stairs past him, a wood elf, her brown hair pulled back in a bushy tail like a squirrel's. She bumps him slightly as she runs, the sound of her feet tapping on the opalescent stairs like music played on glasses of water.

"Sorry!" she calls behind her as she runs on. Severkin hurries his pace, curious about a woman who would run up these stairs. The stairs are more crowded here. Dark elves and some wood elves and even some humans wander in crowds among the stalls, looking at the trinkets and goods being sold. But the squirrel-tailed woman darts a path through the crowd, and Severkin follows in her wake, wanting to get to the over-city quickly.

It isn't much farther to the top, where the stairs open into a huge hall, the floors made of the same stuff as the stairs, with a domed silver ceiling printed with a pattern of spears or arrows interwoven like a checkerboard. The room is cavernous, and lining its walls are more stalls, these selling the finest goods Severkin has seen yet: furs and leather, jewelry that looks real, and fine wines and cheeses. The merchants don't bellow out their goods here; they stand behind their stalls, stiff but smiling as customers in fine clothes make the rounds, inspecting things, asking questions in soft tones.

There is one large archway leading out of the room, with a guard standing beside it in a uniform with an eagle emblazoned on the chest, and wearing a horned helmet. The girl with the ponytail is about to dart through the door, but the guard holds out his hand to stop her. As he does so, Severkin notices the whole room slowly turn their ears to listen.

"Whoa there, Izzorchen," he says with a smile. "Bringing a message?"

"You know I am," the girl says with a smirk. "You just want me to tell you what it says."

"I'm interested in local politics," the guard says, smiling. "Come on. What does Elega say to Rorth today?"

"She is merely suggesting that the guards from over and under send each other blacksmiths to discuss weapon-smelting techniques," the girl says politely. The crowd around them seems to lean in and draw a collective breath.

"That may be what she wrote in whatever you're supposed to hand to Rorth, but what did she say?"

The girl smiles as though she has a particularly amusing secret. "She said that if we're going to defeat the giants, then Rorth's smiths must learn that weapons should be made for fighting, not for bakers to roll out bread with."

The guard bursts into laughter at this, and the crowd around them all chuckle softly.

"Can I go now?" the girl asks.

"Go," the guard says, waving her on. "Best to deliver the written message and not the spoken one."

"I never deliver the spoken ones," the girl says before racing off, her ponytail bobbing behind her. The crowd goes back to politely perusing the stalls, but Severkin can tell that they're done here. They'd come for the show, and it's over now. He approaches the horned guard.

"Greetings," the guard says. "Returning home?"

"I've never been to Wellhall, actually. I came in through the undercity."

"Well, now you're truly home. Do you need directions?"

"Thank you, yes. I'm looking for two places: the barracks, and a pub called the Silver Roof."

The guard nods. "The pub is just around the corner, to the left. On your right. Named for this roof, in fact." He points his chin upward. "Although, technically it ought to be called the Silver Ceiling. But that's harder to say when you've had too much ale, I think. For the barracks, you'll want to head up King's Way—the wide street that runs from here. It'll go outside the mountain and then twist back inside farther up. Just stay on it. It leads to the palace. The barracks are on its right."

"Thanks," Severkin says with a nod, and heads through the arch.

Part of the overcity is carved into the mountain, and smells like melting snow and metal being forged. Buildings blend into rock walls, and in place of a sky, there are huge stained-glass windows, pouring in colored light. It's cold, too. Archways lead outside the mountain, where the city continues to wind upward. King's Way leads right from the archway with the guard through the center of town. Severkin thinks about heading to the pub first, as it's closer, but he decides it would be best to become one of the guard first, in case it gets him a discount on drinks. And Rel had made it sound easy: Just show up, present Rel's letter, and get a little badge.

King's Way is cobblestoned and wide enough for carriages

and wagons to go in either direction while pedestrians walk on the sides. And it's a crowded street, too—a crowded city. Gray elves are everywhere, carrying goods, working at forges and fletcheries. Severkin has never felt so surrounded by his own kind. No one gives him a sidelong glance, the way they would in other cities. A few elves even smile at him and say good day. In other cities, he's usually ignored, if not outright glared at. Gray elves are thought by other races to be conniving, suspicious. Guards always pick him out and follow him with their eyes. Shopkeepers tell him to keep his hands off the merchandise unless he's going to make a purchase. It had made childhood especially difficult, knowing what an outsider he was in the city of Gallia, where he'd grown up. He'd learned very quickly to hide himself, not to be noticed at all. He couldn't blend in with the crowds, but he could blend in with the shadows.

But here he doesn't need to. He can walk down King's Way without anyone giving him a second look. He feels lighter, somehow, like his armor has been too tight for years without his noticing, and now it finally fits.

As the guard said it would, King's Way leads outside the mountain. No door, no gate, just an archway. Severkin walks through it and finds that the city continues, even outside, just as he'd been told. The rock of the mountainside rises up on both sides of the carved street, making it a valley. In the walls on boths sides of him are doors and windows, houses, shops. Above him, the sky is the color of ice, palest blue, polished like a well-kept sword. He follows the road as it curves up and inside the mountain again, and he finds that the city continues and looks just like it did on the level where he first entered.

Severkin keeps walking until he comes to what seems to be the end of King's Way, and the top of the city.

It's eerily similar to the square with the large buildings in the undercity. There, the buildings had gold-and-brown domes, and here, they have gray-and-silver peaks, but the way the buildings are placed all around a square, the tallest opposite the main street, is familiar. The statues might even be in the same relative places. Even the eagle over the door of one of the buildings reminds him of the snake over the guardhouse below. He stops for a moment, examining the statues—all of gray elves, proud warriors he recognizes from storybooks he'd stolen as a child. At the very center of the square is a huge building, which he assumes is the palace. It's all fine lines and arches carved from the palest of gray stone, but halfway up, that changes. There, the building branches out like a tree, and the fine carvings fade away, turning into the rough cracks of a cave again. The palace *is* the mountain, he realizes. It stands right under the center of the dome and holds it up. Maybe the palace even continues farther up, to the very tip, windows carved into the rock, overlooking the world.

As he is staring up, he feels someone looking at him and lowers his eyes again. It is the wood elf from before—with the ponytail like a squirrel's—who was carrying messages between the under- and overking.

"First time?" she asks.

"Yes," Severkin says. "Am I so obvious?"

"The gray elves who've never been here before—they're easy to pick out. To the rest of the world, you're all thieves and killers, but here, you're heroes." She gestures at the statues. "I saw you coming up from the undercity."

"You ran past me. You were delivering a message."

"Delivered. I'm supposed to take another one back down now. Rorth said Elega must have cracked her head—probably bending over and trying to see her feet—to be dumb enough to steal from him. But then he told me to say something more polite."

"You deliver insults between the guard captain of the undercity and Rorth—is he the captain of the guard here? I'm supposed to deliver this recommendation to him."

"He's the prince regent. Husband to our beloved queen and general of the army and captain of the guard. And he's right over there." She points at the building with the eagle over the door. "But he's also in a bad mood. So be careful. And my job is being the runner. I deliver messages between the two. It's just that they both take a few tries before getting their messages ready for sending. Name's Izzy, by the way."

"Severkin," he says, shaking her outstretched hand.

"Well, I'm usually in the Silver Roof after dusk, Severkin, if you want to buy me a drink. All this running up and down the stairs keeps me in great shape, you may have noticed." She wiggles her eyebrows, and Severkin is, for a moment, too stunned to speak. She takes that moment to turn and jog away, her movements, he thinks, perhaps more flirtatious than athletic this time. He grins as she runs, then shakes his head.

He turns and heads toward the building with the eagle over it. Two guardsmen stand outside, their armor the same as the guard's he'd seen at the entrance to the city. They look him over as he approaches but say nothing.

"I have a letter for Rorth," he says to them. "To apply to

be a guardsman." One nods his head, and Severkin takes this as permission to enter. Inside is a huge hall, all in the gray stone, with shields and swords hung on the walls. Severkin eyes the swords, wondering what their value is, but then sees they're only replicas. At the end of the hall is a slightly raised platform with a table and several chairs on it. A few gray elves are there, arguing.

"We don't even know this one. He isn't even a guard!" says one of them, an elf with a long black beard.

"So let's hold off judgment," says another, this one a woman with long hair so dark red it's nearly purple.

"Who are you?" says the last of them, noticing Severkin. This one is clearly the leader—a tall elf with white hair to his shoulders and a small circlet on his head. He wears armor more ornate than the others' and at his neck is a gilded clasp shaped like a hawk, attaching a long yellow cape to his breastplate. Rorth, he assumes. Severkin approaches them and presents his letter with a slight bow.

"My name is Severkin. I assisted a guard named Rel at Bridgefall, and he said I should present this letter to Rorth along with my hope to join the National Guard."

"You're Severkin?" the elf with the beard says.

"You must have come straight here," the woman says. "We just got a note from Elega saying her agent Reunne has requested you for a mission."

"I'm flattered," Severkin says.

"Elega also mentions that she now has the Hammer—she says you were key in delivering it to her," says the bearded elf again, glaring. "Explain yourself."

"I . . . don't know what the Hammer is," Severkin says.

"Rel asked me to assist Reunne in bringing something back to Wellhall. I saw it, but it didn't look like a hammer, and I never knew what it was."

"You let a dwarf have it, though!" the bearded elf shouts.

"Easy, Ind," the woman says. "He's not a guard. He didn't know what he was doing. He merely helped a dwarf get back home."

"Reunne is a gray elf, actually," Severkin says.

The bearded elf—Ind—scrunches up his face at this, wrinkles popping up and his skin darkening like a raisin. "Damn traitorous underelves," he hisses.

"See," the woman says, addressing the elf in the circlet, "he didn't know. We can tell him—send him. And then we'll have the Staff. Then we just need the Spear, and Elega will have to give us the Hammer." She turns back to Severkin. "You're loyal to the gray elves, aren't you?"

"I . . . yes," Severkin says. He thinks this is probably a better answer than to explain his feelings, which are complex and have changed a lot today.

"Are you from here?" Rorth asks.

"No," Severkin says. "I was on my way here, and my ship crashed when a giant emerged from the sea."

Rorth nods. "So you have no real loyalty to the gray elves of Wellhall."

"I am proud of my race," Severkin says.

"Yes," Rorth says, "I believe you. So let me tell you this: the package which you helped Reunne deliver—it is a key part of a great machine. One built eons ago, when the giants were last awake. Gray elf and dwarf worked together then. The machine they built was to fend off the giants. It is the only thing that ever has. There are three components to it. The dwarves now have one."

"But aren't we all working together?" Severkin asks. "To defeat the giants?"

"The question is whether we will be working together when the giants are gone," the woman said.

"We won't," Ind says.

"Probably not," the woman concedes with a smile. "Which is why it is important that we, the gray elves, have the weapon. We defeat the giants, and then, if the dwarves try to go back to their old ways, we use the weapon on them. You understand that, don't you, Severkin?" She smiles, her yellow eyes narrowing to stilettos.

"I do," Severkin says, feeling his muscles tense, preparing for a blow.

"They now have one part," Rorth says. "If we get the other two, they will have to give us the Hammer, to defeat the giants. And we know where the next piece is—and they've requested you go retrieve it, with this Reunne."

"When you do," the woman says softly, "bring it back here. Don't let it go to the undercity. Can you do that?" Her voice is practically a purr.

"Stop flirting, Siffon," Ind says. "He's going to think he's trying to win your hand."

"My hand is still up for grabs," Siffon snaps back. "But I don't think that's what he's interested in."

"Both of you stop," Rorth says, putting his hand between them. "He'll do it because if he brings the Staff back here, I will reward him greatly." He turns to Severkin. "Money, titles—whatever you want. We need this to defeat the giants.

Anything we can offer you is nothing beside that. Bring me the Staff. Can you do that?"

"Yes," Severkin says. Titles? Titles almost always come with power, the power to go wherever he wants, permission to explore ruins, access to historical maps to find lost cities. . . . Oh, yes—he'll get them a staff if it means a key to the kingdom.

"Good. And if you bring it to Elega, I will have you banished from the overcity. Do you understand?"

"Yes," Severkin says.

"Then, welcome to the guard. Siff, get him a badge and tell him where he's going. Ind, you're with me."

The two men stride out of the room, and Siffon smiles again at Severkin.

"This way," she says, heading in the other direction. "I'll explain the mission as we get you a badge." Her armor is tight-fitting, blue-silver scales. A whip hangs from her belt next to a sword.

"You're an advisor to the guard captain?" Severkin asks.

She laughs, a haughty birdsong sound. "I forgot we never really introduced ourselves. We were just so caught up in this mission—Elega wanted Severkin on the mission—who was Severkin? And there you were. . . . I'm Siffon D'Greiges. I assist the prince regent and the queen. Technically, my title is advisor on special projects. Ind, the other one, is the chief advisor on military strategy. He's really not so bad." They walk down a small hallway off the main hall and down a staircase.

"He seemed angry."

"We didn't know Elega had retrieved the Hammer. We'd sent one of our guards with Reunne, of course. One from above, one from below, that's the rule. But apparently, he died. Reunne may have killed him. You should be wary on this mission." Severkin presses his lips shut but wants to come to Reunne's defense. He knows her, and she wouldn't have done that.

They stop in a small room with a desk in the middle of it. A man in uniform but without a helmet or weapons sits behind the desk. Siffon extends her hand.

"Badge for the fresh meat," she says. The guard grins and takes a badge out of his desk drawer and hands it to her. She smiles and pins it on Severkin's chest. She's very close to him as she does this, and he can suddenly smell the chalk-and-roses of her sweat and feel the heat from her body. He swallows.

"Good," she says as they leave the room the way they came, heading back to the main hall. "Now, the mission. You're to meet Reunne at the Tower, in Grayhome, to the north. I'll mark it on your map. The Staff, the piece of the machine you're after, was kept in the Tower after it was broken up, but the new head of the Mages Guild says it's . . . gone missing."

"Missing?" Severkin asks.

"I don't know. She said she needed some help getting it back—help of the skilled-warrior variety. She's a dwarf—so be careful, it might all be a trick."

"Why was the machine broken up originally?"

"The elves and dwarves agreed to separate it so that they wouldn't use it on each other. Which is, of course, exactly what we're thinking of doing now," Siff says, tilting her head to the side as though she finds this amusing.

"How did a dwarf become head of the Mages Guild?" Severkin asks. Though a guard like Rel seems plausible, he assumes head of the Mages Guild is an important role, and it's hard to imagine the elves letting a dwarf have it.

"She ran the university in the undercity. Very prominent and well respected. Wonderful educator. When the dwarves came up, she applied right away for a job at the Tower. As a sign of good faith, she was made vice dean. The dean retired a few months ago and left her in charge. We weren't happy about it, but the Tower handles their own affairs. Her name is Frigit. She's apparently very severe but very good at what she does. And supposedly she has no secret loyalties to Elega. But if they were secret, we wouldn't know about them. The dwarves are very good at keeping secrets."

Severkin nods. He wonders if this is what he sounds like—prejudiced. He doesn't like the idea of being like that. Rel, after all, seemed kind, and Reunne seems to trust the dwarves well enough to work for them. And Severkin trusts Reunne.

"I think I know all I need to, then," Severkin says. "I'll head to the Tower at daybreak."

"Good," Siffon says. They're back in the great hall, but it is empty, and she is standing close to him. "Come back with the Staff, and I'll be very happy. But let Elega have it . . . and I'll be angry. Which won't be nearly as much fun for you."

She kisses him lightly on the cheek and walks away.

Severkin takes a deep breath. It's been an odd day.

THIRTEEN

NICK WAKES up to Dad banging on his door again.

"Breakfast!" Dad calls. "Come on, eat quick, we've got to get going so we have time to go over those questions with your mom before the movie."

Nick closes his eyes again. He doesn't like the idea of having everything he wants to talk to Mom about being picked over beforehand and censored. He lies in bed a while longer. The light in his room is a fuzzy blue-gray. Slowly he sits up and grabs his phone from next to his bed and sends Nat a text saying he probably can't play much today, but he promises to meet up with her tonight, if she's playing. She texts back right away:

I promise too

"Are you coming?" Dad shouts from downstairs. Nick rolls his eyes and stands, then heads downstairs. Dad is eating a bowl of cereal.

"No pancakes?" Nick asks, maybe sounding a little nastier than he meant to.

"I bought some of that instant oatmeal stuff, if you want something warm," Dad says. "Now eat fast; it's already almost noon. We're supposed to visit your mom before three. They're showing a German movie."

Nick groans. "I have to watch a German movie?"

"Yep," Dad says with the grin of a parent making their child learn against their will. "Plus, you need to talk to your mom for your assignment, right?"

"Yeah," Nick says, opening a pack of instant oatmeal and adding it to some water in a bowl, then sticking it in the microwave.

"Probably should make sure you bring it, then, right?"

Nick nods, his head feeling heavy, then goes upstairs and grabs the questionnaire and brings it back to the kitchen. He puts it on the table so he doesn't forget it. The microwave beeps, and he takes out the oatmeal and starts eating. It's plastic-y, lumpy.

Dad takes one of those deep, parental breaths that Nick knows means he's showing how nice he thinks he's being. "Look, I just don't want to upset her like the other day. No getting in her face. No getting upset. Just ask the questions, and if she can't answer them, move on. Okay?"

"Fine," Nick says, shoveling the oatmeal into his mouth.

"Good." Dad smiles—a real smile. He seems happy today. Because he gets to see Mom again, Nick knows. It's good to see that Dad misses her, too, but Nick feels guilty seeing his father's happiness. Why isn't he happy like that?

Nick finishes his oatmeal and heads back upstairs without saying anything. He showers, trims his hair with the giant electric clippers, puts on clothes, and goes online to look at the game forums—to see how much everyone else is liking it, and to tell everyone how awesome he thinks it is.

He knows he needs to be careful on the forums, though, now that the game is out. He hates spoilers. Even before the game came out, he read all about the graphics and controls but not the plot. Luckily the designers didn't talk much about the plot—they said it was so varied depending on decisions you made that talking about it, or even where they got their ideas, would ruin it. They were going to talk more about it after it had been out awhile, at the big GamesCon in New York, in a month. Nick is still so jealous of Nat for getting to go. Maybe she'll film it for him.

The boards that don't have spoiler tags are basically just talking about character creation and controls. He posts a few of his own thoughts—on how real it feels, on how the controls are fluid—before Dad knocks on the door.

"You just walked away," Dad says, coming in before Nick can tell him he's busy. "Something you want to say?"

Nick looks up, shrugs.

"I just don't see why we can't do normal stuff with mom," he says, staring at the Chichén Itzá poster, wondering if he'll ever go to Rome with his family. Maybe he'll go alone, when he's older. Send postcards. "Go out to a real movie."

"Well, this is normal stuff for your mom," Dad says, sitting on the bed. "Maybe not the normal stuff you like to do, but your mom and I watch German films pretty regularly. Or we did. You just never bothered to watch with us. You played your game, or did homework, or watched TV in your room. And that was fine. But now, it's about Mom. So if you want to see her, we're going to do things she wants to do. We've been doing things you want to do for a while, Nick. I think your mother gets to pick now and then."

Nick leans back in his chair and nods. He feels like he's just been blasted with freezing air. "You're right," he says. "I'm sorry. I just . . . Is the movie going to be hard to understand?"

"There will be subtitles. I can't promise you'll like it. But pretend, okay? How about sometime next week, after school, you and I go see a movie you want to see? That sound fun?"

"A movie on a school night?" Nick raises an eyebrow. Dad must feel guilty.

"Yeah," Dad says. "You're old enough. I think you know you'll still have to do your homework first. And . . . we're going to have to change the rules a little now. So I guess we can change them for the better, too."

"Okay," Nick says. "Thanks."

"Thank you," Dad says, standing. "I'm going to go get changed. Come downstairs and we'll head over to see Mom."

Nick nods. He looks at his computer screen. On the forum, someone has just posted a response to him, saying the spear fighting feels especially fluid, and he should try it. The poster's handle is GrayR97. Nick wonders if it's the person who plays Reunne. His character name and handle are the same, after all—she'd know it was him.

"Downstairs in fifteen," Dad says again, interrupting Nick's thoughts.

"Yeah," Nick says, without looking up. Dad leaves, and Nick clicks on GrayR97's profile. It's not Reunne—his bio says he's a male, and he's the same age as Nick. Nick is sure the person playing Reunne is older, and a woman. She just embodies the character so well—the way she explains things, the protectiveness—she's like a mom. Like *his* mom.

In an instant, the idea of Reunne being like mom freezes him. His eyes open wider and air touches the parts normally covered by his eyelids, making them tingle. He inhales so deeply that his chest feels unnaturally huge, and then he realizes he needs to exhale and lets it out like a gale. She had painted those cities from the game, after all. They have a console that could play it there. She knows his character's name—everything about him, in fact. Nick has told her all the stories of Severkin as she watched him play. And when she played, her favorite weapon was the spear. He swallows. He's not sure if the idea is crazy or if it makes perfect sense. Mom playing Reunne.

But then, she would have told him, right? Unless there was some rule against it—they're not allowed to visit every day, so maybe she's not supposed to be communicating with him outside approved visits. They'd have to keep it secret, then.

Nick shakes his head. No. It's a crazy idea. Insane. Mom would tell him. He just misses her. Except, she's definitely playing. The paintings of Wellhall and Bridgefall prove that. But when he asked her, she couldn't tell him. It was like she was wrapped up in blankets. Maybe the disease she really has—whatever it is—was causing that, or maybe the Alzheimer's drugs. That's what that look she gave him was. That wink. Mom playing the game. Mom is Reunne. It's not that crazy.

He puts his shoes on and heads downstairs, where Dad is waiting. They drive with the radio on. Nick looks out at the passing scenery and tries to tell himself he's wrong, Mom can't be playing the game, she would tell him—maybe in-game. Except then she'd violate the in-game-only rules and get kicked off the server. It's ridiculous. But he still keeps turning the idea over and over in his head, like he's handling a precious artifact. Every reason he comes up with that Reunne can't be Mom he can also disprove with one thought. It all fits together: even if it doesn't make sense, it *makes sense*. When they arrive, Nick doesn't realize it at first, like there's a de-lay between his hearing the wheels on the white rocks of the parking lot and his knowing what the sound means.

Mom could be Reunne. And he needs to somehow find out if he's losing his mind. Because if he's not, then Mom is trying to tell him something, and he needs to catch up, because he didn't even realize it was her.

They get out of the car and walk to the porch, the gravel crunching under their feet like broken glass.

"So, if I think the questions are upsetting her, I'm going to say 'next question,' okay?"

"Sure," Nick says. He isn't really listening. He's trying to think of things to ask her about the game. Ways to confirm she's Reunne. Then he can tell Dad about it, maybe the doc-tors. It must mean something. But until he can prove it, he can't tell Dad. Dad'll say he's in some form of denial again and tell him he can't talk to Mom about the game. Figure it out first, Nick tells himself. Figure out that it's Mom, prove it, then we can tell Dad. And that'll blow his mind. Nick can see the shocked look on his face already, big eyes behind glasses, hair bouncing, lips pulling together like a knot to form that perfect "Oh."

Inside, an aide swipes them in and directs them to the

lounge to the side, where Mom is playing cards with a very old woman in a wheelchair. She looks up when they enter and smiles, then says something to the woman in the wheel-chair and gets up. She hugs Nick and gives Dad a kiss on the cheek.

"So good to see my boys," she says. She runs her hands over Nick's head, something Nick would have hated a few months ago but that he doesn't mind now. "What do you want to do? Do you want to go for a walk? There's a lovely little pond behind the house."

"That sounds great," Dad says. "Nicky has some more of those questions for the school project he wants to ask you, if you're up for it."

"Of course!" Mom says, ruffling Nick's hair again. "Anything for my little Nicky."

They walk back outside to the porch and then around to the back of the mansion. There are a few benches here, and a pond. The lawn stretches out like an arena. A few concrete paths weave around the grounds, and nurses stroll back and forth on them, leisurely checking on the patients. Nick sees Jess, Ms. Knight's girlfriend, pushing an old man in a wheel-chair. She smiles at them and nods but doesn't stop what she's doing. A few older patients have easels and share a small fold-ing table among them, covered with paints.

"Is this where you painted those watercolors, Mom?" Nick asks. His father clears his throat.

"Oh, no. I haven't painted outside yet," Mom says. "Just as part of the class. Art therapy, they call it. Next week, we're sculpting. I don't remember ever working with clay before, so I think it will be exciting. Let's sit down here." They sit down on a bench by the pond, Nick to the left of his mother, his father to her right. "So, what did you want to ask me?"

Dad hands him the now crumpled questionnaire, marked up with both Nick's handwriting and Dad's. He looks over the questions.

"I was curious about the watercolors," Nick begins.

"Nick," Dad interrupts. "Let's start with the questions for school."

Nick looks down at the questionnaire to hide his scowl. "Okay," he says, reading the first question. "Mom, can you remember what school was like growing up?"

Mom smiles, then tilts her head, looking off into the distance. "It was so many years ago," she says. "But I remember the uniforms. Bright royal blue. When we were little, it was white shirts with blue scarves, and we did lots of marching. I remember a lot of marching. You had to be one of the Pioneers so you could join the FDJ—Freie Deutsche Jugend, the 'Free German Youth'—they had blue shirts. I didn't really understand why I had to join them, you know, but my parents made me, and when I was older and in the FDJ, I realized it was because if you didn't join, you couldn't really get a good education. The schools were state sponsored, you see. Training to make us good little communists. If you didn't join, you weren't loyal to the government and therefore weren't allowed to learn anything. I wanted to learn other languages, and see other places—I've always wanted to, as far back as I could remember. But the chances of that happening were very small. And there was no way it would happen if I didn't stay in the FDJ, so I did. And it wasn't just that you had to be a member, you had to prove to them you were loyal, show them through actions that you believed in the cause." She looks back down at Nick and smiles.

"How were you supposed to prove that?" Nick asks.

Mom taps her chest. "And they gave us badges! I remember that. Little badges that went right on your shirt. I don't remember if that was the FDJ or the Pioneers, though."

"Did you do well enough to get a good education?" Nick asks.

"Yes," she says, and looks away again. "I got a very good education. I knew it was the only way to get out, to see the world."

"So you were a good communist?" Nick asks. He shifts on the bench. He knows that communism isn't exactly a great thing. People on the news still call each other that. Although some people seem to think it isn't so bad, either. But the communists in East Berlin, he thinks, they weren't good. Everyone agrees on that. So if Mom was good at it . . .

"I did what I needed to do, Nicky," Mom says in a soft voice. "I have regrets, but if the wall hadn't fallen, it would have been my only way out."

"Let's move on to something else," Dad suggests.

"But I want to know—" Nick begins.

"We can do some research at home," Dad suggests. "Why don't you ask something else?"

Nick stares at Mom, hoping she'll speak up, defend herself, say she's fine to keep talking. That the part of Mom that's still totally her will emerge and wink and give him some clues—something so he knows if it's her, and if it is, what she's trying to tell him. But she just stares off at the sky, which is a clear pale blue, like a sheet of ice.

"It was cold in the uniforms," she says suddenly. "That always seemed unfair to me."

"What's next on the list?" Dad asks.

Nick squeezes the paper in his hand so tightly that the edges almost cut him. "How did you and Dad meet?" he asks, reading from the list.

"I was studying anthropology at NYU," Mom says, as if just remembering. "He was TA'ing . . . some other class down the hall. I kept seeing him. He kept seeing me. We paused at the same water fountain. One day he asked if he could take me to the movies, and I said yes. I hadn't been out with anyone else since coming to America. I thought he was handsome and had a nice smile. And he didn't mind my accent, or my stupid questions—"

"None of her questions were stupid," Dad interrupts. "She was trying to learn. That's something about her that made me love her. And she's far smarter than me. Learned everything faster than I ever could."

"I had more room up here," she says, turning to look at Dad and knocking a fist on her head. "It was empty from all the nonsense they'd taught me at home." His parents lean in toward each other, smiling.

"Hey, Mom," Nick interrupts. "Can I tell you about the game I've been playing?"

"Sure, Nicky," Mom says, still smiling at Dad. They were both focusing on each other and ignoring Nick, but he'd seen them do this before—it was gross—and he knew it was a great time to get away with stuff they'd otherwise say no to.

"There's a character in it, Reunne, and I don't know if I should trust her, and I was wondering if you thought I should."

"Nick," his father says, breaking his gaze from his mother's and looking now directly at Nick. "What does this have to do with the school project?"

"I was just asking. I miss Mom talking to me while I played the game."

Dad smiles sympathetically. "Let's finish up the school questions first. Then you can ask about the game."

"Okay," Nick says, frowning. He looks down and smoothes out the questionnaire and keeps asking questions—the safe ones, approved by Dad. This isn't what he wants to know. They go on for about half an hour more, and Nick learns that Mom loved to sew and fixed all her own clothes, and that she used to cook for the whole family. Cooked, sewed, and went to school and studied hard enough to get good enough grades to move on in her schooling and one day get a job that would let her leave Berlin. That's what she wanted more than anything else.

"I knew my life was outside, Nicky," she says, resting her hand on Nick's leg. "So I studied hard and did the best I could. Like you should. Study hard, and you can do whatever you want."

"Yeah, Mom," Nick says, rolling his eyes. Do whatever you want until they say you have Alzheimer's and lock you up.

"It's time for the movie," Dad says, looking at his watch. "Come on, they're showing this one especially for you, Sophie."

"Right," she says, standing. "This will be fun." Nick and Dad stand, and they walk back around to the front of the building, but Nick takes Mom's hand and walks slower so that Dad is a little way ahead of them. He doesn't want Dad hearing these questions.

"Mom," he says, "are you Reunne?" He watches her face carefully, looking for a wink, a smile, an arched eyebrow to let him in on the game.

"What do you mean?" she asks. He walks quickly in front of her and spins so he can look at her eyes. They're soft waves, no froth, no sharpness. Mom stops short in front of him. "What are you doing, Nicky?"

"I just . . . ," he says. "Are you still in there?"

Mom's eyes widen and water a little, and it takes a moment before Nick realizes she's giving him PityFace. He's never seen it from her before.

"I'm right here," she says, hugging his head to her shoulder. "Okay?"

"Yeah, Mom," he says into her skin. She squeezes him tightly, and he lets himself be hugged because it feels warm and safe and reminds him of something good, though he isn't sure what. It's Mom. Not all of her. Not the sharp, clever parts of her, not the brave parts that know she needs to break out of herself before the drugs they give her mess up her brain for good, but there's still enough of her. The parts that love him are still here. And that's good for right now.

Not good for finding out if she's Reunne, though.

"What are you doing?" Dad asks, walking back to them. "I turned around and you were behind me."

"It's okay, Lamont," Mom says. "Nick just needed a hug."

Dad grins. "Okay," he says. "Well, come on. You can hug him during the movie, too."

"Okay," Mom says, letting go. The cool air rushes in around Nick's face, and he thinks he can almost feel his ears pop. And then Mom takes his hand and they walk into the building.

They walk down the hall toward the office where they met the doctor. But this time they turn left and come into a large open room, with a mix of sofas, armchairs, and folding chairs scattered audience-style in front of a big TV. There's a big window at one end, but Jess is closing curtains over it, and the room darkens.

"Hi," Jess says, turning around and walking toward them. "Here for the movie?"

"We are," Dad says.

"Do you have the tickets?" Mom asks.

"Oh, you don't need tickets here, Sophie," Jess says.

"I know," Mom says, her face turning pointed for a moment. "I was making a joke."

"Oh," Jess says, then laughs in a way that Nick can tell is forced. "Sorry. Of course. I'm just a little out of it today."

"Happens to all of us," Mom says in a voice with a touch of edge to it. Nick looks at Mom and she looks at him for a moment and grins, then winks. She's there for a moment, and Nick is about to ask about Reunne, but Jess speaks first.

"Why don't you all sit down?" Jess says. "I'm going to remind a few people that it's movie time."

"Thank you," Dad says. Jess smiles, and leaves them alone in the room. "Let's get a front-row seat." Dad steers them toward a sofa right in front of the TV. They sit down, Nick at one end, Dad at the other, and Mom between them again. The sofa is so plush, it seems to suck him into it.

He stares at Mom, wondering if she's still sharp, but she smiles down at him and he can tell she isn't. The edge that was there for a moment is gone again, but the moment when she'd joked with Jess, that had confirmed it. She's still in there.

Nick just has to figure out how to get her out. Or wait . . . if it is Mom playing, she's clearly sharp when she's playing. Cotton-candy-fluff Mom wouldn't be able to play Reunne.

He looks at the TV. It's huge, and hanging on the wall. Under it is a low table with remotes and electronics on it. Including, Nick notices, a game console. But he doesn't see the game anywhere. In fact, he doesn't see any games or DVDs around. There's a big cabinet in the corner, but he thinks if he opens it and starts looking for the game, his parents will try to stop him.

"This was one of the first German movies I ever saw," Dad says. "It was our third date, I think. I went to the video store and asked for something German, so I could impress her. Turned out she hadn't seen it either, because it was made in West Germany a few years before the wall fell. You remember?"

"It's not the most romantic movie," Mom says with a laugh. "But it was so sweet of him." She kisses him on the cheek. Luckily, at that moment Jess comes back in with a few of the other residents in tow. The women among them are all so much older than Mom, so frail, like handfuls of dried grass. They look like the women at the mall who clutch their purses tighter as he walks past them, and for a moment he has a vision of Mom doing that, of his mom looking at him like they do, but then he remembers Mom isn't like them, which is why he needs to get her out. That look the women give him is the reason he made Severkin a gray elf in the first place. They're always suspected of being thieves and criminals, too.

Mom waves at the old ladies, and they say hello, and she introduces him and Dad to them. Nick smiles as best he can. Mom doesn't belong here, surrounded by grandmothers. Is this how he's going to end up? One day is he going to spend twenty minutes wondering where his keys are till his wife says "Alzheimer's" and locks him up? Is he going to be like Mom, so afraid of himself that he chooses to get locked up in a place like this, spending most of his life with people so much older—missing his kids' lives? He crosses his arms and leans back into the sink of the sofa, letting it drown him. Jess has the DVD in her pocket, and she takes it out and leaves the case next to the player as she puts the DVD in. She presses a few buttons, and the menu screen comes on. *Wings of Desire.* Nick rolls his eyes. Jess hits Play and sits down in the back.

"Why is it in black-and-white?" he whispers to his parents. "You said it was made in the eighties."

"You'll see," Dad whispers back. "Now be quiet."

Nick leans back again, but as soon as the subtitles come on, he feels himself unfocusing, and he doesn't really care. He waits ten minutes, then whispers that he's going to the bathroom and leaves the room.

Without his parents, the home seems creepier. The sounds of medical machines, like giants gasping, footsteps, cackling old people—it may as well be haunted. Nick's not sure he believes in ghosts, but either way, these people, sort of already dead, their minds going, are pretty close to ghosts, and most definitely real. He walks down the long hallway. He doesn't really have to use the bathroom. But he does want to see his mother's room, and maybe search it for some evidence—of why she's here, of her being Reunne. Maybe something in the paintings.

No one pays him much attention except a man in a wheelchair who glares at him, spittle dribbling down his mouth.

Nick walks by him quickly. He remembers the way to Mom's room, upstairs.

The door to Mom's room is closed but unlocked. Nick takes a breath and goes inside. It's meticulously neat. The bed is made; not one piece of clothing is on the floor. But what's weird is all the Post-its. There are Post-its on the window that read *Close before bed* and two on the door that say *Close when dressing* and *Close behind you*. There are a few on the desk, labeling each of the drawers *Makeup, Hair Stuff,* and *Papers*. And one on the photo of him and Dad on her mantel that says *Lamont—husband. Nick—son.* Nick peels that one off, folds it in the middle, and puts it in his pocket. She doesn't need a Post-it to remember him.

He's torn about what to look for—the shoebox of German stuff or something linking her to Reunne? He starts with the watercolors she painted, which are now hanging on the wall. They're absolutely of the game. Wellhall, Bridgefall, and a new one that looks like it could be the undercity—maybe the small garden in front of Reunne's home. But no people. No portraits of Severkin, like he was secretly hoping.

He opens the closet and looks for the shoebox that used to be in her closet at home, but doesn't see it. He opens cabinets and quietly closes them again when all he finds are books. Then he goes through all the drawers. They're each labeled, but Nick knows that if Mom was trying to hide something, she'd put it someplace unexpected, like he would. He goes through drawers of blouses and sweaters carefully, even one with underwear. He looks through the closet, in each of the pairs of shoes. Nothing. He crouches on the floor to look under the bed, and in the dark, he sees something glint. He reaches for it and pulls it back into the light, still kneeling on the floor. It's Mom's old cameo necklace—the ivory-on-ivory woman's profile. He stares at it—it looks like old parchment in the light. It has nothing to do with Germany, he knows, nothing to do with Alzheimer's. She bought it when he was four or five. He hears the door open and stands up quickly, trying to look natural. He leaves the necklace on the floor.

"What are you doing in here?"

Nick turns. It's Maria.

"My mom wanted something," Nick says. "I came up here to get it, but I can't find it."

Maria's eyes scan the room, stopping for just a moment on the framed photo of Nick and Dad. "Uh-huh," she says, looking skeptical, but also on the edge of laughter. "What did she want?"

"A neck pillow," Nick says with surprising ease. He's never thought of himself as a good liar.

"She doesn't have a neck pillow," Maria says, now full-on grinning.

"Well, I guess she got confused," Nick says, and feels dirty for using Mom's not-Alzheimer's as a part of his lie.

"You'd better get back to the movie," Maria says, moving out of the doorway. "She'll miss you if you're gone too long. I'll find a neck pillow and bring it down."

Nick leaves without saying anything, though he doesn't break eye contact with Maria until he's out the door. Then he slowly walks back to the movie room. He creeps back in and takes his seat on the sofa. Mom is leaning on Dad now, her hands wrapped around his arm, her head on his shoulder, eyes focused on the movie and unmoving even when Nick walks in. Dad raises an eyebrow.

"Got lost," Nick whispers.

He doesn't pay much attention to the rest of the movie, not even when it's suddenly in color. Instead, he tries to work out what it is that brings out his full mom—the sharp Mom who plays as Reunne and tries to tell him things with eye movements. Maybe he could convince her to stop taking her meds, or visit her at night—that's when Mom seems to be playing, too. That might be when her mind's keenest. Then they could sit together and go through all her symptoms, what it feels like, and Nick could google them all and figure out what's really going on, and how to cure it. Maybe there's something he's missed that only she can tell him.

When the movie is over, Jess turns the lights back on, and the few residents who are still awake stand and stretch. Jess starts rousing the others.

"*Ich hatte einen sehr schönen Abend mit dir,*" Mom says to Dad. Nick only knows a few words in German, and he hates it when his parents use it like code. They don't very often, though, 'cause Dad is so bad at it. Even to Nick, his accent sounds weird.

"*Es ist noch Nachmittag,*" Dad says.

"What are you guys talking about?" Nick asks. "Can we go back outside? I want to ask Mom some more questions."

"*Ist das deine Wohnung?*" Mom says. "*Hattest du nicht gesagt sie sei sehr klein?*"

Nick wonders if "speaking in German" should be a box on the checklist or if they're just doing this so he can't understand them. Probably that. Maybe box 6, but that's for new problems with words, not speaking a language you've known longer than the one you normally talk in. And she doesn't seem to be having problems with German.

"*Nein, dies ist deine Hause,*" Dad says. Then to Nick: "She's saying she wants to go sleep for a while. I think I'm going to take her to her room, okay?"

"That's not what she said," Nick says, folding his arms. "The word for sleep is *schlaf.* Mom used to tell it to me all the time when I was little."

"She used the word for rest," Dad says. Then he turns back to Mom. "*Sag auf Wiedersehen zu unsere Sohn, dann kannst du dir ausruhen.*"

Mom looks down at Nick and strokes his hair lightly. "*Er ist ja ein ganz Lieber,*" she says. "*Was macht er hier? Das ist doch nicht deine Wohnung, oder? So hatte ich mir unser Rendezvous aber nicht vorgestellt. . . .*" She squints, as if dizzy, and turns back to Dad. "*Was ist los? Irgendetwas stimmt hier nicht.*" Her voice is higher now. Maybe they're fighting. Sometimes they fight in German in an attempt not to upset him.

"Can I ask Mom just one more question?" he says.

"No, Nicky," Dad says. "I'm taking her to bed. *Komm mit, Sophie. Ich bringe dich zum Bett. Dann kannst du schlafen.*"

He takes her by the hand and almost pulls her out of the room, but the expression on her face is angry and confused, and Nick wonders if this isn't a fight between Mom and Dad but between Mom and Mom—his keen Mom wanting to stay, to tell Nick everything now that it's getting later, while the drugs cloud her mind and tell her to go to sleep. Figures Dad would side with the drugs. Nick kicks the foot of the sofa, hard, and sits back down in it. A few of the residents and Jess look over.

"You okay?" Jess asks.

"Yeah." Nick's voice is insincere and he knows it. "I just

wanted to ask Mom something, but . . ." He raises his hand, pointing in the direction his parents went, unable to really explain what just happened.

Jess comes over and sits down next to him. "What did you want to ask her?"

Nick cocks his head. "Do you . . . that is. You know the game, right? Wellhall? That Ms. Knight and I were talking about?"

"Oh yeah," Jess says. "She can't stop talking about it."

"Do they have it here?" Nick asks.

"Yeah," Jess says without hesitation. "I ordered it. When I first started work here, all they had was a TV, but then I showed all the doctors these studies on how gaming actually helps with memory problems, not to mention overall health, and they gave me a budget. I'm in charge of all the games, and Hillary, um, Ms. Knight, I mean, said I had to order this one. Usually I go for the movement games, to keep the residents on their feet, but puzzle ones are good, too."

"Does my mom play it, do you know?"

Jess shakes her head. "I don't know for sure. I'm not in here all the time. Why?"

"It's just something we used to do together," Nick says. "I wanted to know if she still was."

"If it reminds her of you, I'm sure she still is," Jess says, resting a hand on his shoulder for a moment. "Even when they forget why they're doing something, sometimes residents still do them because they know they're important. If it's important to your mom, I'm sure she's playing." She takes her hand off his shoulder. It suddenly feels like a wind has come through, or like he's taken a health potion, and he feels his chest swell a little. Recovery.

"Yeah," he says. "Thanks."

"No problem," Jess says, standing. "And I'll tell Ms. Knight you say hi."

"Yeah," Nick says. "Thanks."

Just then an old man with a walker starts banging on the window, asking why it won't open. Jess flashes a grin at Nick, then runs over to help the man.

Nick stands and walks out of the room, wanting to get away from the man, who is now arguing with Jess. Nick wanders out to the front porch and sits down among the other residents. Some nod at him and smile. Most ignore him. He thinks about what Jess said about residents doing things they know are important without knowing why they're important, but he knows Mom knows what she's doing. It's too conscious—the way Reunne talks about growing up in the undercity is like a lesson—and it's so similar to what he's heard about East Berlin. The food, the being watched. Maybe it's Mom trying to show him what her life was like—answer his questions—the best way she can. He nods and scratches his chin. It makes sense, in a weird way. But that's exactly how Mom would educate him—through the thing he loves most. It's just like when she used to sit behind him, watching him play and telling him what all the stories came from—the history and mythology behind them. But now she's making it her own history.

But it has to be more than that, doesn't it? If it's just Mom showing her history through the game, why wouldn't the soft-eyed Mom know about it? Why is only the sharp-eyed Mom winking at him? She must be trying to tell him something else, too—some secret message he hasn't figured out yet. And while he doesn't know what the message is, he feels sure it's something he can use to get her out. It's sharp-eyed Mom's escape attempt—through him.

"That's where you are," Nick's dad says, suddenly standing next to him.

"Yeah, it was stuffy in there. Why did you take Mom away?"

"She was tired, Nick. That's all." Dad looks down as he says this, won't meet Nick's eyes. "We should get home. Did you get what you needed for your school project? Was it enough?"

"Yeah," Nick says, stepping down the porch steps and onto the white rocks of the parking lot. "I got what I needed."

FOURTEEN

SEVERKIN WANTS to find Reunne. He wants to talk with her again. The desire is practically all consuming. And he knows that if he goes to the Tower, he'll meet her there, but he also knows he has one stop to make before he can go. He promised he'd meet an old friend there, after all.

The Silver Roof is a tall but narrow gray-stone building, standing alone. It has a triangular tin roof, different from the stone domes the other buildings seem to have, more like the roof of the palace he has just come from. Though it's only a little after noon, people are stumbling out of the place as though they've been drinking all night, and inside it's crowded.

It's cramped, too, with a bar along one long wall and a fireplace opposite, and a cluster of tables and chairs between. Severkin glances around, but the crowds of people make it hard to see much besides the merrymakers: they're of all races, drinking and laughing and clapping each other on the back, and there's even some unfortunate singing. He tries to approach the bar but is suddenly grabbed from behind and spun.

"Severkin! I wondered when you'd sneak in here."

Severkin grins at the woman facing him. She's a troll, tall and muscular, with mint-green skin and a blue mohawk so long it trails down her back like a tail. She's in brown leather armor from the top of her neck to her feet, with only her head and hands exposed, and she is wearing a belt from which hang two strips of white cloth that fall nearly to her feet at the front and back. A staff is strapped across her back. None of it is for show; the staff is splintered at its base, the leather armor is worn and scratched in places, and the cloth that hangs from her belt is tattered at the ends.

"Hello, Elkana," Severkin says.

Elkana smiles, her sharp pointed teeth like knives, and leans down to grab Severkin up in a hug.

"Oh, it's been too long," Elkana says after putting him down. "And ye owe me a drink." She nods toward the bar and they walk to it together and Severkin orders them two drinks.

"So what brings you to Wellhall?" Severkin asks.

"The giants, same as you I'd wager."

Severkin nods and sips his beer.

"But they seem to be in a holding pattern. Attacked by the giants each night, the gray elves fight 'em off but don't kill 'em. I looked into joining the soldiers who hold off the giant each night, but it seems so dull. I want to get out there, find the other giants, or whatever woke them, and then get that. Kill the disease, not the symptom, aye?"

Severkin nods. "I agree. But no one seems to know what's woken them."

"I'm thinking it might be related to what put them to sleep," Elkana says, drinking deeply from her pint. "I want to do some research at the library I hear they have at the Tower in Grayhome."

"Actually," Severkin says, lowering his voice, "I've been charged with helping reassemble the device that put them to sleep."

"Really?" Elkana's eyes widen, then narrow. "What is it?"

"I don't know," Severkin confesses.

Elkana half growls, half sighs in disappointment.

"I know we need to retrieve three parts, called the Hammer, the Staff, and the Spear," Severkin says. "I'm meeting another agent at Grayhome. The new head of the Mages Guild there knows where the Staff is. We're supposed to retrieve it."

"Well, it seems our missions are aligned, then. And good thing, too. Ye'll need my magic to get ye that far north without dying. Still shooting yer wee little arrows?"

"I think I'll kill more than you will on our journey up north."

Elkana slams down her empty glass.

"Whoever kills the least has to buy the next round," she says.

"Deal."

⊙ ⊙ ⊙

THEY START out for the Tower after one more round and after checking out the various shops in Wellhall. Most goods are too expensive for them, but Severkin restocks his arrows and buys new boots.

The way out of town is through another giant arch in the

mountain, this one with a wide street leading down like a slide, to the foothills and plains beyond the capital city. Grayhome is far north on their maps, and somewhat west, on a peninsula reaching up into the ocean like a hand stretching for the gods. The ocean there is marked as covered in ice, the earth a tundra. But at least, Severkin thinks as they head down the mountain, it'll be flat.

They discuss strategy as they walk downhill: Elkana has only a few healing spells but can throw fire, lightning, and poison, so Severkin keeps his hands on his blades, ready to run forward and engage enemies head-on as she casts her spells from behind him. The technique works well as they head north, fighting wolves, bears, and bandits. Severkin sometimes wonders if she's waiting till he's weakened their foes so she can get the kill, but by the time they reach the outer borders of Grayhome, she's only killed two more than he has.

They know it's the outer border of Grayhome because of the river. It's frozen solid, and not very wide, but just beyond it, there is another river, and another beyond that.

"The nine frozen rivers," Elkana says. "This is Grayhome. Are ye supposed to meet the other agent here, or at the Tower?" Severkin has filled her in on everything that has happened to him since his ship crashed—all about Reunne, how strong a warrior she is, how kind she is, how thoughtful, how much the two of them will get along.

Severkin looks around. The sun is setting and the tundra reflects back the purplish light, so the whole landscape feels lit by a distant, dying fire. It's cold, and the ground is barren and covered with thin snow, which smells of water and the faintest hint of mint. It's the sort of landscape he knows people would call desolate, but he feels invigorated by its emptiness, by the clarity of the horizon. This is the homeland of his people, and it's still empty enough that he can have a hand in carving it.

"I don't see anyone," he says. "Let's continue on to the city proper and the Tower." The city is only a speck in the distance. They cross the nine frozen rivers carefully—there are no bridges and they must walk on the ice. As they walk, the sky grows darker, not with the setting sun but with clouds, and it begins to sleet, thick drivels of half-frozen water like mucus.

The rivers are slippery to cross, so though they aren't very wide, it's slow going. As they walk onward, the sleet comes down harder, obscuring Severkin's vision and plastering his hair to his face in dark streaks.

They're halfway across the sixth river when he hears the howl. It's close.

"Quickly!" he shouts at Elkana, who nods. This river is not as narrow as the others. They're still a good twenty feet from shore. This doesn't seem to bother the pack of wolves, though. They pad out onto the river without slipping, their eyes trailing the pair, the steam of their breath rising from between the ivory points of their teeth. One of them growls softly, and the pack comes close and begins to circle Elkana and Severkin. There are a dozen, Severkin quickly counts. Normally, this wouldn't be a problem, but with only ice underfoot, he's worried about slipping. And, should one of the wolves tackle him, how strong a fall would the ice take?

"Can you do some sort of protection spell?" Severkin asks. Without thinking about it, he and Elkana have drawn closer together, back to back.

"I can send out a shockwave," she says. "But that would surely break the ice under us. Same with fire. I might be able to poison them . . . but they might still have enough time to kill us a wee bit before it kills them."

The wolves are snarling, forming a full circle around them.

"I guess we'll just have to hope for the best, then," Severkin says. "I'll try to hold them off while—" He's interrupted by a loud crack from shore. The wolves all turn to look. Through the sleet, all Severkin can see is a shadowed figure. There's another crack, and this time a flare of light, too, and the figure is briefly illuminated—Reunne. Finally. Severkin has a hundred questions for her, but now isn't the time to ask them. The wolves stare at Reunne, the noise clearly upsetting to them. This time Severkin watches as Reunne throws something at the ground—there's a small flash and a crack. The wolves look at one another and then take off, away from Reunne.

"Thanks!" Severkin calls.

"Heard the howl, thought maybe someone was in trouble!" Reunne calls back.

"Ye know our savior?" Elkana whispers.

"The other agent," Severkin said. They walk carefully to shore, where Reunne is waiting. She has on a large fur cloak with a hood over her armor.

"Was that magic?" Elkana asks.

"Dwarven firesnaps. Scare off lots of critters," Reunne says, eyeing Elkana warily. "I thought I was just meeting Severkin."

"She's a friend," Severkin says. "She was heading this way, anyway. Is it a problem?"

"No," Reunne says, shaking her head. "But let's not mention it to our superiors. I assume you've been told our mission?" They begin walking again, heading toward the dim lights of the city.

"Yes. Retrieve the Staff. The head of the Mages Guild needs our help with that."

Reunne nods again. "Mistress Frigit seldom asks for help from anybody, so it's probably going to be difficult."

"Ye know the head of the Mages Guild?" Elkana asks, walking a little ahead of them and turning back to stare. "You're not even a mage."

"She was in charge of the academy of the undercity," Reunne says, shrugging. "She oversaw all teaching—weapons, magic. One school to teach everything. You're assigned your classes based on aptitude. She would personally meet with every student and tell them what their path was. And she also met with you if you were . . . unruly."

"Were you unruly?" Severkin asks. "You don't seem the type."

"I owe my discipline to Mistress Frigit. But I was often called to her office. I didn't like the uniforms," Reunne says, her face stoic.

"Ye had to wear uniforms?" Elkana snorts.

"Homogeny," Reunne says, as if reciting. "No one should stand out while a student. We have to learn to accept that we are a small cog in a large machine and that our place has been chosen for us by those wiser than us. Uniforms aided us in understanding that."

Elkana spits on the ground. "That sounds awful," she says.

Reunne says nothing, and they walk on in silence. The sleet falling on the ground sounds to Severkin like a hundred whispers in the dark.

THEY ARRIVE at the city of Grayhome half an hour later. The sun has set and the wind seems stronger than before, but Severkin can see the city clearly by the light from the torches that hang in glass spheres, suspended from lines crisscrossing the sky like the laces of a sandal. Grayhome looks like a crystal formation made of buildings, laid out at odd angles. The buildings are stone, but snow and ice have found every available edge to cling to, so the walls have white lines all over them and it seems the ice crystals have been shattered, with their cracks radiating out through the whole city. Behind the city, the Tower rises up, three times as tall as any other building but of the same style—narrow, with sharp angles. But, unlike the other buildings, it's a pale gray, and where the frost touches it, it seems to glow.

"We should find someplace to rest for the night," Severkin says. "Get warm. We'll see Frigit tomorrow."

"Aye," Elkana agrees. "I don't think I can think straight enough to talk to the head of the Mages Guild till I get some food in me. And grog. And a warm fire by my feet."

"They've probably locked up for the night, anyway," Reunne says. "Mistress Frigit always locks the doors at dinner so no one can go find trouble afterward. Just eat, study, sleep."

"I am not going to like this woman," Elkana says.

"There's an inn right there," Severkin says, pointing at a sign a few buildings away. They stumble toward it and pull the frozen doors open. Inside is both inn and tavern. There is a small bar on the ground floor, with stairs leading up to an open balcony that looks down on the tavern. A huge fireplace has a fire too small for it crackling and smelling of burning pine. There are only a few patrons—mostly gray elves, but also a dwarf and a few sandkin. They look up when Severkin, Reunne, and Elkana enter, but soon go back to their drinks. A bard is tuning his lute in one corner of the room, and the occasional off-key twangs radiate through the room like shivers.

Severkin approaches the barkeep, an unimpressed-looking gray elf woman, and asks for three rooms for the evening and three mugs of ale. She pours the ale and hands out the keys.

"Top floor," she says. "All on the left. That'll be seventy." Severkin hands over the coin for all of them, and they take their mugs of ale to the balcony area upstairs, where they find a table by another fireplace.

"So that was a neat trick ye did with the wolves, and the little explosions," Elkana says. "What did ye call them?"

"Firesnaps. Silver explosive powder wrapped in paper. Throw them at something hard and they make a loud noise. Simple dwarven technology. Children play with them. But I know many wild animals don't like the sound. If you have any lightning spells, they have a similar effect."

"Aye, that's good to know," Elkana says.

"Did you make the firesnaps as a child?" Severkin asks Reunne.

Reunne nods as she drinks her ale. "Yes. They're fun for scaring adults. And it teaches basic explosive principles. The gray elves from the undercity usually aren't taught much more than that, though."

"Why not?" Elkana asks.

Reunne looks as if she is about to say something but pauses and takes another drink of her ale. "We're not the right height," she says.

Elkana laughs.

"I'm serious. The dwarves design their machines and explosives for their height. It is difficult to bend down to the right position."

"I thought ye grew up with the dwarves, though," Elkana says. "A whole bunch of ye."

Reunne looks at Severkin and tilts her head slightly, as if uncomfortable with Severkin having shared her past. Severkin feels a sudden urge to apologize, but the sensation is so new to him, he doesn't act on it right away and instead lets it fill his shoulders with a tingling and his mouth with a bitter taste.

"Yes," Reunne says after a moment. "But there were still far more dwarves."

"Interesting," Elkana says. She puts down her empty mug. "I'd love to chat more, but if you want me ta be any use to you, I'd best be getting to my room ta meditate and replenish my spells. See ye all tomorrow. Don't go on without me."

"We won't," Severkin says, smiling. "Sleep well."

"You as well," Elkana says, and stands, stretching her arms to the ceiling before heading up the stairs.

The fire near them makes the clicking sound of a disapproving grandmother, and below on the main floor, the bard finally stops tuning his lute and begins to softly play.

"So you trust her," Reunne asks suddenly, in a low voice. "The troll?"

"Yes," Severkin says. "I've known her for ages. I . . . apologize if I should not have shared with her where you were from."

"I like being able to pass as a regular gray elf. But you trust her to protect you, fight with you?"

"Yes. We've fought together before."

"Then I will trust her, too. But be careful. You know what they say about trolls—how they're sneaky and clever and prone to sudden bouts of violence if not given what they want."

"People say things like that about gray elves, too," Severkin says, staring at the fire. "That we steal and lie."

"Do they?" Reunne asks, leaning back in her chair. "I've never left the island. They don't speak ill of gray elves here."

"No, I suppose they wouldn't," Severkin says, taking a drink. "This is our home." He smiles at that. At the idea of being in a place where no one mistrusts him. "You never faced prejudice from the dwarves, growing up?"

"Not directed at me. I'm one of them. They may have spoken against those from aboveground, but . . . I'm not one of those."

"So, are you more family with the dwarves," Severkin asks, narrowing his eyes, "or more family with me?" He looks at her, and she looks away at the fire. He thinks of what Rorth and the others had said about Reunne—that she couldn't be trusted. Could he have been imagining her trustworthiness? Was he so desperate for some familial connection that he was seeing her as something she wasn't? He thought she had told him they were kin to show her loyalty to him, but now she seems divided. Or she's trying to cover her lies.

Reunne takes a deep breath.

"I confess," she says after a beat, "when the barrier came down and we could go aboveground, it felt . . . amazing. Being among people who looked like me. I felt more as if I belonged. But then they called me 'underelf' and 'traitor' when they found out where I was from, and I realized I was split—gray elves won't call me kin, though I call them kin, and since the split, dwarves have grown more wary of us elves who grew up with them. They tell me to pick a side. Perhaps, though, as the peace grows, I won't have to choose. My two halves can join."

Severkin nods. "I know how that feels," he says.

"Do you?" Reunne asks. "How?"

Severkin pauses, his mind briefly blank. "I was raised by a human," he says. "I had to find my own identity and build it from books and assumptions and things taught to me. But being here for the first time, among my own people . . . I feel like I can just be myself—as though I don't need to know what it is to be a gray elf, because there are nothing but gray elves, and each one is different."

"I can see that," Reunne says.

"So," Severkin asks, leaning in, "do you think there are people in the Tower who don't want to be there? Maybe under some enchantment, and we need to break it somehow?"

"You sound tired," Reunne says. "And I know I'm tired. I'm to my bed."

"All right," Severkin says, disappointed. "I'll go up, too." They leave their empty mugs and head upstairs, each taking one of the rooms, which have braziers in them, making the rooms warm and smoky. Severkin unpacks his things and hangs his clothes to dry and gets into bed. His door opens suddenly and he sits up, seeing only a silhouette beyond the threshhold.

Reunne walks in, still in her armor, but her spear is gone. She sits down at the edge of his bed, reaches out and takes his shoulder, then covers him with the blankets.

"Sorry," she says. "I didn't mean to disturb you. I just wanted to say . . . before, when you asked me who my family was, I said I was both and neither, and that's true. My father was taken when I was young. By the Sword and Shield, the guards I mentioned who work in the shadows. My father wanted peace with the overworld—this was nearly a century ago. And then he vanished. Before she died, my mother raised me to be quiet and obedient to the dwarves. So I was an outcast even down there. I was the daughter of the disappeared, and I tried to show them I could be obedient, but they never really accepted me.

"So I wanted you to know I still know you're my family. More than the gray elves of the overcity or the dwarves and elves of the undercity. Neither of them accept me—but you do. I can't explain it, but I feel a kinship with you. Maybe it's because you're an elf without the prejudices from either city. Maybe you're the first of my kind who I don't feel judged by." She walks a few steps away from him, looks out the small window. "I'm sorry. I just felt I had to say that. Good night." She turns and walks toward the door without looking back.

"Good night," Severkin says. He watches Reunne leave, closing the door behind her, and then shuts his eyes and lets sleep overtake him.

FIFTEEN

NICK TURNS off the game. It's late. He has school tomorrow and he knows he should sleep, but instead he thinks
about what Reunne—Mom—just told him. Reunne's father
was disappeared. Captured by the Sword and Shield—a similar group, Nick thinks, to the Stasi, East Berlin's secret police.
He's done his research. But he thinks now he hasn't done
enough. He goes to his computer, ignoring the checklist, and
starts Googling "Stasi Alzheimer's" and "East Berlin prison
Alzheimer's," but nothing comes up that actually relates to
East Berlin. Just people with the last name Stasi, or ads for
Alzheimer's treatments on pages about East Berlin. He doesn't
understand what Mom is trying to tell him.

If her father was disappeared, shouldn't she have been
less willing to go into the home? Wouldn't she know what it
was like to have a parent just vanish? Why would she want
that for him?

He googles some more, researches East German prison

camps, "the disappeared," "the imprisoned," his fingers grow-ing numb with the typing, his eyes dim against the bright light of the screen. Nothing, though. Maybe it's a clue to something else. Maybe she's the imprisoned, disappeared one and he needs to break her out, like Reunne would break out her fa-ther. He'll have to ask Reunne more. He doesn't have enough. He knows she's trying to tell him something, but he doesn't know what.

The clock on his computer screen says its 1 a.m., which on a school night is hours past when he should be in bed. He's surprised Dad hasn't come and checked on him. He turns off the computer and lies down in bed, wondering how Reunne would break into a prison and steal a prisoner and, then, how she'd help the prisoner escape her own fear and climb out of the fog she's drowning in.

• • •

"That was awesome," Nat says as she sits next to him in history class. It's the second class, but there's a ten-minute break, so not everyone has come in yet. "You're really good. I was afraid you were gonna suck, y'know. I mean, I'd still play with you, but I didn't want to be held back. I think I might be holding you back, though."

"Nah," Nick says. "You're really good, too." Nick has been wondering all morning if he should tell Nat who Reunne is—who she could be. He's afraid she might think he's crazy, though. If she doesn't think he's a freak just for having a mom everyone thinks is sick. Maybe she'll think both. Probably both.

Having a parent who everyone thinks is going crazy is

akin to going crazy yourself, Nick thinks. He's paranoid that everyone knows, afraid of what they'll feel about him—pity, fear, hate—and he's afraid of the day he loses his keys. Then they'll lock him away, too. Maybe this is what living in East Germany was like.

"I really loved the part where Reunne showed up with those firesnaps. I wonder if she can teach me the explosives skill. That would be good. And I guess I should try to learn a better lightning spell. I bet they'll be selling one at the Tower, right?"

Nick glances up at Ms. Knight, who is writing on the board. Other students are filing in.

"We can't talk about it too loudly," Nick says. "We don't want to spoil it for Ms. Knight."

"You mean she plays?" Nat asks, her eyes going wide. Nick nods. "You're my favorite, Ms. Knight!" Nat shouts. Some other students giggle. Ms. Knight turns around with a perplexed look on her face.

"Thank you?" she says. "Everyone take your seats; class starts . . ." She points at the corner of the room as if expecting the bell there to ring, but several seconds go by before it does, after which Ms. Knight looks pleased with herself anyway.

"Okay," she says. "I've gone over your questionnaires, and I think we're going to have an excellent term and cover a lot of important events. I'm going to put you in pairs and groups where you have similar backgrounds so you can share research and talk about what you've learned from your families. You won't be presenting together, but you will have twenty minutes each week to report to each other what you've learned. So, let's see. Emma Angelov, you're with Nick

Reeves." Ms. Knight points at Nick and Emma—a different Emma from the one he met at the bookstore, one whom Nick doesn't know. She's aggressively blond.

"I think you mean Emma Clarke, Ms. Knight," Emma says. "My family wasn't near Africa." Nick looks at Nat, and they roll their eyes together.

"Nick's family is from Germany, actually," Ms. Knight says. "So pair up."

Emma shrugs, and moves over to sit by Nick. Ms. Knight reads out the rest of the names, and Nat goes over to the other side of the room to sit with her group.

"So, Germany?" Emma asks. She tilts her head at him as if expecting the punch line of a joke she won't really think is funny, so she has to prepare a fake laugh.

Nick nods. "My mom, East Berlin."

"Oh," Emma says, leaning back and pulling her hair behind her ears. "I get it. My grandpa grew up in Bulgaria under communism. I wanted to focus on life under communism."

"My mom was there when the wall fell, so I'm doing that."

"That's cool," Emma says. She tilts her head again. "Sorry if I was out of line with that Africa comment. I guess you don't look *that* black."

"It's fine," Nick says, looking at his desk. It's not fine, but he doesn't want to start in with it. And he knows protesting that there are different ways to be black is just going to get this white girl feeling all defensive. In his sixth-grade class there was one other black kid—Don Robinson—who everyone referred to as "the real black kid" because he played basketball and listened to rap and wore baseball hats with the brims ironed flat. Nick knew there were other ways to be black—he just had to look at his father for that. No one could doubt

Dad's blackness. But the white kids his age always seem to expect the one thing—that pop-culture, edgy-celebrity thing that white suburban kids think of as black—that Nick couldn't provide. He should be used to it by now. But he's just tired of it instead. It bores him. He stares down at his desk, which has TWO RIVERS carved choppily into it. Someone has crossed out RIVERS with a knife and carved smaller, more elegant letters above it: SLIVERS. He runs his hands over the words, feeling the rough edges knives made years ago cut freshly into his fingers.

"I also . . . ," Emma starts, then pauses and tilts her head forward, her eyes big, like she's about to tell him his puppy died. "I want to say I'm sorry about your mom. . . ."

Nick's body flash-freezes. He can feel the bones in his jaw start to crack from the cold.

"I don't mean to be rude," Emma continues, seeing the look on his face. "It's just something I heard, and I was, like, 'He seems so normal.' It must be hard having a mom who's . . . off." She looks at him as if expecting a response.

Nick opens his mouth, and, and takes a gulp of air too fast, so it feels like he's choking, and suddenly he's boiling now, sweating.

"I don't want to talk about it," he says softly.

Emma reaches out and pats his hand. There's no warmth in the gesture; it's like she's petting the ugly dog of a friend.

"Is that why you and Natalie are so close?" She draws out the vowels in Natalie's name when she asks this.

"What do you mean?" Nick asks.

"Oh," Emma says, and looks down at her desk. "If you don't know, I shouldn't tell you."

"Okay," Nick says. He's too exhausted to be curious. Emma

purses her lips, and Nick gets the impression she's disappointed that he's not prying.

"So, let's talk about communism," she says. "Apparently they were totally shut off from the rest of the world, so they didn't know anything. That must have sucked."

· · ·

"Have fun with Emma Angel-Love?" Nat asks at lunch, a few periods later.

"Angel-Love?" Nick asks, peeling a banana.

"That's the nickname she gave herself in second grade. She say anything interesting?" Nick carefully peels the banana, picking at all the threads of peel left behind. "I only ask 'cause she's a huge gossip." Nick nods and continues to stare at his banana. There's a dark brown spot about halfway down, but he likes those spots—they always taste sickly sweet to him, like caramel. "A broch," Nat says after a moment of silence. "She told you about my dad, didn't she?"

Nick looks up at Nat.

"No," he says. "I think she wanted to . . . She said—" He stops. How can he say what Emma said without revealing what she said about Mom?

"What?" Nat says. She starts tapping her fingers on the table one after the other, like falling dominoes, or the tide. "Look, my dad is better now. He went to rehab. He doesn't drink anymore." She says it all quickly, but the words are stale, something she's said over and over. Nick has never explained Mom's situation to anyone. He doesn't know how to make those words stale.

"That's not what she said," Nick says.

Nat turns bright red, but it fades in a flash, and she shrugs. "Well, that's my story," she says. "My dad was a drunk; some friends and I found him passed out on the floor when we came home one day. Now he's better. If you don't want to be my friend anymore, then screw you." She stops tapping her fingers and waits for a moment and Nick thinks about reaching out and putting his hand on hers but doesn't.

"I still want to be your friend," he says. "I don't care about that." He stares at her, and she's smiling. He tries to process this new information: Her dad was an alcoholic. Her dad is better now. It doesn't change his opinion of her. Her dad is a different person from Nat. Just like Mom is different from him.

"She asked if we were friends because she thinks my mom is crazy." Natalie's eyes widen, there's a delay before she speaks. It's her turn now to stare at her bottle of orange juice, the tape off, pulp clustering around the rim like moss. "You knew," Nick says.

"I'd heard something," Nat confesses. "But I didn't believe it. I figured if it was true, you'd tell me."

"It's not true," Nick says. Nat smiles, looks up at him, thinks that's the end of the story. "But I'm the only one who knows that," he finishes.

He forgets to eat lunch as he explains about Mom's supposed illness, about what Alzheimer's is, and how he knows she doesn't have it because of the checklist, how she has something else, about how she's in a home. It feels so good to say it, like his body has been all knotted up before now, and as he talks, the knots untie themselves one by one and he can feel his blood flow, his muscles stretch, his whole body strong enough now to take down a giant. It feels like freedom. He doesn't even notice how Nat's expression has changed until he's done with his story. Till he's told her about Mom's paintings of Wellhall, and that Reunne is Mom. But then he finishes, and looks at her, and she's wearing PityFace, her head cocked to the side, her eyes wide and her shoulders back, her lips pressed into a straight line except for at the corners, which go up, but only slightly—not a smile, just an expression saying "I'm here for you."

"Are you sure she's not really sick?" she asks, her voice low.

The bell rings, signaling the end of lunch, and it feels like the scream inside Nick's head, the scream from a staff through his gut as blood runs everywhere. He gets up to leave without saying anything, walks away, deaf except for the echo of the bell in his ears.

SIXTEEN

NAT TRIES to talk to him in the parking lot after school—he sees her running for him, waving, but he gets on the bus quickly and ignores her. She starts calling him almost immediately, but he doesn't pick up, and then the text messages start:

> I'm sorry
> Please call me I just want to apologize
> I know what ur going thru
> I believe you

This one comes as he's getting off the bus, and Nick stares at it like Severkin would stare at a puzzle-lock on the door to a vault. Is it a lie told out of guilt? Truth? What does she believe, exactly?

He goes inside, but the house is empty, Dad still at work. He goes up to his room and turns on the game, then stares at his phone again. He doesn't know if she really believes him. Maybe he didn't explain it well enough. Maybe he should have told her about the things his mom used to do in the game. There was one quest he especially remembers, which started with a slip of paper on his pillow reading, "The Queen in Bluegarden who doesn't sit on a throne." Bluegarden was a huge city, overseen by Queen Delilah, but she was always on her throne. Severkin spent an hour exploring the city before he realized that one of the citizens' pet cats was named Queenie. He'd pickpocketed the cat—something Nick didn't even know was possible, but apparently his mom had figured it out—and found a note.

He recognized the note from another quest. It was a note between lovers, just a scrap of paper, but Nick saw it in a different context now. It said "We'll meet where there is a tree that was once a woman." In the original quest, they were talking about an overgrown statue in an abandoned city. But this wasn't that quest. This was something Mom gave to him. He'd gone online, remembering Mom saying it was based on Greek mythology, and looked into Greek myths where women had been turned into trees. The big one was when the nymph Daphne was turned into a laurel tree. Nick had known what to do then. There was a gardener who ran the royal greenhouses in the city of Serelle, and her name was Laurel. Severkin searched every tree in Laurel's greenhouse until he found an enchanted dagger.

In the game, when a player enchants an object, the player can rename the item. The dagger was called the Golden Apple. This one took more puzzling out. He knew the myth of the golden apple, how it caused the Trojan War, but there was no golden apple in the game, no Trojan War. The war in the game was based on World War I. He turned the idea over and over in his head and examined the enchantments on the dagger—improved accuracy. And then he realized that a golden apple was the starting point of the Trojan War, so he should go to the starting point of the war in the game—a pastry shop in the city of Jevo where the assassin had been having coffee, not knowing his conspirators had failed to kill the prince. Like in World War I, a wrong turn had put the prince in the assassin's sight. The assassin shot the prince, and war began. In the game, the pastry shop was still doing business, so Severkin snuck in one night after it had closed, and in the basement, amid the bags of flour and sugar, he'd found an amulet called Severkin's Sight, which not only improved his accuracy but let him see people through walls. It had been an awesome quest.

He thinks maybe if Nat knew about that—and about the other quests like it—maybe she wouldn't have been so skeptical. He looks down at the text messages again.

I believe you

He calls Nat's number, and she picks up before the first ring is over.

"Thank you," she says quickly. Her voice sounds sticky.

"What do you believe?" Nick asks. He keeps his voice cool.

"What?"

"You said you believe me. What do you believe?"

"That maybe your mom was misdiagnosed."

Nick takes a deep breath, and it feels like the first breath he's taken in a while. "Thank you," he says. In the background, he can hear murmuring, people talking. "Where are you?"

"My mom's restaurant," she says. "Late lunch crowd. I'm in a corner booth. I'm supposed to be working on my homework."

"Me too," Nick says.

"I'm really sorry I didn't believe you. It's just . . . I thought Reunne was an NPC, so when you got to that part . . ." She trails off.

"You don't believe it's my mom, do you?" Nick doesn't mind this as much. He knows it sounds crazy, and he has no proof. But that's okay. It's a new theory. He'll get some proof. And now Nat can help him.

"It just sounds kind of crazy," Nat says. There's a beat where Nick stares at his feet and notices one of his shoelaces is untied. He kicks both his shoes off. "Sorry, I shouldn't have said crazy."

"I know," Nick says, and stares at his feet. "It does sound weird."

"Why wouldn't she tell you?"

"I don't know, exactly. I feel like there's the real her but that she only comes out sometimes. The rest of the time, it's like she's lost in this fog. I think it could be the drugs they're giving her at the home."

"It's like a conspiracy," Nat says. "That's why it sounds so weird."

"I know that," Nick says. "But I'm going to prove it's her. Then they'll have to let her come home." Nat is silent, but Nick can hear people talking in the background and a sudden sound like water being poured on a fire, all sizzle and smoke. "Will you help me?" he asks.

"How?" Nat says. "We can't break character on the server. You can't just call her 'Mom' and see what happens."

"I know," Nick says, staring at the menu screen on the game. It shows the mountain of Wellhall, the clouds swirling around it while the eerie sound of violin strings and vocals, more like weeping than singing, play in the background. While he watches, the screen darkens as the clouds around Wellhall swell out like waves, and then the screen shows the Tower, white and gleaming as snow falls gently around it. "Just . . . If I can prove it to you, will you back me up?"

"Okay," Nat says. "But if you can't . . ."

"Then maybe it's not her," Nick concedes. "Maybe I'm just going crazy like my mom."

"It's not crazy to want your mom to get better," Nat says. "I know that."

"Thanks," Nick says. The game has started up, but he turns it off now. He wants to play when Nat's on. "I'm going to do some homework now. But you'll be on the game tonight? You'll help me prove it's my mom?"

"I'll help you investigate," Nat says. Which is close enough, Nick thinks. "See you then," he says.

SEVENTEEN

SEVERKIN WAKES up to the bright light of snowy places. It streams in through the window like a banner and casts a white circle, like from a magnifying glass. He rises, then washes his face in the basin in the room. The water is ice cold and wakes him up. After dressing he goes and knocks on the doors of his comrades. Elkana's room is empty, the door open. Reunne's door is closed, and she doesn't immediately respond to his knock. Severkin takes inventory of his weapons while waiting. He could use more arrows.

Reunne opens the door. "Ready to get started?" she asks.

Severkin nods, a smile on his face. "I think Elkana is already downstairs."

They head downstairs, and Severkin studies Reunne, the way she walks, and the lines around her eyes. He thinks of her missing father and wonders if it haunts her, knowing he might still be out there, alive, waiting for her to rescue him. At the bar, Elkana is devouring a plate of meat and eggs. They sit with her and eat some breakfast, although not so large as Elkana's.

"This is going to be fun," Severkin says to Elkana.

"Maybe," Elkana says cautiously.

When they're done with breakfast, they head outside and walk toward the Tower. The city is different in the daytime, with only a gentle snow falling. Now it looks like they're walking along the edge of a giant snowflake, and the Tower is the farthest tip. There aren't many people out in the streets, but those who are have their heads down, watching for ice, and so don't pay Severkin and his companions much heed.

Up close, the Tower is less tower-like than from afar: narrow and tall, but deeper than expected. A huge archway with a gate opens onto a courtyard, and behind that is another large door through which Severkin assumes is the Tower proper. But he doesn't spend much time looking at it because he's distracted by the students in the courtyard. They all shovel snow in unison, like soldiers, and they all wear matching robes—in bright blue.

"Blue robes," he says.

"Same color she made us wear in the undercity," Reunne says. Severkin tries to exchange a look with Elkana, but when he catches her eye, she just looks confused.

"Did you have to shovel dirt?" Severkin asks.

"Some," Reunne answers, walking carefully around the edge of the courtyard so as not to interfere with the students. "Marching, too. Lots of marching. 'Physical activity for the spirit and the mind,' she called it."

"Shoveling snow has never helped with my magic," Elkana says.

"Have you tried it?" Reunne asks.

"Nah. I just know from instinct. Maybe this isn't the place for me ta join up after all." They'd circled the courtyard and come to the large doors, which Reunne opens. Inside, the Tower is surprisingly large, made all of stone, with narrow, swordlike windows cut into the walls, leaving only thin punctures of snow light in their wake. These slices of light from the windows crisscross to form a white spiderweb on the floor. The room is empty except for one man in a blue robe behind a desk in front of a stairway. He looks up as they enter but doesn't say anything until they're very close to him.

"The Tower is off limits to nonstudents," he says in a whisper.

"We're from the guard," Severkin says, taking out his new badge. "We were sent for."

The man studies the badge, then nods. "Mistress Frigit is on the top floor. Please do not step into any of the other rooms." He immediately returns to staring at his desk, as though the conversation has exhausted him.

The three walk past him and up the staircase. As it ascends, the walls close in around it, with only the occasional door and landing. Elkana tries one of the doors and it opens slightly. She nods at Severkin.

"I bet they have some good equipment," she says. "And enough of it that they wouldn't mind a little going missing."

"Mistress Frigit keeps very tight records," Reunne says before Severkin can respond. "And besides, we're guards. We don't steal from citizens."

Elkana stares at Reunne and then at Severkin.

"You don't steal?" she says.

Severkin shrugs and purses his lips. "Not in front of her, anyway," he whispers, and Elkana chuckles.

Reunne is already half a flight above them, so they run to catch up and nearly bump into her. She's standing in front of the door at the end of the stairway. She knocks.

"Enter!" calls a brisk voice. They open the door and walk into the headmistress's office, the top of the tower. It's bright, because the ceiling is clear glass, showing the silver blue of the sky above them. The ceiling dips down into the wall in places, like melting snow, providing a view of the city and the frozen wastes to the north. Bookshelves lined with old tomes are placed against the wall where there are no windows, and a cast-iron stove sits to one side, the smell of herbs and smoke coming from it. In the center of the room is a low desk, and sitting behind it, looking over a huge book, is a dwarf. She glances up when they enter. She's small even for a dwarf and wears the same bright blue as the students below, but with a yellow collar at the neck of her robe. She has eyeglasses that make her eyes seem like little black dots, and her gray hair is slicked back so tightly into a bun that it's nearly invisible.

"You're the guard?" she asks.

"Yes, Mistress Frigit," Reunne says. "You may remember me—"

"I don't have time for that," Frigit interrupts, raising a palm. "You're here for the Staff, but I don't have it. It was stolen. You'll retrieve it, along with the other stolen items, and eliminate the thief. Is that clear?"

"Is there a reward?" Elkana asks.

"You'll be paid by the guard, I assume," Frigit says in dripping, unimpressed tones. "And you'll be helping to stop the giants, which strikes me as a reward unto itself."

"What if we wanted ta join the Tower?" Elkana asks. "I'm not in the guard. I'm just helping."

"A troll in the Tower?" Frigit says, standing. She looks Elkana up and down, shaking her head in wonder. "Do you actually know any magic?"

"I do," Elkana says, her hand suddenly glowing red hot. "And a troll using magic is no stranger than a dwarf using magic."

"I dare say it is. But very well. If you assist in this quest, you will be given access to the Tower as a member. I assume you're not going to be taking classes or working in the courtyard."

"Hadn't planned on it." Elkana's hand snuffs out with an audible gasp.

"Good. You might terrify the students. Anyway, as I said, assist and you can have access. You can all have access." She waves her hand as though tossing peasants spare change. "Now, the thief. A human named Helena Halja. She was the headmistress of the Tower. Not the one before me but the one before that. She left under unseemly circumstances. Accusations of necromancy, disgusting things like that. Apparently, she took a lot of the Tower's most valued artifacts with her when she left, and no one thought to check. Also, my predecessor was an idiot."

"Do you know what she took, exactly?" Severkin asks. He sees hundreds of artifacts, filled with secrets, dancing in front of him.

"No, not exactly. But I'll trust you to give her lair a thorough search and bring back whatever you find."

"And where is this lair?" Reunne asks.

"I'm not entirely sure," Frigit says, sitting down. "But if one is to put stock in rumor—and unfortunately there's really nothing else to put stock in in this instance—she had a home in the mountains to the northeast. A little manor. Why anyone would have a manor there is beyond me and, frankly, should have been a sign that the woman wasn't meant for higher education, but there it is. Start there. I'm sure you'll find something. You are the professionals, after all." And with that, she looks back down at her book.

"That's it?" Elkana asks.

"Thank you, Mistress Frigit," Reunne says, and heads for the door, motioning for Severkin and Elkana to do likewise. Elkana looks like she wants to say more, but they exit and Reunne shuts the door behind them.

"That was helpful," Elkana says, heading down the stairs, taking two at a time. "A mansion in the hills kinda over that way." She waves a clawed hand.

"She didn't seem to remember you," Severkin says to Reunne.

"She might have," Reunne says, "and just not cared. But she's had many students. I wouldn't be offended if she'd forgotten me."

"She definitely didn't have any interest in small talk," Elkana says. "I'm just hoping this is worth it. I should have asked what resources the Tower has. Spell making? An enchanting room? I'd rather not go kill some necromancer just so I have access ta an impressive herb garden."

"With Mistress Frigit in charge, there will be much more than that," Reunne says.

"Well, good," Elkana says. "Before we head out, I'd like to see if I can purchase a lightning spell."

"I need more arrows," Severkin says.

"I could use some better armor," Reunne says. "Let's meet at the gate to the city—but be quick. I want to find this place before nightfall."

The three of them split up to arrange their equipment and supplies. The city is more alive now but still frozen, and the people move too slowly for Severkin; they seem not quite awake, or even alive. The shopkeepers sigh when he buys from them, their breath creating small clouds in the cold air. Their fingernails are so pale they look like ice. Severkin asks around, tries to find out about the mansion in the hills, about Helena Halja, but the citizens just look at him with frosted, empty eyes. No one knows anything, but the arrows he buys are sharp. Severkin is at the city gates first, but Reunne is right behind, and Elkana shows up a moment later.

"The shopkeep at the spell shop said we should follow the last of the frozen rivers to the east, till we hit a graveyard. He said we should be able ta see the mansion from there, if the weather's clear."

"We'd better hurry, then," Severkin says, looking at the horizon. Some clouds are moving in from the south, bubbling and dark.

Reunne takes the lead, as hers is the only short-range weapon, but the progress is quick, now that the day is clear. As they hike, Elkana fires off questions at Reunne like the sparks that occasionally pop and crackle out of her fingers.

"So what was it like, then, growin' up in the dark?"

"I have nothing to compare it to. But in retrospect, I'd call it . . . limited. Information was controlled by the government, so we knew only what they told us, ate only what they provided," Reunne says, stepping over a frozen puddle.

"That how ye got in with the guard, then? National service?"

"Yes, about."

"About?" Elkana asks, throwing some sparks at a wolf that has been staring at them from the woods. It yelps and runs off.

"I wasn't drafted, if that's what you're asking. There just weren't very many other choices that I was qualified for or that paid nearly as well. Or that gave me the opportunity to see outside the undercity. I traveled all under the land. Once or twice I even headed to the surface."

"In all your travels, what's the oddest disease you've come down with?" Severkin asks.

"I don't know," Reunne says. "Why all the questions?"

"Just gettin' ta know ye better," Elkana says.

They encounter a few more wolves, which they dispatch easily, and once, a huge bear that provides more of a challenge, but they recover quickly and reach the graveyard just as the clouds reach them and it begins sleeting in slow, thick tears. Mist seems to rise from the gravestones, which are half buried under frost and look long neglected. A single rooster, somehow escaped from a nearby farm, wanders the graves, dusty red and starving.

"Do ye see anything?" Elkana asks, her arm over her head in a futile attempt to stay dry.

"There," Severkin and Reunne say simultaneously, both pointing to the same spot.

"Heh," Elkana says. "Almost like ye two are related."

"We have the same blood," Reunne says.

Severkin smiles. "I sometimes feel like you're the gray elf

mother I never had," he says in a forced half laugh, as though trying to make a joke of it.

Reunne smiles at this and places a hand on his for a moment.

"And you're a great history teacher," he adds.

"History?" Reunne asks, pulling her hand back. "I'm not that ancient. Though I suppose I am educating you about your roots."

"History . . . ," Elkana says, as if thinking about something.

"Yes. He's a gray elf who doesn't know about gray elves," Reunne says. "So I've been teaching him. But now I'd rather we head to that mansion and retrieve the Staff."

Severkin nods and looks at Elkana, smiling in triumph, but she won't meet his eye. They find a rough path, barely visible, at the far end of the graveyard, where the clawlike rocks jut suddenly out of the ground, a wall of stone fists. As they begin their hike, they are almost immediately set upon by a pair of bears. Elkana's hands crackle with electricity as Severkin notches an arrow.

"So do ye think of Severkin as kin?" Elkana asks, throwing lightning at the bears. "What with your both bein' gray elves, even though he was raised overland?"

"We're blood," Reunne says, spinning her spear to ward off one of the bear's claws. "Can we talk about this later?"

"Well, yeah, but ye had a different upbringing," Elkana says, rolling out of the way as the other bear charges her. Severkin releases the arrow, and it hits the bear's flank with a *thunk* but doesn't slow it down.

"As you did from the rest of your blood, I'd wager," Reunne

says, stabbing at the other bear with her spear. "What does it matter?"

"Just want to know what yer relationship is." Elkana rubs her palms together and lets out an electric crack that stuns both bears.

"He's too young for me, if that's what you're asking," Reunne says, plunging her spear through the chest of one bear. "He's all yours."

Elkana chuckles. "He's on the scrawny side. I'm undecided."

"I'm plenty fit," Severkin says, and slashes the throat of the other bear for good measure.

"We should stay quiet," Reunne says. "We're getting close, and I don't want to set off any alarms if we can help it."

By the time they reach the manor, climbing over the last hump with their hands, it's pouring sleet and so dark that they can barely see one another. There's a tall fence, like steel lace, around the manor, but the gate swings open and shut in the wind. Reunne grabs it and holds it open so the others can pass through.

"Do we just knock?" Severkin asks at the door.

"And say what?" Elkana says. "'We heard ye stole some stuff, would ye mind giving it back, please?'"

"I think perhaps stealth would be the best way to approach this," Reunne says, nodding.

"Excellent," Severkin says. "I'll lead the way." He kneels down and takes out his lockpicks. It's a little difficult to work with the wind and sleet, so it takes him twelve seconds to pick the lock, nowhere near his personal best. No guards come running when they walk inside, no alarm sounds. In fact, once they close the door, it becomes completely silent, the storm outside a memory. The only sounds are of their footsteps on the dirty marble tiles and of their breathing, like whispers in the dark.

"This place looks abandoned," Elkana says, summoning a floating orb of white light that circles her like an obsessed firefly. Severkin looks around. She's right. Not just abandoned but sacked: paintings torn from splintered frames, rooms empty aside from the occasional table too heavy to move or chair too worthless to steal. The floors are coated with dust and mold so thick and undisturbed it looks like rugs. They make a thorough examination of the manor, upstairs and down, but there's nothing, not even rats. Severkin bites his lower lip in frustration. Where are the artifacts?

"Maybe we have the wrong manor?" he suggests. "Maybe there's another farther up the mountain."

"No," Reunne says, and begins tapping on the walls. "There's something about this place. The silence. It doesn't feel right."

"I agree," Elkana says. "This place feels off. Something is here. I don't know if it's the Staff or artifacts or something else, but something is here."

"I think a secret passage," Reunne says, tapping another wall.

"That's not the best way to look for them," Severkin says.

"Oh?" Reunne asks. "Then you do it."

Severkin nods and takes a large breath. He closes his eyes, and when he opens them again, his vision is different, highlighting small details that seemed normal before and connecting them to other small details. This ripple in the dust wasn't made by the wind, his senses tell him, and over here is a fingerprint on the smudged candlestick. Not every detail is relevant, he knows, but his mind collects the information and processes it. It's a trick his adoptive father taught him—the Treasure Hunter's Sight. He taps a lamp and smells the dust in the corner of what was probably once a study; he leads them all around the house, examining each clue. He can't do this for very long, so he hurries, almost running around the house, until a small scratch in the wooden panel of the bedroom wall and the faint smell of coal dust lead him to a wall sconce, long since broken, so it looks like the stem of a flower, its glass bloom lost to time. He twists it and the wooden panel in the wall clicks slightly and depresses. Severkin closes his eyes again, and when he opens them, he sees normally.

"Well done," Elkana says, patting him on the back. "That's a good trick."

"People like you would work for the Sword and Shield," Reunne says, "before the undercity was joined with the over again."

Severkin glances back at her when she says this, unsure if she means it as a compliment, but her face is unreadable. He pushes the wall panel open and the smell of frost and dirt wafts into the room. Beyond is a tunnel hacked into the rock, leading downward.

"What are the Sword and Shield?" Elkana asks.

"In the undercity," Reunne says, "they were guards who kept themselves hidden—disguised among the citizens."

"Like secret police," Severkin says, walking carefully down the tunnel.

"That . . ." Reunne considers for a moment. "That is an accurate description, though I've never heard it said thus."

"That sounds unfriendly," Elkana says.

Severkin nods, then puts a finger to his lips. The others crouch low and walk quietly, following him down the tunnel. At the end is a huge cavern, lit by torches so far apart they seem like stars in the darkness. The room is so gigantic, Severkin isn't sure how it can exist under the mountain.

"No guards," Reunne whispers. "This is making me uneasy."

Each torch is on a stand above a table positioned along the edge of the circular room, and then, farther in, another circle, and another within that. In the center is a very large table with a lantern hanging over it. The nearest table has a glass box on it, and in the box is a pair of gauntlets, green and gleaming. Severkin kneels to look at them. They're covered in ancient Orcish script, which he's only passingly familiar with. He recognizes the words for *strength* and *hands* but not much else. He reaches to open the glass box, but a gesture from Elkana stops him.

"The arrangements of the tables is magical," Elkana says. "They may be trapped, or alarmed."

"Can you disarm them?" Severkin asks.

Elkana looks around the room. "There's nothing nearby to disarm. . . . It's difficult ta explain. There are no spells, but the tables are arranged sorta like certain runes. . . . They're traps only in that you must open them the right way. There's no disarming. . . . There's only not-setting-off."

"So, how?" Reunne asks.

"I'll need ta look around more carefully ta find out," Elkana says. "Watch my back."

"I'll take the center," Reunne says. "Look out."

Reunne nods and heads toward the center of the room,

looking carefully about her as she walks, spear drawn. Elkana ventures farther into the room and begins investigating the torches and glass boxes. Severkin follows her, though he's more interested in the contents of the glass boxes than the boxes themselves. There are ancient human tablets, encrusted with jewels, and old pendants with troll runes that glow a faint purple. There's a pair of swords, sharp and ice blue, hilts shaped like a hawk and a snake, respectively, and those are just the first three items they walk past. The room is filled with ancient treasure, and Severkin wants it all.

"The pattern is all about the center," Elkana says. "Maybe ye shouldn't . . ." Severkin and Elkana turn, but Reunne has already reached the center. As she crosses into the circle of light thrown by the central lantern, a low ringing fills the room, like a giant bell.

"Get back!" Severkin shouts to Reunne, who runs to join them.

"Treasure hunters?" comes a woman's voice like smoke, echoing through the room. "Did the Tower finally realize what they were missing? Or are you the type who just enjoy exploring?"

"The giants are wakin' up!" Elkana shouts. "Ye have something we need ta put 'em ta sleep again, is all!"

The woman steps out of the shadows from where Severkin was sure there was no woman a moment ago. She looks human, or like she was once human. She's pale, with long dark hair, but more noticeable is the black leather mask that covers half her face. There's no eyehole in it, no nostril, just leather polished as dark as the ocean. And to keep it fastened, there are two straps that wrap around the side of her face that's still there, one under her mouth, one over her eye, buckled in place.

"Ye're Helena, are ye?" Elkana says. "Wouldn't want ta be invading the wrong underground lair."

"I am Helena," the woman says, walking toward them. She wears a long robe that covers most of her body, but Severkin notices that one of her hands is a different color from the other, and on that hand, the thumb doesn't match and is sewn in place. "And I know the giants are waking. I've known for a while."

"So you'll give us the Staff?" Severkin asks cautiously. "So we can put them to sleep?"

"No," Helena says, still walking closer. Not walking, really, floating. Reunne brandishes her spear, the blade slicing the air just in front of Helena.

"Why not?" Severkin asks.

"I need it," she says, stopping just short of Reunne's spear. "I use it."

"For what?" Reunne asks.

"For this," Helena says, and suddenly the room begins to vibrate. From between two torches on the far side of the room, a great shadow appears and walks toward them. Severkin can see flashes of it as it passes through rings of light: a hand the size of his body, a foot that could crush mountains.

"You see," Helena says, turning around. "I have no problem with giants. I imagine one day the rest of you will figure it out, too. They're not so very hard to kill. But once they're dead . . . that's when the fun begins."

The shape has reached the center lantern now, and Severkin can see it clearly: a giant, once. But now it's just the corpse of one, eyes filmy white, teeth rotten, flesh blue and mottled with death. Helena walks toward it, and without saying anything, it extends its hand and she steps onto it. It lifts her up to its head, where she gets off. The head has been leveled—the top removed—and bolted in place is a flat disc, and on that . . .

"Is that a throne?" Elkana asks. "Look, I understand the whole Queen of the Undead aesthetic, but a throne bolted onto the head of a giant's corpse? Haven't ye heard of overkill?"

Helena sits down in the throne, and suddenly the undead giant swings a fist and Severkin only just manages to dodge out of the way. The room shudders, and stones fall from the ceiling like hail.

"I haven't had intruders in such a long time!" Helena calls from her throne. Her voice echoes off the walls. "I've missed this!"

The giant makes a fist again and goes to hammer Severkin, and again he rolls out of the way just in time, but a shard of rock comes flying at his leg and he can feel the fierce pain as it slices a line in his flesh. He doesn't have time to tend to it, though. He looks up and sees that Reunne has engaged the beast, swiping at its legs with her spear. It turns its attention to her, but she's quick. Using her spear as a pick, she stabs it into the giant's leg, then grabs hold of the spear and begins swinging from it in acrobatic circles. The giant shakes its leg, but she's holding on tight. With a sudden movement, she springs upward, her spear coming with her, the velocity sending her as high as the giant's shoulder, where she stabs it again. But this time she's in easy reach, and the giant goes to slap her off. Severkin readies an arrow and shoots it at the giant's hand, stunning it enough that Reunne can climb higher onto its shoulder. She grabs her spear out of its skin and goes to slice at the giant's neck, but before she can, it begins shaking and suddenly charges forward, head down. Reunne leaps as she begins to fall and manages to land in a crouch, unhurt. The giant, meanwhile, has skidded to a stop. Helena sits on her throne for all this, apparently unaffected by the movement.

"We need to take her out!" Severkin shouts, but Elkana is a step ahead of him, and as he says this she lets loose a spell she'd apparently been preparing all this time. A huge burst of flame flies from both her hands like a pillar, right at Helena. Helena turns and for a moment looks worried, but with a flick of her wrist, the giant's hand flies up to block the fire. Severkin watches the dead flesh on the giant's palm crackle and turn black under the fire's blast. When Elkana stops the magic, a burned circle of skin falls off the giant's hand like a shattered mirror. Reunne charges the giant's leg again, but Severkin wants to take out the master, not the servant. He notches an arrow and lets it fly at Helena. She doesn't see it until it hits her in the arm. Then she looks up, spots Severkin, and raises an arm. Suddenly the giant is less interested in Reunne and more interested in Severkin, and it charges. Severkin dodges, but not quickly enough, and feels stone flying up to stab his arms and legs.

But Severkin isn't the only one taking damage from the giant's attacks. The lamp closest to him has fallen and gone out, plunging his slice of the cavern into darkness. His night vision kicks in, and he looks up to see Helena frantically searching, her head twisting left to right and back. She can't see, he realizes. He notches another arrow and lets it fly, this time hitting her in the waist. She cries out but doesn't fall. A moment later, there's another blast of fire from Elkana, which the giant blocks again. Because Helena can see it coming.

Severkin rushes over to Elkana, his body now sluggish and oozing blood.

"Oh gods," she says, seeing the stripes of blood down his arms and legs. "Ye look like the peppermint-candy sticks human children eat."

"The light," Severkin says.

"Don't go toward it," Elkana says. "I'll heal ye, just give me a moment."

"No," Severkin says. "We need to take out the lights. She can't see in the dark."

Severkin feels the faint tendrils of magic speeding over his skin from the ground, like being caught in a flock of birds that suddenly take flight. The pain eases, but only somewhat. He's stopped bleeding, but now he feels bruised.

"Take out the lights," Severkin repeated, and Elkana nods at him, her eyes going wide at something over his shoulder. Severkin turns to see that the giant has Reunne in its hand and is crushing her. Without thinking, he lets fly an arrow at the fist holding her. The giant's hand loosens, and Reunne slips out, somersaulting to the ground and landing in a crouch. She takes off, heading for Elkana, and the giant's attention is now on Severkin. Elkana has crossed to a nearby lantern, and with a kick and a quick jab with her staff, it's down and out. She's enveloped in darkness. But Severkin can see her, as can Reunne. And Elkana's night vision, while not as good, is still better than that of a human's, like Helena.

Helena is focused on Severkin now, and the giant is

charging at him again. He dashes over to another lantern and pushes it over. It crashes down, and the torch flickers on the ground for a moment before sputtering out. Darkness again. But the giant hasn't stopped coming. Its foot glances off Severkin's back as it charges past him to the spot where he was standing just a breath ago. Severkin flies forward, the pain from just that small impact like a crack in his muscle that quickly splinters outward. He can feel its red tendrils leaping up his body as flakes of him fall away, like a crumbling stone wall. He has no foundation anymore. He falls, face-first into the dirt.

He can hear his name being called over the ringing in his ears, and he forces himself up onto his knees. He can't die now. If he dies now, here, in this cave, he'll never know the truth about Reunne. She'll continue the mission without him. She won't need him. He'll never see her again. He has to get up.

His knees are bloody and the dirt from the floor cakes them like matted fur. The giant is close. He needs to get away. Maybe Elkana can heal him again. He staggers forward, then turns to where the giant was. It is kicking blindly in the dark, and on her throne, Helena is screaming furiously. There are a few torches still shining, but as Severkin watches, Elkana tears them down in neat strokes from her staff. The cavern is in total darkness. And within it, Reunne strikes. Severkin's body is weak, and he can barely shoot any more arrows, but he tries to help, firing at Helena enough to keep her nervous while Reunne does the real work. She hacks at the giant with her spear and, as before, swings her way up its body, part acrobat, part warrior. When she reaches the left shoulder she straddles it, bracing herself as she begins to hack away at the neck. With Severkin's night vision, the blood looks black to him, almost like water, but its rotten smell manacles his lungs and chokes him to his knees. His eyes water.

He looks up and can see the blur that is the giant's head roll slowly from its shoulders, and from the head a figure flies off, hovering in place. Severkin blinks and sees it's Helena, screaming. Reunne is still on the giant's shoulders. If she jumps now, she could grab on to Helena, kill her. The giant's body begins to fall. Severkin is in its shadow, and he tries to stand, to get away before it crushes him, but his muscles ache, and the poison spray of the blood is still choking him. He knows he's about to die, crushed by an undead giant's falling corpse. He lets out a low moan as he realizes his quest here is over, and he watches Reunne leap into the air, ready to strike Helena down. Vengeance at least, he thinks, and closes his eyes.

He feels something knock into his body, and he begins to fly, the wind on his face, and then he hears the sound of a waterfall. And then feels lightning on his face.

"Get up," Reunne says. Severkin opens his eyes. He's alive. Still in pain, but alive. "Drink this," Reunne says, and hands him a red vial. He sits up, then chugs its contents down. It tastes like licorice and cherries, and he can feel his blood start to perk up, his body suddenly trying to live again.

"What happened?" he asks.

"I saw you about to get crushed, so I grabbed you out of the way," Reunne says. "Can you heal him?" she asks of Elkana, who has just run up to them. "Helena is getting away."

Elkana begins chanting and Severkin can feel his muscles

and skin start to stretch and reconnect, feel the blood go back into his body.

"Why didn't you kill her?" Severkin asks Reunne. "I saw you had the chance."

"Then you would have died," Reunne says, as if talking to an idiot.

Severkin flushes as Elkana's spell takes effect. He feels himself rubbed with warm oil, the rushing feeling of birds flying again, and then a mint-tinged wind. He stands. He's almost as good as he was before the battle.

"That was my last one," Elkana says. "I should meditate for a moment, or I won't be able ta cast it again for a while."

Reunne stands and looks over her shoulder. "She's long gone. We're going to have to track her anyway. Take your time."

"We should see if anything here could help us, too," Severkin says, looking around at the shattered glass cases.

"Good idea," Reunne says. "She may be raising another giant."

Severkin watches Elkana sit down and cross her legs. She closes her eyes and starts murmuring something that sounds like the same phrases repeated over and over, a list of things. Her lips move like the petals of an opening flower. He turns away and scours the now pitch-black cavern, looking for surviving artifacts. He gathers the gauntlets he saw before, which seem to enhance strength, so he gives them to Reunne. A medallion provides a larger well of magic to draw from, so he slips it over Elkana's shoulders as she meditates. There are other trinkets, too: arrows that freeze their target, a cloak that shields the user from lightning, and there, among a hill of glass fragments, the pair of swords he saw before, one's hilt a hawk, the other's a snake. The snake sword makes his surprise attacks deadlier; the hawk sword makes his arms move faster as he swings them. He slips these into his other swords' sheaths when Reunne's back is turned. He doesn't want to have to give them back to Frigit when they return, and Reunne would probably scold him like a mother for stealing.

"All right," Elkana says, standing. "I'm set as I can be. Didja see which way she ran?"

"Up," Reunne says, pointing. There's a cave in the wall.

"Well, let's get going," Severkin says.

EIGHTEEN

"SHE SAVED me," Nick says at the lunch table. "If she were an NPC, she wouldn't have done that."

"Yeah . . . ," Nat starts. She opens up a plastic container and pushes her shoulders back. Then she opens the box and takes out a pair of chopsticks. "But that doesn't mean she's your mom. And the designers said these AIs are super advanced, so they seem human." She uses the chopsticks to fish out a small yellow column and takes a bite, then looks around.

"I thought you said you didn't bring your mom's food to school," Nick says.

"Yeah," Nat says. "But . . . I don't know. I just felt better knowing there was someone else I ate with who was like me. I mean, I know you're not any part Chinese, you don't identify as *hapa*, and that's fine. It's not really about you. It's about me. I can't explain it."

Nick shrugs but feels his face warm slightly. "Cool,"

he says. "It looks good. And if we agree she's a real person, then—"

"Do you want a bite?" Nat interrupts. Nick looks down at the peanut butter sandwich Dad had made him. For some reason, Dad had tried toasting the bread, and it was blackened at the edges, giving it an unpleasant smoke-and-wood flavor. He doesn't know why he doesn't make his own sandwiches. Mom used to make them, so he'd never had reason to before, but now he does.

"Sure," he says. Nat expertly plucks another column from her box and places it on Nick's tray. "What is it?"

"*Har gao,*" Nat says, and shrugs, popping another into her mouth. "Shrimp dumpling. Not kosher, but delicious," she says, eating. Nick picks his up with his hands and takes a bite. It washes his mouth with flavor, bright and briny, then savory, like a match lit on the tongue.

"It's really good," Nick says. "I haven't had really good food in ages."

"You should come to the restaurant!" Nat says suddenly. "After school."

"I don't know . . ." Nick looks down. He's supposed to take the bus home and wait for Dad to finish teaching. He could ask Dad to pick him up at the restaurant, but then he'd meet Nat, and for some reason Nick doesn't want that. He takes another bite of the *har gao.* "There'll be food?" he asks.

"Oh yeah. It's late lunch hour—the place is half-empty. I usually spread out in a booth and study, and Mom brings me snacks. Your dad won't mind, will he?"

"He'll have to pick me up there," Nick says.

"That's perfect!" Nat says. She takes another *har gao* out

of the container and puts it down on Nick's tray. Nick snaps it up.

"What's perfect?" he asks between the two bites it takes for him to finish the roll.

"Well, you know the GamesCon in the city this weekend and how I have tickets? I was going to go with my parents, but I asked my mom yesterday if instead of one of them . . . I could take you." She takes another *har gao* from the container but drops it for a moment, then looks down and picks it up. "Only for Sunday, but that's the day the Wellhall people are talking."

"That would be awesome," Nick says. He watches her hands. He feels electric—the thought of going to GamesCon is a fantasy come to life. If he can go.

"My mom said it would be okay . . . but she'd have to meet your dad, and he'd have to okay it. Since she'll be taking us."

"Okay," Nick says. "I'll go with you after school. I can text my dad."

"Great!" Nat's face relaxes, and Nick realizes how nervous she was, how her freckles had been swarming like anxious bees.

"What is that smell?" says Charlie, sauntering over to their table. Nick and Nat lock eyes and simultaneously sigh.

"Its food, Charlie, go away," Nick says softly.

"Someone puts something that smells like that in their mouth?" He leans over the table they are sitting at, staring at Nat. "No wonder you hang out with her. Her standards seem pretty low."

"'Cause she'll put anything in her mouth," one of the guys behind Charlie says. The rest of them chuckle. Nick wonders where Charlie got this gang from. Did he hire them, like you do in video games?

"I'm telling you this for your own good," Charlie says, turning back to Nick, "'cause we're friends: You can do better."

Nick stares down at the table. He knows he hasn't made eye contact with anyone since Charlie came over, but somehow he can't lift his head like he knows he should. To defend Nat. To stare Charlie down. The silence goes on long enough that Charlie straightens up into a winner's posture.

"Later," he says, walking away.

"Sorry," Nick says, finally looking up at Nat. Her face is blank, and he's not sure if she's mad at him.

"You don't need to apologize," Nat says. "He's the *schmuck*."

"Yeah, but I should have said something," Nick says, and looks down at the food Nat gave him.

"I can stand up for myself," she says, shaking her head. "And besides, you talk back to him, it just goes on longer. Let him get his moron out and walk away. I can't believe you used to be friends with him."

"We played video games together."

Before Mom's bad day, anyway. Charlie always invited him over, and he had good snacks, good drinks, and his mom was never home since the divorce. It was awesome. Even the last time, before Nick became a freak, had been fun.

"Get the power up, get the power up!" Charlie had shouted, pointing at the screen. Nick had the controller. He was better at the levels that had you racing through stuff instead of just shooting hordes of bad guys. Nick spun the space commander over a rock to grab a weapons upgrade. "Nice!" Charlie said, and raised his hand to give him a high five. Nick paused and slapped him on the hand. He didn't turn to face Charlie, but he felt himself smiling stupidly, widely. "You really rock at this stuff, Nick."

"Thanks," Nick said, unpausing the game.

"I feel like you're my secret weapon," Charlie said, taking a soda out of the minifridge in his room. "Like, no one else at school who plays this is really friends with you, so they don't know how good you are."

Nick laughed. "I'm not a weapon," he said. "I'm just good with my hands." He paused. "All the girls say so."

Charlie snorted his soda, spitting foam onto the rug. "Dude, don't try to be smooth. It doesn't work for you."

Nick laughed, feeling his cheeks warm slightly. He focused on the game, moving the guns quickly enough, dodging lasers. Better to focus on that instead of how idiotic he must have sounded.

"Seriously, though," Charlie said, stretching out his legs on the floor. "You never talk about girls. Do you like girls?"

"I like girls," Nick said. He couldn't look away from the screen to face Charlie. He had to focus on killing the aliens.

"It's cool if you don't," Charlie said. "We live just outside New York City. You can like guys."

"I like girls," Nick said, his voice a little more insistent than he meant it to be.

"Cool," Charlie said. "Me too." He took a long drink of his soda. "So, you like any particular girl?"

"What, like from school?" The space commander had a minigun now, he was fending off hordes of aliens. Normally, Charlie would take the controller at this point, but he wasn't asking for it, so Nick kept playing.

"Yeah, from school," Charlie said. "Who do you think is hot? Who do you want to ask to the end-of-the-year dance?"

"I don't know," Nick said. "Jackie's cute."

"Yeah, she is," Charlie said, slapping Nick hard on the back. Nick swallowed. He felt like he was being tested. Charlie's hand was still there, squeezing his shoulder. It wasn't that Charlie was so much more popular, or so much cooler, or anything like that, but Charlie was a guy. That guy. The guy Nick sort of wished he was sometimes, who could make everyone laugh, who could talk to anybody. If he were in the game, he would be Severkin, but without the bows and knives. He'd probably go in for an axe. But Charlie didn't play as Severkin. He played as a mage named Donnell and shot fire from his hands at anything that moved. Charlie's hand pulled back, and Nick realized it had been there for a while, gently rubbing his shoulder.

"I'm going to tell Jackie you like her," Charlie said. "I'm going to be your wingman. We're going to make this happen."

"No," Nick said quickly. "Please don't." He wanted to turn around, look Charlie in the eye, make it clear that he was serious, but the space commander was jumping through anti-grav tunnels and shooting at aliens, so he couldn't look away from the screen. His hands got sweaty, thinking of Charlie whispering in Jackie's ear, Jackie's nose turning up in disgust, the giggling whenever she saw him in the corridors. Most kids didn't really know who Nick was, and he was okay with that. He didn't want to become the guy who was stalking Jackie.

"Why not? You need a girlfriend. We all need girlfriends. Junior high will be so cool. There'll be more girls to choose from." He took another long drink from the can of soda, then crushed it in his hand and tossed it away. "But first we're gonna get you and Jackie together." He slapped Nick on the back again, hard, and this time the controller flew out of his hand. "Dude!" Charlie said, grabbing the controller off the ground. "Don't get us killed just 'cause your hormones are distracting you."

"Sorry," Nick said, happy to lean back a little, not focus on the screen. "But seriously, don't talk to Jackie. I appreciate it, but . . . I'll ask her myself, when I'm ready."

"Yeah, yeah," Charlie said, his eyes reflecting the screen. Charlie wasn't good at carrying on a conversation and playing at the same time. Nick leaned back and wiped his sweaty hands on his jeans.

"How about you?" Nick asked. "Who do you like?"

"What?" Charlie said, half turning around then whipping his eyes back to the screen.

"What girl do you like? You know mine." He looked up at the screen, where Charlie was taking out a scantily clad green alien woman in a metal bikini. "Or maybe you don't like girls?" Nick joked, trying to sound like Charlie. "We live just outside New York City—it's okay to not like girls."

Onscreen, the alien woman pressed her hands around the space commander's throat and squeezed until the screen went black.

"What?" Charlie asked, his voice cracking a little. He didn't turn around. "You think I'm gay?"

"What?" Nick said. "No—I was just doing what you did. . . ." He shivered, afraid he'd done it wrong again. He shouldn't have tried to imitate Charlie. He wasn't smooth.

"Oh," Charlie laughed, turning around. "Right." He laughed louder. "Dude, I was being serious—I mean, no one is going to think I'm gay, but you're . . . harder to figure out." He punched

Nick's shoulder, knocking him back a little, then returned to the game and hit Continue.

"I like Jackie," Nick said. "I'm straight."

"Who cares?" Charlie had said back then. "You're not going to do anything about it." The space commander came back on the screen, his gun at the ready, aliens surrounding him. "So, I think we get a new power next level. Immunity or sleep grenades?"

"Maybe he just leveled up," Nick says to Nat now, shaking off the memory. "Or switched classes or something when he got to junior high."

"*You* leveled up," Nat says, staring at him. "He got hit with an intelligence-draining spell. If he was ever cool to begin with, which I somehow doubt."

Nick smiles. After they'd beaten the space commander game, he hadn't seen Charlie for a while, and then there was Mom's bad day. After that, everyone noticed Nick. They called him the "son of that freak," or "the son of that poor woman," or "the son of" something else. Charlie stopped talking to him, stopped responding to his texts, even when the DLC for the Space Commando game came out. Nick got angry for a little while, and wrote lots of emails to Charlie that he never sent, and then the summer came and his parents were talking about the home, and he forgot all about it. His brain was filled with other things.

"Thanks," Nick says, taking out his sandwich. No more *har gao* are forthcoming. "But back to my mother . . ."

"Reunne," Nat says, her voice soft as the feathers on a flying arrow.

"Right," Nick says. "Reunne. She saved me."

"I know," Nat says. She looks up at him, tilting her head. "But I don't think that proves anything."

"But everything she said does," Nick says, his hands suddenly darting out without his meaning to. "It's just like East Berlin. She knows about my project, so she's helping me. I've been doing all this reading, and the secret police in East Berlin, the Stasi—they called themselves the 'shield and sword' of the Communist Party."

"Okay," Nat says, nodding. "But that could be part of the game. The last one was based on Greco-Roman mythology and World War One. They use historical influences and various mythologies. So it's probably intentional."

"Yeah." Nick nods. "But she's using that, you know? She's telling me about what it was like growing up in that world. She recognized what the game was based on and is using it to create a history. She did that with the last one, too. When I was out from school, she'd play the game and set up these, like, treasure hunts and archeological digs in the game. And then she'd write me these little notes and leave them on the controller. They all related back to Greek mythology and World War One stuff, too. Like, she was teaching me. But now she's doing it from inside."

"That's so cool, that your mom played like that," Nat says. "My parents don't get it at all." She takes a long drink from her water bottle.

"Plays," Nick says after a moment.

Nat nods slowly, then starts putting her trash together on her tray. Without asking, she takes Nick's trash, too, and piles it all together.

"It's just a big coincidence," she says, standing with the

tray of trash. "That the game would also be based on the place your mom is from."

"I know," Nick says. He feels heavy, like if he were to stand, he might fall through the floor. Maybe he's crazy. "She just feels so real."

"She does," Nat agrees. "She really does. So maybe it is a coincidence. A really great one. Or maybe your mom is online, manipulating stuff in the game so it suits the story she wants to tell better. Maybe she reverse-pickpocketed all those blue robes onto the mages. I mean, we never really hear about the Sword and Shield stuff from anyone else." She gets up and throws out their trash. Nick watches her. She's in jeans today with a bright blue T-shirt. Her hair is held back with a white headband, but otherwise it flows loose down her back. The blue streaks swim through it like perfume, and for a moment, Nick wonders if the texture of the streaks is different from the rest of her hair.

Nat sits back down. "You okay?" she asks. He wants to say something, but his voice is suddenly clamped down by his throat, so he just nods. "We should get to class."

They stand and head out of the cafeteria, walking toward history.

"Thanks," Nick says as they stop at his locker so he can get his history books. "For believing me. I know it sounds crazy, but . . . just the way she looked at me, how she winked. It's like she's trying to set up this puzzle, and I feel like if I can just solve it . . ."

"I get it," Nat says, leaning against the locker next to his. Nick looks over and stares at her for longer than he probably should, smiling, then starts turning the combination lock, trying to remember the right numbers. He feels almost like he's levitating, but then a locker a few down from his slams shut and he plummets back down. Nick glances over. It's Charlie and his friends again, snickering together.

"She's, like, ten years older than me," Charlie says, bragging. "She's fine, huge boobs. And at the wedding, she was all like 'We're gonna be family' and pulled my head into them. It was awesome." He was lying, Nick knew. Charlie hated his new stepmother. Or, at least, he'd hated her when his dad had run off to California with her, leaving him and his mom. Maybe things had gotten better at the wedding. The other boys start laughing, and one of them high-fives Charlie.

"You hit that!" one of them shouts, and Charlie nods, laughing. Nick realizes he's staring at them instead of at his books and quickly looks back in his locker, but it's too late. Charlie felt the stare, and turns his eyes on Nick and Nat, a wolf grin on his face.

"Yo, freak," he says. He walks over to them, and Nick focuses on taking books out of his locker and putting them in his bag. The task seems much more complicated when he puts so much attention on it.

"Go away," Nat says.

"I hear you're a half-breed, like freak here," Charlie says. "So does that make you like a Chinese wigger? A wink, maybe?" Nick looks over at Nat, who is bright red, like she's been punched in the stomach. If Nick were Severkin, really Severkin, he would say something that would reduce Charlie to tears and have the whole hall laughing. He would saunter off with Nat. But Nick isn't Severkin. He stares at Nat as she blinks a few times, then turns away and closes his locker, not quite slamming it. He takes Nat by the arm and tries to walk away, but Charlie grabs his backpack and pulls him back. Nick lets go of Nat and turns around, his eyes on the ground.

"You forget who I am, freak?" Charlie asks. "Your mom forget me, too? Maybe I should go over there one day, tell her I'm the female body inspector and ask her to lift her skirt up again so I can get a photo."

"Charlie," comes a voice trying to sound stern, from down the hall. Nick looks behind him. Ms. Knight is walking toward them. She's trying to stomp, he thinks, but it's like a fawn trying to be an elephant. Charlie lets go of Nick's backpack and Nick turns away, heads down the hall. "You okay, Nick?" Ms. Knight asks as they walk up to her. Nick nods without looking up.

"What a bitch," Charlie fake-whispers to his friends, loud enough that Nick can hear it from down the hall. "I heard she slept with Principal Aran to get the job." His friends laugh like excited donkeys.

"What did you say?" Ms. Knight asks, but her voice is shaky, too high, up and down, sounding like a cuckoo clock. Charlie and his friend walk the other way down the hall, ignoring her, still laughing.

"You didn't have to do that," Nick says softly, and looks up. He feels bad for putting Charlie's focus on her, and on Nat.

"Well," Ms. Knight says, her voice firm, "I thought I did. Come on, you two, you have my class next."

"That was cool of you, Ms. Knight," Nat says, her color returning to normal.

Ms. Knight nods but doesn't look at them as they walk into the classroom. They're the first ones there, and sit down in the back. Ms. Knight takes a piece of chalk and starts writing something on the board.

"I have so much English homework," Nick says, seeing all the books in his bag as he takes out his history notebook. "Have you finished *Romeo and Juliet* yet?" Nat doesn't answer, and he looks up at her. She's focused on Ms. Knight, her head tilted slightly, like a drop of water about to fall off the corner of a rooftop after a storm.

"Do the teachers know about your mom?" she asks in a near whisper.

"What?" Nick asks, whispering back without knowing why. He swallows. Ms. Knight knows, but he's not sure about the other teachers. He hopes not.

"Like, is it in your file or anything?"

Nick shrugs. "I don't know," he says. "Why?"

"I'm wondering if Ms. Knight would know."

Nick looks over at Ms. Knight. She erases something on the board with her sleeve, then rewrites it. "She knows," he says.

"Are you sure?" Nat asks. Her whispers are becoming excited, like a faucet turned on low sputtering into high.

"Yeah I, . . ." Nick pauses, not sure what to share. "She saw me at the home my mom's at. She figured it out."

"What if it's her?" Nat blurts out, loudly enough that Ms. Knight turns for a moment. More students are coming in, too. Nick stares at Nat, her eyes wide, freckles like glitter. She's figured out a secret, she's won a battle. Nick looks over at Ms. Knight, who is wiping chalk dust from her hands and surveying the board. A stray thread of hair falls over her face, and she pulls it behind her ear.

"I . . . ," Nick says. "I guess. Maybe."

The bell rings, and Ms. Knight starts class. She picks up a piece of chalk and points it in front of her like a spear, and Nick feels like he's been stabbed in the chest.

• • •

In class, they're separated and Nick has to talk about communism with Emma Angel-Love again, who tries to ask him more about Nat's dad. He keeps his eyes on the textbook and instead discusses the Free German Youth and the similar programs throughout other communist countries.

After class, he waves at Nat, getting ready to head to biology, but she holds up a finger and he waits as she packs up her things—slower than she needs to. When they're about to leave, they're the last ones there besides Ms. Knight, who is erasing the board.

"Ms. Knight?" Nat asks.

"Yes?" Ms. Knight stops, and smiles at Nat. "Something I can help you with?"

"It's about . . . the game," Nat says. Nick feels his pulse freeze, each slow beat of it releasing ice water into his blood.

"Wellhall?" Ms. Knight says. "Nick told you I play it?"

"Yeah," Nat says, and adjusts her backpack straps and looks Ms. Knight in the eye. She looks like a large cat, not crouched in fear, but studying. "And that's really cool. We just want to know where you are in the game so we don't give anything away when we're talking before class."

"Oh," Ms. Knight says, pulling her hair back behind her shoulders and turning back to the board, erasing the blur of chalk words. "Don't worry about that. That's sweet, but really.

I don't pay much attention to what you're talking about before class. I just assume it's none of my business." Behind her back, Nat shoots Nick a look, her eyebrows like bowstrings rising into curves, then snapping flat.

"Well, yeah," Nick says, hoping it's what Nat wants, "but just in case. So we know when to whisper."

"Oh," Ms. Knight says, and she stops erasing and stands straight up but keeps her eyes on the board. "Well, I crashed, of course, but I haven't even made it to Wellhall yet. I'm in Brightbank. I'm playing a cleric, so I figured I'd join the Temple there, do some of those quests. Haven't started, though." She starts erasing again. "Lessons to plan, homework to grade. I bet I have less free time than you two."

"Thanks, Ms. Knight," Nat says. "We'd better go. We're going to be late." She takes Nick by the arm and directs him toward the door.

"See you tomorrow," Ms. Knight calls. "Happy gaming."

Out in the hall, Nat pulls Nick into a corner, earning some stares and chuckles from passing classmates.

"She's not far enough," Nick says. But he isn't sure. Ms. Knight as Reunne makes sense—she knows about Mom, knows about the project he's doing on her—even sees his notes on it. And she seems cool. She could be one of the TV teachers who gets overly involved in the lives of students "going through something." She could be trying to Make Learning Fun. She wouldn't know that Nick would think it was Mom. She wouldn't know how awful a betrayal it could be.

Nat shakes her head. "It's her. She was totally lying back there. Did you see how she wouldn't make eye contact? Mom says that's a sure sign of lying." She looks down at her feet.

"She taught it to me so I would know when my dad was lying about being drunk. And in the game," she says, looking back up, "Reunne is teaching you, like you said. Teaching. I think she's trying to help you with your project."

"I don't know . . . ," Nick says. "Maybe. But Reunne seems . . . older. Doesn't she?" He's not sure anymore. It's like the ground is shaking.

"It's easy to act in-game. I don't remind you of Elkana in real life, do I?"

She does, but Nick suspects telling her she reminds him of a troll isn't the best move. "Well, you're both really forthright," he says. "Direct. Take-charge."

"I'm not really like that," Nat says, but her freckles seem to glow for a second, halos of red around them like stars.

The bell rings.

"We're going to be late," Nick says.

"I'll meet you at the buses after school."

"See you then." They separate and head for their classes, but Nick pauses to turn and watch her for a moment, the memory of her blushing fading in his mind.

The rest of the day is a series of glitches, pixels freezing then leaping ahead, so Nick keeps feeling as though he's missed something. He can't stop thinking of Reunne: his mother, NPC, Ms. Knight, some other player entirely? It's not that the idea of Ms. Knight playing Reunne seems impossible, just uncomfortable. He hasn't said anything out of character to Reunne—that would get him kicked off the server—but he still feels as though he's connected with her in a way that . . . if it was Ms. Knight, would be weird. Icky. He doesn't want her to be Ms. Knight.

He doesn't want to tell Nat this, though, so when they sit together on the bus later, he stays quiet. She was so excited about her theory, and he can't prove it's wrong. He just hopes it is. She sits next to him and playfully bumps her shoulder into his. He's texting Dad where to pick him up later. The bus smells like hot plastic and sweat.

They ride in silence for a moment. "I'm not saying it's impossible that it's your mom," Nat says suddenly, as if she knows what he's thinking, or as if she's picking up from a conversation she's been having with him in her head for a while. "It's just that if I had to choose between your mom and Ms. Knight, Ms. Knight seems more . . ." She circles her hands around each other like she's raising a drawbridge. "Realistic," she says finally, the drawbridge shutting into place with a concrete thud. Nick takes a long breath. "Sorry," she says. "I could be wrong. I don't know your mom. But Reunne is always there when we're playing—and Ms. Knight is working when we're in school."

"And my mom could be waiting for us." Nick looks out the window at the passing suburban houses, all pale and small. "Or doing stuff when we're in school and then coming back to meet us. Learning about the world so she can link her history to it. Like switching all the mages' robes."

"Yeah," Nat says, nodding. Nick can see her reflection in the window. "But would your mom be allowed to play as much as she wanted?"

"You think she's sick, don't you?" Nick asks, still looking out the window. He sees her face in the glass again, staring at him. Her eyes open wide and fill with the row of trees they're passing by.

"I don't know," she says. "But doctors believe she's sick enough to be in this home. So I think she's probably a little sick. Maybe not as bad as everyone thinks . . . but . . ."

"It's hereditary," Nick says. "If you think she's sick, you think I'm sick, too." He regrets it the moment he says it. His tone was mean, metal. He stares out the window.

"I know," she says. "What I don't know is if your mom is sick. I don't know. I know you don't think she is, and your dad thinks she is, and there are doctors, and her, and I've never met any of them. So I don't know. And I don't know how you can be angry at me for not knowing."

Nick turns around and looks at her. Her expression is steelier than he's ever seen it. She looks like a freshly forged shield.

"You're right," he says. "I'm sorry. I'm angry at everyone for not knowing. It's like I keep getting pricked with ragebrew. Do you ever feel like that? Like suddenly one word can make you so frustrated, and you know it's wrong, but you can't help it?"

"All the time," Nat says, and nods. "And when my dad was drinking, and people didn't really know, they'd say stuff, like stupid little things, like how his tie was crooked at a dance recital or something, and I'd get so mad. I stepped on a girl's foot once. I mean, I made it look like an accident, but it was on purpose. I was in heels, too."

"You dance?" Nick asks, his vision suddenly filled with images of Nat in sparkly dresses, like on the celebrity dance shows on TV.

"I used to. I stopped when Dad went to rehab." She looks away at the rubbery back of the seat in front of them. Someone has written *Suck it* in silver pen. She twirls her pendant in her hand. It looks like a lace glove made out of thin gold, with a single green stone in the center. She twirls it back and forth. Nick isn't sure what to say, and wonders if this is how Nat feels every time he mentions his mother. "This is our stop," Nat says.

The bus deposits them down the street from the shopping center with the Chinese restaurant and the bookstore. They walk down the sidewalk in silence.

"Sorry if that was weird," Nick says as they enter the shopping center. "I didn't mean to bring up your dad's . . ."

"Alcoholism," Nat says without a hint of embarrassment. "Don't worry. I stopped dancing because Dad was sick, but I could have restarted if I wanted. I just didn't want to."

"If you want to talk about it or anything . . . ," Nick says.

"I'm okay. Do you want to talk about it?"

"Me?" Nick looks up at her. "Why would I want to talk about your dad?"

"Some people do. Makes them feel better to talk about it. I can answer questions, if you want. What he drank—gin, mostly, but he wasn't above vodka or beer. How much—I'm not sure. He had a few G and T's when he got home from work every day, but he definitely drank at work, too, and drank some more where we couldn't see him. Want to know what sort of drunk he was? He was fun, actually. Probably why it never seemed like a problem. He was cheerful and funny and thought everything was great." She lists all these traits in a voice as even as a blade's edge. He can see Elkana meditating, reciting small chants to herself. It's like that.

"Sorry," he says. "I didn't mean to . . ."

"You don't have to apologize," she sighs. They're in front of the restaurant but she stops. She turns to face him and looks him straight in the face. "Don't talk about it in front of my mom, okay? But don't worry, you didn't do or say anything wrong or anything like that." Her voice is cheerful, reassuring, but forced, like a greeter at one of the big chain stores in the mall.

Nick nods. "Okay," he says. "I just . . . I felt bad."

"You shouldn't. If you still do," she says, opening the door to the restaurant, "that's more your issue than mine."

Nick has been in here once before, but it was years ago, and his memories are of just a lot of red, and the smell of things frying in oils, and spices he didn't know the names of. It's still all that: red walls, black wooden tables shiny as oil spills, and a gold ceiling, but now he sees it as Nat's place, too. He sees how the staff smiles at her and how she walks to the back to a circular booth and sits down as though the booth is hers. This is clearly Nat's home. He wonders what her mom is like. And her dad—aside from all the alcoholic stuff she just told Nick. Is he repentant now? Sadder? His own dad is sadder now. Because he's given up—he won't fight like Nick does. And he's lost his wife. Nick follows Nat down the aisle, pausing for a moment as a server whisks past him. His dad has really lost Mom. Nick's only just met Nat, and just the idea of losing her feels like a punch in the stomach. For his dad, it must be . . . something he can't think about. Nick sits down next to Nat in the booth and smiles at her, trying not to think about Dad. Dad will be fine once Mom is home. Almost immediately after Nick sits, a server sets a tray of food down in front of him and Nat.

"Thanks, Mike," Nat says. Mike smiles and walks off. "My mom will be out in a sec, now that she knows I'm here. Depends how the kitchen is." She looks around the restaurant; it's about half full, and the people eating are doing so slowly. "I'm guessing two minutes." She starts unpacking her backpack. "Want to start with history homework?" she asks.

"Um, sure," Nick says. He'd been hoping to talk more about Reunne. But he gets out his books and a pen and piles them all up like Nat has.

"You should eat, too," Nat says, motioning at the food. "Scallion pancakes. They're really good." She grabs one and takes a bite. Nick does likewise. They're delicious, fried dough and green bits.

"Is this your new friend?" asks a voice coming down through the rows of tables. It's a large voice, slightly accented with New York, where every word sounds like it's somehow squeezed "eh" into it, in both tone and feeling. Nick turns. He recognizes that the woman must be Nat's mom: a round woman in a white chef's jacket. They don't have much in common physically; Nat is slender and her face is oval, whereas this woman is all circles: cheeks, face, body. But they share a presence; they seem bigger than they are—Nat's mother more so than Nat. She's short, and really not very large, but she takes up the whole restaurant. All eyes are on her, and her eyes are on Nick.

Nick stands immediately and offers his hand for her to shake, like his mother taught him. "Hi, Ms. Asher-Woo." He's unsure if he should have just called her Ms. Woo, but she smiles in a way that makes him think it doesn't matter.

"So nice to finally meet you, Nick," she says, and shakes

his hand. She's warm, and smells so strongly of garlic and oil that touching her makes him hungry. Her expression is filled with a joy that Nick recognizes only because he hasn't seen it for so long—the expression of mothers: the lines around the eyes that are like lists of things they love and worry about, the cheeks that are full and seem to rise like someone taking a deep breath of air before diving into the water. He hasn't seen that expression in over a week, and he used to see it all the time, and now he has to take a deep breath, because it feels as though he's the one underwater.

The feeling lasts only a moment, though, till Ms. Asher-Woo lets go of his hand. "You can call me Jenny, though. I hope you like the food."

"It's amazing," Nick says. "My dad can't cook at all. I haven't eaten food this good in weeks."

"Oh, poor thing," Jenny says, an eyebrow raised in an expression Nick has seen Nat make. "I'm glad you like it. You and your family are welcome here for dinner anytime."

"Thanks," Nick says.

Jenny walks past Nick and leans over the table to give her daughter a kiss on the forehead. "Now get to studying. As long as you keep studying, the food will keep coming."

"Thanks, Mom," Nat says, rolling her eyes but smiling. Jenny vanishes back down the rows of tables and into the kitchen, and Nick sits back down.

"Your mom seems cool," Nick says.

"She's happy I can still make friends, with everything that happened," Nat says. "You alleviate her guilt."

"So we have to read chapter six in the book, right?" Nick says, reaching for another scallion pancake.

"The studying is just for my mom," Nat says. "If she knew we were talking about the game, she wouldn't feed us. She was serious about that. Just turn the pages in your textbook now and then and we'll be fine."

"Oh," Nick says, wondering why she couldn't have told him this earlier.

"Sorry, I guess I just assumed you'd know," Nat says, opening her textbook. "I don't usually bring friends to the restaurant. I mean, I usually do study. But . . ."

"That's cool." Nick opens his textbook and stares down at it for a moment. "So . . . Ms. Knight."

Nat puts her arm over her open textbook and lays her head on top of that, looking at Nick. "Yeah, sorry for just springing that idea on you then bailing."

"That's okay," Nick says. "But it did stay with me all day."

"You think it's her?"

"I don't know," he says. He takes another scallion pancake and begins eating it.

"I know you want it to be your mom," Nat says, "but that's not enough."

"I know," Nick says between bites. "It's just that if I start thinking it's not my mom—if it's Ms. Knight or even an NPC—then I'm afraid I won't be looking for whatever messages my mom is trying to tell me."

"But if it's not your mom, you're looking for messages that aren't there," Nat says. She bites slowly into her pancake and chews it as if trying not to make noise. "But I did have an idea," she says. "You might not like it."

Nick finishes the pancake and stares at his fingers, which shine with oil. "What is it?" he asks.

"We google her." Suddenly the sound in the restaurant becomes louder—the click of silverware, the murmur of conversations, the footsteps of servers walking the aisles. One of them places a plate of food down in front of them. "Thanks," Nat says. The new food smells like chili peppers and peanuts. "Reunne, I mean," she says to Nick.

"We can't look her up online," Nick says. "We'll ruin the game if we see any of the story."

"Yeah," Nat says, taking some of the new food. "But I figured out a way around that. I'll find the Wiki for the game, and I'll go to that, and just type in Reunne. I won't look at anything else. If there's a whole page for her, I'll look at it."

"And that'll probably mean she's an NPC," Nick says. "If there's a whole page for her. And she's not Ms. Knight. And she's not my mom."

"Not necessarily. If she only plays on the Character server, people who have encountered her might think she's an NPC. Anyone can add to a Wiki." Nick nods. "But her page will tell us if she's only encountered on the main quest, or if she's been seen elsewhere or anything. It might tell us she's an NPC . . . but maybe not. It depends how much info there is."

Nick wants a reason to tell her no, but he can't think of any. So he just nods again, feeling his lips press themselves tightly together.

"Oh, quick, look at your book—my mom is watching," Nat says, her face suddenly contorting into a mask of seriousness, eyes narrowed, one eyebrow raised. Nick stares down at his book. "Okay," Nat says after a moment. She turns to her bag and takes out her phone. "I'm looking her up now. You okay?"

"Yeah." He watches Nat type on her phone's screen, each

artificial click noise sounding like loud footsteps. He closes his eyes and pictures Reunne's face, the lines around her eyes, the hollows of her cheeks.

"This isn't helpful," Nat says finally.

"What?" Nick opens his eyes.

"It's just a stub. 'Reunne is a gray elf warrior.' That's it." Nick exhales deeply, the air rushing out of him so fast he feels a cool breeze on his face.

"So she must be a person," Nick says. "If she were an NPC, people would say so, right?"

"I . . ." Nat shakes her head and slips the phone back into her bag. "I don't know. It doesn't mean anything, really. Except that she's a mystery. Which we already knew."

"More to us than to other people," Nick says.

"Yeah," Nat says. "So we're still stuck. Although . . ." She types a few more things into her phone, then smiles brightly. "Elkana has a stub, too," she says, excited. "Elkana is a troll. Well, that's not very informative."

"So Reunne could be a person," Nick says. Nat types some more into her phone.

"Severkin doesn't come up, though," she says, frowning. She looks up at him. "Sorry. Want me to add one?"

"That's okay," Nick says. "I barely interact with anyone but you and Mom, anyway." He pauses, realizing what he's just said and how silly it sounds. "Reunne, I mean," he says quickly, and takes a bite of his food. Thankfully, Nat pretends not to notice.

"I guess we have to find out more about Reunne, then," she says. "And Ms. Knight."

"And I need to find out more about my mom." Nick irons out the pages of his textbook with his palm.

"How? The questionnaire is turned in."

"I'll figure something out." He stares at Nat.

She looks down at her textbook. "But how are we going to find out about Ms. Knight?" she asks. "Think she'd tell us about her character?"

"If it is her," Nick says, "and she doesn't want us to know . . . then, no. But . . . there is someone else I can ask."

"Who?"

"Her girlfriend, Jess. She works at the home my mom's at. I ran into them in the parking lot. That's how she knows. . . . I'll need to come up with an excuse for asking, though. Like I want to make sure I'm not playing with my teacher or something . . ."

"That should work," Nat says, nodding. "And we can keep trying to figure out what Reunne is trying to tell you in the game. If she is your mom."

"Yeah," Nick says, flipping a page in his textbook.

"If we finish the main quest, then that'll tell us if she's an NPC, won't it? Like if she dies at the end . . ." Nat pauses. Nick feels a sudden cold shudder rock him. "Sorry," Nat continues. "But if . . . in the quest, she does something, or if at the end she says something like 'Nice adventuring with you. If you need my help again, you can find me in my home,' and then you can go there to get her to join you. NPCs always do stuff like that when their quest is over."

"So we just need to finish the main quest," Nick says. "I never do the main quest first."

"Me neither."

"Well, thanks for doing it now," Nick says. "It'll be worth it. If it is my mom, then there'll be a clue—like we use the artifacts we're collecting to do something, and that's a symbol for what she's trying to tell us. How to get her out of the home, probably."

Nat is silent for a long while, staring at her book. Nick thinks maybe her mom is watching again. She nods, then puts a hand on her textbook. "We should probably do some actual work, then. Otherwise we won't have time to play tonight."

They begin going over chapters of history, algebraic formulas, and literature that they know is classic but feels like more of the history reading. Nick tries not to think about Reunne. He tries not to think about Ms. Knight or his mother, but they all seem to stare back at him from the words and numbers on the pages: his mother's closing eye in the shape of an *a*, Ms. Knight wielding her chalk like a spear in a *K*, Reunne turning away from him to fight an oncoming wolf like a *7*. The game plays on in his mind, even when he's not near the console.

"Do you get this?" Nick asks, referring to the algebra in front of him.

Nat looks up at his page, then raises an eyebrow. "'Cause I'm Asian, I'm good at math?" she asks.

Nick thinks she's kidding, but just in case, he says: "No, no, I just mean—" But she stops him with a laugh.

"I think you have to move the *x* to the other side of the equation," she says, pointing at the page. Their fingers are close, his pinky angled like an arrow flying from the bow of his curved hand. Nick can feel her staring at him, so he looks up, and he can feel her hand getting even closer, the heat of it like a fireball. It's amazing how much heat comes from just her pinky finger. Enough that the back of his neck starts to sweat. But then her eyes flicker and she pulls her hand back, staring up past Nick. Nick turns to see his father, hands in his pockets and a grin on his face that makes him like like a gremlin who's just stolen a giant bag of gold.

"Hi, Dad," Nick says.

"Hi," Dad says, still grinning. "You must be Nat?" he asks, turning his eyes on Nat. "Short for . . . Natalie?"

"Yeah," Nat says, standing and extending her hand. "Nice to meet you, Mr. Reeves."

"Very nice to meet you, too," Nick's dad says, pronouncing the word "very" in a way that makes Nick's face feel hot.

"I guess I gotta go," Nick says, starting to pack up his things before his father says something else.

"Wait," Nat says. "My mom wants to meet you, Mr. Reeves."

"I'd like to meet her, too, if my son is going to be studying in her restaurant."

"I texted you," Nick says, putting the last of his stuff away. "Besides, I get real food here."

Nick shrugs his backpack on and turns toward the door. Jenny is already coming down the aisle toward them. Nick needs to make this fast: They'll meet, he'll get permission to go to the GamesCon, and then they'll flee. If it starts going long, he'll have to find a way to cut it short.

"Hello there," Jenny says, extending her hand to Nick's dad. They shake. "I'm Jenny, Nat's mom." She smiles at Dad, her face glowing. Without turning her face from him, she says, "Nick, what do you think you're doing? You're not going anywhere. Sit down—all of you. More food is coming. Natalie's father won't be back from the city until late, but we can eat and chat without him."

Nick opens his mouth but can't think of anything to stop this from happening. He looks anxiously at Dad, hoping he'll want to leave. Maybe he really wants to cook tonight.

"That sounds wonderful," Dad says as he sits. Nick looks helplessly at Nat, who shrugs, a giggle clearly dancing under her lips. With a sigh, Nick takes off his backpack and sits down, his bag a heavy weight at his feet.

•   •   •

It doesn't go as awfully as Nick had imagined. Yes, there are quick knife slashes of embarrassment from his father, but they seem to tear at his clothes rather than his skin. Sure, he's naked and trying to retain some dignity, but at least it doesn't hurt. And Nat gets just as bad from her mother as Nick gets from Dad. Sometimes servers rush out and whisper something in Jenny's ear and then she has to go to the kitchen for a few minutes. Those are the worst times, when Nick's dad stares at Nat, and then at Nick, and then back at Nat, letting the silence fill with suggestions. But the food is really good, spicy and flavorful and not burned, and best of all, Dad gives permission for Nick to go to the GamesCon.

"That sounds great, actually," Dad says after Jenny mentions it. The meal is over, and small glasses of steaming, woody tea have been put in front of them. "Nick is always playing that thing, and I don't understand it. I think it would be good for him to see people talking about what goes into making it, all that stuff. I don't really get it . . . but I know it's a whole world: mythologies, characters. Interactive books, my wife calls it. She says the series has strong mythological and anthropological roots, too. She plays with Nick."

For a moment—less than a moment, really, just the time it takes to begin to inhale—Nick thinks Dad knows. Thinks Dad knows about Reunne being Mom and has just confirmed it. But then he realizes that's not what Dad meant at all.

"Played," Nick corrects him. Or secretly plays without their seeing each other because you couldn't convince her to stay at home. Jenny looks over at him, then up at Nick's dad expectantly, but when no explanation is forthcoming, smiles politely. She takes a sip of her tea. "Ah . . . will I need to get Nick's mother's permission as well?" she asks, staring at her teacup.

"No, no. I'll talk it over with Sophie," Nick's dad says. He pauses and looks down at the table. "We're not divorced. She has early-onset Alzheimer's and is at Sunrise House."

"Oh," Jenny says, immediately pressing her hand into Lamont's arm. "I'm sorry, I didn't realize."

"That's all right," Dad says. "You're actually the first person I've told who didn't know . . . us." He looks over at Nick, and his face is bad graphics—the shimmer in his eyes too bright—old-looking, a last-gen game. Nick looks down at his tea. The graphics there are more sophisticated, the swirl of steam over the tea delicate, like silk, pixels barely visible. He feels Nat's hand on his knee, but just for a flicker. A quick healing spell, and then it's gone. "It's good for me to be able to say it," Nick's dad finishes.

"Well, I'm very sorry to hear about it. And who knows? Maybe they'll cure it in the next few years—and then she can come home."

"Who knows?" Nick's dad says, raising his tea to his lips, the steam momentarily covering his face like a veil.

They crack open fortune cookies, and Nat helps Nick pronounce his "Chinese word" before pointing out that fortune cookies are an American thing and aren't served in China.

"Customers expect them," Jenny says, taking a bite of hers. "Besides, they don't taste too bad, and mine says I always bring others happiness."

"At least you don't get those awful cryptic ones anymore," Nat says, then turns to Nick. "They were from another company. They said crap like 'He who does this thing is happy' or whatever. Stereotype of the oriental mystic kinda stuff. Such BS."

"Language, Natalie," Jenny says.

"I just said two letters," Nat says. "Am I not allowed to say letters?" She grins at Nick, and Nick grins back.

"Thank you, Jenny," Nick's dad says. "It was an amazing meal." He starts getting out his wallet, but Jenny waves her hands for him to put it away.

"My treat," she says. "And I'm glad you enjoyed it. You and Nick are welcome here anytime."

"I'm sure Nick will take advantage of that, with the way I cook."

"I hope I'll see more of you, Nick," Jenny says, and suddenly gives him a large hug. She's soft, and smells like all the food they just ate mingling with the woodiness of the tea. He hugs her back.

"Thanks," Nick says. He turns to Nat, but he can feel both Jenny and Dad watching him expectantly, so he just lifts his hand in a wave. She smiles and waves back.

"See you later," she says. "Got to catch Helena."

"Yeah," Nick says. "See you in a bit."

Nick and Dad walk through the aisles between the tables and outside, where the smells from the restaurant fall away in a sudden wave, leaving only the disappointing smells of the parking lot, exhaust and burned tires. The sun isn't down yet, still low on the horizon, but it feels chilly already.

In the car, his father turns to him and Nick leans his head back on the headrest, willing himself not to look at his father.

"You didn't mention Nat was a girl," Dad says.

"Didn't think it mattered," Nick says. His father makes a sound that clearly starts as a laugh but that he tries to hide in a cough.

"Well, she seems very nice," Dad says. "She's Chinese American?"

"Her dad is Jewish," Nick says. "Half-white, like me."

"Ah," Dad says. "Well, she seems very nice. And I liked her mom, too."

"*She* can cook," Nick says, folding his arms.

"Yeah, but I bet she couldn't teach a class on the African American Experience in the Early Nineteen Hundreds, like I did today."

"Probably not," Nick says, chuckling despite himself. Dad starts to laugh, and it doesn't make much sense, but Nick laughs, too. They drive the rest of the way in relative silence, one of them occasionally laughing again and setting the other one off.

Inside the house, Nick is about to run upstairs to play the game but first turns to Dad.

"Thanks," he says. "For letting me go to the GamesCon."

"Of course," Dad says, picking the mail up from the floor. "But promise to take photos. I hear there are weird costumes at those things."

"Okay, Dad."

Nick watches his father wander into the kitchen, staring at the mail. He turns the light on in the kitchen, and his silhouette is curved over the mail, his shoulders broad like a shield. Nick runs upstairs to play the game.

NINETEEN

SEVERKIN STARES at the tunnel Helena fled through.

"I can get us up," Reunne says. "Just give me a moment."

"You all right?" Severkin asks.

"Fine," Reunne says. "Just preparing." She takes a deep breath. "Now I'm ready. Elkana?"

Elkana rises from her meditative pose. "Whenever you're ready."

"Very well," Reunne says, and suddenly charges the wall, spear forward like the tusk of a boar. She rams into the wall with enough force to dislodge some stone, leaving a tiny alcove. Then she withdraws the spear and rams it into the wall again a little higher up, then again, just above that. She's creating a ladder, Severkin realizes. Reunne steps back and continues to hurl her spear at the wall with an accuracy not quite as precise as Severkin's but impressive nonetheless. She retrieves it by climbing the already present handholds and pulling the spear out as she jumps down. Within minutes, she's created a ladder of handholds.

"Let's go," she says.

They climb up the wall and follow the tunnel at the top. It slopes downward and is lit only when Elkana uses fire magic on the nearby torches, and they flicker into unsteady life. The path flattens out, and looking around, Severkin realizes they must be beneath the graveyard at the foot of the mountain. There are tombs and coffins lining the walls; skeletons some ambitious graverobber has picked clean lie slumped against the wall.

"Can I ask you something?" Severkin asks Reunne. She shakes her head and puts her finger to her lips.

"This doesn't feel right," Elkana whispers. There's a creak of old hinges opening and one of the torches on the wall goes out in a whisper of cold air. "Necromancy," Elkana says just as one of the skeletons reaches out and grabs Severkin around the ankle.

Severkin kicks it away, but then another skeleton, held together by and smelling of dried mud, rises and attacks them. Severkin punches it once, and it scatters like rolled dice and doesn't get back up. But it's a small victory, as more corpses, in varying states of decay, start to crawl out of their coffins and pull themselves up. Many of them are clutching weapons they were buried with. Severkin takes out his blades, Reunne takes a defensive stance with her spear, and Elkana's hands burn with fire. As the undead surround them, they attack. Severkin cuts through the leather of dried flesh with his blades and Elkana burns it, while Reunne stabs and leaps over the corpses, her spear finding the rotting holes in their backs.

They take out the first wave easily, but as they move deeper through the caves, the onslaught continues. And the labyrinthine nature of the tunnels doesn't help, either—dead ends become traps as the walls spawn undead to attack them. Severkin starts keeping track of where they've been by whether or not the corpses are out of their coffins or not—which isn't always an accurate method. They fight for what seems like hours but must stop a few times for Elkana to meditate and for Reunne and Severkin to catch their breaths.

Severkin instinctively knows they've found Helena when the corpses stay dead in the coffins lining a large metal door.

"Remember," Severkin says, his hand on the door, "she can't see in the dark. If we can, we should exterminate light sources."

"Aye," Elkana says. "If she raises more corpses—small ones, mind—I'll handle those with fire. You two focus on her. If she pulls another dead giant out of her arse, I may need a hand."

"Good," Severkin says. "Let's go."

Inside is a larger chamber than they've been in for a while, but not nearly as large as where they fought the giant. It looks like a workroom, with horizontal slabs set up against the walls, bodies lying open on them in varying states of dissection. Helena leans against one of them, sewing up a large cut on her arm. She looks at them, her one eye glowing a faint red. Thin lines of black have dried around her mouth. She quickly pulls the thread away, and with a gesture, the corpses in the room come to life. They grab nearby weapons or surgical tools and come at Severkin and his companions.

These corpses seem faster than the others, and smarter, too. Severkin wonders if it's due to the work they've had done on them. He dodges under a bone saw and rolls across the room, focusing on Helena. Behind him he hears a heavy *thump* and *whoosh* as Elkana creates a wall of flame that consumes the undead. There's no screaming when the corpses die their second death. It's unnerving.

Reunne is already on Helena, who is fighting with a staff of deep purple energy that smells like blood and gas. Severkin hangs back, trying to stay hidden in the chaos of the flames and fighting. Behind him, he hears more explosions of fire. Reunne tries to stab Helena, but Helena's staff twists into a rope and encircles Reunne's spear and arm, locking her in place. Severkin sees his opening and charges Helena from behind, thrusting upward and through her chest. He feels both his blades emerge on the other side and pulls them back. They drip black liquid. But Helena doesn't fall. She laughs instead, her staff unwinding from Reunne's arm like a tentacle.

"This is foolish," Helena says, spraying black spittle with her breath.

"The head!" Reunne shouts, but Helena turns and clubs Reunne with the staff, throwing her across the room, then spins on Severkin.

"Elkana!" Severkin shouts. "Done with those corpses yet?"

"Not really!" Elkana shouts back from beyond a wall of fire.

Helena's staff whips out for Severkin's feet and he jumps to dodge it. She advances on him, and following Reunne's advice, he tries to decapitate Helena with a slash of his sword, but she ducks out of the way, still laughing. Suddenly the wall of fire to their side explodes outward and a huge pillar of fire comes through it sideways, knocking into Helena. She stumbles to the side, and Severkin leaps.

Helena's body has been alive too long, the black blood making it too soft, the marrow rotting, and his blade carves through her as though she were overly ripe fruit. Her head falls with a dull splat on the floor. There's a sound like all the air going out of the room, and the fire evaporates. Severkin stares down at the body, waiting for it to come back to life.

Reunne walks across the room to them. "She really dead this time?" she asks.

Elkana approaches and looks down at Helena. "She's fairly dead," Elkana says. "This isn't my field, but I think she's beyond the place where she can do any harm." She pauses, staring down at the body. "Still, I think we should burn her with fire, just in case." She makes fists, which light up in flame.

"Wait," Reunne says, and kneels down. Severkin kneels as well, searching the corpse for anything of value. He takes some gold, a few rings. Reunne takes a simple silvery tube from the corpse's hand. "Now," Reunne says, backing away, "I have the Staff."

"That's it?" Severkin asks. "It's small."

Reunne shrugs. "It is what it is," she says, and starts to tuck the Staff into her belt.

"Perhaps," Severkin says, and holds out his hand, "you wouldn't mind if we took this one back to Rorth, rather than Elega? Rorth felt as though it was . . . unfair that the dwarves had the Hammer. This may make things more even."

Reunne looks down at the Staff. "Rorth and Elega are fighting because they think once the giants are gone, they'll turn it on each other, aren't they?"

"Aye," says Elkana, crossing her arms. Her hands still glow.

Reunne shakes her head, her eyes still on the floor. "I hate all this fighting so much. I thought *peace* . . . eh. Foolish." She looks up at Severkin. "Why would you give it to Rorth?"

Severkin opens his mouth but pauses. "I think to stop the giants . . . if we give it to Rorth, we make them bring everything together. They each have a part."

"There are three parts," Reunne says.

"So, two to one, one to the other," Severkin says. "As long as one doesn't have them all, they'll have to work together, right? And then they won't be able to turn on each other. They'll each take back their own pieces . . . and if they're smart, hide them again."

"Oh, aye," Elkana says, and shakes her head. "And then a hundred years from now, another group of adventurers will have ta go through all this again."

No one says anything, which Elkana takes as her cue to spew fire from her hands at Helena's body, turning it to ash and a sickly-sweet-smelling smoke that makes Severkin's eyes water.

"Take it, then," Reunne says, handing Severkin the Staff once the smoke has cleared. "And let's find a way out of here."

They find a convenient door that leads them back to the entrance of the cavern, though it had been hidden there. They trudge back through the debris of the giant's cave and up to the abandoned mansion. When they get outside, it's just turning to dawn.

"Thank you," Severkin says as they head down the mountain, "for saving me from the giant. You could have taken Helena out right then. It was . . . kind of you to save me instead."

"That's what we do for one another," Reunne says, kicking snow as they descend a steep slope.

"We?" Severkin asks, wondering if she means warriors, comrades, gray elves, or something more.

"Wolf," Reunne says, pointing out a scraggly-looking lone wolf. It stares at them briefly, then runs off. Reunne walks quickly, making as if to chase it, but gives up once she's slightly ahead of Severkin and Elkana.

"Do you feel all right?" Severkin asks Reunne as they walk. She looks over at him, one eyebrow raised.

"I may be older than you, but I'm not out of breath from a little walking."

"No," Severkin says quickly. "I just mean, the skeletons, the necromancy—we should be sure you haven't gotten any diseases."

"I cured all those," Elkana says. Severkin looks over at her and tries to make his look significant. She nods, seeming to understand.

"Maybe there are diseases only us gray elves can get," Severkin says. "Know of any of those? Or what they might be called?" he asks Reunne. "I forget, does witstiff affect only us?"

"No," Reunne says. "It can affect anyone. But it's really only a bane for spell casters. Wouldn't be a big problem for me."

"Still," Severkin says, "maybe there's a cure for it that you know?"

Reunne shakes her head. "Just what I buy in the apothecary," she says. "Wolf."

They kill another pack of wolves, but when Severkin tries to bring up illnesses again, Reunne just shakes her head.

"I'm not a healer," she says. "These are questions for a cleric."

They walk a little farther along in silence until Elkana starts singing troll ballads. Severkin isn't sure how they're supposed to sound, but they remind him of the sound of his own heart after sprinting, and it makes him anxious. It seems to have the same effect on Reunne as she waves them goodbye just before they arrive at the foot of Wellhall.

"This is a quicker way to the undercity," she says, pointing at a small trap door in the ground. "And I'll need to tell Elega we got the Staff. She probably won't be happy I gave it to you."

"Thank you again," Severkin says. "For everything. Maybe we'll see you for the next one?"

"Oh, the Spear," Reunne says, nodding. "I hope so." And she pulls open the trap door and disappears down it.

Unfortunately, Elkana doesn't stop singing until they reach the guard hall. Severkin flashes his badge at the guards, who let him pass but give curious looks to Elkana. Inside, Rorth is on the throne, and Ind and Siffon are arguing in front of him. Rorth looks up when they enter and smiles, then stands up and walks toward them. Ind and Siffon immediately quiet down.

"Do you have it?" Rorth asks.

"I do," Severkin says, taking the Staff out of his pouch and handing it to Rorth with a slight bow.

"Excellent," Rorth says, staring at the Staff. "Just as the diagrams show." He walks back toward his throne, and Severkin and Elkana follow. "We'll send you for the Spear as well. Who is this troll?" he asks, suddenly noticing Elkana.

"A friend," Severkin says quickly. "She was invaluable in retrieving the Staff."

"A troll," Rorth says, nodding. "That's good. Neither an

elf nor a dwarf. Elega can't object, but this troll's your friend, you say?"

"I can speak for myself," Elkana says.

"Of course," Rorth says. "My apologies, lady. Thank you for your help. We shall make you a guard at once, and you shall accompany Severkin in retrieving the Spear."

"I shall, shall I?" Elkana asks, putting a hand on her hip.

Rorth raises an eyebrow. "I hope so," he says.

The doors open again, and Izzy runs in, panting and pink, her squirrel ponytail bobbing behind her.

"Ah, what does Elega have to say, Izzy?" Ind asks.

"Madam Elega says she is most pleased with the retrieval of the Staff and hopes your lordship will keep it well guarded." Ind harrumphs while Siffon and Rorth smile. "She also says that she does not yet have the location of the Spear, but she believes she has found someone who does. She requests that you send the gray elf Severkin to her, so she may instruct him further. If she is willing, the troll Elkana is also welcome." Izzy bows, her hands clasped behind her back.

"Ooooh, I'm welcome," Elkana says in mock excitement. "Think I should get a fancy dress 'n' all that?"

"You shouldn't mock it," Siffon says. "It's rare for non-dwarves to be invited into the undercity's guardhouse. You might be the first troll who goes there . . . willingly, anyway."

"Excellent," Rorth says. "Tell Elega that my agents will be there when they're good and ready, and shall take their time doing so. I may suggest that if she grows bored waiting, she attempt to locate her feet, which I'm sure she hasn't seen in decades." Izzy salutes and runs out the door.

"Is she really gonna tell her all that?" Elkana asks.

"She'll rephrase it," Rorth says. "Now get a badge from Siffon here, and then get going. I want the Spear in my hands quickly."

"But ye just said—" Elkana starts, but Severkin grabs her arm and steers her toward the side door to the guards registry, where Siffon is waiting. They head down the hall Siffon took Severkin down the first time.

"So you're his . . . friend?" Siffon asks, sounding a little disappointed.

"Aye," Elkana says. "Who are ye?"

"She's Siffon," Severkin says. "The spymaster."

"I wouldn't call myself that," Siffon says as they arrive in the room with the badges. She takes one from the guard on duty and hands it to Elkana, then signs a few papers.

"Spymaster?" Elkana asks. "Then ye must have files on Wellhall residents, right?"

Siffon blinks a few times as her face evens out into a cool mask. "I have no idea what you mean," she says.

"Oh, aye, that," Elkana says. "But do ye have one on Reunne, the gray elf we've been working with from the undercity?"

"I told you," Siffon says. "I have no idea what you mean." The even lines of her mouth and eyes are starting to turn angry.

"Well, thank you," Severkin says, heading back down the hall. "We'll return with the Spear."

"But she can tell us about Reunne," Elkana says, looking at Siffon, who glares back. "Oh, fine. We'll be on our way. But if Reunne kills us when we're not looking and ye could have stopped it, I expect a proper fancy funeral funded by the state." Siffon cracks a smile but instantly levels her face again. Severkin and Reunne head out of the guardhouse and down to the city, heading for the undercity.

"So, Elega," Elkana says. "Ye met her?"

"No," Severkin says. "But I hear she doesn't like gray elves."

"Ah, well, this'll be loads of fun, then," Elkana says.

TWENTY

NICK WAKES up reaching out into the air. He'd been dreaming of Mom making bacon at the stove. She'd looked like that old ivory cameo of hers, pale, posed, and delicate, and the kitchen had smelled like home again. There's no smell in his room but the one coming from his dirty laundry in a pile in the corner. He dresses and goes downstairs.

Dad is reading the newspaper and eating cold cereal. Nick goes over to the stove, where he'd dreamed the phantom of his mother, where he sometimes sees her shadow even when he's awake. He doesn't use the stove himself, never really looks at it, but now he studies it. It's simple, white, clean of food stains, but a thin stubble of dust has begun to crop up on the sides. Behind it, the wall is painted white, except that there's a blackened column, like rising smoke. He notices the range hood is blackened as well, shadowy claw marks on the metal. He tries to think of the last time he actually looked at the stove. Has it been like this for a while? He leans forward—the paint in the center of the black smoke on the wall is chipping away in a vertical line. Nick reaches out and pushes a flake of it away with his fingernail. It crumbles and falls behind the stove, leaving a small white triangle along the crack.

"What are you doing?" Dad asks from behind him.

"How long has this been like this?" Nick asks.

"What?" Dad asks. Nick looks behind him. Dad is still staring at the paper.

"This burn," Nick says, and turns around and flicks another piece of paint out from around the crack.

"That's old," Dad says. Nick goes to the cupboard, takes out a bowl and pours cereal and milk into it, then sits down across from Dad.

"I don't remember any fires," Nick says.

"You must not have been here," Dad says, and flips a page of the newspaper. Nick notices how his father raises it to cover his face slightly, like a mask. Severkin would think he was hiding something. So does Nick.

"You're the only one who would burn anything," Nick says, taking a spoonful of cereal, "and I'm always here when you're cooking."

His father lowers the top half of the paper and stares at Nick through his glasses. "Maybe you were upstairs, playing your game, or sleeping, or possibly studying, though I know that's a long shot."

Nick feels the prick of the ragebrew, coursing up his arms, making him hold the spoon so tightly it starts to burn his hand.

"It's not fair, the way you and Mom don't tell me things," Nick says. "You make all these choices that change my life and you don't tell me why. It's like . . ." Nick searches his cereal bowl for a weapon to hurl at his father. "It's like I'm a slave," he says. It's crude, disrespectful to his ancestry and the ancestry of thousands of others, but it'll hurt Dad. And that's what he wants.

Dad looks down, contemplating the last few pieces of cereal floating in his bowl. It becomes quiet. Nick expected anger, yelling, one of the various lectures he's heard before, but there's just silence. Finally Dad takes a deep breath. He looks up.

"You're right," he says. Nick feels his skin cool and his hairs stand on end, all reaching out for something. "It's not fair," his father says. "And it's not what all the books and counselors say to do. They say to be open and honest. But your mother . . . she loves you so much, you know that, right?"

Nick nods.

"The burn marks are from a fire your mother accidentally set about a week before she left. She was cooking . . . something, I don't remember. Got confused, added something, and whatever was in the pan went up in flames." His father puts the newspaper down on the table, irons it with his arm. "She panicked; I grabbed the fire extinguisher. You were upstairs, the music on, reading some magazine about your game. When you came down for dinner, you asked about the smoke and Mom said she'd burned something." He tilts his head to the side and smiles a little. "Which wasn't a lie."

Nick takes a deep breath. He looks down at his cereal, which has grown soggy, and mashes it with his spoon. What box on the checklist is for setting fires? 1, 2, 3, and probably 8, too. Does he have to check them all, or can he just pick one, he wonders. But no, the ragebrew in his blood tells him, that's not enough. Not enough to leave her family. It was just a fire so small he hadn't even noticed the damage until now.

"So she went away," he says, "'cause, what? Because she had a cooking accident? Then *you* should have been locked up a long time ago."

"She's not locked up, Nick!" Dad says.

Nick gets up and empties his cereal bowl into the trash. "I'm going to be late for school," he says, and heads back upstairs. Dad doesn't follow.

When he comes back downstairs, his father isn't around, so Nick leaves for the bus and then for school. But his frustration continues throughout the day. He can feel himself unfocusing in class, can feel the late summer air coating his body like cotton balls, softening everything outside him, making it fuzzy and distant. The only time things come back into focus is at lunch.

"So I'm going to send you a playlist," Nat says, taking out her phone. It has a bright purple case. "I wanted to tell you in person, though, so you didn't think I was just sending you some random link." He takes out his phone and looks at the link she's sent him, to a playlist called "Nick." He clicks the Save button. He's unsure of what to say. It's all gotten so confusing, and he keeps thinking about the crack running up the burned paint in the kitchen.

"Thanks," he said.

"It's the music I listened to when my dad was in rehab," she says, putting her phone away. It's not, like, super sad or anything. It's like power music. Music that makes you want to punch things. It's stupid, I know, but I just thought maybe you could use it."

"It's not stupid," Nick says. He forces his best smile for her. He puts his phone away and looks back up at her and opens his mouth to tell Nat about the crack in the wall, but then stops. He doesn't want to share it. "I'll know more after I talk to Jess on Friday," he says instead. "She can tell me if it's Ms. Knight or not."

Nat smiles, but her eyes flicker down for a moment, like she's disappointed. "What are you going to ask her?"

"What her character looks like. That seems like something Jess would know, even if she only sees Ms. Knight playing."

"Cool," Nat says. She looks down at the remnants of her food and the plastic table. "You okay? You seem kinda weird today."

Nick looks up at her and studies the blue streaks in her hair. They're growing out and start a few inches down, just showing up out of the black like the aurora borealis. "I had a fight with my dad this morning. It's not important."

Nat starts packing up the remnants of her lunch, piling the trash like a hill on her tray. "My folks made me go to a shrink when my dad went into rehab," she says, taking Nick's crumpled brown lunch bag. "I hated it. Didn't help, except for one thing: the shrink said it was good to say things aloud. Makes you confront them. I spent hours in my room saying 'My dad is an alcoholic. My dad is sick.' Sounds creepy, but it helped."

"Like when you listed all that stuff yesterday?" Nick asks, thinking of her chanting her father's drinking habits.

"Yeah." Nat nods. She gets up and takes the tray over to a trash bin. Nick watches her sweep all the trash away and put the tray on top of the others. She comes back over, and Nick stands and they walk out together. "Sometimes it just helps to say a thing," Nat says. "When you're ready."

"Thanks," Nick says. But he doesn't say anything else. He doesn't say *My mother lit the stove on fire.*

Nat shrugs and then reaches out and squeezes his shoulder. "See you in history," she says.

The rest of the day and the next go quickly. School is driving relentlessly forward, and as his teachers are fond of saying, this is junior high now, things are tougher. Nick can't even go near the game for the rest of the week; he has math quizzes and papers, and what Dad said about his not studying sort of stung. He'd always been a good student. A-minuses, mostly, not those pure, diamond A's, but good. Mom had always praised him for that, helped him study. It's harder on his own. He locks himself in his room, where the air seems thick and hot and salted with some sort of sleeping gas. He tells himself that Severkin studied—Severkin knows all the ancient languages, the ancient cultures. If Nick wants to be anything like that, he needs to study, too. He listens to Nat's playlist, and he likes it, though it's usually not what he listens to. It's loud and angry and feels like a lightning storm over the ocean. After a few songs, though, it calms down. It's just rain.

Dad isn't exactly pretending that they didn't fight, but he's not talking about it, either. Nick doesn't say anything to him, and Dad doesn't say anything to Nick besides "What do you want on the pizza?" and "I'll pick you up after school tomorrow so we can go see Mom." Otherwise, they're strangers haunting the same empty house.

• • •

Nick gets in the car Friday after school after waving goodbye to Nat. He thinks he did okay on the math quiz, and his paper on East Berlin is going well. But today is more important than school. Today he has to find out more about Reunne—from Jess, and from his mother. If Reunne is trying to tell him something, he needs a clue from outside the game.

"I'm going to talk to your mom today," Dad says when they've been driving for a few minutes. "About telling you more about why she's in the home. Okay?"

"Sure," Nick says after a moment. He doesn't know what else to say. He thinks he should be happy—Dad is finally listening to him—but instead it's like his stomach is so heavy, it's pulling the rest of his body down. He slouches back into the chair, scooting down so the seat belt pushes into his chin. It doesn't help.

"I don't know if she'll be okay with it, though. It's really her story. It's not even much of a story. But she has her reasons. She loves you and wants to protect you."

"How can she protect me?" Nick asks. "And from what? Alzheimer's? If she's sick, I'm going to get sick. If she's not sick, I'm not. All she has to do is admit she's not sick." The heaviness in his stomach starts to roil, and he remembers being Severkin on the ship at the beginning of the game: the shuddering underfoot, the huge rolling wave that pushed him away.

"She's sick," Dad says, voice like a hammer. "You have to accept that, Nick." He looks over at Nick, then his eyes dart back to the road. "But it doesn't mean you'll get sick. We don't know that for sure. There's just a chance."

"Yeah, a big chance," Nick says, folding his arms. Dad is silent.

They pull into the white gravel parking lot without either of them saying anything else. The crackling of the gravel under the car sounds like crumbling rock.

Nick opens the door before the car is even parked and walks quickly toward the porch so Dad can't catch up. A nurse swipes him through with a nod and he runs upstairs to Mom's room, but she's not there. He walks back downstairs to the desk, where his father is standing.

"She's painting out back," he says. They walk outside and around the back, the old people staring at them, one asking his father to get them more iced tea. Nick and Dad ignore them. Out back, in the grass, Mom has an easel set up. The grass is almost as high as her knees and seems to fade into her. Or she into it. She doesn't see them at first and instead focuses on her easel and the palette of paints in her hand. Her back is straight and her hair is loose, occasionally flying out in the breeze. She wears a white skirt and sweater. She looks like she's painting the back of the home, but as Nick gets closer he can see her easel, and the painting on it is of him. At least, he thinks it's him. The eyebrows are too thick, and the skin isn't brown but gray. The whole painting is gray, except for his eyes, which are brown. That part she got right.

"Hi, Mom," Nick says when they're close enough for her to hear them.

She turns and smiles. "Nicky," she says. "I'm trying to paint you. It's hard from memory. . . . Come here and stand over there so I can fix it." Nick walks around to stand in the grass in front of his mother. She's blocked by the canvas except for her legs and one elbow. Dad goes and stands behind her, watching her paint. "No need to look so worried, Nicky,"

Mom says, poking her head out around the side of the easel. "Relax." Nick tries to relax but is suddenly very aware of his arms and how they hang wrong, and his posture, which has never been good. "Don't think about it," she says. "Why don't you tell me about school. How is your paper on me coming?"

"It's not really on you," Nick says, trying putting his hands in his pockets. That feels weird, though, so he folds them over his chest. "It's about the fall of the Berlin Wall. I've been doing lots of research. I know how it was sort of a mistake that they opened it, but then everyone gathered at the gate and it came down."

"Arms down," Mom says. "Yes, I remember that. So many people."

"You were there?" Nick asks.

"Oh yes," she says, her face obscured by the canvas and her voice like a strong breeze, or a heavy sigh. "It wasn't intentional. I was out walking." She sounds as if she's going to say more but then pauses for a long time. Her arm stops moving. "Can you turn a little to your left, Nicky?" Nick turns obediently. "Good, thank you. But yes, I saw the crowds. I'd been walking for hours, so I hadn't heard anything on the radio. I had to ask someone what was happening. I stopped a young man on the street and asked him, and he said, 'They're opening the wall, sister.' I remember that. I wasn't a revolutionary before, but that night anyone young, anyone who had been raised under the shadow of the wall, we were brothers and sisters. It was almost a new word, not the old *brother, sister, comrade*. It was something else. So I followed the crowd and I watched from a distance—I didn't want to be arrested, they would have taken away my chance at a good job, and after all the work I'd done getting so far in school, I couldn't risk it. So I watched. And then, suddenly, the wall was open. I wish I could say it was like light flooded in or something romantic, but it was like . . . like when your ears pop on a plane. Noises become louder and clearer, but they're still the same noises. That's what it was like that night. Of course, over the next few weeks and months it all started to change. But that night, it was like having your ears pop." She leans out from behind the canvas and looks him in the eye, then makes a popping noise with her lips. Nick smiles.

"Finally, a smile," Mom says. "Now hold it so I can paint it."

Nick tries to hold the smile but it becomes strained, then painful. "I can't hold it anymore," he says.

"That's all right, I got it, I think. Come see." Nick walks around to look at the painting. Not much has changed—it's still grayscale except for his eyes. But it looks more like him now, he thinks. Except maybe the expression. The expression is too hard. Even with the smile, he looks like a wall. He turns away and looks at Mom instead.

"It's nice, Mom. But tell me more about the wall. Where were you?"

"Oh, I don't remember exactly," she says, looking up at the sky. "I was a long way from home, I remember that. But I wasn't so close to the wall that I could hear the crowds." She shakes her head. "Sorry. I just followed the others. I don't remember where I was."

"Where were you going?"

"I was just out walking, Nicky." Her voice lowers slightly. "I don't want to talk about that. That night was very good for a lot of people, including me. But it wasn't all good. Now tell me what you really think of the painting."

Nick looks back at the painting. "I think I look angry," he says. "But otherwise it's really good."

"You don't look angry," Dad says. "You look worried. Paint him so he looks more relaxed, Sophie."

"No, I like it this way. I think he looks like he cares. That is the face I want to see on my wall—my son, caring."

"I do care, Mom," Nick says, taking Mom's hand.

"Why don't we take the painting up to your room," Dad says. "We can hang it there. Then I need to talk to your mom alone for a little while, okay?"

"Yeah," Nick says. "But the paint is still wet."

"Oh, right," Dad says. Nick wonders if he should make a checklist for Dad. Check off box 8—"Decreased or poor judgment." "Well, maybe you can go find a nurse to let them know it's done? While I talk to your mother?"

"Sure," Nick says. He'll find Jess. He needs to talk to her anyway, and alone is better. His parents walk over to the bench they were sitting on the other day, and Nick walks away, trying not to look too purposeful. He checks the media room first, but Jess isn't there, so he asks at the desk and they direct him to a room down the hall.

The door is open, and Nick walks in slowly. Jess is sitting by a patient's bedside, checking a tube that goes into the patient's nose. This room is one of the more hospital-like ones, with floors that glare under bright lights.

"Your hair is so pretty," the old woman in bed says to Jess. "You people have the best hair." She reaches out and strokes one of Jess's braids as Jess reaches over her.

"Thank you," Jess says in a tone Nick has heard before. Has used before. "Looks like you're all set here. Want me to turn on the TV?"

"Oh yes," the woman says. Jess turns it on and walks out of the room, nodding at Nick as she does so. Nick follows her.

"Did you want to talk to me?" Jess asks.

"Do you get questions about your hair a lot?" Nick asks. They're walking to the media room.

"Old white people. Yeah. Sometimes I try telling them it's not okay, but they forget, or pretend to. Part of the life."

"Yeah," Nick says.

Jess stops in the media room and starts collecting stray DVDs and matching them to their cases. "Did you want to ask me about my hair, too?"

"Oh, no," Nick says rubbing his hand over his own buzzed hair. "I wanted to ask if you knew what character Ms. Knight plays—in Wellhall."

Jess looks up at him, an eyebrow raised. "Why do you want to know that?"

"Is there a reason I shouldn't know?" Nick asks, suddenly wondering if Nat was right. His heart speeds up a little.

"I get that she's a cool, young teacher and all, but she's still your teacher. You can't hang out with her in the game to get better grades." Jess stands, no longer focused on cleaning up, just focused on Nick. "She likes you—don't worry about being a suck-up. That'll freak her out."

"No, no . . . ," Nick says, putting up his hand. "The opposite. We know she'd be uncomfortable, so we just want to make sure if we see her in-game, we can stay away. It'd be weird if she found out she was playing with her students."

Jess nods. "Okay. That's really mature of you. But I don't know how helpful I can be. I mean, I watch her play, but usually I'm in bed, and it's just sort of happening. I don't pay much attention."

"Do you know what her character looks like? Or what weapon she uses?"

"Yeah . . ." Jess looks down at the DVDs in her hand. "I think she uses a spear—or a staff. Something like that." Nick swallows.

Maybe Nat was right. "Anything else?"

"It's a female character. Red hair, like hers. I think she wears a red-and-white dress or robe—but that changes, right?"

"Yeah," Nick says, exhaling. Reunne does not have red hair. Ms. Knight isn't Reunne. Nat was wrong. Nick cracks a grin. He knew she was wrong. She should have believed him from the start. He knows his own mother. He feels a laugh start to bubble up inside him but pushes it back down.

"And I think she's a priest, or a warrior priest or something. Is that specific enough?"

"Yeah," Nick says. "Is that the only character she plays?"

"Oh yeah. She loves that character. Besides, she only has time for one." Jess puts all the DVDs back on the shelves and walks out of the media room, and Nick follows.

"Thanks," Nick says. He uses all his energy to keep his body still, not jump up in the air and holler so loud Nat can hear it that he was right. His mom is playing the game. His mom is trying to tell him something. She's trying to tell him something and he has no idea what.

"No problem," Jess says. "How's your mom?"

"She's really good," Nick says. "I'm thinking of springing her out of here."

Jess laughs, but seeing Nick's face, the laugh fades. She stops in the hall and looks at him. "You're not serious, right?"

Nick shrugs. "I just don't think she's as sick as everyone says."

Jess puts a hand on Nick's shoulder and leaves it there. "They haven't really told you anything, have they?"

Nick shakes his head. But he knows enough. He knows his mom is Reunne, and that means something. He just has to figure out what.

"That's not fair," she says. "Not fair to anyone." She kneels slightly so she's at eye level with Nick. "Your mom is great. She's one of my favorites. She's funny, doesn't do any of that little micro-aggressive racist crap—sometimes even calls other patients out on it—and she loves you so much. You're all she talks about. Have you seen what she's painting?" Nick nods. "And she's in here so much, watching people play Wellhall, painting it afterwards. Sometimes she talks to them as they play, too." Jess pauses, looks away for a moment, then looks back at Nick. "She calls them Nicky."

"And she plays, too," Nick says. Jess keeps staring at him, saying nothing. "She plays, too," Nick repeats, louder.

Jess stands up. "I don't know. I'm not in there all the time. Maybe." She turns and starts walking again.

"Thanks," Nick says, pushing a polite smile onto his face. He knows his mom plays. And she doesn't know how sick his mom is. She's not even a doctor.

"If you ever want someone to talk to," Jess says, stopping and turning to face him again, "I'm always around." She smiles, but it's a smile that's trying to hide PityFace, and Nick has to work hard not to roll his eyes. It's not her fault. She doesn't know, after all. No one knows but him. But if Reunne isn't Ms. Knight, then it has to be Mom. He feels himself evaporating, all the weight that he possessed gone, like he has used one of the potions in-game that let you carry a heavy load without affecting movement. No, not like that, he realizes, because the load is gone. Now if he can only figure out what Mom is trying to tell him in the game—what the sharp-eyed, smart part of her wants to say. It has to be some way to get her out, some symptom the doctors haven't noticed that points to something besides Alzheimer's. Maybe just the fact that she's playing online with him would be enough for the doctors— she found him online, right? All he has to do is prove it's her.

He still has to do that, he realizes, walking back outside to his parents. The actual proving. She won't admit she's Reunne. He might know it, and she might know it, and Nat might know it, but until Dad and the doctors know it, it doesn't count. Or he can get her to admit it. Get Mom to realize that playing the game is enough to show how well she is.

He stops when he gets around to the back of the home. His parents are still on the bench, Dad's hands small explosions while he talks, Mom staring straight ahead, leaning forward, hands clasped in the hammock of her skirt. He can't make out what Dad is saying, but it's loud. It sounds like a distant foghorn. Nick is behind them, so they haven't seen him yet. He thinks of Severkin and creeps forward, his steps carefully placed to muffle sound. He watches his shadow, careful it doesn't fall into their line of sight.

"He has to know," Dad is saying. "He's so angry, Sophie. It's not fair to keep all this from him."

"I don't want him to fear what happened to me," Mom says, her voice quiet as dripping water. "I don't want him to even imagine what happened to me happening to him."

"You prefer he not know anything? I think he doesn't even realize how sick you are."

"Let him live like that, then," Mom says, straightening up. "It's better than living how I lived."

"Sophie," Dad says as his hands come down in his lap like lead. "I may just tell him anyway."

"No," Mom says, turning to look at Dad, but as she does so, she sees Nick out of the corner of her eye. Her face goes from carved wood to cotton smiles. But her eyes are sharp. "Nicky," she says. "Did I show you the painting I'm doing of you?" Nick nods slowly, wondering if this is box 1 or 3, "Memory loss that disrupts daily life" or "Difficulty completing familiar tasks."

"You showed him already," Dad says, putting his hand on her shoulder. "Remember, he modeled for you?"

"Of course I remember," Mom says, rolling her eyes. "I'm just making a joke." Nick forces a laugh. No boxes to check after all.

"Did you find a nurse, Nick?" Dad asks.

"They were all busy," Nick lies. "I wasn't sure if I should bother them."

Dad stands, hands on his thighs, a slow unbending. "I'll go find one, then. Stay with your mother. Don't upset her."

Nick takes Dad's place on the bench, and Mom rests her hand on his knee. Nick's dad pauses, staring at her hand.

"He won't upset me," Mom says. Dad stares a moment longer at Mom's hand, then nods and walks away.

"He worries too much," Nick says.

"It's good that he worries," Mom says, looking out at the grass. "Did I show you the painting I did of you?"

Nick laughs. "That joke is getting old, Mom."

Mom giggles, a strangely young sound, like a baby's giggle. "Sorry," she says.

"So when are we going to get you out of here?" Nick asks. "I know you're Reunne. I know you're teaching me about your history through Wellhall. But I don't know what else you're trying to tell me—what's really wrong with you? How do I get you out?"

Mom is silent, staring at a sparrow that has landed in the grass a few feet away. The grass hides most of it, but when it pecks at the ground, its tail feathers bob up like a prairie dog.

"I don't think I'm supposed to leave," Mom says finally.

"You can do whatever you want," Nick says. "It's your life."

"Oh, Nicky," his mother says, her hand squeezing his leg. "It's not completely mine. It's yours, too."

"And I want you at home," Nick says, laying his hand over his mother's. "Come home."

"Look," Mom says standing, "it's Lamont." Dad is coming toward them, Maria alongside him.

"Did you see this painting of you?" Maria asks Nick as they get closer. Nick nods. "Did you know your mom could paint like that? I had no idea."

"She's good at everything," Nick says.

Maria laughs. "Good son," she says. "Well, why don't I take the painting into the studio and mark down that it should be hung in your room when it's dry, Sophie? That sound good?"

"Thank you," Mom says, nodding.

"And it's about time for your pills, too. You want me to bring them out?"

"Yes, thank you," Dad answers. Nick rolls his eyes. Maria takes the painting and goes inside, and Dad hovers, then sits down on the other side of the bench. "It's a nice place, isn't it, Sophie?"

"Oh yes," she says. "Very peaceful, and everyone is so nice. Lots of old people, though. That's why I'm always so happy to see you." She leans her head on Dad's shoulder and Nick stares at the sparrow in the grass again, which has been joined by another. This place might not be so bad, he thinks, but it's not for her.

Maria comes back out, rolling a little cart of cups of pills and water. She plucks one cup of each and walks them over to Mom. Mom downs them without question.

"She's been getting tired after her pills," Maria says to Dad, like Mom isn't sitting right there.

"Oh," Dad says. "Okay, why don't we take her upstairs, then, and let her rest? We'll be back Sunday."

"I have GamesCon," Nick says.

"Oh, right. Sophie, Nick is going to a big convention in the city for that game he likes so much."

"How exciting," Mom says. "That's the one with the mountain with the two cities in it, right?"

"Yeah," Nick says. He looks at Dad. "I never told her that," he says. "I think she's playing it from here."

"Are you playing Nick's game here, Sophie?" Dad asks, looking at Maria. Maria shrugs.

"They have it here," Nick says. He opens his mouth to say *And I know who she's playing* but closes it. He doesn't have proof yet. But this is a good first step. He'll have to let Dad in on it slowly so he doesn't blow up and tell Nick he's wrong.

"Oh, the game, right," Mom says. "The one with the mountain? Beautiful to look at. Strong basis in Nordic and Germanic mythology, I think. It's amazing what these game makers can do now. I don't think I'm very good at it, though." She looks as if she's trying to figure out what to say to him, but after a moment, winks instead.

"See?" Nick says. Dad stares at Mom, smiling. Maybe this will be enough.

Mom yawns loudly without covering her mouth.

"Okay," Maria says. "I think we should get her upstairs. Want to go take a nap, Sophie?"

Mom nods slowly. Nick waits for Dad to stop them, to say *But if she's playing the game, like my son says, maybe she's not sick.* But he doesn't. Nick takes a deep breath. He's proved Mom is playing the game. Next he needs to prove that she's sending him messages in it. But this is a good start. He feels filled up with something warm that expands his chest, giving him strength. A strength potion, maybe.

He and Dad help Mom upstairs, where Nick gives her a hug. "See you soon," he says. He and Dad get back into the car and Nick gets out his cell phone as they drive home and texts Nat:

> Ms. Knight plays a redhead priestess. And Mom said today she plays. Reunne must be Mom.

He waits a minute, but Nat doesn't text him back.

> C u on the game 2nite

he texts her.

"It's nice that your mom is still playing the game, isn't it?"

Dad asks. He's smiling. "She's such a wonderful woman. You know that, right?"

Nick looks up, not sure whether to be confused or offended.

"Of course I know that," he says. I know it better than you, he thinks. Nick knows exactly how amazing she is—fighting through whatever it is in her head that's keeping her down, and communicating with him the one way she can. But he doesn't say all that. Dad's not ready yet.

When they get home, Dad says he's going to go grade papers and that Nick should do his homework. They can order a pizza. Dad seems to feel sad when he spots the empty chair and the pizza box still in the recycling from the last time they ordered, but Nick knows that once Mom is home, everything will be better.

TWENTY-ONE

SEVERKIN AND Elkana approach the building with the snake over its door cautiously. Severkin can feel eyes on them—not just the guards in front of the building, but from all around, watching the foreigners step up to the dwarven guardhouse. But this is where they'd been told to go. Elega was going to tell them how to find the Spear.

They walk up to the guards under the snake, and Severkin clears his throat.

"We're, uh—" He stops as the dwarves silently part to let them pass.

"Anyone can just walk in, then?" Elkana asks.

"We knew you were coming," one of the dwarves says. Their helmets cover their faces and make their voices echo, so it's impossible to tell which dwarf said it. Severkin and Elkana pause, not sure if they should just walk in. "You are Severkin and Elkana," one of the dwarves says—possibly the same one. "We were told what you look like, we were told you would be arriving, and we were told to allow you passage. Go quickly. Elega is not a patient warrior."

Severkin nods and pushes open the huge doors behind them. They're heavier than they look and he has to use both arms.

The inside is remarkably similar to the guard hall of the gray elves, but darker. There's no pomp here, no carpets and carved columns. Instead the columns are made of chipped onyx, and the floor is bare granite tile.

Reunne waits inside, leaning against one of the columns.

"That was fast," she says. "Follow me."

She walks down the hall, but at the end of it there is no throne, only a table and chairs, all empty. She turns down a side hallway and leads them downstairs and through narrow metal doors. Eventually they come to a large room lit with covered torches but still dark because the walls and floor are nearly black. At one end of the room is a huge desk, and behind it is a dwarven woman, her head covered with a black skullcap, her iron-colored hair pulled back in a braid. She has a large nose that turns down slightly and eyes that seem to reflect what little light is in the room like mirrors. She stares at them as they enter, expectant.

"Come, sit," she says. She motions to the chairs in front of her desk, four of them, one already occupied, though the occupant doesn't turn to look at them. Reunne does as the woman—Elega, Severkin assumes—asks, and Severkin and Elkana do the same. Elega does not stand, but she lays her hand on her desk, her fingers curled as if she's clutching a sphere. "Reunne says you've proven useful, so we accept you into these hallowed halls," Elega says. She speaks quickly and with a voice like an old man clearing his throat. "But you must understand that this information we have acquired is secret. If you reveal what we are about to tell you, we will hunt you down and kill you, ally or no."

"I think Rorth would raise some objections to that, yeah?" Elkana says.

"Rorth doesn't care about you, troll." The words fly out with a little spittle, and Elega laughs. "And besides, the way we'd do it, he wouldn't know it was us. You'd just disappear."

"We understand," Severkin says.

"You too, Reunne," Elega says, and nods at her.

"Of course," Reunne says. Elega stares at her for a beat, her eyes moving up and down Reunne's face like she's doing a math problem.

"Good. This is Efem," she says, nodding her head at the occupant of the fourth chair, and Severkin glances over at him. He's a clean-shaven dwarf, which is unusual, and his hairline is high. He has a long, thin frown like a bridge, and the wrinkles on his face and around his turtle eyes suggest the frown is his default expression. But despite all that, he is strangely forgettable.

"I am in charge of the Sword and the Shield," he says in a low voice that carries. There's a cold silence. "This is one of the secrets you are not allowed to tell."

Reunne nods, and Severkin imitates her. After a moment, even Elkana nods slightly.

"One of the things we do is run a prison," Efem says. "For provocateurs who spoke out against our war with the over-world, back when such a war was happening, of course. We believe one of our prisoners knows where the Spear is. We will take you to her, and you may question her yourself."

"Why is she still in prison?" Elkana asks. "The war with the overworld is over. Shouldn't she be set free?"

"Technically," Efem says, "Sindry did more than just speak out. She led an entire colony in revolt, trying to escape to the overworld and begin a town there."

"I still don't understand," Elkana says. "Dwarves go ta the overworld all the time now."

"She broke the law," Elega interrupts. "The fact that the law she broke has since been repealed is irrelevant. Her sentence stands."

"That doesnae seem right," Elkana says.

"Our laws are our laws," Elega says, her hand inching toward Elkana like a spider. "You are here to help stop the giants. We don't want your opinion on anything else."

"Also," Efem says, "as we mentioned, the existence of this prison is secret. Who is in it is secret. If we just started letting them go, then it wouldn't be secret anymore." His hands, which have been immobile and folded in his lap, raise slightly, like they're inhaling.

"So no one knows that the prisoners are in prison?" Severkin asks.

Efem nods.

"They just disappeared," Reunne says softly. Severkin looks over at her, but her expression is unreadable, empty. Severkin knows she's thinking of her father. He wonders if she might explode at them, demand to know where he is, but she stays quiet. Becomes quieter, even, as though her body is perfectly still.

"Precisely," Efem says.

"But why bring us to this prisoner at all?" Reunne asks. "Surely you could get all the information you want from her?"

"She's particularly obstinate," Efem says, his tongue rolling inside his mouth as though trying to rid himself of a bad taste. "We think seeing overworlders may convince her to help." He nods slightly at Elkana.

"Ah," Elkana says. "Now I see why I've been invited along. She's never seen a troll before, eh? It'll make her believe us when we say you're at peace with the overworld now and we need her help with the giants."

"Exactly so," Efem says. "Our interrogators told her the truth of the matter flat out, and she laughed at them. Our other usual techniques did nothing. We think you may be able to convince her of the truth." Severkin frowns, trying not to think about what the "usual techniques" must be.

"And why do you think she knows where the Spear is?" Severkin asks.

"Records," Elega says. "She and her fellow provocateurs were part of an excavation colony. We sent them into a cave where we thought there'd be resources to hollow it out in preparation for a new colony. They did their jobs for a while, but then Sindry found something—something that matches the description of the Spear. Shortly thereafter, they tried to escape—started digging a tunnel to the surface. Assumed no one was monitoring them."

"That was incorrect," Efem says. "A loyal dwarf revealed their plan, and now they all reside in Number Seven."

"Seven?" Elkana asks. "So there are six others?"

Efem stares at her silently until they realize he won't be answering.

"But we couldn't find the Spear," Elega says. "She hid it somewhere." Severkin and Elkana stare at each other in the silence. The black walls make Elkana's skin seem to glow like the algae monsters he and Reunne had fought.

"Can we . . . ," Reunne starts. She purses her lips then opens them again. "Can we promise her freedom? In exchange for what she tells us?"

"You can promise her whatever you want," Efem says, his hands inhaling again. He pauses, waits for his exact meaning to sink in. "Any other questions?" No one says anything. Severkin shakes his head. "Good, then we'd best be off. We'll take some tunnels out this way," he says, standing. He's not wearing any armor, just black breeches and high-collared jacket. "Number Seven is well hidden, so it may be a long journey."

"Bring back the Spear," Elega says, but she's staring at papers on her desk.

Severkin, Elkana, and Reunne stand, and Efem leads them out the way they came, then down another hallway and more stairs. Halfway down the next hall, he presses a brick and the wall swings open. The doorway is low, so they must duck to enter it, and once inside, it's pitch black. Efem takes out a torch and lights it, then closes the hidden door behind him. They walk, bent over and silent, a few hundred feet before the tunnel opens up and they can stand straight again.

"This will be a long walk," Efem says. "I have more torches if you'd like." He hands out torches to Severkin and the others, who light them and follow him in silence. The road is roughly carved into the underground, the ceiling low and gnarled like natural earth, not the neat stone ceilings of the undercity.

Severkin hangs back from Efem and waits for him to get a

little ahead before whispering to Reunne, "Are you okay with this?"

Reunne nods slowly, her eyes fixed on Efem's silhouette. "Let's get the Spear," she says. "Then maybe I can learn something about . . . that." Her voice is barely a whisper, more like an exhale with notes.

They walk ahead in silence for a long while, Efem leading them down twists and turns so numerous and dark that Severkin loses all sense of where they are. They're outside the undercity, that much he knows. But in what direction, or how far, he can't be sure.

Finally the tunnel's roof rises slightly and the ground underfoot becomes more polished. There is a large metal door built into the side of the wall and Efem produces a key from somewhere in his robes and unlocks it. They all follow him inside.

Here, the air smells not like dirt but like metal, and the room is large enough that Severkin imagines he can feel a breeze. It is lit by a huge chandelier and torches, but it still feels glum, dark. The marbled tiles on the walls have a green tinge. The staircase that dominates the room seems to glow gray. A guard in a uniform Severkin hasn't seen before is standing in the center of the room. When Efem enters, he nods slightly.

"The prisoner is already in the interrogation room, sir. Number three," the guard says. He wears no helmet and his chain mail is black. The same Sword and Shield emblem is at his collar.

"Very good. I'll take them." The guard nods and disappears through a door in the side of the room. Efem walks up the staircase, and they follow him. Severkin looks at Reunne, but her eyes are blank, reflecting the light of the room like glass.

"We have very careful systems in place. Most of the prisoners haven't seen any other prisoner for years. They have no contact with the outside world besides the guards. We have total control over their lives." He leads them up the stairs and through a door into another room. A few guards patrol the perimeter looking at what Severkin first thinks are windows, but then he remembers they're underground, and he sees that while the walls are coated with glass, they're not windows. At least not in the conventional sense. The room is a dome, and the walls flicker with magic, showing fuzzy, faded images of prisoners in cells. Small cells. Most of the prisoners are dwarves, but a few of them are gray elves. The rooms are all identical. Windowless, cramped, with a bed that looks like a plank and a small hole in the ground that Severkin assumes is a toilet. The walls are stone but covered in a ribbing of some sort, like veins.

"We can see all the prisoners from here," Efem says.

"That's some magic," Elkana says.

"Yes," Efem says. "And you'd be wise not to try to replicate it. We lost more than a few mages creating this room. But it's worth it. Everyone is constantly surveilled this way."

"And it's limited to just the prisons?" Severkin asks, remembering the feeling of being watched in the undercity.

"Do you see the ropes along the walls of each cell— coating the walls?" Efem asks, ignoring Severkin's question. "The slightest tug on those, and a bell rings in the halls. If a prisoner tries to kill themselves, or becomes violent, we can stop it immediately. Some prisoners we keep perpetually drugged, or enchanted—keep their minds fuzzy, so they can't even think of escape." Severkin doesn't ask his question again. He knows no answer is forthcoming. Efem walks along the wall, his palm outstretched, hovering over the images of the cells and prisoners until he comes to one and stops. "This is where you'll be going," he says. The room the illusion shows is different—black walls, a table in the center, and a dwarven woman sitting at it. "That's Sindry. I'll take you to the interrogation room now. The walls are coated in thick leather—it cleans easier—but there are the ropes underneath the leather. If anything goes wrong, just press down anywhere on the walls and the guards will come in."

He leads them out of the room at the opposite end they entered from. The corridor here is wide but low. The doors are all dark, with small rectangular windows covered with bars. There isn't a single sound besides their footsteps and prisoners breathing short, whimpering breaths.

"And we can promise her freedom?" Severkin asks Efem when he stops in front of a door. Efem turns and looks Severkin in the eye, a smile curling up into his cheeks like syrup being poured into stirred porridge.

"You can promise her whatever you need to," he says.

"So you said," Severkin says, "but will those promises be honored?"

Efem lets his lip curl up, amused. "She's a traitor. You might not understand what that means down here, but I'm sure Reunne does." Severkin turns to Reunne, who stares at the floor. "Reunne, will promises to traitors be honored?"

Reunne looks up and at Severkin. "She's never getting out of here. She's never going to leave—no matter what we do.

The only thing we can do is try to get the Spear. Even if that means lying."

Severkin looks Reunne over until she stares at the floor again. She's always seemed so strong, but now she seems flattened, crushed under the weight of the mountain. He wants to get her out of here. He wants to bring her to the overcity and show her what freedom can feel like.

"You can do whatever you want to her," Efem says, causing Severkin to look back up at him. "But find out where the Spear is." He gestures at the closed door, palm open and up. "She's waiting."

Severkin isn't sure whether the "she" he refers to is Sindry or Elega, but he opens the door and walks in. He'll probably have to take the lead, he thinks. Reunne seems practically catatonic, and Elkana doesn't have his nuance. He walks into the room.

It's circular, and the walls are coated in oil-black leather that glimmers in the light from a caged set of torches on the ceiling, too high to reach. There's a table in the center of the room, and behind it sits Sindry. Severkin takes a moment to study her. Her hands are manacled to the table and are thin and bony. Her face is, too, her cheekbones rising like the curve of a shovel over a ditch. She looks like she hasn't eaten in years. Her hair is a dull gold color and cut short. Her eyes are thin, suspicious lines, but they widen into blue surprise when she spots Elkana.

"Hi," Severkin says.

Sindry keeps staring at Elkana, then turns to Severkin, her eyes narrowing again.

"I think you know why we're here."

"No," Sindry says, her voice deep and scratched.

"We're looking for something we need to put the giants to sleep again. We think you know where it is."

"Oh, this story again. The giants are awake, are they?"

"Yes," Severkin says, "and the under- and overcities have made peace."

Sindry snorts. "Why am I still in here, then?"

Severkin looks at Reunne and Elkana. None of them has an answer.

"You committed a crime," Reunne says finally. She doesn't look up at Sindry. "That it is no longer a crime doesn't mean you didn't commit one." Severkin wants to reach out and take Reunne's hand. She could be talking about her father, for all she knows.

"I admit," Sindry says, trying to lean back, but the manacles on her wrists keep her in place, "the troll costume is impressive."

Elkana raises an eyebrow. "Ain't a costume."

"You're a real troll?"

"Aye. From the overworld. The giants are real, and we need your help puttin' 'em back to sleep."

Sindry stares at Elkana.

"It's a spear," Severkin says, hoping for an opening. "You found it while excavating."

"Not exactly a spear," Reunne says. "More like a huge spear tip or an arrowhead. Four edges like a cross . . ." She looks at Elkana. "Got paper and charcoal?" Elkana nods and hands Reunne some from her bag. Reunne puts them down on the table and sketches a detailed drawing of a tall arrowhead with sharp edges and prongs, lines along the middle.

Severkin wonders for a moment how she knows the item in such detail and why he doesn't but assumes it's because Rorth didn't want him to know.

"Yeah, I remember it," Sindry says, still staring at Elkana.

"Ye wanna tug on my ear or something?" Elkana asks.

"Can I?" Sindry says. Elkana's eyes go wide, and she glances at Severkin, who nods.

"Fine," Elkana says, and leans over the table so Sindry can touch her ear. Quickly, Sindry darts in and bites Elkana's ear. Elkana yells out, pulling back. Sindry's mouth is red with blood, and Elkana has one hand on her ear and the other glowing with fire.

"Sorry," Sindry says quickly. "I'm sorry . . . I just had to make sure you're real. Not an illusion."

Elkana stares at Sindry a moment more before letting the fire in her hand dissolve. "Real enough, then?"

"Yes." Sindry nods. "So is it true? You're from the overworld?"

"Aye," Elkana says. "Him, too. Not her, though. But we trust her."

"And we really do need the Spear to stop the giants," Severkin says.

Sindry is quiet for a long while, staring at her hands. The blood dries and crackles on her lips, and she licks them, smearing it in a streak.

"I haven't seen anyone else in so long," she says. "Just the guards. What's the undercity like now? Now that we're at peace?"

Severkin looks at Reunne, who is still staring at her hands.

"Much the same," Reunne says finally.

Sindry nods. "Things are slow to change," she says. "They look fast, but they're not."

"But if we stop the giants," Severkin says, "this joint force of under- and overworld, maybe that'll bring us a step closer."

Sindry shakes her head. "No. Not down here. Down here, the high protect themselves and only themselves. The Sword and Shield will protect the Sword and Shield. You'll never convince them of peace."

"They'll fall in time," Reunne says softly.

Sindry sighs, the sounds like dead leaves. "Maybe," she says. "But hope lies with above, not with below. Below must change into above. And this thing you want to find . . ."

"The Spear," Severkin says.

"Yes," Sindry says. "It's powerful. It lets you . . . not control others' minds, but plant thoughts in them. And understand what they feel, which lets you argue to their beliefs more persuasively. It's how I convinced the whole colony to try to escape. It let me . . . peer into them. You can't let the Sword and Shield have it. You can't let anyone have it."

"We'll be careful," Severkin promises. "But we need it to stop the giants. Afterward, we'll hide it again." He knows this isn't true. The side that ends up with the artifacts will want to hold onto them to keep the other side in check. But maybe he can persuade them that the best way is to split them apart and hide them again. That would be the best for everyone. "But we need it. Or else all of Wellhall, above and below, will come toppling down."

Sindry wipes a bit of Elkana's blood from her lips and stares at it on her hands.

"I wonder if that would be so bad," she says so softly Severkin can barely hear it.

"There's hope now," Severkin says, and reaches out for her hands. He takes them in his, and they feel light, like dried reeds that could crumble under his touch.

Sindry looks up at him. "You promise?" she asks. "That there's hope?"

"I promise," Severkin says. He realizes it's the one promise he can keep.

"I hid it in the clay pits," Sindry says after a moment, and as she says it, it's like part of her leaves her. She seems even thinner somehow, without her last secret. Severkin wonders if it was the only thing keeping her alive, and whether now that he's just made her give it up, she'll die. And if she does, will he ever know? He knows the answer to that question: no. He'll never know anything about her again.

"Thank you," Severkin says.

"We shut the clay pits down," Sindry says. "There was an infestation of mud flies. I hid it in their nest—the highest one. Don't let them have it, when you're done. Steal it back, throw it to the deepest part of the ocean. Promise?" She tries to reach out, but her hands are still manacled to the table.

"I promise," Severkin says.

And then they sit in silence a moment more. Sindry stares at her hands, and Severkin wishes there were something else he could do. But he knows that there isn't. She'll be here until she dies, and she'll probably be buried here, under an anonymous gravestone.

"Thank you" he says, and turns to go. Reunne and Elkana follow him outside, but before closing the door, he looks back at Sindry—pale and sharp angled, hair like old gold, a forgotten statue, crumbling apart underground.

Outside, Efem is gone. A guard—possibly the one from earlier—stands in his place, waiting.

"I was told to give you this map. It will tell you how to get to the abandoned colony and then how to get back to the undercity after that."

Severkin takes the map and unfolds it. It shows their starting location as a cavern far from the city.

"Is this where we are?" he asks, looking up at the guard. But the guard has a face mask on, and suddenly there's a strange smell in the air, and Severkin feels his eyelids droop and his body fall to the ground.

⊙   ⊙   ⊙

SEVERKIN OPENS his eyes in a large cavern lit only by torches on the wall, clearly not anywhere in the prison. In his hand, on top of the map, is a note, which he opens and reads:

> *Sorry for the dramatics, but it was the best way.*
> *—Efem*

Severkin crumples the note in his hand and looks around for Elkana and Reunne. Elkana is just a few feet past him, starting to stand, shaking her head as if dizzy.

"Not very hospitable, was that?" she asks, when she sees Severkin. "We're just out of there, right? Not trapped in some new prison or something?"

"I think so," Severkin says. "Do you see Reunne?" They peer through the dimness of the cavern, and Severkin sees some movement at the far end. "There, maybe," he says, and they walk toward it.

It's Reunne, waiting at the end of the cavern, doing what appears to be exercises with her spear, fluid motions one into the other, almost dancelike.

"Reunne, you all right?" Elkana asks. "This isnae some kinda seizure, is it?"

Reunne stops and puts her spear back in the scabbard on her back. "Exercises," she says. "I needed to . . . think."

"Was all that difficult?" Severkin asks, meaning their seeing the prison, her seeing a place like where her father is probably kept. Was probably kept. It sounds stupid as soon as he says it, but Reunne is kind enough not to glare.

"Let's move on," Reunne says. Severkin nods and opens the map. The colony doesn't look to be very far from their starting position, and he wonders how far they are from the prison and how long they were unconscious.

They start walking and along the way find themselves fighting off the occasional creature—giant rats, mouths foaming white, and huge bats like living shadows. Nothing overpowering, though, nothing unexpected. They're soon on what looks to be an abandoned main road, or main tunnel, he supposes. It's well paved, but the stones are dusty and the air smells stagnant. Spiderwebs hang like lace arches over the road, and sometimes large spiders climb down them and Severkin and the others fight them off.

"So," Severkin says quietly, "do you think your father is being held in one of those prisons?" He turns to look at Reunne. She doesn't look back at him. For a moment, he's not sure she even heard him.

"Maybe," she eventually says. "Or he's dead."

"You want to break him out?" Severkin asks. "I'll help. Maybe he's been kept drugged. There must be a way, though."

"I don't know," Reunne says. "I don't know *if* he's being kept, or how, or where." She spins on him. "How can I save him when I don't know anything?"

"I . . . ," Severkin says. "I don't know. But you can still try. Make plans."

"I'll try," Reunne says, turning back to the road. "Once the giants are asleep again, I'll do more than try."

They walk on a while more in silence until the road ends at the colony. There's an arch and a sign over it in Dwarvish that names it Far Northeast Colony. Dwarves aren't much for interesting names, apparently. They go through the arch and look around at the ruins of a colony that was never completed. It's lit by a gentle glow of purplish mold on the high ceilings. It would have looked like a small version of the undercity, if it had been finished. But the walls of buildings are only half up, and machines lay rusting on the roads. The cavern, at least, was hollowed out. And there's one large building in the center, with a domed roof and a few statues in front. There are street signs for streets that never existed. It feels like a city, if a city were a thought you'd just forgotten.

"I don't like this place," Elkana says. "Let's find the clay pits and be out of here." Severkin looks down at the map, which is sectioned off into zones: algae ponds, brick workshop, housing, clay pits. The clay pits are across the cavern, so they set off, walking down the barest outlines of streets.

"Why'd they need clay pits, anyway?" Elkana asks. "Dwarves use it fer their skin or some such?"

"Bricks," Reunne says. "It's a special sort of clay, but if you find it, it can be strained and mixed with algae to create bricks that are strong and that glow slightly. It's not hard to find, but we use it up pretty quickly, so all colonies are built near clay pits."

As they get closer to the clay pits, Severkin hears a buzzing, at first like a background hum, but then growing louder.

"She said there was an infestation, right?" he asks. "Mud flies?"

"They build nests from mud or clay," Reunne says. "Nasty things—they bite. But I can't imagine they'll be too much trouble. We can burn them out if we need to."

Another arch marks the entrance to the clay pits. The buzzing is loud now, so loud Severkin needs to shout.

"Sounds like more than just an infestation!" he yells. There are two statues on either side of the archway, of noble dwarves standing in finery, weapons in front of them. But they've been colonized. Along the curves of their faces, in the angles of their necks and chins, are long clay tubes, like pan-pipes, with holes along their sides. As Severkin stares, a fly the size of his thumb darts out of one and into the archway. Severkin shines his torch after it. He can see a thousand flies, easily, filling the air like a cloud.

"Ye want me ta just burn 'em?" Elkana asks.

"Can you think of a better idea?" Reunne asks.

Elkana rolls her head on her shoulders and steps forward and raises her hands, letting loose a tide of fire through the arch. For a moment, the buzzing seems to soften, but then it grows loud again as hundreds of mud flies come out through the arch, dodging Elkana's flames. Severkin raises his hands to his face, expecting them to bite, but instead they all fly to one area, a little way off, and assemble. They contract as one, like a heartbeat, and pulse out again, this time not as a cloud but as a shadow—a shadow of a dwarf. Severkin feels his skin shiver, and quickly draws an arrow and fires at the fly-dwarf, but of course the arrow goes right through it. There are more of these dwarf-shaped swarms forming and charging them.

"How are they doing that?" Severkin asks. No one answers. One of the fly-dwarves is upon him and jumps at him with such force that Severkin stumbles backward, hit all over by a hundred stones. And then the stones start to bite. They're not mere flea bites, sting and itch. They're the bites of sharp axes or arrows. He can feel blood running into his eyes.

"This ain't working!" Elkana shouts. She's being swarmed, too, and so is Reunne. Severkin tries running into the clay pits.

"Let's just get the Spear and get out!" he shouts. Reunne and Elkana follow him, Elkana letting off bursts of fire now and then, trying to keep the flies down.

The clay pits are slippery and wet. The floor is ankle deep with gray water, and beneath that, the clay underfoot squelches. All around them, mud-fly nests rise from the ground like organ pipes, coating the walls, the columns the dwarves had put up, the machines they used to harvest the mud. Carts, sieves, conveyor belts, all misshapen, coated in thick tubes of clay like armor.

"She said she put it in a nest," Severkin says, trying to swat more of the insects away. They bite his hands and neck, every bit of exposed skin. He can feel himself growing tired with pain.

"So which nest?" Elkana shouts, blasting more of the insects with fire.

They try to see through the swarms of bugs and the darkness, but not even Severkin's night vision can see past the flies. They try climbing some of the nests, but the tubes fall away in their hands, and more mud flies stream out of them, angry and buzzing.

They take different forms—the dwarf shadows again, and the shapes of giant flies—but always in a swarm, always delivering the feeling of a thousand needles to the face and hands. Elkana has to stop throwing fire to cast her few healing spells on herself, Reunne, and Severkin.

Severkin sees a glint in the darkness only because he's turned his head upward, hoping the flies won't sting his eyes that way. It's at the top of one of the largest nests—a thick column of pipes as tall as a house, and on top, a pointed roof that shines slightly at the peak.

"There!" he shouts, and points. Elkana lets loose a blossom of fire, to clear out the flies for a moment in hopes of seeing the object clearly. But in the dark, all they can see is a metal point.

"How can we get up there?" Reunne shouts. "I can't climb it with my spear—the clay is too soft."

"And I can't climb it with my hands," Severkin says. They've clustered around the base, and Elkana has put a ring of fire around them. The smoke seems to keep the flies away better than the actual fire. But outside the ring, the strange dwarven silhouettes wait, something between a swarm and an army.

"What about that?" Elkana asks, pointing at an old

machine. It looks to be a large metal grate on a wheel, designed to scoop the clay up and hold it in the air to drain it. Two handles wind the grate—like a platform—up or down around a central bar, like an orbit. But it clearly needs to be hand-wound now, the engines all long dead.

"If I stood on that and leapt," Reunne says, "I think I'd be able to grab it and tear it down, yes."

"All right, then," Elkana says, and hurls a fireball at the grate. The clay nests embedded in it shatter, and it creaks loose.

"You'll need to hold the grate just right," Reunne says. "Otherwise it won't be high enough."

"Let's do it," Severkin says. He rushes forward, the flies swarming him like a clinging rain. Reunne jumps onto the grate, and Elkana and Severkin stand on either side of it, where the handles are.

"Now!" Reunne shouts, and both Severkin and Elkana turn the handles on their sides. They turn slowly, grinding through decades of old mud and rust, groaning against Severkin and Elkana's efforts. The flies sting at his fingers as Severkin turns, and the blood runs over his hands, making them slippery.

"Careful," Reunne says. "Almost there. No, too far, back!" Severkin switches direction, winding the platform back toward the top of its orbit. "There," Reunne says, and he holds the handle in place, even as it strains to go back down. He hears a clang from above him and feels the platform push back, and he lets go. He looks up, and through the fog of flies he can see Reunne dive for the Spear and grab it, pulling it down and into the muddy nests with her.

And suddenly the insects stop.

They're still there, buzzing and biting, but their intelligence seems to be gone. They take no shapes, and their bites become less strategic, less frequent. Severkin runs over to where Reunne has landed in the mud, the Spear below her. She lies there on her stomach, and for a moment, he thinks she's dead, but when he kneels beside her, she shifts and rolls over, the Spear clutched in her hands. It's not as big as he thought it would be, only the size of both his hands together.

"You all right?" he asks. Elkana runs over and puts up another circle of fire, but this one is weaker, Severkin notices, the flames lower.

"I'm fine," Reunne says.

"Then let's get out of here," Severkin says, and pulls her up out of the clay. They run for the arch, and the flies don't follow when they leave the clay pits.

When they're safely away from the nests, and the buzzing is just in their imagination, not their ears, they stop and catch their breath. Reunne is coated in clay, a paler gray against her blue-gray skin. It covers her armor and hair, too, so she looks like a living statue.

"That was unexpected," Severkin says. "I never thought flies would be such a problem." He looks at his hand, which is bubbling with red spots as if diseased. He wonders if Reunne isn't better off coated in clay.

"I can take care of the bites," Elkana says. "Just give me a moment ta meditate." Severkin nods, and Elkana sits and starts quietly chanting. Severkin and Reunne walk a little way off.

"Can I see it?" Severkin asks. Reunne pulls the Spear out of her bag, where she must have put it as they ran. It looks exactly like the drawing she'd shown him—it even gleams, despite having been stuck in the mud all those years. She hands the Spear to him. It feels cool in his hand, but nothing happens. "I thought, touching it . . . I'd feel that . . . that mind thing Sindry talked about," he says.

"According to records, she had it in her home for a while," Reunne says. "I think it takes a few days to kick in." She pauses, peels some of the clay from her face. "But I can tell you what you're thinking without it."

"Oh?"

"Yeah. You're wondering how you can convince me to let you take it to Rorth, instead of letting me take it to Elega."

Severkin smirks. "Maybe," he says.

"You don't need to convince me," Reunne says. "After to-day . . . that place. I don't think the gray elves are much better, but they have to be better than that."

"Well . . . ," Severkin says. "Yeah. That went easier than I expected."

"Just tell them you grabbed it from the nest—don't say I turned it over to you."

"Are you sure? You could get Rorth to honor you in some way."

Reunne shakes her head. "Your being honored is enough for me. I'm proud of you."

Severkin feels his skin warm at that, and not just from the fly bites. He looks at Reunne, the wrinkles in her face highlighted by the clay she couldn't scrape off, and he wants to say a hundred things, but knows he can't, and instead just says "Thanks."

"All right," Elkana says, coming over. "Line up fer Doctor Elkana's magical disease-ridding cure-all."

Severkin and Reunne look at each other and chuckle, and then Elkana raises her hands and Severkin can feel all the poisons leaving his body like rising steam.

TWENTY-TWO

NICK WAKES up late, his ears still buzzing with the sound of the mud flies. There's no smell of burning food, so he assumes Dad is also sleeping in. Nick's stomach is rumbling, so he gets up to go downstairs for breakfast before turning on the game. As he descends, he makes a list in his head of what he needs to do today, a new item for each step he takes down the carpeted staircase: finish all his homework so he can go to GamesCon tomorrow, play as much of the game as possible so that if there are spoilers he'll be past them already, convince Mom through the game to come home.

In the kitchen, he pours himself water then gets out a bowl for cereal.

"Nick, could you come in here for a sec?" Dad calls from the dining room. Nick finishes pouring the cereal, adds milk to it, then walks into the dining room, eating his breakfast. His father is dressed, clean, and clearly had been lying in wait. He sits at the center of the table, on the long end. Nick sits across from him. There's a plain manila folder on the table in front of Dad. It's as thick as Nick's history textbook. To Dad's right is Mom's old shoebox.

"We need to talk," Dad says. His tone is serious without being angry. Nick's brain races over things he could be in trouble for: the one that leaps to mind is talking to Mom about breaking out. Did Dad overhear it as he got close? Nick eats a spoonful of cereal as calmly as he can, and swallows. "Your mother doesn't want me sharing all this," Dad says, laying hands on the manila folder as though it's a bible. "But . . . I don't think it's fair to you anymore. She's not coming home," he says, and Nick takes another bite of cereal, willing himself not to contradict his father out loud. "So, I think you should know why she's there. But please, don't tell her you know all this, okay?"

Nick nods cautiously. "What are you telling me?"

"I'm going to tell you about your grandfather," Dad says. Nick puts his bowl down on the table, as it's suddenly too cold to keep holding. He doesn't want to eat any more, anyway. He thinks about leaning forward, arms a triangle on the tablecloth, sucking the information out of his father, but finds himself instead leaning back into the formal plank of his dining room chair. Dad reaches into the shoebox and pulls out an old photo of a smiling white guy. The image is all sepia, the background paneled wood. It's Grandpa. Nick takes it and looks at it a moment before putting it down next to his cereal.

"So tell me," Nick says.

Dad shakes his head and snorts, like it's funny. "It doesn't sound like a big thing when you tell the story," he says, and looks up. He has an expression like one Nick sometimes imagines he must have when he looks at his mother's empty chair in the kitchen. "It happened the night the wall fell. She said she was out walking, you remember?"

Nick nods.

"And you know your grandfather was sick—he had Alzheimer's. Early, too. But he was older than your mother is now. Ten years in. Your mom was doing all she could to complete her education and take care of him, and all she wanted was to leave. It was hard for her, Nick. If she did get what she wanted—if she was allowed to leave—she didn't know what would happen to her father. There were some facilities . . . nothing nice. But her father refused to even admit he was sick. People realized, of course. Which meant the government knew. She was terrified that one day she'd get to travel, but when she came back he'd have vanished, having been taken away or just having wandered off.

"But that night had been the worst. Her father had forgotten her. Had woken up from a nap, come into the kitchen, and not known who she was. He didn't know who *he* was, either—he was somewhere else in time, in his mind. Your mother thinks he thought he was a young university student again, and that she was . . . a girl he'd met at a party the night before. He was in his underwear, and he walked up to her—she was reading at the table—and started rubbing her shoulders. Then his hands went lower, and he started . . ." Dad fumbles for words, but Nick knows what he means. The few bites of cereal he had are congealing in his stomach. He looks at the cereal left in his bowl, which is now so soggy that there's not much milk visible. Just glue made of cereal.

"Anyway," Dad continues, "he started groping her. And

when she tried to push him off, tell him who she was, he just laughed. He thought it was a game. He put his arms around her and tried to . . . She fended him off. And she left him there, alone in his underwear. That's what had happened before she was out walking."

Nick stares at the manila envelope and tries to process what his father has told him. It seems like a campfire ghost story. He wonders how many sheets of paper are in the folder. Two hundred? His history textbook has at least three hundred pages, but those pages are slick and thin, more like ink poured into the shapes of words and left to dry than actual paper.

"Do you understand?" Dad asks.

"Mom is afraid of molesting me," Nick says, nodding. It sounds ridiculous out loud.

"Not exactly," Dad begins, but Nick looks up at his father and starts to laugh.

"That's all?" he asks. "Mom is afraid she'll forget who I am and, what, go all cougar on me?" He shakes his head. "That's not going to happen," he says. He looks his father straight in the eye and smiles, because he knows he's about to win with the next question: "Do you think that's going to happen?"

His father is silent, and Nick feels his body swell, a too-full-balloon feeling of triumph.

"This is your mom's file," Dad says instead. "All her tests. All the doctors' reports. I think you should read it."

Nick stares at the folder as Dad pushes it across the table. It's so full, it could pop open any moment and throw pages around the room like hail.

"I have to do my homework," Nick says, feeling his smile

fade. "I won't have time tomorrow, with GamesCon. I'll read it later." He stares at it, halfway between him and his father. A manila dam, holding back a flood. Nick scoots back from the table and laughs again.

"Mom's not going to molest me," he says, taking his bowl. "And we both know it. I'm going to get her out of there."

"Nick, you can't get—"

"Homework," Nick says, and leaves the room before the conversation can start again. It was a whirlpool, that conversation. He and Dad kept circling and circling, going farther down, but nothing ever happened. No one got swallowed up and vanished with a pop, like when you get caught in a whirlpool in the game. That makes so much more sense, Nick thinks. Vanishing with a pop.

TWENTY-THREE

SEVERKIN, ELKANA, and Reunne enter Wellhall through the dwarven passages, the city outlined in torches that roar like hearthfire and light up the underground skyline like fireflies. Their skin is still sticky with clay and sweat, but at least the bites are gone and they don't itch. Severkin feels the weight of the Spear in a bag tied to his belt, but it's a good weight, like a medal—the weight of triumph.

"You sure you don't want to come with us and deliver this to Rorth?" he asks Reunne. "There's going to be a lot of thanks."

Reunne shakes her head. "I'm going to have to explain to Elega how I lost the final piece to you. I'll say it was sly trickery or something like that." She shrugs.

"Oh, aye, play in ta the gray elf stereotypes," Elkana says.

"It will convince her. That's the important part," Reunne says. "Besides, I really want to take a bath." She pulls at more dried flecks of clay on her face. "I'll walk you as far as Bilrost Hall, though."

Dwarves stare at them as they walk past, and for a while, Severkin thinks they must know what he has in his bag, how they're here to save the kingdom. But then he realizes it's not that, it's them. Two gray elves and a troll. People shy away from them, put their hands on the satchels of money they have around their waists, to make sure they're still there. It's like everywhere else he's been, except the overcity. Maybe, he thinks, he can actually make a home in the overcity, where people don't stare. They'll probably give him a mansion with what he's about to do.

At the Hall, Reunne waves them goodbye.

"I'll come get you as soon as we're done," Severkin tells her. "There are some cities we haven't seen yet. You'll come with us, right?"

"Of course," Reunne says, reaching out and rumpling his hair. "We're family."

"Great," Severkin says, throwing a look at Elkana. "So, we'll see you in a bit—maybe you could come up to watch them use the weapon and put the giants to sleep."

"I'll try," Reunne says. "If Elega lets me. I'd better get to see her, though. The quicker I get the being-screamed-at part over with, the quicker I can make it topside."

"See you soon, then," Severkin says. Reunne nods and walks off, heading back to the main square. Severkin and Elkana begin hiking up the stairs to the overcity.

"She said we were family," he says to Elkana.

"Aye, I was there. I heard it," Elkana says with a roll of her eyes. "But she was probably speaking metaphorically, unless you think you're still young enough to be adopted?"

Severkin barks a laugh. "I suppose it depends on how much older she is."

"You're too old to need a mommy."

Severkin shrugs. "I wouldn't know. I never had one."

They walk up the huge stairway slowly, stopping to look at some of the stalls closer to the surface. When they finally make it to the overcity, Elkana suggests a celebratory drink, but Severkin tells her no, not until they've handed over the Spear—then there'll be many celebratory drinks, which Elkana agrees to.

They flash their badges at the guards and go into the main hall, where Rorth is yelling at Izzy, her squirrel ponytail bobbing with repressed laughter.

"Tell that shriveled crone I'd sooner strap fruit bowls to the heads of my soldiers than throw away coin on these flimsy things she's calling helmets."

Elkana bursts out laughing, and Rorth, Ind, Siffon, and Izzy turn, noticing them for the first time. Izzy winks.

"Ah!" Rorth says, beckoning them closer with his hands. "Tell me you have the Spear."

"We have the Spear," Severkin says, taking it out of his satchel. In the light, it gleams a dull pewter. Ind rushes forward and grabs it from Severkin's hands.

"Forget that message," Rorth says to Izzy, a smile rippling over his face. "Tell her we have the Spear and the Staff, and we hope she will bring us the Hammer as quickly as possible so we can put the giants to rest. Quicker than you've ever gone." Rorth waves a hand and Izzy is out the door in a shot.

Ind has been studying the Spear carefully, turning it over in his hands, studying the blade edges.

"Amazing," he says finally. He gives it to Rorth, who studies it for a moment before handing it back.

"It looks like a spearhead to me," he says. "But Ind knows best. He's been studying this."

"It looks just like the diagrams," Ind says, and nods. "Same runes and such. If I may go get the Staff, I'll show you how they fit together."

"Go," Rorth says, and Ind hurries away like a gleeful child. "And now, you," he says to Severkin. "I promised you riches and rewards, did I not?"

"You did," Severkin says, trying not to appear too eager.

"So what would you like?"

"A home, here in the overcity, if there is one," Severkin says. "One where I may keep the relics of my adventures."

"A collector, are you? Very well." He nods at Siffon, who nods back. "And what about you, troll?"

"Well, ta call me by my name would be a nice start," Elkana says, causing Rorth's eyebrows to raise. "But, aside from that, I'd appreciate access. Throughout the kingdom. Not just ta be able ta study at the Tower, but also ta investigate the various closed-off locations where magical tombs are hidden, and of course, all the libraries."

"Easy to grant, Mistress Elkana," Rorth says. "And both of you shall be paid in gold, as well. Siffon will work out the details."

"Siffon will pass it along to someone whose job it is to work out the details," Siffon corrects.

Ind comes running back in, the Staff in one hand, the Spear in the other. He presents them both to Rorth, who nods. Ind then puts the two together. The Staff slips into the Spear, forming what looks to Severkin like an oversize arrow with no feathers.

"Odd," Ind says. "I thought there would be glowing . . . or something to affirm I'd done it right."

"Is there a chance you've done it wrong?" Rorth asks.

Ind shakes his head. "No, it's all in the diagrams. First the Staff into the Spear and then the Spear into the Hammer—it will give way to the point. Then one simply places both hands on it and thinks what they want the giants to do, and it is done. If Your Majesty places your hands upon it and thinks only that he wishes the giants to sleep for eternity, then . . . they should. Or for at least another thousand years."

Suddenly the doors to the hall burst open. Izzy comes back in, sweating and red faced.

"That was fast, even for you, Izzy."

"She's coming," Izzy says, then bends over, gasping for air. "She's coming here now."

"Ah," Rorth says, smirking. "Let's prepare, then. Ind, set that thing on a fancy pillow or something. And get the diagrams so we can show her we're ready for her contribution to our saving the world."

Severkin and Elkana find a place to the side, out of sight, as the court busies itself to receive the dwarven guard captain. Tables and chairs are brought out, guards put in place. Siffon goes over a few files with Rorth. When the door swings open and a guard announces Elega, everyone is already at ease.

Except Elega. She is clearly annoyed with having to come here, and her gray face is lavender with frustration and possibly exertion, from the steps she had to walk up. She's thrown on a long purple cloak that trails on the ground. As she walks into the hall she notices Severkin and glares at him. She's accompanied by two other dwarves, both as old as she is, one with glasses, the other with an axe.

"So you got the Spear," she says, hopping into the chair prepared for her. "Bully for you. I have the Hammer. Can we get this over with?"

"Elega," Rorth says, sweeping down from his throne, his armor like melting gold. "I am honored to have you in my humble court."

"I'm sure," Elega says in a tone that makes it clear she doesn't believe him and also doesn't care. "And I'm honored to be here. But can we please put the giants to sleep? Up here you just see the ones that make it aboveground, that are already fully awake and fighting. I have colonies built into what we thought was stable rock that becomes unstable as the giants shift and start to wake. Every moment, I could be losing citizens."

"Of course," Rorth says, looking slightly ashamed. "Ind?"

Ind comes forward with the Staff and Spear on a pillow, which he lays on the table in front of Elega. Elega takes the Hammer—a sphere of metal—from a pouch at her side and puts it down. "Now, sire," Ind says. "You take the Spear and plunge it into the Hammer. It will open itself." Rorth takes the Spear and lifts it over the Hammer.

"Don't try any of your gray-elf trickery with me, Rorth," Elega says. Rorth nods and plunges the Spear down.

It skids off the sphere of the Hammer and instead buries itself in the wooden table. Everyone is silent, and the sound of the Spear vibrating in the wood seems to fill the Hall.

"You must have done it wrong," Ind says. "Sire," he adds quickly.

Rorth shakes his head and pulls the Spear from the table

and tries driving it into the Hammer again, but more slowly. Again, the Hammer doesn't open.

"Let me try," Elega snorts. Rorth ignores her and tries again, but again nothing happens except for the scratching sound of metal sliding on metal. Elega grabs the spear from Rorth and slowly pushes it down into the Hammer. It slides off again.

"Something is wrong," she says. She motions to her attendant without the axe, and he comes over and takes the Spear from her. He turns it over in his hands and stares at it, then closes his eyes and mumbles something.

"This isn't the Spear," he says. "Or the Staff." Everyone is silent. He stares at the Hammer on the table. "And that's not the Hammer. They're cunning replacements, but the magic from them is . . . just an illusion. Magic to make something look magical. Cheap spells anyone could do." Severkin feels the eyes in the room shift toward him, and he feels his armor grow warm.

"We didn't know," he says. "We didn't even know what they looked like until we found them. And neither of us was there when they found the Hammer." He can hear his voice growing higher as he says this. There are no easy exits. The windows are all several feet off the ground, and then he's not sure he could bring Elkana with him.

"That's true," Siffon says. "We were careful not to give him descriptions of the items, as we weren't sure if he was trustworthy."

"Is this some trick?" Rorth demands, turning on Elega. "Did you conspire with him and that other gray elf who brought these things back?"

"I told you, I want the giants asleep more than you do. If I had the artifacts, I would just use them! This is no trick."

"Severkin," Siffon says, advancing toward him. "How did you know what the Staff was?"

"The necromancer who had it—she was using it to control a dead giant. I inferred," Severkin says, crossing his arms.

"Although," Elkana adds, "it was Reunne who picked it up and said it was the Staff." Severkin glares at Elkana, who won't meet his gaze.

"And how did you know what the Spear was?" Rorth asks.

"Reunne had drawn it before . . . ," Severkin confesses. He can see what's happening. He's not sure how to fight it, though.

"They look just like in the diagrams," Ind says. "He brought the right things back! We're just not using them correctly."

The room is silent a moment, and Elega sighs.

"Reunne," she says.

"What?" Rorth asks.

"The gray elf I sent to retrieve the objects . . . Her family is descended from the original makers of them. She probably knew what they looked like before she found them."

"So?" Severkin asks.

"I thought it made sense," Elega says. "And I like Reunne—she's very winning. Observant, manipulative, clever."

"Trustworthy?" Siffon asks.

Elega shrugs. "Is anybody in this damned city trustworthy?"

"So you think she replaced all the objects with fakes?" Rorth asks. "To what end?"

"I don't know," Elega says, shaking her head. The wrinkles in her face seem to slide downward as she frowns.

"No," Severkin says. "It can't be Reunne. Someone must have gotten to all the artifacts first—a long time ago. Replaced them with fakes."

"Except that Helena was using the Staff," Elkana says softly. "It worked then." Severkin turns on Elkana, who still won't meet his gaze. From the corner of his eye, he sees Elega whisper something in the ear of her attendant holding the axe. He quietly leaves.

"But . . . ," Severkin says. He doesn't know how to finish the sentence.

"I'm sorry," Elkana says, laying a hand on his shoulder. "I know ye came ta think of her as family."

"She's being framed," Severkin says in a voice only Elkana can hear. "I don't know how, but this is a setup. I'll go find her. I'm sure she'll have some insight into how this happened. I bet it was Efem, somehow, something to do with her father."

"She's probably long gone by now," Elega says to Rorth. "But we'll find her. You can look, too, if you wish. In the meantime, I'm going back to the undercity. We'll have to look into new ways of stopping the giants."

"This is your fault, Elega," Rorth says, pointing a golden-armored finger at her.

"Maybe so," Elega says, her head nodding up and down. "But I'll fix it."

Rorth begins yelling at her, and Elega stands there taking it, but Severkin doesn't pay attention to what they're saying.

"I need to go find her," he says to Elkana.

"I'll come," Elkana says.

They head for the exit, where Siffon stops him with a light touch on the shoulder.

"If you find her, and she has them, bring them to us. We'll give you both everything we promised," she says. Severkin nods.

They walk back through the city quickly, and down the hall stairs. They pass the dwarf with the axe, whom Severkin smiles at. They'll find Reunne first. They'll ask her what's going on. Nothing beyond that will happen until they've talked. There must be an explanation.

Severkin and Elkana are silent as they run down the steps, careful not to slip on the spiraling rainbow. In the undercity, Severkin heads to where he remembers Reunne's house being. The city is a maze, and dwarves cross the streets to avoid them, but he relies on his instincts, and he knows he's close when he starts seeing other gray elves, their heads down, their eyes on the ground. Shadows pulse around them, some with dwarves in them, others just alive with their own darkness. It takes a while, but he finds the house again, the courtyard with the fountain.

He pulls the gate open quietly and stands in the courtyard, listening to the water splashing like a hundred whispers in the dark. Then he goes forward and knocks on the door. There's no answer.

"Should we wait?" Severkin asks Elkana. She raises her eyebrows at him.

"Pick the lock," she says. "If ye want to prove she's innocent, then ye pick the lock and find the evidence."

Severkin nods, then quickly picks the lock and opens the door. Inside, the fire is roaring, the air smells of incense.

"Reunne?" he calls out. There's no answer.

"She was just here, if she's gone," Elkana says. They search the house—upstairs and down, where the memory wall is. There's no sign of her. "Do that thing ye do," Elkana tells Severkin. "Where you find clues. Maybe ye'll find out where she went."

Severkin nods and closes his eyes. When he opens them again, the house is different. He looks upstairs and down and notices things he didn't see before; on the memory wall, there are carvings of a snake cut in two, and a hawk, broken-winged. He finds old journals about the creation of the Hammer, Staff, and Spear and how to use them. And in the room downstairs, next to the memory wall, he finds an incense burner, cold, with fingerprints on it. He pulls it down.

The memory wall swings back, revealing a wide chamber beyond. In the center of the chamber stands Reunne, waiting. On a stone table behind her are the Spear, the Staff, and the Hammer, already assembled, forming an orb with a crown.

"I was just deciding what to do with the giants when I heard you call my name," she says. Her voice is different—smoother, less like the wrinkled-paper sound of an older woman and more like scented oil. "So what do you think I should do? Destroy the dwarves first? Or the elves?"

"Neither," Elkana says. Severkin nods.

"Why not just put the giants to sleep, like we wanted?" Severkin asks. "Wasn't that the plan?"

"Oh, that's their plan," Reunne says, walking toward them. "Rorth and Elega. Gray elves and dwarves. I had a different plan. Get rid of them all." She's close to them now, and Severkin can see Elkana taking a defensive pose, her hands lighting up. But Severkin can't believe it.

"Why?" Severkin asks.

"Really?" Reunne asks. "You've walked down here. You've seen the way dwarves stare at us—can you be so shocked I want them gone? And the gray elves above . . . Well, maybe they're kind to you. But not to us undercity elves. We're called traitors, glared at and avoided as much as we are in the undercity."

"So . . . you'll kill them?" Severkin asks.

"Yes," Reunne says. "Destroy Wellhall. Start from scratch. No old prejudices. And I'll be leading the charge. After I stop the giants."

"After ye use them ta destroy Wellhall," Elkana says. "Very nice."

Reunne shrugs. She's standing right in front of Severkin now, and he feels cold, frozen. He knows he should be angry, but he feels the opposite of that. Or something so far away from anger that there's no comparison. It's separation. Out-of-body. And then he feels the knife go into his gut. He clutches his stomach and looks down, watching with wonder as his hands turn red with something like spilled watercolor.

"Mother," he says.

"Mother?" Reunne says. "That whole family bit usually works on you outlander orphans, but you really took it to a new level. Mother," she laughs. Her laugh is strangely beautiful, which Severkin knows is an odd thing to think at this moment. It echoes and separates, like a duet. There's a low rumble to it, like drums, and then a higher melody, like a flute. And then the laugh ends with a crackle as Elkana hurls lightning at Reunne. Severkin stumbles backward, watching Reunne easily dodge Elkana's magic.

Severkin takes out his swords and feels them like hot coals

in his hands. This is really happening. She just stabbed him. He has to kill her.

Reunne has her spear out already, though, and has leapt across the room, planting it firmly in Elkana's side, so Elkana collapses in a heap. Then she turns on Severkin, a smile on her face. Behind her, Elkana is struggling to get up, her hands blazing. Reunne leaps at Severkin, but he throws his swords up, blocking her spear.

"You kept some swords from Helena's trinket collection, did you?" Reunne asks. "Naughty boy. Mother is going to have to punish you." Reunne kicks out, their weapons still locked, and Severkin tries to spin out of the way, but the wound in his side flares with pain and he falters backward. Reunne kicks out at him and he falls to the ground. Behind Reunne, Elkana is standing again, using her staff like a cane, and she throws fire at Reunne, hitting her in the back. Reunne cries out, her voice a tear of thunder, then turns on Elkana and, with a wide swing from her spear, decapitates her.

Severkin stands, his body aching, and lifts his swords up, ready to charge Reunne. Reunne smiles. The air smells of burning skin and cloying incense. Reunne charges, and Severkin charges, too, but just as he sees an opening and stabs for Reunne's chest, she leaps over him and lands behind him. He starts to spin, but he can feel the spear tip go into his body, cutting through muscle and ribs like they were cheap plaster. The blade tip emerges from his chest, slightly off-center, red-slicked. He stares down at it and feels the swords drop from his hands.

Reunne pulls the spear out, and Severkin collapses. She doesn't even say anything, just walks back toward the stone table with the artifacts as Severkin's vision fades to black. It's a peculiar sensation, dying. The pouring out of blood from pierced organs. Like deflating. Like melting. He can't see Reunne anymore, but he can sense her body at the table, leaning over the objects. The last thing he hears is her humming something—a familiar folk melody. He tries to remember where else he's heard it, but can't, and then he dies.

TWENTY-FOUR

NICK IS distracted from the GAME OVER screen by the buzzing of his phone on his bed. He blinks, for what may be the first time in an hour or maybe just a few seconds. He's not sure how long it's been since Severkin died. He turns around and picks up his phone. He has a text message from Nat.

U ok?

Yes

he texts back. "Okay" is actually fairly accurate. Not good, not bad. Not really anything. He feels as though he should be experiencing the prick of ragebrew—should be hurling his game console out the window and crying, but instead, he feels okay. Rubbery. Plastic. Dense and unfeeling. Okay.

Want 2 tlk?

Nat texts.

No

Nick stares at his phone and gets up. He goes to his desk, where his homework is set up, waiting to be completed. He thinks of the hard facts within them, and the hard facts that have been surrounding him for so long without his seeing them, like ice, or bricks, being stacked one by one, closing in like an igloo, and he's never even realized.

Still on for gamescon tmrw right?

Nat asks.

Yes

Nick texts.

Excited 4 it!

he adds as an afterthought. And he is. Somewhere in the back of him, he is. But now he's okay, and he's going to do his homework.

When he finishes, the sun is three-quarters of the way down the horizon. His stomach rumbles, which is odd, because he doesn't feel hungry. But he knows he should eat. So he goes downstairs. Dad is at the stove. He's making grilled cheese, butter on both sides, and it's not even burned. He slips the sandwich off the frying pan and onto a plate. He picks it up and turns to see Nick, and Nick sees for the first time that his father has been giving him PityFace for months, maybe years, maybe his whole life.

"You want this one?" Dad asks. Nick nods. He sits down at the kitchen table and eats the sandwich while his father makes another. "I used to make these in college. I thought I would have forgotten how, but I still got it. First thing I ever made for your mother."

"It's good," Nick says. He can tell his voice is toneless, robotic, but he's not entirely sure how to fix it.

Dad sits down opposite him and takes a bite of his grilled cheese. "You okay?" he asks. Nick is tired of people asking him that. "I mean, I know you're not. But I guess what I'm asking is if you've started to process what I told you this morning?"

You told me Mom has early-onset Alzheimer's, Nick thinks. The same thing you've been telling me for over a year. "Yeah," Nick says.

"Do you want to go over her file? I can just talk you through it, if you want."

Nick shakes his head. "I don't need that," he says. "I get it."

"All right," Dad says. "Want a Coke or something?"

"Yeah," Nick says. Dad pours him a glass and sets it down in front of him. Nick takes a long sip. The bubbles are ice-cold and stab at his throat in a way he likes. Dad eats his grilled cheese silently. "Did you know?" Nick asks.

"Know what?" Dad says through his chewing.

"When you married her. When you had me. Did you know what would happen to Mom?"

Dad puts his sandwich down and swallows. "I knew it was a possibility, yes. Your mom told me."

Nick is silent. He stares down at his own grilled cheese, with two bites taken out of it, and lifts it to his mouth again. "That was really unfair of you," he says. His voice is still toneless. "To have a kid anyway." He takes a bite. For a while, all he can hear is his own chewing and the fizz of the Coke in his glass, like something breaking.

"You're right," Dad says after a while. "It was. But I'm not sorry."

The soda-fizz sound grows louder for a moment, and Nick looks at his glass, at the beige fuzz on the surface. "Me neither," he says.

Dad stands and runs his hand over Nick's head like Mom does, then gets himself out a beer and opens it.

"How did Grandpa die?" Nick asks, and starts to eat his sandwich again. His fingers feel more alive now, and the smell of the cheese suddenly hits him and makes his mouth water.

His father leans back against the counter and takes a long drink of his beer. "I don't really know," he says. "Your mom wouldn't talk about it, and I never pushed. I just know that he died sometime soon after . . . what I told you about. And then she left."

"Was she scared? When Grandpa got sick?"

Dad nods. "Yeah. Are you scared? 'Cause I'm terrified."

Nick nods. His sandwich is finished, so he drinks the rest of his Coke.

"Can we watch a movie?" Nick asks.

"Sure," Dad says. "What do you want?"

"You pick," Nick says, standing up. "But not a documentary. I have to go text Nat about tomorrow."

"Okay," Dad says. Nick goes upstairs and picks up his phone. He types out the text message and whispers it aloud when it's done. Then he takes a deep breath and hits Send, then runs back downstairs to watch a movie with Dad.

Reunne killed us. Reunne is not my mom. My mom has Alzheimer's.

. . .

Nick doesn't sleep well. He has the nightmare again, but there's no Reunne tearing off a Mom mask this time. His classmates and teachers just laugh, and then they stop, and Nick feels that dread in his stomach again, the heavy, unbalancing sensation of something being wrong with the world, like there's an earthquake going on that no one else seems to notice. He wakes up in the middle of the night badly needing to pee and then can't get back to sleep for what seems like hours. His room's not that warm, but his body feels damp with some sort of heat, and the sheets stick to him like webbed fingers.

When his alarm goes off, he's not sure if he ever made it back to sleep or if he just closed his eyes and went brainless for hours. His eyes feel hot.

He rolls out of bed and takes a long, cool shower, hoping to wake himself up, and it helps a little. Downstairs, Dad is drinking coffee, and Nick pours himself a cup, even though he doesn't like it, and then pours as much sugar into it as he can before Dad gives him a disapproving look.

"I didn't sleep great," Nick says, sitting down. "I want to be awake for the GamesCon today."

"Sorry you didn't sleep well," Dad says, frowning. "Was it because of what we talked about?"

Nick shrugs and drinks the coffee. It tastes like hot ice cream.

"You should eat something, too, or else Jenny will think I'm a bad dad. Maybe some toast?"

"I'll make it," Nick says, and finds some bread in the fridge and puts it in the toaster. He watches the toaster, afraid that if he ignores it, he might burn something. Then Dad reads the paper and Nick quickly finishes his coffee and toast, staring out the window, willing Nat and Jenny to show up. He wants to throw himself into GamesCon. He wants to forget about Mom, just for a day, and focus on the game and the things he loves. And maybe seeing the game laid out, dissected by its creators, will make him realize how stupid he was to hope it was more than just a game.

A blue station wagon pulls up and honks once, and Nick stands so quickly his chair skids back.

Dad laughs. "You have everything you need? You want some cash?" he asks.

Nick shrugs, not willing to turn down money but too proud to actually ask for it.

Dad hands him a few twenties. "I'll walk out with you."

At the car, Nat opens a door in the back for him and Nick hops in while Dad and Jenny talk through the window.

"You okay?" Nat asks.

Nick nods without looking at her. "I really want to have a good time today."

"Okay," Nat says brightly. "Let's do that, then."

"Bye, Nicky!" Dad calls, waving through the window. Nick waves back, and then Jenny pulls away.

"Thank you so much for this," Nick says to Jenny and Nat.

"My pleasure," Jenny says. "Just no getting in trouble. Don't want to upset your dad. Sounds like you two have enough on your plate as is."

Nick takes a deep breath. He doesn't want to talk about it.

"So I have a map," Nat says, pulling out a floor plan. "It says what booths are where, and this list says what events will happen when."

Jenny drives to the train station, and they take the train into New York. Nick has been here before, for Dad's lectures, for trips, for lots of stuff, and so, apparently, has Nat, since they both know the way to the subway from the train, even when Jenny forgets it. They all take the subway across town, and then they get out and Nat leads them on a long walk to the edge of the island. The whole time, Nick and Nat plan their day. Nick knows it's not going to be E3—he's not old enough for that—but from the booths and events, it looks like it's going to be even better than he thought.

It's happening in a big convention center next to the river, two stories, high ceilings. They show their tickets and get laminated badges on lanyards to wear around their necks. Outside, people are milling around handing out leaflets, dressed in costume. Some people don't even seem to be affiliated with the convention—they must have just seen other people wearing costumes and run home to put on their own, happy to have found a place to wear them. There are superheroes and villains, robots, people from every video game Nick has played and from hundreds he hasn't.

"This is so cool," Nat says once they're inside. There are fewer costumes here, but more people.

"Don't let me lose sight of you," Jenny says. "If we get separated, text me right away."

"Okay, Mom," Nat says, and runs into the crowd. Nick chases after her. "First," she says, "we wanted to see the demo for the new Wellhall DLC. That'll be over there." She points just as Jenny catches up, then leads them across the arena that is the convention center. Nat ducks and weaves through the swells of people, like a huge ocean. People of all ages, in costume or not, are staring at the bright lights and TV monitors showing off games all around them. They go through a section devoted to farming games, where giant cow statues wink at them, and then past a sci-fi racer area, where the sound of hover-thrusters powering up is so loud Nick has to cover his ears. With his ears muffled, the sound effects and noise of the crowd fade to a series of murmurs and pulses, like the sound of rushing blood and a beating heart. He pushes through the crowd, trying to keep Nat in sight, and for a moment the world slows, and the thought comes to him that he can't wait to tell his mother about this. And then the thought comes to him that there would be no point.

He shakes his head, takes his hands off his ears so that the boom of the sound effects can sonically disintegrate his thoughts. When he looks up, he thinks for a second that he's lost Nat in the crowd, but she emerges from between two tall men like curtains and grabs his hand, pulling him after her, and she's smiling so widely that he can forget—and not worry about what forgetting means.

They find the line for the Wellhall DLC demo, and Jenny catches up to them, shaking her head at her daughter, who shrugs apologetically. As they wait in line, they can see the people ahead of them playing the game on the big screen, so big the characters are larger than life, the swords and arrows that fly around violently oversize. The demo of the DLC has them hacking through a jungle on an island south of Wellhall. The dwarves here have been separated from their kin for so long that they've developed their own language and have an entirely different culture, where their ancestors are depicted as roots and mushrooms and worshipped as gods. Nick and Nat play for a while, but they have to use pre-generated characters made to show off the demo, and without Severkin and Elkana, it's just not the same. Still, the change from the mountains and caves of Wellhall is a good one, and Nick is excited to explore it further when it's finally released. They're only allowed ten minutes of play time, though. Then it's the next person's turn.

Nick and Nat leave the demo booth and wander over to where Jenny is leaning against a wall, reading a book with apples on the cover.

"So where to next?" Nat asks, taking out her map again. "I think maybe the presentation of the new Farmland game?" She bites her lower lip. "Don't laugh, but I really like them. The cows are so cute."

Nick tries hard not to laugh but fails. "We can go see it, sure," he says.

They find the hall the presentation will take place in, and there's a big line in. The doors haven't opened yet. Jenny stands with them, still reading her book, and Nat starts talking to Nick in a soft voice.

"So . . . do you want to talk about last night? Reunne?"

Nick shrugs, and memories come flooding back. Mom is sick; he was crazy to think she was in the game. Probably should check all the check boxes for himself. Mom might forget him altogether, and then at some point, he might forget himself.

"I . . . ," he says. The people in front of them are in

costumes—giant overalls with big shiny yellow buttons and hats that look like cow heads, googly-eyed and ridiculous. But they look happy. "My mom is sick," he says, looking down. The people in front of them are wearing shoes made to look like cow hooves. "I should have accepted that . . . but instead I came up with a whole other story. I'm crazy, like she is."

"It's not crazy to want your mom to be well," Nat says softly. "And it's not even crazy to get so caught up in imagining a world where she's okay that you start to think it's real. I did that all the time. I lied to people. I told them my dad was off on a business trip instead of in rehab, even though everybody knew. I told them he'd gotten a new job, that he was buying me presents. . . . I invented this entire story. This alternate universe where my dad wasn't sick—he was a total *mensch* and everything was great." She turns away from Nick and looks at a cow-hatted person. "I like that hat," she says. She turns back to Nick. "You just invented a better story. You mixed it up with the story of Wellhall. Way cooler than mine, where he was going to bring me back snow globes from his business trips."

"Snow globes?" Nick asks.

Nat is staring at the ground. She shrugs. "I don't even like snow globes," she says. "I think I had one once, but I broke it. But it seemed like something a good dad would do. Your version of a mom who wasn't sick fought giants. Way cooler than snow globes."

"Yeah," Nick says, and laughs a little. What he doesn't say, what he thinks would probably be mean to say, is that Nat's dad always had the possibility of getting better. Mom doesn't.

"So, you okay?" Nat asks, looking up at him. Her freckles are like seeds.

"Not really," Nick says. He doesn't want to lie right now. "I'm losing my mom. But I'm . . . figuring it out."

"Well," Nat says, her voice more cheerful, "that's something." She reaches out and lays a hand on Nick's arm and then immediately drops it when Jenny glances up from her book and tries to pretend she didn't notice.

The presentation of the new Farmland game is so cute, Nick feels a little ridiculous being in the audience, but Nat seems to really love it, her feet tapping on the ground every time a new giant-eyed animal is revealed onscreen. Nick tries to pay attention, but he finds himself with his eyes glazed over and suddenly remembering something his mother once told him about ancient Egyptian or modern Japanese culture. Sometimes he looks up very quickly, thinking an image on the screen is his mother, or Reunne, but it's always just a farmer taking care of the large-headed animals. He wonders if he should feel sadder. He thinks he should. But somehow it's as though the sadness is all just outside him, and he's in a small green bubble, curled and fetal, and the sadness is dripping into the bubble through a small hole at the top, like red tears. He absorbs one tear, and then another falls. A small, ever-present sadness, like walking in wet socks.

He doesn't know if it would be better to feel all the sadness at once in a great flood. He doesn't know if he'd survive that. Which might be why the bubble formed in the first place, and he just lies in it, listening to the *drip-drip-drip,* like a leaky faucet that can never be fixed.

When the Farmland presentation is over, the organizers invite people to the booth down the hall to play the demo. Nick and Nat wait in line, planning the rest of the things they want to see, and when Nat gets to the front of the line to play,

Nick goes around to the front of the booth and buys a cow hat for five dollars and puts it on Nat's head while she's playing. She laughs, and Nick realizes that the good thing about the bubble is that it's not just sadness in there. There are other things, too.

They run around the rest of the Con, playing demos of games they haven't heard of that look cool on the giant over-head screens. They take photos of people in costume. At one point, they spot a man dressed like Rorth, and they ask if they can have their picture taken with him. He says "Sure," and Nat hands her phone to her mom, and they pose for the photo on either side of Rorth, looking as much like Severkin and Elkana as they can without makeup. It's not a bad photo, even if Nat forgot to take her cow hat off. Nat emails the photo to Nick right away, and then it's time for the Wellhall Creator Panel.

The line to get into it is long by the time they get there, which is forty minutes before it starts. They look at each other anxiously, both afraid to voice the possibility that they might not get in. The line is filled with people dressed like they come from the world of Wellhall. Trolls and orcs, elves of all kinds. One woman even looks like Reunne, and Nick can't stop staring at her, until he notices she has a huge sword instead of a spear.

When the doors open, the line instantly starts pushing forward, and Nick and Nat push with it. Luckily, the auditorium is huge, and they get seats—to the side and in the middle, but decent seats in what quickly becomes a completely full auditorium. The presentation starts twenty minutes later than it's supposed to, but eventually a blogger from a games magazine gets up to the podium and starts introducing the makers of

Wellhall: the producers, designer, lead writer, and art director. Nick is disappointed by how regular they look. Just guys in polo shirts and jeans, thinning hairlines, glasses. The lead writer isn't white, and one of the producers is a woman, but the other three could practically be clones with different hair colors and waist sizes. Still, they created Wellhall, a world so real that Nick thought it *was*. . . . He hears a *drip* in his mind as another splash of sadness fills his bubble. He focuses all his attention on the people on stage.

There's a lot of applause, and then the blogger starts asking them questions. The first one is about where the ideas came from, and the first thing one of the producers says is "East Berlin." Nick feels Nat's hand clamp down on his knee. She's worried for him, but actually, he feels relieved. There was a reason he saw it all in the game. It *was* in the game. It just wasn't Mom.

"We started out thinking about divided cities," the producer says, his hand cycling in front of him. "Because we knew that was what we wanted. It was time to bring dwarves back. We knew we couldn't have a game in Wellhall without dwarves, not after all the history we'd built up. So the dwarves are allies now, but shaky ones. And they live in the same city. Where else was like that? Berlin. It was the obvious one. There were others, too, of course. Beirut, Frankfurt, Padang Besar, even Rome and Vatican City. We ended up using all of them, but Berlin—maybe because there was more recorded history to pull from—ended up being the focal point. That's where we started with Wellhall. Plus, it's in Germany, where they have all these great myths with elves and dwarves already. So we brought in giants, too."

"Actually, it ended up being more Norse than Germanic, in that respect," the lead writer says, pushing up his glasses. "There's a lot of crossover, but Germanic mythology is so varied, it was hard to pull from."

"Right," the producer says. "So Berlin is Wellhall, and then the other cities, since they're also divided, sort of, they're other cities. Like, Ariav is like Rome."

"We blended a lot," the writer says. "But Berlin was definitely our main inspiration. Right around and after the fall of the Berlin Wall. All that tension, all that spying. We wanted this game to feel more like a spy thriller in many ways, with betrayals and double agents and all that."

"Visually," the female producer says, "we went to Berlin, too."

"Yes," the art director says, as if surprised to be onstage. "We have some pictures, actually . . . if this works. . . . Can you dim the lights?" The lights on the audience dim slightly, and the wall behind the game designers lights up with a black-and-white photo. It shows crowds of young people marching through a street. "I was really inspired by the images of the Berlin Wall falling, and also by the graffiti on the wall itself." He flips through more photos, some showing graffiti, some showing people waiting in line. "I like their eyes," he says. "The way they're both defiant and nervous, looking around like they're going to be shot at any moment." He flips to another photo. This one shows a bunch of people waiting in front of a gate. A young woman stares directly at the camera. Nick feels his body suck in air and hold it. The woman is his mother. "This is the night the wall fell. People lined up to leave, but then they came back. They just wanted to see what was on the other side. That's how we thought of the stairs, too—almost touristy." The photo changes. It's a poorly lit street. "And the shadows. Oh, we loved the shadows. We have this one guy who just did shadows in the undercity. He's amazing. That's why the shadows down there feel so alive."

There's more applause, but Nick is wondering if his body will exhale in the next few seconds, because he thinks he might be drowning in the recycled air of the auditorium. Nat looks at him and squeezes his knee. He exhales.

"That was my mom," he whispers. The blogger asks about dwarves, and some of the audience boo.

"Are you sure?" Nat asks.

Nick nods. "She was in line to leave," he says. And remembering what his father said about what his grandfather had done that night, he doesn't blame her.

"You okay?" Nat asks.

Nick nods and blinks away the wetness in his eyes. "Just shocked," he says.

He wonders if she left for good that night. He wonders if he can ask her. It wouldn't be so hard to just run away. Never go back to a father who couldn't remember you. Maybe that's what she's doing now—running away so Nick doesn't have to.

That's why Dad didn't know what happened to Grandpa, why Mom wouldn't talk about it. And now she's put herself away not because she's afraid for herself, but because she's afraid that one day Nick might do what she did and walk away, and then he'd have to live with the guilt she has now. Maybe. He isn't sure. Maybe he could ask her.

He turns his focus back to the stage, where the director is

talking about the new technology they used, a program design they called Omni, where every aspect of the same story was changed by simple decisions.

"Like the main quest," he says, leaning into his mike. "That thing can go literally thirty-two different ways depending on where you come into it, what NPCs you meet. And it all has to do with decisions you make before it even starts, like your race, and where you get the quest. A lot of people end up adventuring with Siffon, but some people have to do the maze quest with Rel, and some people have to fight Helena with Reunne."

"Spoilers!" the blogger says, and everyone laughs.

"Yeah, yeah," the director says. "The point is, there's, like, infinite replay. Almost all the quests will be totally different the next time around if you make different choices."

"Just like real life," the writer says, and the audience applauds loudly.

• • •

The panel goes on for about two hours, total. They talk about storylines, forthcoming DLC, and advantages of playing as a dwarf, and they show off concept art and design models. It's amazing. For Nick, the shock of seeing his mother fades for the rest of the presentation. Instead, he absorbs the room, the people onstage who created this world and the people in the audience who live in it. People like him.

Afterward, the blogger tells everyone to get in line and come up onstage to get autographs and shake hands with the designers and stuff, and Nick and Nat get in line.

"That was awesome," Nat says.

Nick nods.

"It's like meeting God," she says.

Nick doesn't answer.

"I think I want to design games," Nat says. "You think I'd be good at it?"

"I think you'd be great at it." Nick nods. "Elkana is like a story herself."

"Thanks."

"I want to see that photo again," Nick says. "Think they'll show it to me, if I tell them it's my mom?"

Nat shrugs. "You can ask," she says, her voice rising in a slow question.

When they get up onstage, Nick asks them all to sign his game case, and they do, but when he gets to the art director, Nick asks where he got the photo.

"Which one?" the art director asks.

"It was a young woman, standing in line the night the wall fell," Nick says.

"Ah," he says, pulling out a tablet and flipping through pictures. "History buff?"

Nick shakes his head. "I think the woman is my mom."

The art director looks up at him, his expression unbelieving.

"She was there," Nick says. "When the wall fell."

The art director smirks, looks around like he's being punked.

"My dad is black," Nick says. "My mom is white. German. East German."

The man looks back at Nick and nods, slowly, starting to believe.

"Is this the photo?" he asks, holding it up.

Nick looks at it. His mother, not much older than him, stares back. The lines around her face are gone, her hair is longer, but it's obviously her. Nick nods.

The art director looks at the photo and then back at Nick. "Yeah, actually, I can see it. That's so wild. Is she here?"

"No," Nick says. "She's . . ." He takes a breath. "She's sick. I actually thought that . . ." He stops himself. This guy doesn't need to know what he thought about Reunne, doesn't need to know his story. "She's sick," he says.

"I'm sorry, man," the art director says. "I hope she gets better."

"Thanks," Nick says. "Any chance I could have a copy of that photo?"

"Sure," the man says. "Give me your email and I'll have someone send it off to you. And, hey, here." He reaches behind him into a big cardboard box. "Have a T-shirt."

"Wow, thanks," Nick says, taking the shirt. It's black and has both the hawk and snake symbols from Wellhall on it.

"I hope your mom gets better."

• • •

Nick holds his T-shirt up for Nat as he walks down the stage stairs after everyone has signed his game case.

"Cool!" she says.

"It's a pity present," Nick says softly. "I told him my mom was sick." He giggles. "He told me he hopes she gets better." He laughs aloud now, but Nat looks concerned, so he makes himself stop. They walk toward the exit. "I think you should have it," he says.

"That's okay," Nat says.

"No, I want you to have it as a thank-you," Nick says. "For taking me."

"Are you sure?" Nat asks.

"Absolutely," Nick says, and hands her the balled-up cotton. He smiles to himself and tries not to laugh again.

There's not much else to do, but they look around at the other booths and take photos with people in costumes until Jenny says it's time to go. They take the subway and the train back to Two Rivers, looking at photos from the event, replaying it, reciting all the small details so they don't forget them. Nick hugs Nat and Jenny and thanks them again.

"It was a really great day," he says, and he means it. "I'll see you on the game in a few hours."

At home, before he tells Dad about the day, he goes upstairs to his computer. The wallpaper is still the checklist. He stares at the little boxes and the ironed-out words describing symptoms he's never really understood. Then he goes to his email and downloads the photos from the day that Nat sent him, and the one the art director sent him, of Mom. He makes the photo of him and Nat in the cow hat and the guy who looked like Rorth his new desktop. Then he prints out the photo of Mom and goes downstairs to show Dad.

TWENTY-FIVE

SEVERKIN PULLS the gate open quietly and stands in the courtyard, listening to the water splashing like a hundred whispers in the dark.

"Come on," he says to Elkana. He kneels down to pick the lock—in six seconds, a tie for his personal best—then quietly pushes the door open. They creep into the house, but it's silent. Severkin doesn't need to search. He knows instinctively where Reunne is.

They walk downstairs and approach the memory wall. Elkana reaches up and starts tugging at the incense burners, but nothing happens. She shrugs at Severkin. Severkin examines the wall, traces the lines of history with his eyes, looks up to the name Grayfather at the top and at Reunne's name at the bottom, linked by name after name after name, like a long chain.

Then, with all his might, he kicks the wall. It shakes under his foot, and gravel and sand spill down it in a momentary waterfall. He can taste the stale dirt as it enters the air.

"Now she knows we're here," Elkana says, drawing her spear.

"I don't care," Severkin says, and kicks the wall again. A crack splinters up and down it from where his foot has struck. Small pieces crumble off the surface of the wall, leaving triangles of clean stone behind. Severkin kicks again and again. The crack grows, fires out across the whole wall, a spiderweb, a nebula. He kicks again, and a small hole appears, right over a name he never bothered to learn. Some ancestor of Reunne's, erased from memory. He kicks again, and more names and pieces fall, more holes form, and then he kicks again and again until the wall crumbles down to nothingness with the shudder of a dying beast. The other walls tremble. They walk into the chamber beyond, where Reunne is standing.

"I take it you're angry," she says.

"You lied," Severkin says. "You pretended to be something you weren't."

"Don't we all?" Reunne says, tilting her head. "That's no reason to destroy a family relic."

"Ye seem ta have gotten yer hands on some others," Elkana says, nodding at the Spear, the Staff, and the Hammer, which are on a low stone table behind Reunne.

"That's true," Reunne says with a smile. "And I like these better."

"Why be so nice to me?" Severkin asks. "Why make me feel like we were family?"

"So you wouldn't notice when I slipped the Staff out of your bag and replaced it with the copy I'd made from my ancestor's notes," Reunne says with a shrug. "You lonely orphans from faraway places are all the same. You come here, a place you finally fit into, where you aren't looked down on, and you're just filled with love and a need to connect. I gave that to you."

"Even though no one ever gave it to you," Severkin says.

Reunne narrows her eyes. She takes her spear off her back and points it at them. "If you plan to give my relics back to your precious overcity elves so they can have the glory I should have, you're going to have to kill me."

"I know," Severkin says, drawing his swords. "I've been looking forward to it."

Reunne leaps, and Severkin spins out of the way, avoiding her downward thrust. Elkana shoots an arc of lightning at her, and Reunne turns on her, spear outstretched like a whip. She nicks Elkana, but Elkana leaps back. With Reunne's back to him, Severkin charges forward with his blades. She turns just as he is about to strike, the point of her spear coming around toward him like a comet. Severkin kneels into a slide, cresting under the spear and slicing at Reunne's torso. She staggers back with a grunt, and Severkin's swords are edged with red.

Elkana, seeing Reunne stagger, gestures toward her, and suddenly a wall of flame erupts between them, setting Reunne alight. Reunne lets out a shriek like a cornered wolf and leaps into the air, away from both of them, the fire on her armor extinguishing from the force of her jump. She spins on them, waiting for them to come to her, but Severkin doesn't give her what she wants, and instead, in one fluid motion, drops his blades and takes an arrow from his quiver. He lets them fly one after another at Reunne while Elkana pelts her with fire and lightning. Reunne dodges and deflects with her spear but quickly realizes she's put herself at a disadvantage and charges Severkin. Severkin ducks, grabbing his swords, and leaps over her as she's about to batter into him, spear first. He lands back to back with her and can feel her swinging her spear around, so he somersaults forward, out of the way, then spins to face her. Her face is covered with blood and her wrinkles are pulled back into a snarl. Severkin smiles. Elkana throws fire again, forcing Reunne to leap forward. Severkin runs at her, his blade extended above his head. He feels the weight as Reunne is split on his blade, the pull of her skin like a strong wind on a ship's sail. When she falls to the ground, a deep wound runs from just below her neck to her navel. Her breathing is wet and thick. She manages to roll over and look up at Severkin. Her teeth are bloodied and look like meat. Severkin kneels beside her.

"The thing is," he says, "if you had just come with us, presented the objects to Rorth, you would have been accepted. It's not that I don't feel pity for you—you're between worlds, hated by everyone. I've been there. But when you told me I was family, I believed it. I would have made you my family."

Reunne spits at him, blood and phlegm sticking to his face.

"We're not family," she says. And then she dies.

"I know."

TWENTY-SIX

"THAT WAS amazing," Nat says at lunch. "You cut her in two! It was kind of gruesome, but it was really cool, too. Is it bad that I think that? Does it make me a sociopath?" She puts some of her food down on Nick's tray—a spring roll. Nick picks it up and takes a bite. Nat is wearing the T-shirt he gave her. It's two sizes too big, but she's cut the collar off so part of her shoulder is showing—also freckled—and it looks good.

"Do you want to cut people in two in real life?" Nick asks.

"Ew, no," Nat says, scrunching her face up.

"Then I think we're fine."

"Hey, freak," comes Charlie's voice as he approaches their table. Nat rolls her eyes and Nick tries not to laugh but still finds himself smiling. Charlie can't hurt him now. Charlie trying to hurt him is . . . funny. "What are you laughing at?" Charlie asks. His friends have swarmed up behind him. "You forget I could kick your ass?"

"What spell are you thinking of getting next?" Nick asks Nat.

Charlie slams his palm down on the table so hard that Nick's tray rattles. "Don't ignore me, freak," he says. "Or did your mom forget to teach you manners?"

Nick turns his eyes on Charlie and thinks about how they were once sort-of-friends. Now all he sees is Charlie's small eyes and the shadows of people he's trying to impress looming behind him like a panel of judges. Nick takes a deep breath.

"You know what, Charlie," Nick says, the words shooting out before he decides to say them. "My mom is sick. So yeah, she forgets things. And if you want to make fun of me or her for that, then go ahead. All it does is make you look like an asshole. I wouldn't do that to you—no matter what I knew about you or your family. But, sure, if you want to make fun of me because it makes those idiots behind you laugh and like you, fine. I'm happy to help you with your social life."

Nat inhales sharply through her teeth, looking down at the table, but grinning. From behind Charlie comes a pipe of nervous laughter, but that makes Nat start to giggle, and suddenly she's throwing her head back and laughing loudly enough that people are staring. Charlie is red, and Nick knows he's probably about to get punched, but surprisingly, Charlie just stares at Nat, like he's waiting for her to stop laughing, but she doesn't, so instead he just walks away, his shadows following him silently.

Nat's laughter dies down. She puts another spring roll down on Nick's tray, which he eats greedily.

"Should I ask my mom to start packing me two lunches?" Nat asks.

"Is that an option?" Nick asks. "Because, yes. Unless she wants to teach my dad to cook."

Nat laughs. "She might be willing. She likes you guys."

"Hey, Nick!"

Nick looks up to see Ms. Knight walking toward them, with Jess at her side.

"Hi," Nick says, and to Jess, "What are you doing here?"

"I'm treating her to lunch in our glamorous dining hall," Ms. Knight says. "Was Charlie bothering you just now?"

"No." Nick shakes his head, smiling.

"Well, I just wanted to say hi," Jess says. "You going to come visit your mom soon?" she asks quietly.

"Tonight," Nick says.

"I'm off all of today," Jess says. "But if you come around this weekend, I already asked permission so you can play that game with her. Just call ahead and I'll reserve time and everything."

"Thanks," Nick said. "That would be great."

"C'mon, leave them alone," Ms. Knight says. "They have to eat so they have energy for my class later."

"Okay, see you later, Nick," Jess says, waving.

"See you!" Nick says. Jess and Ms. Knight walk away and wave at them as they leave. Nick turns back to Nat, who is grinning lopsidedly at him. "What?" he says.

"You're just very popular today," Nat says. He laughs. "So you're going to see your mom tonight?"

He nods.

"Oh well. I was going to ask if you wanted to come study."

"Sorry," he says. "But I'll be on the game later tonight. We have a reward to collect. And I want to join the Thieves Guild. You in?"

"Yes," Nat says. "Time to get out of Wellhall, see some other cities."

"Cool," Nick says. "And maybe I can go to your mom's restaurant after school tomorrow?"

"Yeah," Nat says. "We have to finish those damn history papers. You done with yours?"

"Almost," Nick says.

● ● ●

After school, Dad picks him up and they drive to the home. It's a chilly day—really starting to feel like fall now. Nick is wearing shorts, and being outside gives him goosebumps from the chill. The sky is old-sword gray, and the parking lot's white stones seem like pebbles without the bright sunlight. Nick takes off his seat belt and turns to Dad.

"I want to see her alone," he says.

Dad looks up at him and starts to shake his head.

"Please," Nick says. "I won't upset her. I just need to . . . say goodbye."

"It's not goodbye, Nick."

"I know," Nick says. "I didn't mean like, goodbye-goodbye. Just . . . the goodbye I should have said when she first moved out."

Dad takes off his glasses and rubs the space between his eyes. "Why now?"

For a moment, Nick thinks of telling him—about Reunne, about his fantasy and how it toppled around him but somehow didn't kill him. Didn't even hurt as much as he thought.

He wants to tell him he's still angry but not as much, that he feels like he's moved up a level, and he needs to do this to figure out where to put his new skill points. But he doesn't think Dad will get it.

"'Cause of what you told me," Nick says.

"Don't tell your mother what I said," Dad says quickly.

"I won't," Nick says. "But can I see her alone, for just a few minutes?"

Dad inhales deeply. "Okay," he says. "But the nurses and staff will still be there."

"That's okay," Nick says, getting out of the car. They walk to the porch together. No one is outside today; it's too cool. Inside, at the desk, Maria is writing something on a clipboard and absently scratching the back of one leg with her foot.

"Hi," Nick says.

Maria turns. "Hi," she says, cautiously. "You guys aren't normally here Monday."

"I know," Nick says. "Do you know where my mom is?"

"Pottery," Maria says, her worry lines appearing on her forehead. "But she's not expecting you. . . . She might be confused."

"That's okay," Nick says. "I just want to talk to her." Maria looks up and behind Nick to Dad, and Nick watches her expression as they have one of those silent conversations that they think kids don't pick up on.

"Okay," Maria says. "I'll show you there."

He follows Maria down a few halls and into a lower level, where the windows are just on the top halves of the walls. There are six or seven residents down here, and four nurses. The residents are all at pottery wheels, and a woman in a smock goes around helping them. Mom's pot is low and wide, more like a bowl. He starts walking toward her, then backs up a few steps to where Maria is leaning against the wall, watching him.

"I'm sorry if I was rude that first day we met," he says to Maria.

Maria shrugs but smiles faintly. "I've seen a lot worse," she says. Nick nods and walks over to Mom. He studies her profile. She's so pale in the light of the basement, almost glowing. He sees the cameo necklace dangling from her neck and feels a moment of guilt, remembering how he left it on the floor. There's an empty stool next to her that he sits down on.

"Hi," he says.

She looks up from her pot and smiles at him.

"Hello," she says. Nick expects something more, but she's focused on her pot. Her hands press on the sides of the pot, coaxing them upward, taller and thinner, as it spins.

"I wanted to talk to you about the night the wall fell," Nick says. Mom looks up at him again and smiles, the lines around her eyes crinkling into stars.

"You look like my son," she says, and looks back at her pot. "He's such a good kid, but he's at that age, you know? I worry."

Nick swallows. His ears are ringing like he's just been punched, and he can feel himself blinking away the water building up in his eyes. Worse than being punched—beaten. Drained. By his mother. A few more drops of sadness fall into his bubble, one after the other, making echoing splashes. But he's lived through his mother killing him once already, even if he was wrong about it, so he swallows and takes a breath, then forces himself to speak.

"I *am* your son," he says.

"Oh no," Mom says. "My family only visits on the weekends."

"Oh," Nick says, looking down. "Right." He watches her hands on the clay again. The pot has gotten so tall now that at the edge the clay is paper thin and she can't keep it even. It ripples, like the edge of a scallop, and then it tears.

"*Scheisse,*" Mom says. She coaxes the clay back down, tries to repair the damage, but it's uneven now and toppling inward.

"I wanted to ask about the night the wall fell," Nick says. "The Berlin Wall. And about your dad."

"I remember that very well," Mom says, her eyes focused on the clay. She's pushed it back down and started anew. It's a plate now, rising into a bowl. "I remember . . . something awful had happened. To me, just before. And I was walking along, and people ran past me, excited. And then more people, so I stopped and asked them what was happening, and they said the wall was open. They were going to see the West. And that's what I'd always wanted, just to escape. To get out of East Berlin, so I ran after them." She coaxes the bowl up into a vase, more carefully now, bending the rim slightly outward. "I waited in line—well, more of a crowd—for a long time. And then I walked through. It was so easy—the guards had given up by then, so I just walked through. Through the stone and the barbed wire and the other wall beyond it. And then I was in the West. It was . . . beautiful. Lots of light, even though it was nighttime. Brightly colored advertisements everywhere." She carefully curls the rim downward, keeping it separate from the rest of the vase underneath. It looks like the jet of a fountain, the water spilling over when it reaches the top, or maybe a tree. "And I thought to myself that I could stay there. I could just stay, and no one would know I'd gone. I could travel to America. I could see the world." She lifts her hands away and stops the pottery wheel. The vase stays in place. "It's for my husband," she says. "Do you think he'll like it?"

"Yeah," Nick says. "Dad will love that. But what happened next? What happened once you'd crossed the wall?"

"Oh, I went back," she says with a shrug. "I had responsibilities. I wandered around first, of course, but that night I went back, and I felt miserable the whole walk home. And then when I got home, my father was gone. He'd gotten out and gone who knows where. They found him a week later, dead in a river. I was so . . . so, so relieved." She turns and looks at Nick. "Does that make me a bad person?" she asks.

"No," Nick says. "Not at all." He lays his hand on Mom's hand, feeling the slick gumminess of the clay covering her hands like gloves.

"I hope my son never feels that way about me," Mom says. Then she lifts her hand away from Nick's, and raises it in the air. The woman with the smock comes over and looks at it.

"Very nice work, Sophie," she says. "Beautiful." She turns to Nick. "Isn't she talented?"

"Yeah," Nick says, though he feels like they're talking about her like she's a child, which makes him feel weird.

"I'm sleepy," Mom says. The woman in the smock waves to the nurses, and Maria comes forward.

"You want to lie down, Sophie?" she asks. Mom nods.

"Why don't you say goodbye?" Maria says to Nick. Nick hugs his mother, who seems surprised but pats him lightly on the back. Nick tightens his grip, then lets go. And then she hugs him back, too, and Nick knows that, for this moment, it's not just some parts of her but every part of her that's hugging him back. Every part of her loves him.

"Bye, Mom," he says. "I'll be back on Saturday."

Mom nods.

"Can you find your own way?" Maria asks.

"Yeah," Nick says. "I can."

He walks slowly up the stairs and down the halls, noticing the other residents; white hair, polite smiles, expressions like curious cats. They're all inside today, and when he passes a rec room, he sees them all gathered around a TV, one of them with a game controller in his hand. He steps in and watches the old man play Wellhall for a while. He's a knight, hitting goblins with a sword.

"Get 'em!" one of the other residents shouts. The others all laugh and start shouting what else to do next: "On your left!" "Watch your back!" "Cut him in two!" Nick grins and walks away. Dad is talking to Jess at the front desk. They don't notice Nick approaching.

"It's always hard," Jess says. "But I think you're doing a good job. You can ask him, too, you know."

"Ask him if I'm being a good father?" Dad asks. Nick stops where he is. "How does one even ask that?"

Jess shrugs. "I don't know," she says. "Just . . . check in."

Nick steps out and walks quickly up to Dad.

"Thanks, Dad," he says, so they know he's there. He hugs Dad tightly. Dad hugs him back.

"What for?" Dad asks.

"For letting me talk to Mom," Nick says.

Dad nods.

"And for taking us to Nat's mom's place for dinner. I'm too exhausted to try your cooking tonight."

Dad laughs and then rests his hand on Nick's head. "Okay," he says. "Thanks, Jess. Say hi to Ms. Knight for us."

"Will do," Jess says, smiling. "See you soon?"

"We'll be back," Nick says.

TWENTY-SEVEN

"WELL," SEVERKIN says, drinking his third mug of ale, "you ready to head out? I hear there's a ruin near Blackwater that no one has ever come out of alive."

"Ooooh, sounds fun," Elkana says. "Are ye sure ye don't want ta see yer new home first? A big ol' mansion right up against the wall of the mountain must have quite a view. And we went ta a lot of trouble for it." They get up and head through the crowd of drunks and revelers for the door. Rorth had happily given them their requested rewards once they'd returned the artifacts. He'd gripped the object, and it had hummed slightly, and it had seemed to work. There hadn't been any more giant sightings in days.

"It'll be here when we get back," Severkin says as they stumble out the door. He takes a big gulp of air. It's dark out, and the night winds of the high mountain have worked their way inside. Rorth had said he had a new mission for them—to find out what woke the giants in the first place, so they could make sure it didn't happen again. They'd get to that. Eventually.

"Well, just don't forget about it," Elkana says. "Be a shame never ta use that beautiful house."

"It'll be a museum one day," Severkin says. "Filled with the treasures of my adventures. And we'll be old, and we'll charge a gold piece for a ticket and totter around giving tours and telling young people about how we fought the Wizard of Someplace and got the Sword of Something."

Elkana laughs.

"They'll be very impressed," Severkin says. They start walking for the gate out of the city, the cold winds sobering them as they go.

"Why have ye roped me in ta this now?" Elkana says. "Cannae I just die in valiant battle?"

"No," Severkin says, taking her hand for a moment, then releasing it. "I'll need you around, to make sure I don't forget the stories, the adventures."

"The name of the Sword of Something?"

"Yeah, like that," Severkin says. They've reached the gate and look out at the sky. It's dark, and to Severkin, the stars smile like freckles.

"Well, let's move on, then," Elkana says. "Gotta have these adventures if ye want ta make yer museum happen."

Severkin nods and takes another step forward.

ACKNOWLEDGMENTS

AS WITH any book, I have many, many people to thank for helping me fine-tune it into what it's become. Without their support and advice, this book wouldn't exist.

First and foremost, I need to thank my friends Ann and Amy, not only for talking me through their multiracial experiences, but also providing me with academic texts, kind feedback on my missteps, and enthusiastic support for something I often felt anxious writing. They've inspired me in this writing in more ways than I can count.

None of this would have been possible without my agent, Joy. She is my fiercest advocate, my most stalwart defender, my consigliere, and one of my dearest friends. I owe her way more than I can ever say. Thanks to everyone over at David Black, including Luke, Susan, Emily, Antonella, Sarah, and, of course, David himself.

My editor, Steve, deserves thousands upon thousands of cat photos for his ever-precise and valuable feedback, and for dealing with my rambling nature. I cannot thank him enough for taking a risk on this book, unwieldy and patchwork as it was, and helping to shape it into what it is today. I don't know what the right emoji is for "eternal gratitude," but if I did, I would tweet it at him indefinitely.

Dr. Alexis Eastman, my dear friend, cannot be thanked enough. I went into this knowing only a small amount about Alzheimer's, and how treatments and facilities run, but she not only took me through it all, step by step, but read and re-read the book to make sure everything felt medically sound. Also my mother-in-law, Beverley, and my sister-in-law, Angela, both nurses, for talking me through some aspects of care.

I want to thank the entire team at Knopf and RHCB, especially Nancy, Adrienne, Melanie, Dominique, Katherine, and the hardworking publicity team. Also the folks who created this amazing cover: Nicole and Julie.

I have many, many readers to thank, people who read this—sometimes multiple times—and gave me feedback and advice on how to better it. My writing group—Laura, Robin, Paula, Holly, Margel, and Dan—especially deserves thanks for reading this so many times. Also Christian, Leslie, Jackie, Sarah, Teri, and Teri (no relation). Their notes were invaluable. And, of course, my amazing mother, who has read all of my books many more times than anyone else, and is still surprised when I leave out apostrophes.

I also need to thank my youth advisory team—Macie, Elyn, Barry, MacKenzie, and Kristin—for helping me to understand how young people talk (on their phones, mostly, it turns out).

And Staab! My wonderful former housemate and all-around amazing human being deserves credit not just for his feedback about perceptions of Germany, but for all the actual German he corrected. Especially the swearing. Also Boris, who talked to me about growing up under communism.

Thanks to my old college professor Elizabeth Hamilton, with whom I took some East German cinema classes, and my friend Mary for encouraging me to take them with her. I learned way more about the Cold War through those classes than I ever did in high school, and the images in and feeling of many of those movies helped to guide the feeling of this book.

As always, I owe eternal gratitude and love to my parents for their endless support and encouragement.

And Chris, for being Chris.